Anonymous

General Index to the Remains Historical and Literary

Vol. I-XXX

SALZWASSER VERLAG

Anonymous

General Index to the Remains Historical and Literary

Vol. I-XXX

Reprint of the original, first published in 1863.

1st Edition 2022 | ISBN: 978-3-37500-079-0

Verlag (Publisher): Salzwasser Verlag GmbH, Zeilweg 44, 60439 Frankfurt, Deutschland
Vertretungsberechtigt (Authorized to represent): E. Roepke, Zeilweg 44, 60439 Frankfurt, Deutschland
Druck (Print): Books on Demand GmbH, In de Tarpen 42, 22848 Norderstedt, Deutschland

GENERAL INDEX

TO THE

REMAINS HISTORICAL AND LITERARY

PUBLISHED BY

THE CHETHAM SOCIETY.

VOLS. I.–XXX.

PRINTED FOR THE CHETHAM SOCIETY.

M.DCCC.LXIII.

PREFACE.

THE CHETHAM SOCIETY, established in March 1843 for the publication of Historical and Literary Remains connected with the Palatine Counties of Lancaster and Chester, and issuing to its members three volumes annually, has now reached its sixtieth volume.

For some years the growing extent of this series of Publications has pressed upon the Council of the SOCIETY the necessity of some arrangement whereby its large stores of valuable but miscellaneous information could be rendered more perfectly available to the Historian or Archæologist. A similar feeling has lately led to the issue of an Analytical and Descriptive Catalogue of the publications of a kindred Society (the CAMDEN), prepared by Mr. J. G. Nichols, which affords a distinct view of the character of each work and gives a general idea of its contents; and so far serves the office of a guide. But it has all along been felt by the Council of the CHETHAM SOCIETY that a mere descriptive Catalogue, however well executed, would after all prove comparatively useless; and that, with a large and varied

collection of works such as we are now considering, what is really wanted is the power of ascertaining at a glance whether the special subject on which the student desires information is mentioned in the volumes, and if so where the passage or passages containing it may be found, and that this want could only be adequately supplied by a comprehensive and well-considered General Index; and it was in compliance with their request (conveyed through the PRESIDENT) to prepare such an Index, that the Compiler of the present volume undertook, more than two years ago, that first instalment of his task, the result of which is now in the reader's hands.

The first thirty volumes of the CHETHAM SOCIETY'S Publications present the issue for the first ten years of its existence, and include the following works:*

Vol.
I. Brereton's Travels.
II. Civil War Tracts of Lancashire.
III. *Chester's Triumph.*
IV. Life of Adam Martindale.
V. Memorials of the Rebellion of 1715.
VI. *Potts's Discoverie of Witches.*
VII. *Iter Lancastrense.*
VIII, XIX, XXI, XXII. Gastrell's Notitia Cestriensis, 4 vols.
IX. The Norris Papers.
X, XI, XVI, XX. Coucher Book of Whalley Abbey, 4 vols.
XII. The Moore Rental.

* For the full-length Titles see the List of Publications given in the Prospectus prefixed to this volume.

XIII. Diary and Correspondence of Dr. John Worthington. Vol. I.
XIV. Journal of Nicholas Assheton.
XV. Lyfe of Saynt Werburge.
XVII. Warrington in 1465.
XVIII. Diary of Rev. Henry Newcome.
XXIII. *Robinson's Golden Mirrour.*
XXIV. *Chetham Miscellanies.* Vol. I.
XXV. *Cardinal Allen's Defence of the Surrender of Deventer.*
XXVI, XXVII. Autobiography of Henry Newcome, 2 vols.
XXVIII. Jacobite Trials at Manchester.
XXIX. The Stanley Papers. Part I.
XXX. Documents relating to the Priory of Penwortham.

Separate Indexes to volumes III, VI, VII, XXIII, XXIV, XXV, distinguished in the above list by being printed in *italics*, and which are the only works that were left unsupplied at the time of publication, have been printed and are appended to the present volume, from which they can be detached at pleasure for insertion in their respective places.

A few words upon the plan on which the General Index is compiled may facilitate its use. At first an attempt was made to supersede altogether the special Indexes by embodying in it the whole of the information they contain, including every paginal reference. This attempt, however, was soon relinquished as alike misleading and unmanageable. For example: the proper name of Ashton, under its three forms of Ashton, Asheton and Assheton, occurs in sixteen of the separate Indexes, embodies four hundred and thirty-eight distinct references, and occupies thirteen columns or six and a half pages of small type. Now,

bearing in mind that some two or three centuries ago orthography formed no part of the general system of education in England, and that men and women spelled or misspelled even their own names on pure phonetic principles, satisfied apparently with any combination of letters that would convey the required sound,—let any one propose to himself the problem of tracing for the purposes of an Index the personal identity of each individual *Nicholas* or *Ralph* through such a mass of references, and then remember that every other personal name given in the volume would have to be similarly treated, and he will have some idea of a portion of the task which presented itself to be encountered on such a plan. Moreover the Indexes are by various hands; and small differences of plan which come out on close investigation still more confuse the problem. The increase of bulk and of consequent expense which such a plan (were it practicable) would involve, may be gathered from a comparison of the six and a half pages of small type mentioned above, with the space actually occupied by the name in its threefold form in the present volume, viz. five half-lines.

Without going into detail upon plans which were tried only to be relinquished, it may suffice to say that the one finally adopted resolved itself into the construction of a key to the existing Indexes, which should bring together under one alphabet the whole of their subjects, giving reference for the sake of clearness and brevity to the volume only, but classifying where required and systematising the informa-

tion, so as to guide the student with the least possible loss of time *through the separate Indexes* to the subject matter he might be in search of. This is what is attempted in the present volume, which is meant to hold somewhat the same relation to the separate Indexes that a general map of England holds to a county atlas.

One or two explanatory observations will still be necessary:—

The reference to a work is in every case to the volume containing the Index: thus, as Vol. XX. is the fourth volume of the *Whalley Coucher Book*, and contains the two Indexes (locorum *et* nominum), a reference to any name in the *Coucher Book*, is always made through that volume.

A few references are followed by a note of interrogation (?). Where this occurs it indicates that the Compiler, in his process of verification, has failed to find the passage or name referred to. Where he has been able to detect the error the paginal reference is added, unless when the subject occurs within a page or two of the one indicated, or can be easily traced by the Table of Contents, in which case it has not been thought necessary to notice it.

It now only remains for the Compiler to hope that the arduous but not unpleasing labour, which has led him in thought during the leisure hours of so many months to the grey towers and battle fields, the cloistered walks and old manor houses of the two Palatine Counties, so rich in traditions and associations of the Past, and brought him face to face with its historical celebrities and local worthies,

may prove of the value and service which have been anticipated for it. Should such happily prove to be the case, the thanks of all who may make use of the volume will be mainly due to the learned and indefatigable President of the Chetham Society who first prompted the undertaking, and by his counsel and aid, freely rendered whenever asked, has lessened its difficulty and accelerated its progress.

C. S. SIMMS.

March 4th, 1863.

GENERAL INDEX.

VOLS. I.—XXX.

𝔑 indicates Names of Persons.

AARAM chapel, xxii.
Abbadie, Dr., xxviii.
Abbey of St. Werburge, xv. *See* Werburgh.
Abbey of Whalley, xiv. *See* Whalley.
Abbeyfield, co. Chester, xiv.
Abbey gate, Chester: fairs to be held there only, xv.
Abbeys, their dissolution the cause of pressing for soldiers, vii.
Abbot *or* Abbott, 𝔑, ii, vii, xiii, xiv, xxii, xxviii.
Abbotes kytchyn, xx, (*tit.* Whalleye).
Abbots, imputed attempt to restore in Scotland, i.
Abbotsbury, xiii.
Aberdeen, i, xiv.
Abingdon, xiii.
Abingdon's *Antiquities of the Church of Worcester*, xxii.
Abington *or* Habington, William, xxix.
Ablard, Anthony, xiii.
Abraham, 𝔑, viii, xiii, xxvii.
Abraham's sacryfyce of Isaac depaynted on arras, xv.
Abram, 𝔑, xxii.
Abram hall, Wigan, xxii.
Abringeham, Joh. de, xx.
Abstract (the), by Henry Newcome, xviii.
Aburne *for* Aldbourne, co. Wilts, xiii.
Abuses in the Church not to be reformed by private men, xiv.
"Academy day" at Stonyhurst, xiv.
Accidents in Newcome's family, xviii.
Accres, 𝔑, ix.
Accrington, xiv; account of, xxii.
Accrington Nova, xxii.
Acheden, Emma de, xx.
Achetun *or* Aughton, manor of, xxii.
Ackers, 𝔑, viii.
Acre's field, xix.
Act Books of the bishops of Chester, xiv.
Acton, co. Chester, viii, xx.
Acton, 𝔑, viii, ix, xx, xxii, xxiv.
Actors, their contempt of municipal authority, xxix.
Acts of parliament, 1661–3, xviii.
Adam, derivation of the name, xiii.
Adam and Eve depaynted on arras, xv.
Adam and Walbank, xiv.
Adams, 𝔑, viii, xiii, xix, xxvii.
Adams's (Thomas) *Mystical Bedlam*, xiv.
Adamsom, 𝔑, xxvii, xxx.
Adburgham, 𝔑., xvii, xxii.
Adda brought from the North by Peada to preche to his people, xv.
Adderley, Sir Charles, xviii, xxvii.
Adderton- *or* Adwalton-moor, battle of, ii.

Addertons and Lelands, XIV.
Addison, 𝔑, XII, XIV, XXII, XXIV.
Addy, William, XIII.
Adeldryde, saynt and vyrgyn, doughter of prynce Ermenred of Kent, XV.
Adelgenda, Marniscius de, his bee-hive, XIII.
Adelhere, prynce of Eest England, XV.
Adelwlf, kyng of West-Saxons, XV.
Adla, kyng of Southsex, XV.
Adlington, chapelry of Prestbury: account of, VIII; hall of, VIII.
Adlington, co. Lanc., XII, XIX.
Adlington hall, Standish, notice of, XXII.
Adlington, 𝔑, VIII, IX, XXII.
Admarsh, in Bleasdale forest, XXII.
Admarsh chapel, school and poor, XIV.
Admiralty (the), address to queen Anne upon, IX.
Adoulfus, kyng, defeats the Danes, XV.
Adsword, hamlet of Cheadle, VIII.
Advertisements of post horses between London and Lancashire, XII.
Adwalton, co. York, XIV.
Ady, Thomas, his *Candle in the Dark*, VI.
Æsop, IV.
Affliction, Newcome's reflections upon, XVIII.
Africa, IX.
Agar, Thomas, XXIV.
Agatha, saynt, depaynted on arras, XV.
Agden, township of Rosthorne, VIII; hall, notice of, VIII.
Agdon, township of Malpas, VIII.
Agecroft hall, Eccles, XIV; description of, XIX.
Aggelay, terra de, XX.
Aghendole, meaning of the word, VI.
Aghton, 𝔑, IX, XXII.
Agincourt, battle of, XVII.
Agnes, saynt, depaynted on arras, XV.
Agreement in religion between Papists and Lutherans, XIII.
Agrippa, Cornelius, VI.
Ague cured by a conversation, XIII.
Aigburth *or* Aigburgh hall, Garston, XII; notice of, XXII.
Ailsa isle, I.
Ainderton, township of Bebington, VIII.
Ainsworth, township of Middleton, XIX.
Ainsworth, 𝔑, XIII, XIX, XXII.
Ainsworth's (W. H.) *Lancashire Witches*, XIV.
Air pump, invention of, by Boyle, XIII.
Aisgill, Joshua, VII.
Akenrode, XX (*tit.* Castelton).
Alabaster quarry near Cardiff, I.
Alanson, Thomas, XII.
Albans (St.), XIV; its monastery founded by Offa, XV.
Albemarle, dukes of, XIX, XXII; earl of, XIX.
Albertus de Alesco, XIV.
Albo Monasterio, Simon de, abbot of Chester, VIII.
Albrincis, Ewan de, abbot of Furness, XXII.
Alburgham, John, VIII.
Alcancoats hall, Colne, notice of, XXII.
Alchemist (the), XVIII.
Alcock, 𝔑, VIII, IX, XII, XXII, XXVII.
Aldcroft, 𝔑, VIII.
Aldeburgh, uncle to Sir William Brereton, I.
Aldeford. Ric. de, XX.
Aldelem *or* Audlem, Thomas de, VIII.
Aldelyn, Tho. de, XX.
Alden, John, vicar of Prescot, IV.
Alderley, IV; account of, VIII.
Aldersey and its divisions, VIII.
Aldersey, 𝔑, VIII, XIV, XVIII, XXII, XXV, XXVII.
Alderswell, a field in Warrington, XVII.
Aldetunstead, XX (*tit.* Briddestwysel).
Aldford, account of, VIII; lords of, patrons of St. Bridget's, Chester, VIII.

Aldford, 𝔑, viii.
Aldholm, Alward and Alicia de, xix.
Aldilegh, H. de, xx.
Aldingham in Furness, account of, xxii.
Aldithelegh, Henr. de, xx.
Aldport, in Manchester, xviii, xix. *See* Alport.
Aldred, archbishop of York, i.
Aldulph, kynge of Eest England, xv.
Ale, eight sorts of, xiv.
Alehouses frequented by the gentry, xiv.
Alençon, duke of, xxv.
Allerstone, co. York, i.
Alexander, 𝔑, viii, xviii, xix, xxvii.
Alexander's *Collection of Proverbs*, xiii.
Alforde, Francis, xxii.
Alfred *or* Alured, kyng: legendary notices of, xv.
Alfred *or* Aufrey, a Saxon, holds the manor of Downham, xxii.
Alfrichesholm, xx.
Alfryde, sone to Oswy kynge of Northumberlande, xv.
Alfrydus of Beverley, historian: notice of, xv.
Alington, Mr., xiii.
Alker, William, vi.
Alkincoats, xxii. *See* Alcancoats.
Alkrington hall, notice of, xix.
All Lostock, viii.
Allcocke *or* Allecock, 𝔑, xii, xxiv.
Alle, kynge of Northumberlande, xv.
Allen, 𝔑, iv, vii, viii, xii, xiii, xviii, xix, xxii, xxv, xxvii.
Allen controversy (the), xviii.
Allenson, 𝔑, ix, xxviii.
Allerton in Childwall, ix, xii, xviii; notice of, xxii.
Allestree, a London bookseller, xiii.
Allestry, Dr., xviii.
Allet, William, xxii.
Alleyn, Edward, founder of Dulwich college, xxix; notice of, xiii.
Allibone (Mr. justice) complains of Protestant non-attendance, xxviii.
Allifein, in Holland: account of, i.
Allin *alias* Anguish, Sir Richard, xviii.
Alliteration, singular specimen of, xxiii.
Almery, John, xiii.
Almond, 𝔑, ix, xiii.
Almoner (the) of Lathom, xxii.
Alnot, servaunt to Werburge: legend respecting, xv.
Alnwick, i, v.
Alport lodge, Manchester, ii. *See* Aldport.
Alport, 𝔑, viii.
Alpraham, township of Bunbury, viii.
Alresford, xiii; rector of, xiv.
Alrichesholm, xx (*tit.* Staneye).
Alsager, township of Barthomley, viii.
Alsager, Mrs., viii.
Alsley, Mr., xviii.
Alston, 𝔑, xix, xx, xxii.
Alt, William, xix.
Alta camera, meaning of, xvii.
Altaclif, xx (*tit.* Wythenhull).
Altar (Roman) converted into a font, xxii.
Altar, behaviour at the, i.
Altarage at Bolton, xix.
Altcar, co. Lanc., ix; account of, xxii.
Alte, xx.
Altedge, township of Ashton-under-Line, xix.
Altemersh, xx.
Altham, co. Lanc. xiv; notice of, xxii.
Altham, 𝔑, vi, xxii.
Althill, township of Ashton-under-Line, xix.
Althorp, 𝔑, xxix.
Altlees, township of Ashton-under-Line, xix.
Alton, co. Hants. xiii; co. Stafford, xxiii.
Altrincham, township of Bowden, viii.

Altune, XX (*tit.* Gerstan).
Aluandelay, Ric. de, XX.
Aluetham, XX; brok, lode, de capella, XX.
Aluetham, 𝔑, XX.
Alum mines near Hoghton, co. Lanc., XIV.
Alvanley, township of Frodsham, VIII; its chapel, XVIII.
Alvanley, baron of, VIII.
Alvaston, co. Chester, VIII.
Alve *now* Alvechurch, diocese of Worcester, XV.
Alvetham, XXII. *See* Aluetham *and* Altham.
Alvetham, 𝔑, XXII.
Alverthorpe, co. York, XXII.
Alythwait, Cartmell, co. Lanc., VIII.
Amato, John Roderigo, VII.
Amber Witch, eulogium on, VI.
Ambrose (St.), purtrayture of, on arras, XV.
Ambrose, 𝔑, II, IX, XII, XVIII, XXII, XXVII.
Amery, 𝔑, III, IX.
Ames, William: notice of, XIII.
Ameson, John, VIII.
Amey, Mrs,, XVIII, XXVII.
Amherst, John, XXII.
Amisse, Mrs., schoolmistress, XIX.
Amort, half-dead, III.
Amounderness, XIX; account of, XXII; rural dean of, VIII.
Amsterdam, XIII: description of, I.
Amyrault *or* Amyraldus, Moses: notice of, XIII.
Anabaptists, XXVII.
Anatomical models, account of, XIII.
Anatomy of Melancholy, XIV.
Ancestry of Rev. H. Newcome, XVIII.
Anchoret, the word explained, VIII.
Ancient, a flag or pennon, III, XIV.
Ancient Heawood, XVIII.
Ancient monuments, Dr. Dee's plan for their recovery and preservation, XXIV.
Ancoats hall, Manchester, XVIII; notice of, XIX.
Andell, Mr., XII.
Anderson, 𝔑, XXVII.
Anderton, township of Budworth, VIII.
Anderton, co. Lanc., XIX.
Anderton, 𝔑, II, V, VI, VIII, IX, XIV, XIX, XXII, XXVIII.
Anderwick castle, I.
Andirton, Rob. de, XXX.
Andlezargh, co. Lanc., XIX.
Andover, XII.
Andow, 𝔑, XII.
Andreas, 𝔑, XIII.
Andrew, 𝔑, I, XVII, XXVII.
Andrew's (St.) day, XIV.
Andrew's (St.) church, London, XIV.
Andrewes, 𝔑, II, XXVII.
Andrews, 𝔑, IX, XIII, XIX, XXVII.
Angelo (St.), dungeons of, XIV.
Angels, curious questions concerning, XIII; their hierarchies, orders, &c., XV.
Angier, 𝔑, II, IV, XIII, XVIII, XIX, XXVII.
Anglesey, lord, IX.
Anglesey, a field in Warrington, XVII.
Anglezark, XIX. *See* Andlezargh.
Angling, remarks on, XIV.
Angrona, XIII.
Anguish *or* Allin, Sir Richard, XVIII.
Angus, Umfravill earl of, XIX.
Anhalt, prince of, XIII.
Anima separata non dormit, discourse on, XIII.
Animadversions on Bishop of Worcester's Letter against Baxter, XVIII.
Anion, John, VIII.
Anjou, duke of, IX.
Anlaf, king of Ireland, XV.
Anlasargh, 𝔑, XX.
Anlubry, in Over Whitley, VIII.
Anna, kynge of Eest England: legendary notices of, XV.

Annales Cestrienses or Chronicle of St. Werburgh, VIII.
Anne, queen of England, V, IX, XII.
Anne, queen of Denmark, XIV.
Annernon, Jane, VII.
Annesley, 𝔑, XII, XIII, XXVII.
Annotations (English), XVIII.
Annuities bill, IX.
Annus Mirabilis, notice of, XIII.
Anointing of Witches, VI.
Anselm, archbishop of Canterbury, VIII, XV.
Anson, 𝔑, XIX.
Anthem (Latin) by Rogers, XIII.
Anthony, brother, XXVII.
Antichrist, the pope believed to be, XIII.
Antidote against the Poyson of the Times, a tract by Martindale, IV.
Antigua, IX.
Antilia, XIII.
Antley (Lower), Accrington: notice of, XXII.
Antoninus *or* Athelredus, archbishop, XV.
Antoninus Caracalla, XXII.
Antoninus (Marcus), edition of by Gataker, XIII.
Antrim, John marquis and second earl of, I.
Antrobus, hamlet of Over Whitley, VIII.
Antrobus, 𝔑, VIII, XXVII.
Antwerp, I.
Apeltre *or* Appeltree, William de, XX, XXII.
Aphthonius, grammarian, IV.
Apologetical Narration, XVIII.
Apologia Catholica, VIII.
Apologists, the five, IV.
Apology for John Wickliff, VII.
Apolyn (saynt), purtrayture of on arras, XV.
Apparitors, VIII.
Appelton, XX.
Appleby, co. Westmoreland, military proceedings at, II, V; co. Leicester, XII.
Appleby, Simon, his evidence at the Manchester trials, XXVIII.
Appledore, co. Devon, I.
Apples from the orchard of Jesus College, XIII.
Appleton, township of Budworth, VIII.
Appleton house in Grappenhall, VIII.
Appleton, Thom. de, XX.
Apricots from Whalley abbey, XIV.
Apslow, Dr., XXIV.
Apthomas, a village near Berwick, I.
Aquarius, Willm. de, XX.
Aquinas, St. Thomas, XIII.
Arbalest, arbalête à jalet, XIV.
Archæologia Scotica, IX.
Archæological Journal, XIV.
Archbishopricks in Ireland, I.
Archbold, 𝔑, XIX, XXVII.
Archer, a millenarian writer, XIII.
Archery, practise of, XIV.
Archie, a court jester, I. *See* Armstrong.
Archilleslack, XX (*tit.* Merland).
Archolm cum Cawood, XXII.
Arclyd, township of Sandbach, VIII.
Ardeley, Nath., XIII.
Arden, 𝔑, VIII, XIV, XXII.
Ardern *or* Arderne, 𝔑, II, IV, VIII, XIII, XIV, XVIII, XIX, XX, XXII, XXVII, XXVIII.
Ardes, lord of, XII.
Ardwick, upper and lower, XVIII, XIX.
Arglass, countess of, XXVII.
Argyle, earls and dukes of, V, XXVII, XXIX.
Arie, R. Jehudah: notice of, XIII.
Arimathea, Joseph of: his tomb at Glastonbury, I.
Arithmetic, treatise on, IV.
Arius, how to avoid the error of, XII.
Arkel. *See* Erynach.
Arlebuggin, *or* Arnoldsbiggin, XIV.

Arlecden, co. Cumb., VIII, XXII.
Arley, co. Chester, VIII, XIV, XVII; park and chapel, notice of, VIII.
Arlington, lord, XIII.
Armada, the Spanish, XIV.
Armagh, bishop of, XXVII.
Armenian Christians, XIII.
Armetriding, 𝔑, XXII.
Armetruy, Joh. de, XXX.
Arminians *and* Arminianism, I, IV.
Arminius, Grotius's lines on, XIII.
Armistead, William, XXII.
Armitage park, XIV.
Armitstead, Rev. John, VIII.
Arms, college of, XIV, XXIV.
Armstrong, Archie, the king's fool, XIII, XIV. *See* Archie *and* Jests.
Armstrong, Rev. Mr., XXII.
Arneway, 𝔑, III, XX.
Arnheim defeats the Imperialists, I.
Arnold, Dr., XIII.
Arnoldesrode, XX (*tit.* Heleye).
Arnset hall and tower, XXII.
Arnson, Mathew, VIII.
Arosmythe, 𝔑, XVII.
Arpeley, a field in Warrington, XVII.
Arragon, Catherine of, XIV.
Arran, isle of, I.
Arran, lord, XXII.
Arras depaynted with pyctures and hystoryes manyfolde, XV.
Array, commission of, II.
Arrow, Woodchurch, co. Chester, VIII.
Arrowsmith, 𝔑, XXVII, XXVIII.
Arscot, Tho., XIII.
Arstandincroft, XX (*tit.* Whiteword).
Arthur, kynge, XV.
Arundel, co. Sussex, IX.
Arundel, earls of, XIV, XX.
Arundel, 𝔑. XXII.
Arundel marbles, VII.
Ascham, Roger, amusements of, XIV.
Ascham's murder, XII.
Ascroft, 𝔑, XII, XXII.
Ash, 𝔑, XVIII, XXVII.
Ashbrook, 𝔑, XII.
Ashburnham, lord, IX; John earl of, XXII.
Ashby house and park, XXIX.
Ashdum, batayle at, XV.
Asheley, 𝔑, XVII, XXIV.
Ashenhurst, John, XXVII.
Asheton, 𝔑, IV, VII, XIX, XXII.
Ashfield, colonel, IV, XXVII.
Ashhurst, 𝔑, XIV, XIX.
Ashhurst's (Sir Henry) *Life of Nathaniel Heywood*, XIX.
Ashley, Poynton, co. Chester, VIII.
Ashley, 𝔑, VIII, XII.
Ashmole, Elias, XXVII; notices of, XIII, XVIII.
Ashmolean Society, Berkshire, XIV.
Ashover, co. Derby, XIV.
Ashton, 𝔑, II, IV, VIII, IX, XII, XVII, XVIII, XXII, XXV, XXVII, XXVIII.
Ashton, township of Ashton-under-Line, XIX; township of Tarvin, VIII.
Ashton hall, near Lancaster, II.
Ashton-under-Line, II, VIII, XIV, XVIII; account of, XIX.
Ashton-in-Makerfield, IV; account of, XXII.
Ashton-upon-Mersey, IV; account of, VIII.
Ashurst, 𝔑, II, IX, XII, XVIII, XXII, XXVII, XXVIII.
Ashworth, 𝔑, XIX, XXII.
Ashworth, co. Lanc., XIV; account of, XIX.
Askew, 𝔑, XXII.
Askrigg, XIV.
Asland river, Croston, XXII.
Aspden, 𝔑, XVIII, XXII, XXVII.
Aspinall, 𝔑, XXII, XXVII.
Aspinwall, 𝔑, XII, XVIII, XXII.
Aspiwalsiche, XX (*tit.* Cromton).
Aspley in Penwortham, XXX.
Aspul, Ann, XXII.
Assassination justified, XXV.
Asselle, an old word for "as well," XIV.

Asshawe, 𝔑, XIX, XXII.
Asshe, Richard, of Aughton, XIV.
Asshe-cullord close, XIV.
Asshes, XX (*tit.* Whalleye).
Assheton, 𝔑, VI, VII, XIV, XVII, XIX, XX, XXII.
Assheton chapel in Middleton church, XIV.
Assheton's Journal, XIX.
Assheworth, 𝔑, XIX.
Associated classis of Cheshire, IV.
Astall, VIII.
Astbury in Middlewich, account of, VIII; Newcome preaches at, XVIII.
Astelegh, Ric. de, XX.
Asterley, Rob. de, XX.
Astle, co. Chester, VIII, XIV. *See* Astall.
Astley, township of Leigh, XIX.
Astley hall, notice of, XXII.
Astley, 𝔑, VI, VIII, XII, XXII.
Aston, IX, XX.
Aston chapelry, co. Chester, account of, VIII.
Aston, 𝔑, II, IV, VIII, IX, XII, XIV, XIX, XX, XXII, XXVIII.
Astuna, 𝔑, XXX.
At-ale, atten-ale, alehouse, XIV.
Atheism, Newcome's inclination to, XVIII.
Athenæum, Marsh's two letters to, XXIV.
Atherstone, co. York, I.
Atherton, 𝔑, II, IX, XII, XIII, XIV, XIX, XXII.
Atherton, co. Lanc., XIX.
Atherton hall, notice of, XXII.
Atherton street, Liverpool, XII.
Athurton, Sir William, XVII.
Atkinson, 𝔑, XIV, XIX, XXII.
Atkyns, Sir Robert, XIII.
Atlantis (New), by Lord Bacon: continuations and imitations of, XIII.
Aton, Mr., XXVII.
Attiscros, old hundred of, VIII.
Aubrey, John, XII, XIII, XIV, XXIV.
Aubrey, Rev. Thomas, VIII.
Audenshaw, township of Manchester, XIX.
Audilegh, Hugo de, XX.
Auditor, Mr. (Fanshaw), XIV.
Audlem, co. Chester, account of, VIII.
Audlem, Thomas de, VIII.
Audley, origin of the Stanleys from, XXIX.
Audley, lord, I.
Audley, 𝔑, XIV, XVIII.
Audry (in some chronicles Edeldritha and Etheldreda), abbess of Ely: legendary account of, XV.
Audyel, Henr. de, XX.
Augeninus, Martinus, XX.
Aughton, co. Lanc., IX, XIV; account of, XXII.
Augustine (St.), XII, XXII.
Aulym *for* Audlem, VIII.
Aurengzebe, IX.
Aust passage over the Severn, I.
Austen, 𝔑, XIII.
Austin friars, account of the, XVII.
Austyn, who was sende from saynte Gregorye to convert England; legendary notices of, XV.
Avenant, Mr., XXVII.
Averroes, XIII.
Awardescroft, XX (*tit.* Salebury).
Awbrey, Dr., XXIV.
Axtell, XII.
Aykebergh, XX.
Aykebergh, Adam de, XX.
Aylesbury, earl of, VIII.
Aylmer, 𝔑, XXII.
Ayndoe, Thomas, XII.
Ayners, Thom. de, XX.
Aynhoe, living of, XVIII.
Aynolesdale, 𝔑., XX.
Aynsley *or* Ainslie, Mr., V.
Aynsworth, 𝔑, XIX.
Ayntre, 𝔑, XX.
Ayr, account of, I.

Ayres, a bencher in Lincoln's Inn, XIV.
Ayry nourishmente, a term for the Puritan exercise, XIV.
Aysgarth in Wensleydale, XIV.
Aytock, Robert, XXII.
Ayton town and castle, I.
Ayton, lord, I.
Aytoun, Roger, XIX.

BABEAU, Monsieur, XXIV.
Baberham, XIII.
Babington, Dr., XIII.
Babington conspiracy (the), XXV.
Babthorpe, 𝔑, XIV.
Baccheness in Haerlem, I.
Bacchus, Silenus and the satyrs, XIV.
Bacford, XX.
Bacford, 𝔑, XX.
Bache, in St. Oswald's, Chester, VIII.
Bache, Mr., XXVII.
Bachelors (knights) eaten out by the baronets, XIV.
Backford, co. Chester: account of, VIII.
Backgammon, XIV.
Backhouse, William, attorney, XXVIII.
Bacon, friar, a manuscript by him asserted to be in Trin. coll., Dublin, I.
Bacon, lord, VI, XIII, XVIII, XXII.
Bacon, Nathan, XIX.
Badajos, wager respecting, IX.
Badbie, Edward, XIV.
Baddeley, co. Chester: account of, VIII.
Baddestwysel, 𝔑, XX.
Baddiley, William, XVIII.
Badelesmere, Gunceline de, XX.
Badger- *or* bowson-hunting, XIV.
Bag lane, Warrington, XVII.
Bagaley, Mr., of Newton, XXVII.
Bagerley *or* Baguley, William, XXII.
Baggaley *or* Baggerley, Humphrey, II.
Bagge lane, Chester, VIII.
Bagmere near Brereton in Cheshire, superstition connected with, I, XIII.
Bagnald, 𝔑, XVIII, XXVII.
Bagnall, 𝔑, I, VIII.
Bagot, Ric., XXVII.
Bagott, Alexander, curate of Stalmine, XXII.
Bagshaw *or* Bagshawe, 𝔑, VIII, XVIII, XIX, XXVII.
Bagshot, XIII.
Bagslade, XX.
Bagslate, XIX.
Baguley, co. Chester, VIII.
Baguley, 𝔑, VIII, XIX.
Baile, Mr., XXVIII.
Bailey, 𝔑, VIII, XII.
Bailey's *Dictionary*, XVII.
Bailton, William, XXII.
Baily (lieut.-general), capitulates to Cromwell at Warrington, II.
Bainbridge, XIV.
Baines, 𝔑, XXII, XXVII.
Baines's *Lancashire*, II, VI, IX, XII, XIV, XVIII, XIX.
Bains, 𝔑, XXII.
Baker, 𝔑, IV, VIII, XIII, XXVIII.
Baker's *MSS.*, XIII, XIX.
Balard gift, XII.
Balcarres, earls of: acquisition of landed property by, VIII, XVII.
Balderstone, in Rochdale, account of, XIX; in Blackburn, account of: XXII.
Balderstone, 𝔑, XXII.
Baldingstone, near Bury, XIV.
Baldock, XIII.
Baldreston, XX.
Baldreston, 𝔑, XX.
Baldwin, 𝔑, VI, VIII, XIV, XVIII, XXII, XXVII.
Baldwin on *De Prestigiis*, XVIII.
Baldwyn, schoolmaster of Colne: notice of, VI.
Baleman *or* Baileman, John, XXII.
Balfrunte, 𝔑, XVII.
Balista, Geoffrey le, XXII.
Balistarius, Walterus, XX. *See* L'Arbalastier.

Ball, 𝔑, XII, XIII, XVIII, XXII, XXVII.
Ball, name of a familiar spirit, VI.
Ballad of *The Distracted Puritan*, quotation from, XIV.
Balle, 𝔑, XIII, XX.
Balliehack, Ireland, I.
Ballyskene, Ireland, a stately house, I.
Balsac, XIII.
Balschagh, 𝔑, XX.
Balshaw's house, Liverpool, XII.
Balthasar, Christophorus, historian: character of, XIII.
Balthrop, Mr., physician, XXIV.
Baltimore, the lords, I, XXVIII.
Balyden, Simon, vicar of St. Oswald's, Chester, VIII.
Bamber, 𝔑, IX, XII.
Bambourg, John de, presbyter, XXII.
Bambridge, 𝔑, VIII, XXIX.
Bamfeild, Mr., of Sherborne, XVIII.
Bamford, 𝔑, IV, VIII, XIX, XX.
Bamford hall, Bury: notice of, XIX.
Bamfurlong hall, Wigan: notice of, XXII.
Bamuille, Phil. de, XX.
Bamvile family, notice of, XXV.
Banaster, 𝔑, XXII.
Banastre, 𝔑, XII, XIV, XX, XXII, XXX.
Banbury peerage question, account of, XIV.
Banchouse, XX (*tit.* Warton).
Bancks, Legh, XXVIII.
Bancroft, 𝔑, XIII, XIV, XXII, XXVII.
Band, captain, at the siege of Manchester, II.
Bandini's *Commentarii de Vita et Scriptis Joannis Baptist Donii*, XIII.
Ban-dog, why so named, III.
Bands worn by Taylor the water poet, XIV.
Banester, Christopher, vice-chancellor of duchy of Lancaster, II.
Bangor, rural dean of, VIII.
Bangor monastery, legendary account of, XV.
Banister *or* Banistre family, of Preston: notice of, XXII.
Bank hall, formerly Bank top, near Burnley, XIV.
Bank hall, Croston: notice of, XXII.
Bank hall, Walton, XII; notice of, XXII.
Bank hill, Bowden, long the residence of the Vawdreys, VIII.
Bankes, 𝔑, IV, IX, XXII.
Banks, 𝔑, VIII, XII, XIX, XXII, XXVIII.
Banks's *Extinct Baronage*, IX.
Banne, 𝔑, IV, XVIII, XXVII.
Bannister, 𝔑, VI, XII, XXVII.
Banquet to Lord Strange at Manchester, II.
Baptism and baptismal regeneration, legendary notices of, XV.
Baptism of witches, VI.
Baptismal ceremonies at Amsterdam and Edinburgh, I; at Manchester, XVIII.
Barbadoes, connection of England with, XII.
Barbar, Mr., XXVII.
Barbor, 𝔑, XVII.
Barbor's land, Warrington, XVII.
Barcroft, 𝔑, XIV, XIX, XXII.
Barcroft hall, Burnley: notice of, XXII.
Bardenay, Lincolnshire: legendary notices of, XV.
Bardesley, Edmund, XIX.
Bardsley, Richard, XXVII.
Bardsea, 𝔑, XXII.
Bardsea hall, Urswick, co. Lanc.: notice of, XXII.
Barers, XX (*tit.* Aluetham).
Baret, Elizabeth, XIX.
Barker, 𝔑, VIII, XIII, XVII, XX, XXII, XXVII, XXVIII.
Barking, co. Suffolk, XIII.
Barkley, a preignaunt poete, XV.
Barkstead, 𝔑, IX, XVIII.
Barlæus, Caspar, on Elizabeth princess palatine, XIII.

Barlow, 𝔑, I, VIII, XIII, XIV, XVIII, XIX, XX, XXII, XXVII.
Barlow hall, Manchester: notice of, XIX.
Barnecroft, XX (*tit.* Whalleye).
Barn-hey, Liverpool, XII.
Barn chapel in Manchester (Newcome's), XVIII.
Barnard, 𝔑, XXII.
Barnardiston, sir Samuel, XXVII.
Barnes, Henry, XXII.
Barnet, near London, XIV.
Barnet, 𝔑, IX, XVIII, XXVII.
Barns, 𝔑, VIII, XXII.
Barnshaw-cum-Goosetrey chapel, Sandbach: account of, VIII.
Barnside *or* Bernesete hall, Colne: notice of, XXII.
Barnstable "fair and pleasant," XIII; haven of, I.
Barnston hall, Woodchurch, VIII.
Barnston, 𝔑, VIII, XIV.
Barnton, township of Budworth, VIII, XIV.
Barnwell, XIII.
Baron, 𝔑, XXII.
Baronetage, XII.
Baronets, observations respecting, XIV.
Baronius, Cæsar: notices of, VII, XIII.
Baroue, 𝔑, XX.
Barrat, William, IV.
Barret *or* Barrett, 𝔑, VIII, XIII, XVIII, XIX, XXII, XXVII.
Barrett MSS. in Chetham library, XVIII.
Barrie, co. Glamorgan, I.
Barrington, XIII.
Barrington, captain, II.
Barritt, —, XII.
Barron, Thomas, XVIII.
Barrow, co. Chester: account of, VIII.
Barrow, 𝔑, VIII, IX, XIII, XIV, XXII, XXVIII.
Barrowclogh, XX (*tit.* Whalleye).
Barry, 𝔑, VIII.
Barrymore, earl of, VIII.
Barrymore, William, VIII.
Barsley, 𝔑, XVIII, XXVII.
Barterley, township of Bartomley, VIII.
Barterton, township of Budworth, VIII.
Bartherton, township of Wibunbury, VIII.
Bartholinus, Caspar: notice of, IV.
Bartholinus, Thomas, the Dane, VI.
Bartholomew fair, revival of, XVIII.
Bartlet, Mr., XIV.
Bartomley, co. Chester: account of, VIII; massacre at, II.
Barton, XIII.
Barton, township of Farndon, VIII.
Barton, near Preston: St. Lawrence's chapel in, XXII.
Barton manor, Eccles, XX; notices of it and the hall, XIX.
Barton, 𝔑, IV, VIII, XII, XIV, XVIII, XIX, XX, XXII, XXVII.
Bartron, sir Thomas, XXII.
Barue *sive* Barrow, XX.
Barvis, Rev. Cuthbert, XIX.
Barwick, 𝔑, VIII, XIII, XVIII, XXII, XXVII.
Basford hall, Wibunbury: notice of, VIII.
Bashall, XIV.
Βασιλικον Δωρον, for whom written, III.
Basil, XIII.
Basylyus (saynt) purtrayed in ryche tysshewe, XV.
Basingwerk, XV; notices of the abbey, VII, VIII.
Basingwerk, Willm. abbas de, XX.
Basire, Dr. Isaac: account of, XIII.
Baskawe grange, VIII.
Baskervyle, 𝔑, VIII, XVIII, XXVII.
Basle, singular will of a rabbi at, I.
Basnett, 𝔑, VIII, XIX.
Basnett-street, Liverpool, XII.
Bass island, notices of, I.
Basteen, Mr., of Dover, XXVIII.

Bastwick, Dr. John: sufferings of, IV.
Bataile of Brampton, extract from, XXIX.
Bate, Elizabeth: murder by, XVIII.
Bateman MS. of the "Song of Lady Bessy," XXIX.
Bates, ꝶ, XIII.
Bath, co. Somerset, XIII; notices of, I, IV, XXV.
Bath and Wells, Robert Burnell bishop of, VIII, XX.
Bath, Robert, vicar of Rochdale, XIV, XXII; notices of, II, XIX.
Bath, Mr., XVIII, XXVII.
Bathegrall, Will. de, XX.
Batho, Edward, VIII.
Bathurst, Dr. Ralph, XIII.
Batterise in Bowland, XIV.
Battlefield college, notice of, XXII.
Battler at Oxford, fees of a, XII.
Battles, Anglo-Saxon: legendary notices of, XV.
Battori, Stephen, king of Poland, XIII.
Bautrie, XIV.
Bawdrie (baldric), a girdle, XIV.
Bawes, XX (*tit.* Walton).
Baxenden, XIX.
Baxter, ꝶ, IV, VI, VIII, XII, XIII, XVII, XVIII, XXVII.
Bayle's *Dictionary*, XIII.
Baylegh, XX.
Baylegh, Joh. de. XX.
Bayley, township of Ribchester: chantry founded there, XXII.
Bayley, ꝶ, VIII, XII, XIV, XVIII, XIX, XXII, XXVII.
Baylie, Nicholas: notice of, VII.
Bayliffe of St. Werburge, his crime and punishment, XV.
Baylue, a Dutch high-sheriff, I.
Bayly, Dr., physician to queen Elizabeth, XXIV.
Baynes, ꝶ, II, XXII.
Baynham, ꝶ, I, XII.
Beachin manor house, Codington, Cheshire, VIII.
Beachley passage, on the Severn, I.
Beak, Mr., XXVIII.
Beal, ꝶ, XIII.
Beale, ꝶ, XIII, XIV, XXVII.
Beamont's *Warrington in* 1465, XXII.
Beard, William, XVIII, XXVII.
Beards, angelical and thanksgiving, XIII.
Beardsall, Jo., XXVII.
Bearsill, Mrs., XVIII.
Beast market *or* Heath street, Warrington, XVII.
Beasts, instruments for mannes salvacyon, XV.
Beatson, IX.
Beauchamp's (lady) gardens, XIII.
Beauclerc, ꝶ, IX, XXII.
Beaucliffe hall, Eccles: notice of, XIX.
Beaumaris, Anglesey, IX.
Beaumont-cote, in Skerton, Bolton-le-sands: notice of, XXII.
Beaumont hall, XXII.
Beaumont, ꝶ, I, V, VIII, XIII, XIV, XX.
Beawsee, manor of, XVII.
Bebington, co. Chester: account of, VIII.
Beby, John, and Anna his wife, XVIII.
Beccy, a holy preeste from the North, XV.
Becher, John Joachim: account of, XIII.
Beck, ꝶ, XVIII, XXII, XXVII.
Beck's *History of Furness Abbey*, XXII.
Becke, Tho., XXVII.
Beckermet, the churches of, XXII.
Becket, ꝶ, VII, VIII, XVIII, XXII.
Beckington, Thomas de, bishop of Wells: notice of, I.
Becon on the support of poor scholars, VIII.
Beconsall *alias* Hesketh Bank, co. Lanc.: account of, XXII.

Bede, venerable, xv; his tomb and monument, i.

Bedell, bishop, xiv, xviii.

Bedford, in Leigh, co. Lanc., xii, xix.

Bedford, Ingelram de Gynes earl of, xxii.

Bedford, John duke of (temp. Henry VI.), xxii.

Bedlam, visits to, xviii.

Bedlam (Tom of) the Tinker, a play, xiv.

Bedlam (Tom à), a tune, xiv.

Bedlams (Tom o'), licensed beggars: account of, xiv.

Bedlo *or* Bedloe, Tom, a masque character, xiv.

Bedsteads of the reign of James I. described, xiv.

Bedwin, ix.

Bee, 𝔑, xiii, xxvii.

Beech, William, killed in church by lightning, xxvii.

Beecher, Mr., xiii.

Beechton, township of Sandbach, viii.

Beer (charter-), "thick muddy stuff," i.

Bees and beehives, i.

Bees (St.), college of, xiv.

Beesley, Richard, xxviii.

Beeston, township of Bunbury, viii; surrender of the castle, xxvii.

Beeston, 𝔑, viii, xiii.

Beeston's *Workes*, xviii.

Beetham church, in Westmoreland: notice of, xix.

Begging corn, a Cheshire custom, vii.

Behmen, Jacob, xiii.

Beighton, 𝔑, xviii, xix.

Beirne, xii.

Bek, 𝔑, xx.

Bekansgill *or* Vale of Nightshade, in Furness, xxii.

Beke, Thomas, xix.

Bekyngham, Elias de, xx.

Belasyse, 𝔑, viii, xix.

Bele, riv., xx.

Belefeld, 𝔑, xx.

Belfast, ix, xii; notice of, i.

Belfeld, 𝔑, xiv, xix.

Belfield, Arthur, of Clegg hall: notice of, viii.

Belfield hall, Milnrow: account of, xix.

Belfore, Mr., xxvii.

Belgrave in Eccleston, co. Chester, viii.

Bell, 𝔑, i, ii, iv, ix, xiii, xviii, xix, xxii, xxvii.

Bell inn, Gray's-inn lane, xiv.

Bell, to bear the: probable origin of the adage, iii.

Bell-founding "antichristian," xviii.

Bells in Edinburgh, i.

Bellamont, earl of, xxviii.

Bellarmyne, iv; his *Works*, "foure books of," xix.

Bellasis, Mr. sergeant, xxii.

Belle, John, xvii.

Bellford, near Holy isle, i.

Belling's *History of the late Warre in Ireland*, xii.

Bellingham, 𝔑, v, viii, xiv, xxii.

Bellis, 𝔑, viii, xix.

Bello-Becco. *See* Erynach.

Bellocampo, Walterus de, xx.

Bellomonte, 𝔑, xx.

Bellot, 𝔑, viii.

Bellum Papale, by James, vii.

Bellusbe, Harry, ix.

Bellyn's lande, Warrington, xvii.

Beloe's *Anecdotes of English Literature*, xiv.

Belot, 𝔑, xxvii.

Belsetanabbe, xx (*tit.* Bilyngton).

Belson, Mr., xiii.

Belton's field, Halton, Cheshire, viii.

Belvoir castle, old panelled picture of Henry VII. at, viii.

Benbow, captain: reasons for his execution at Shrewsbury, ii.

Bendall, captain, iv.

Bendger, sir Thomas, auditor to queen Elizabeth, xxiv.

Bendyshe, sir Thomas, ambassador to Constantinople, XIII.
Benedycte (saynt) and his couent purtrayed: his rule monestycall adopted by saynt Werburge, XV.
Benefice (the), Wild's comedy of, annotated by Newcome, XVIII.
Benfield, Amadæus, VII.
Benfield, Dr. Sebastian: notice of, VII.
Benn, 𝔑, IX.
Benn-street, Liverpool, XII.
Bennet, 𝔑, VIII, XVIII, XXIV.
Bennett, 𝔑, I, VIII, XII, XXII.
Bennison, 𝔑, XXII.
Benoilt, Thomas, clarencieux: his Lancashire visitations, XXIV.
Benson, 𝔑, VIII, XIV, XIX.
Benson's *Relation*, a rare tract in Chetham library, XIV.
Bentham, Christopher, a Liverpool printer, I.
Bent, 𝔑, XVIII, XXVII.
Bent hall, Oldham, in 1849 a hat warehouse, XIX.
Bentivoglio (cardinal) on Stanley's surrender of Deventer, XXV.
Bentivolio, *i.e.* Dr. Nathaniel Ingelo, XIII.
Bentivolio, character of the work of that name, XIII.
Bentley, 𝔑, IV, VIII, XIII, XXVII.
Bently, IX.
Bentwood, in Rochdale, XIX.
Benuille, 𝔑, XX.
Beorswyde, quene of Deiram, mother of St. Hilda, XV.
Berckley, Mrs.: singular dream respecting, XXVII.
Berdeshull, 𝔑, XX.
Berdeword, Willmus de, XX.
Berdisley, 𝔑, XVII.
Bereford, Willmus de, XX.
Beresford, Mr., XXVIII.
Berewyk, Patricius, XX.
Bergen, walls of, I.
Bergh, Ad. de, XX.
Berisford, Mr., XVIII.
Berkeley, Mr. Gawain, minister of Scarisbrick chapel, XXII.
Berkenhead manor, account of, VIII.
Berkenhead priory, in Wirrhall, VIII.
Berkenhead, 𝔑, VIII.
Berkenhend, XII.
Berkshire, property of the Garways in, IX.
Berlin, superstition at, I.
Bermudas, the: Waller's lines upon, XIII.
Bernard, 𝔑, XIII, XX.
Bernard's *Catalogue*, VII; *Guide to Grand Jurymen*, VI.
Bernardi, John, XXVIII.
Bernardus, cocus, XXX.
Bernderlond, XX. (*tit.* Kyuerdale).
Berne, Switzerland, XIII; account of a thirteen years' abstinence from food at, I.
Berneston, Gilb. de, XX.
Bernier's *Abridgement* of Gassendi's *Philosophy*, XIII; *Account of the Court of Aurengzebe*, IX.
Bernulphus, kyng of Mercians, defeated by the Danes, XV.
Berry, 𝔑, VII, IX, XVIII, XIX, XXII.
Berta the kynges doughter of France married to Ethelbryc of Kent, XV.
Berthualdus, archbishop of Canterbury, XV.
Bertie, Montague, earl of Abingdon, VIII.
Berwick, description of, I; taking of, XXIX.
Berwick, duke of, XXVIII.
Beseley, Chris., VIII.
Besse, aunt, XIV.
Best, Henry, XIII.
Beswicke, 𝔑, V, XIV, XVIII, XIX, XXVII, XXVIII.
Beswicke Evidences, XIX.
Betham, 𝔑, I, XXII.

Bethom church. *See* Beetham church.
Bethone, 𝔑, XX.
Betley occupied by prince Rupert, II.
Bets on the war with France in 1706, IX.
Beverley, 𝔑, XIII, XXVII.
Bewerton, township of Aldford, Cheshire, VIII.
Bewerton, township of Audlem, Cheshire, VIII.
Bewsey hall, Warrington: notice of, XXII.
Bewsey tragedy, origin of the, XVII.
Bexton, Joh. de, XX.
Bexton, township of Nether Knutsford, VIII.
Bexton hall, Rosthorne, in 1845 a farm house, VIII.
Bexwicke, 𝔑, IX, XIX.
Bexwicke bridge, near Manchester, XIX.
Beyton, Rob. de, XX.
Beza, XIV; portrait of, I.
Bibby, John, XIV.
Bibles, notices of various, XIII.
Bibliographia Gallica universalis, XIII.
Bibliography, English: great want of a body of, XIII.
Bibliotheca Chymica by Borell, XIII.
Bickerstaff, Margaret, XXII.
Bickerstath, 𝔑, XX.
Bickersteth *or* Bickerstaffe, co. Lanc., IV.
Bickersteth *or* Bicksteth, Thomas, IX.
Bickerton, 𝔑, VIII, XXVII.
Bickley in Malpas, VIII.
Bideford, co. Devon, I.
Bidston, co. Chester, I, XII; account of, VIII.
Bierley family, trial of some of its members for witchcraft, VI.
Bigg, George, XXII.
Bigland, 𝔑, XXII.
Bigland hall, Cartmell: notice of, XXII.
Bigot family, incidental notices of, VIII.
Bikeden, XX (*tit.* Whiteword).
Bikerton in Malpas, VIII.
Biley grange, Middlewich: notice of, VIII.
Billiard, Jarvis, "a judicious apothecary," I.
Billiards, XIV; played by Newcome, XVIII.
Billing, 𝔑, VIII, XXII.
Billinge *or* Billing, XIV; account of, XXII.
Billingsgate, XII.
Billingsley, Mr., XVIII.
Billington, 𝔑, XXII.
Bills, Yonker de, a famous empiric: account of, XIII.
Bilson, frauds of the boy of, VI.
Bilyngton, XX.
Bilyngton, 𝔑, XX.
Binby village, near Budworth, VIII.
Bindloss, 𝔑, II, VIII, XXII.
Binghall, Mr., of Acton, XXVII.
Bingham's, John, *Tactics of Ælian*, XIV.
Bingley, Robert Benson lord, XXII; notice of, VIII.
Biographia Britannica, astonishing judgment of the writer of Ashmole's Life in, XIII.
Birch, near Manchester, IV; account of, XIX.
Birch, 𝔑, II, IV, IX, XII, XIII, XVIII, XIX, XXII, XXIV, XXVII.
Birch, its value as a lamia-fuge, VI.
Birch MSS., XIV.
Birch's *Elizabeth*, XXIX.
Birch's *Life of Cudworth*, XIII.
Birchall, 𝔑, VIII, XXII.
Birchard, Walterus de, XX.
Birchehalgh, XX (*tit.* ffarneworth).
Birchgreue, XX (*tit.* Reued).
Birchehos in Farnword, XX.
Birchenley, near Rochdale, XIX.

Birches, Ric. de, xx.
Bircheyn, Joh. de, xx.
Bircle cum Bamford new (in 1846) church, Middleton, xix.
Bird, 𝔑, viii.
Birdpolt, co. Dorset, xiii.
Birkenhead, ix; surrendered to the parliament, ii. *See* Berkenhead.
Birkenhead priory, the Liverpool granary of, xii.
Birkenhead, 𝔑, ii, iv, xxvii.
Birkley, William, a pseudonym of John Austen a Roman-Catholic writer, xiii.
Birkyn, Jac. de, xx.
Birley, Isabel, establishes a free school at Kirkham, xxii.
Birmingham, alleged conflict at, ii.
Birnard, 𝔑, xiv.
Birom, 𝔑, xvii, xxii.
Biron, 𝔑, xiv, xix, xx. *See* Device.
Birthday (or "baptizeinge day") of Henry Newcome, xviii.
Births (the three) of man: nativity, baptism, burial, xv.
Birtles, township of Prestbury, viii.
Biscoe, Edward, xxii.
Biscopham, Ric. de, xx.
Biscopheym, xxii.
Bishopricks in Scotland and Ireland, i.
Bishops-Auckland, portraits in the palace at, i.
Bishops-Castle, ix.
Bishops' sees removed by William the conqueror, xv.
Bishopsthorpe, account of, i.
Bispham, 𝔑, viii, xxii.
Bispham in Amounderness, account of, xxii.
Bispham halls in Billinge and Croston, notices of, xxii.
Bixteth *or* Bixstath, 𝔑, xii.
Bixteth-street, Liverpool, xii.
Black's (W. H.) *Catalogue of the Ashmole MSS.*, xiii.
Black knight of Nappa, *i.e.* sir Thomas Metcalf, xiv.
Blackadder, John: imprisonment of, i.
Blackborne huntsman, payment to, xiv.
Blackburn, vi, viii, xiv, xix; account of, xxii; occupied by the parliamentary forces, ii.
Blackburne, 𝔑, viii, xix, xxii, xxviii.
Blackburnshire, copyholders of, xiv.
Blackelache, xx (*tit.* Spotlond).
Blackenhall, township of Wibunbury, viii.
Blackett, sir Edward, viii.
Blackhead's (Stephen) conspiracy with Robert Young against bishop Spratt, xxviii.'
Blackiston *or* Blackstone, 𝔑, i, ii.
Blackledge, 𝔑, xxii.
Blackleech, James, xxii.
Blackley chapel, incident of the plague at, iv.
Blackley hall, near Middleton, xiv.
Blackmore, 𝔑, ix, xii, xviii.
Blackpool, a hamlet of Poulton, xxii; Vauxhall, near Blackpool, a seat of the Tyldesleys, xiv.
Black rock, Magu island, Ireland, i.
Blackrod, account of, xix.
Blacks (for mourning) forbidden by John Bruen, xiv.
Blackstone, sir Philip, ii.
Blackstone edge, fortifications and skirmishes upon, ii.
Black-stone examination at Glasgow described, iv.
Blackwall (Swarte-wael) in Voornland, i.
Blackwell, Mr., iv.
Blacon, tithes of, viii.
Blaew, xiii.
Blage, Peter, chantry priest, viii.
Blagge, Margaret, afterwards Mrs. Godolphin, xiv.

Blair, sir James Hunter: marriage of, I.
Blaire, captain, XXVIII.
Blak riv., XX.
Blake, 𝔑, VIII, XII.
Blakeacre in Farington, XXX.
Blakeburn, XX; de capella, XX; constab., XX; vicarii et personæ de, XX; Adam de, XXX.
Blakeburne, 𝔑, XX.
Blakeburnschir senescalli, XX.
Blakebuttes, XX (*tit.* Bacford).
Blakeclogh, XX (*tit.* Spotlond).
Blakecroft, XX (*tit.* Aluetham).
Blakehurst, William, XVII.
Blakelache, XX (*titt.* Carleton parva, Chadewyk, Whelton).
Blakeley, co. Lanc., account of, XIX; its meeting-house pulled down in 1715, V. *See* Blackley.
Blakelowe, XX (*tit.* Eccles).
Blakepughul, XX (*tit.* Chadewyk).
Blakerode, Hugh de, XIX.
Blakesawe, XXX.
Blakesik, XX (*tit.* Whiteword).
Blakslade, XX (*tit.* Spotlond).
Blakeston, Mr., XIII.
Blakestrindheued, XX (*tit.* Whiteword).
Blakey, 𝔑, XXII.
Blanche meadow, Warrington, XVII.
Bland, 𝔑, VIII, XIV, XVIII, XIX, XXVII.
Blanshard, Gilb. de, XX.
Blare, James, I.
Blasdale, James, XIX.
Blasshes in Penwortham, XXX.
Blaston, Gilb de, XX.
Blawith, co. Lanc., account of, XXII.
Blayborne, William, IX.
Blaynborne, John, IX.
Bleacsley, a taylor, XIII.
Bleamore, Mr., XXVII.
Bleasdale, the Parkinsons of, XIV.
Blease, Mr., VIII.
Blencowe, 𝔑, XXII.
Blesedale peramb., XX.
Blesdikius, XIII.
Bletso, Dr., XXVII.
Blevin, Thomas, XXII.
Bliss (Ashmole's *Way to*), character of, XIII.
Blome, XII, XVIII.
Blomeley, sir John, clerk, VIII.
Blondel, David: account of, XIII.
Bloodworth, sir Thomas, knt., and his daughter, XII.
Bloomsmithy *or* wood-rents, XXII.
Blore-heath, battle of, VIII, XVII.
Blosse, rev. sir Francis Lynch, I.
Blount, 𝔑, XIII, XXV.
Blount's *Law Dictionary*, extract from, XVII.
Blue-coat schools, Chester, VIII.
Blundell (Ince-), township of Sefton, XXII.
Blundell, 𝔑, II, VIII, IX, XII, XVII, XIX, XX, XXII, XXVII, XXVIII.
Blunt's *Committee*, extract from, XII.
Blythe, 𝔑, VIII, XIV.
Boardman, 𝔑, XVIII, XXII, XXVII.
Boate, Mr., XXVII.
Boats (passage-) between Haerlem and Amsterdam, I.
Boccalini, Trajan: account of, XIII.
Bochart, Samuel: account of, XIII.
Bodin *or* Bodinus, John, XVIII; notices of, VI, XIII.
Bodkin, a game, XIV.
Bodleian library, VII, XIII.
Bodley, sir Thomas, VII.
Bodmin, XII.
Boggard-hole, near Hoarstones, Pendle, VI.
Boguslaus, XIII.
Bohemia, Elizabeth queen of, I, XIII; her marriage, XIV; princess Elizabeth her daughter, I, XIII.
Bohemian brethren, XIII.
Bohemian Persequution, XVIII.
Bohun, 𝔑, XX.
Bois-le-duc, fortifications of, I.

Bold, 𝔑, II, IV, IX, XII, XIV, XVIII, XIX, XX, XXII.
Bold chapel in Farnworth church: account of, XXII.
Bold hall, Farnworth: account of, XXII.
Bolden, John, XXII.
Boleign, Stephen earl of, XXII.
Boleyn, sir Thomas, XIV.
Bolinbroke, Henry de, afterwards Henry IV., XXII.
Bolingbroke, St. John viscount, IX.
Bolland, XIV.
Bollin fee, Wilmslow, VIII.
Bollin hall, Wilmslow: notice of, VIII.
Bollin river, VIII.
Bolling family, XIX.
Bollington, township of Bowden, VIII.
Bollington, township of Prestbury, VIII.
Bollington, township of Rosthorne, VIII.
Bolton in Bowland, XIV. *See* Boulton.
Bolton-le-moors, VIII, IX, XII, XIII, XIV, XVIII; account of, XIX; incidents in, during the Civil wars, II, IV.
Bolton-le-sands, VIII; account of, XXII.
Bolton-upon-Swale, XIX.
Bolton, duke of, VIII.
Bolton, 𝔑, I, VIII, IX, XIV, XVIII, XIX, XX, XXII, XXVII, XXVIII.
Bonaventura's *De Alis Seraphim*, where to be found, XIII.
Bonaventure, ship, I.
Bond, 𝔑, XIII, XXII.
Bonebury, VIII.
Bongrace, a sort of hood, I.
Boniface "the idol-saint" of Bunbury, Cheshire, XIV.
Boniface, pope, XV.
Bonk, XX (*tit.* Spotlond).
Bonke-street, Warrington, XVII.
Bonkhouses, XX (*tit.* Aluetham).
Bonner, Edmund, bishop of London, XXIV; notices of, VIII.
Bonney's *Life of Jeremy Taylor*, character of, XIII.
Bonvile, William lord, XXII.
Boodle, Mr., XVIII.
Book of the Garter by Ashmole, XVIII.
Booke of Martyrs, XVIII.
Book borrowers and promisers, XIII.
Books, Newcome's favourite, XVIII.
Booker *or* Bowker, 𝔑, XVIII, XXVII.
Bookland, a free-tenure charter, VII.
Booth hall, Bury: account of, XIX.
Booth-lane, near Sandbach: battle at, II.
Booth, 𝔑, I, II, IV, VI, VIII, IX, XII, XVIII, XIX, XXII, XXVII, XXVIII.
Booth's Salford chapel, XVIII, XIX.
Boothman, Jane, VI.
Booths hall, within Worsley, Eccles: account of, XIX.
Booths hall, Rosthorne: notice of, VIII.
Booths-town, Eccles, XIX.
Bootle mill, profits of, XII. *See* Botyll.
Bootle, 𝔑, II, IX, XII, XIV, XVIII, XXII.
Borderers, how they fought at Preston, V.
Bordley, William, minister of Hawkshead: his letters to bishop Gastrell, XXII.
Bordman, 𝔑, VIII, XIX.
Bordrigge, James, XXII.
Boreel, Adam: account of, XIII.
Borell, Peter: account of, XIII.
Borlase's book on Ireland, XII.
Boroughbridge, co. York., VIII.
Boroughbridge, deanery of, VIII.
Boroughreeve of Manchester, Richard Halliwell, vintner, XIV.
Borowgh, William, a Muscouy pilot, XXIV.
Borrett, Mr., XXII.
Borromeo's tomb, XVIII.
Borsley chapel, VIII.
Borwick, in Warton: account of manor, chapel and hall, XXII.

Boscobel, xiv.
Boseley, in Prestbury: account of, viii.
Bossen, hamlet of Cheadle, Cheshire, viii.
Bostock, township of Davenham, viii; hall, notice of, viii.
Bostock, 𝔑, viii, ix, xxii.
Boston, bad character of, xxvii.
Bosvile, Thomas, of Edlington, xviii.
Boswell, 𝔑, vii, xiii.
Boswell's *Sale Catalogue*, extract from, xxiv.
Bosworth, 𝔑, xxiv.
Bosworth, battle of, xxix.
Boteler, 𝔑, viii, xvii.
Botfield, Beriah, of Norton hall, xxiii.
Bothe, 𝔑, xix.
Bothestede, xx (*tit.* Stanword).
Bothestudyerdh, xx (*tit.* Whiteword).
Bothome, xx (*tit.* Bilyngton).
Bothomley, Rob., viii.
Botiler, 𝔑, xx.
Botiller, 𝔑, xvii, xxii.
Botley, Samuel, xiii.
Botsaccus, xiii.
Botteley, John, viii.
Bottiger's *Geschichte von Sachsen*, extract from, xviii.
Bottoms hall in Mottram, notice of, viii.
Bottoms hall in Whaley, notice of, viii.
Botyler, John le, xxii.
Botyll (Bootle), co. Lanc., ix.
Bouchier, Thomas, advocate, viii.
Bouderuydyng, v, xx (*tit.* Bilyngton).
Bouderuydyng, 𝔑, xx.
Bougerelle's *Memoir of Peter Gassendi*, xiii.
Boughey, Mrs., viii.
Boughton, Chester, xix; account of, viii.
Bouillier's (Francisgne) *Historie et Critique de la Révolution Cartésienne*, xiii.
Boules, sir John, ix.
Boulogne, Stephen earl of, afterwards king of England, xxii.
Bouls *or* Boals, William, ix.
Boulton, xiv, xix.
Boulton, 𝔑, ii, viii, xii, xx.
Bound, Cuthbert, minister of Warmwell; his testimony to "a wonderful matter," xiii.
Bourbon, duke of, xiv.
Bourchier, sir Henry: extracts from his correspondence, vii.
Bourdehowse, xx (*tit.* Whalleye).
Bourding, meaning of, vii.
Bourgeois, sir Francis: his bequest to Dulwich college, xiii.
Bourignon, Antoinette: her "long line" of works, xiii.
Bourn, Sam., xiii.
Bourne, 𝔑, ii, xiii, xiv, xviii, xxii, xxiv, xxvii, xxviii.
Bousfield, James, xxii.
Bouskill, James, xxii.
Boussel, Rob., xx.
Boutefeus, meaning of, iv.
Bovill, W. de, xxii.
Bows, various makes of, xiv.
Bowden, co. Chester, i; account of, viii; Adam Martindale's experiences at, iv.
Bowden, 𝔑, viii, ix, xxii.
Bowen, tide-surveyor, ix.
Bower, 𝔑, xix.
Bowes, 𝔑, xiv, xix, xxii.
Bowing at the altar not enjoined, i.
Bowker, 𝔑, ii, xiii, xviii.
Bowland and its forest, xiv.
Bowles, 𝔑, xiii, xxvii.
Bowling, xiv.
Bowling greens, xiv; notice of one at Liverpool, ix.
Bowet, Henry, archdeacon of Richmond, afterwards archbishop of York, xxii.
Bowman, 𝔑, xxii.

Bowson, local name for a badger, XIV.
Bowyer, Foster and John, VIII.
Bowzing gentlemen, XIV.
Box trees in form of soldiers, I.
Boydell chapel in Grappenhall church, VIII.
Boydell, 𝔑, VIII, XVII, XX.
Boyle, a favourite author with H. Newcome, XVIII.
Boyle, 𝔑, VI, IX, XIII.
Boylesnape, XX (*tit.* Barton).
Boylston, Dr., XIII.
Boyne river at Drogheda, I.
Boynton ("treacherous" colonel) slain at Wigan, II.
Boys, John, D.D., fellow of Chelsea college, XIII.
Brabazon, Edward lord, earl of Meath, XII; Mary his wife, I.
Brabin, Robt., one of the electors of Henry Newcome, XXVII.
Brabine, John, founder of Chipping school, XXII.
Bracebridge, 𝔑, VIII.
Bracebrugge, Galfr. de, XX.
Brackley, viscounts, XIV, XIX.
Bradborn, John, VIII.
Bradbury, 𝔑, VIII, XXII.
Braddall, Jo., parliamentary captain, XIV.
Braddon, Mr., IX.
Braddyll, 𝔑. II, VIII, XIV, XIX, XXII, XXVIII.
Braddyll hall, Langho, Blackburn: notice of, XXII.
Bradebrok, XX (*tit.* Wythenhull).
Bradehull, 𝔑, XX.
Bradelegh, 𝔑, XX.
Bradeley, township of Malpas, VIII.
Bradeley, William, vintner, York, XIV.
Bradell *or* Braddyll, John, II.
Braderuyding, XX (*titt.* Eccleshul, Reued).
Bradeschagh, XX (*titt.* Stanword, Whiteword).
Bradford, township of Manchester, XIX.
Bradford, co. York, I, XIV; defeat of Fairfax at, II.
Bradford (East-), near Clitheroe: notice of the manor of, XIV.
Bradford, earls of, VIII, XIX, XXII.
Bradford, 𝔑, I, VIII, XIX.
Bradford's *Letters*, XVIII.
Bradley, co. Stafford: account of the lease rent of, VIII.
Bradley, township of Frodsham, VIII.
Bradley halls in Barthomley and Budworth, notices of, VIII; in Eccleston and Chipping, notices of, XXII.
Bradley manor, Warrington, an ancient seat of the Haydocks: description of, XVII.
Bradley, 𝔑, VIII, XXII, XXVIII.
Bradocke, William, XII.
Bradshaigh, 𝔑, VIII, XXII.
Bradshaw, 𝔑, II, IV, VIII, IX, XII, XIV, XVIII, XIX, XXII, XXVII, XXVIII.
Bradshaw hall and chapel, Bolton-le-moors: accounts of, XIX.
Bradwall, township of Sandbach, VIII; hall, notice of, VIII.
Brahe, count Nielson, XIII.
Braithwaite, 𝔑, XXII.
Bramber, IX, XII.
Brambley, co. York, IV.
Bramhall, archbishop, I.
Bramhall, bishop, XIII.
Brampton, arrival there of the insurgents, V.
Brand's *Antiquities*, XIV; extract from on witchcraft, VI.
Brandearth, fields at Warrington, XVII.
Brandenburgh, elector of, XIII.
Brandlesholme, Henry de, and Alice his daughter, XIX.
Brandlesholme hall, in Elton near Bury: notices of, XIV, XIX.
Brandon, 𝔑, VIII, XIV, XXVIII.
Brandt (Gaspar) and Van Cattenburg's *Life of Grotius*, XIII.

Bras, 𝔑, xx.
Brasington, xiii.
Braules, xiv.
Brawdrick, a "barbarous" Yorkshire robber, iv.
Bray *or* Braye, 𝔑, viii, xix, xxii.
Braynes's expedition to Jamaica, ix.
Brazenose college, Oxford, ix; notice of, xii.
Bread turned to stone, i.
Bread silver, xxii.
Breares, 𝔑, xiv.
Brearley, 𝔑, xiv, xix.
Breda, xiii; declaration of, xviii.
Bredebury, Stephanus de, xx.
Bredekyrk, 𝔑, xx.
Bredow, co. Worcester: Dr. John Prideaux dies at, xiii.
Breerlyclose, xx (*tit.* Whalleye).
Breers, 𝔑, ix, xxviii.
Breise, Patrick, vii.
Brendebotheker, xx (*tit.* Whiteword).
Brendescoles, xx. *See, in same vol.*, Stanword *and* Whelton.
Brandescoles, Ric. de, xx.
Brendewod per div., xx.
Brendewod, 𝔑, xx.
Brendlegh in Penwortham, xxx.
Brennan in Bowland, xiv.
Brent, sir Nathaniel, xiii.
Brentford, battle of, ix.
Breres, 𝔑, xix, xxii.
Brereton, co. Chester, xii, xiii; account of, viii; some of Pell's *MSS.* once remaining at, xiii.
Brereton green, viii.
Brereton hall, account of, viii.
Brereton, 𝔑, i, ii, iii, iv, v, viii, xii, xiii, xviii, xix, xx, xxiii, xxvii, xxviii, xxix.
Brereton's (sir William) *Travels*, xiii.
Brerewood, 𝔑, iv, viii, ix.
Brescy, Rob. de, xx.
Bresseux, xiii.
Bret, Dr., xxvii.
Bretargh, William, and his descendants, xxii.
Bretharue, xx.
Bretharue, Rob. de, xx.
Bretharwe, xx (*tit.* Wolueton).
Brethergh, lieutenant: notice of, ii.
Bretherton, 𝔑, ii, ix, xxii.
Bretland, 𝔑, viii.
Breton, Alanus de, xx.
Breton, Rog. de, xxx.
Brett, 𝔑, xiii, xiv.
Brettargh, Mr., of Aigburth, ix.
Brettestrete, xx (*tit.* Dounom).
Bretton, 𝔑, xviii.
Breuse, Hugo de, xx.
Brewer (rev. J. S.) on Antonio de Dominis and Thorndike, xiii.
Brewerton *for* Bewerton, viii.
Brewery at Shrewsbury, i.
Brewyer, serjeant-major: victory of, ii.
Brexen, Willmus de, xx.
Brexis, Hugo de, xx.
Brian, Ralph, i.
Brickley hall, Wigan, xxii.
Brick-making at Dort, i.
Bricticus, kyng of West Saxon, xv.
Bridde, James, xix.
Briddestwysell, xx.
Briddestwysell, 𝔑, xx.
Briddock, 𝔑, xviii.
Brideoak, 𝔑, ii, viii, xviii, xxii.
Bridge, peculiar use of the word, xvii.
Bridge (the), Liverpool: why built where never water runs under, xii.
Bridge at Warrington, historical account of, xvii.
Bridge hall, Bury: account of, xix.
Bridge-Trafford hall, Plemstow, Cheshire: notice of, viii.
Bridge-street, Warrington, xvii.
Bridge's alley, Liverpool, xii.
Bridges in England and Scotland, notice of some of the finest, i.
Bridge, 𝔑, viii, xii, xix.

Bridgeman *or* Bridgman, ℞, I, II, IV, VI, VIII, IX, XII, XIII, XIV, XVIII, XIX, XXII, XXVII.
Bridgeman's chapel in Bolton church, XIX.
Bridgeman's chapel, Great Lever, Middleton: account of, XIX.
Bridges, Mr., XXVII.
Bridgett, Mrs.: her evidence at the Manchester trials, XXVIII.
Bridgewater, account of, I; siege of, XVIII.
Bridgewater, dukes of, XIX; earls of, I, XIV, XIX.
Briebec in Normandy, sir Bertine Entwisle (a hero of Agincourt) viscount and baron of, XIX.
Brienne, secretary of Louis XV. of France, XVIII.
Briercliffes (the), a gloomy and fated race, VI.
Brierley, ℞, XIV, XIX, XXII.
Brierwood, Robert, of West Chester, XXVIII.
Brieux's (M. de) happy and elegant lines on the death of Bochart, XIII.
Brigge, Ric. de, XX.
Briggs, ℞, VII, IX, XXII.
Brigheye, XX (*tit.* Whalleye).
Bright, ℞, II, XIII, XXIX.
Brightmeade, XIX.
Brightmet, co Lanc., XIV.
Brighton, Joh. de, XX.
Brikerton, VIII.
Brill, Holland, I.
Brimesburgh, Saxon monastery of, VIII.
Brimsage, township and hall in Bromborough, Cheshire: account of, VIII.
Brindle, co. Lanc., VIII; account of, XXII.
Brinsop hall, Dean, XIX.
Brisco, captain, XXVII.
Briscoe, Michael: "a godly minister" at Turton and Walmesley, IV, XIX, XXVII.
Bristol, IX, XII, XIII, XVIII; description and various notices of, I. *See* Brystowe.
Britannia Baconica by Childrey, notice of, XIII.
Britholm, XX (*tit.* Aluetham).
British Bibliographer, XXIX.
Britland, Mrs., XVIII.
Britons, legendary notices of the, XV.
Brittaine, Spencer, XVIII.
Britton, John, XIV; his *Memoirs of Aubrey*, XIII.
Brixtar, Mr., IX.
Broadbent, Caleb, XVIII.
Broadhead, Caleb, XVIII, XXVII.
Broadhulme, near Manchester, XVIII.
Broadhurst, ℞, XIX, XXVII.
Brochol, Roger de, XXII.
Brocholes, ℞, XX.
Brock, ℞, VIII.
Brockbank house, Liverpool, XII.
Brockbank, Christopher, XII.
Brocke, William, of Upton: account of, VII.
Brockfurlong in Farington, XXX.
Brockhole and Braddyll, estate so named, XIV.
Brockholes, ℞, XIV, XIX.
Brockholes hall, Preston: notice of, XXII.
Brockholls, Nicholas de, XXII.
Brocklesley, ℞, VIII.
Brodehalgh, XX. *See in same vol.* Spotlond.
Brodehalgh, ℞, XX.
Broderode, XX (*tit.* Spotlond).
Brodestone, XX (*tit.* Sadelword).
Brodhalgh, XX (*tit.* Chadewyk).
Brodryddynge, XX (*tit.* Whalleye).
Brodwere, Tho., VIII.
Broghill, lord, XII.
Broghton, XX.
Brok, XX (*tit.* Heleye).

Broke, lord, justice of the common pleas, XXIV.
Broke, Thomas, priest of Padiham, XXII.
"Broke the deere," *i.e.* dispersed them, XIV.
Broke-akyr, Orford, near Warrington, XVII.
Broke-hey, Orford, near Warrington, XVII.
Brokelehirstsike, XX (*tit.* Bilyngton).
Bromborough, Cheshire: account of, VIII.
Bromfield, 𝔑, VIII, XIII, XXVIII.
Bromhale, 𝔑, VIII.
Bromhousefeld, XX (*tit.* Eccles).
Bromley, 𝔑, I, VI, VIII, IX, XII, XIV, XIX, XXII, XXVIII.
Brompton, Pat.: rectory of, VIII.
Bromyard, XVIII.
Bromycroft, 𝔑, XX.
Bromyhurst, Joh. de, XX.
Bromyrode, XX (*tit.* Castelton).
Brook's *Lives of the Puritans*, XIV; correction of, XIX.
Brookbank, 𝔑, XII, XXII.
Brooke, 𝔑, I, IV, VIII, XII, XIV, XIX, XXII, XXVII, XXVIII.
Brookes, 𝔑, IX, XVIII, XIX, XXVII.
Brookhouses, township of Whitegate, Cheshire, VIII.
Brooks, 𝔑, II, XXII, XXVIII.
Brooksbank, Mr., fellow of Christ's college, Cambridge, XIII.
Broome, William, of Didsbury, XIX.
Broome and Knight, Messrs., XXII.
Broomhill, township of Barrow, Cheshire, VIII.
Brotherton, 𝔑, IX, XII, XVII, XXII, XXVIII.
Broughton, co. Flint, VIII.
Broughton in Furness, account of, XXII.
Broughton in Preston, IX; account of, XXII.
Broughton, township of Manchester, XIII, XIX.
Broughton towers in Furness, and Preston, notices of, XXII.
Broughton, 𝔑, VIII, IX, XIII, XXVII.
Brouncker, 𝔑, XIII.
Broune, 𝔑, XX.
Browedge school, Cartmell: account of, XXII.
Brown *or* Browne, 𝔑, II, IV, VI, VIII, IX, XIII, XVIII, XIX, XXII, XXVII, XXVIII.
Brownes, Mich., XIV.
Brownists at Amsterdam, divisions of the, XIII.
Brownists and Puritans, imputed acts of, XIV.
Brownlow, 𝔑, XII, XIX.
Brownrig, Dr., bishop of Exeter: character of his sermons, XIII.
Brownrigge, Christopher, XXII.
Brownrigge, Giles, founder of Kirby-Ireleth school, XXII.
Brownswood, William, curate of Douglas, co. Lanc., XXII.
Brownsword, 𝔑, XIII, XVIII, XIX, XXVII.
Browsholme hall, in Bowland, XIV: account of, XXII.
Browsholme MSS., XIV.
Broxholme, early and correct form for Browsholme, XIV.
Broxton, hundred of, VIII.
Broxton, township of Malpas, VIII.
Broxup, John, XVIII, XXVII.
Bruarne, Dr., Christ's-church college, Oxford, XXIV.
Bruccioli's (Antonio) *Commentary upon the Canticle of Canticles*, VII.
Bruce, 𝔑, V, VIII, XIII.
Bruce's *Annals*, IX.
Bruch hall, Warrington: notice of, XXII,
Bruche brook, heath, hey and holte, all in Warrington, XVII.

Bruche manor, Warrington: description of, xvii.
Bruche, 𝔑, xvii.
Brucker's *History of Philosophy*, xiii.
Brudenell, sir Thomas, bart., first earl of Cardigan, xiv.
Brudenell, lord, xxviii.
Bruen *or* Brun, Robert le, viii, xiv.
Bruen, John, of Bruen-Stapelford: notice of, viii; full and detailed account of, xiv.
Bruen, Sarah, xiv.
Bruen, Mr. and Madam, xxvii.
Bruera chapelry, Cheshire: account of, viii.
Bruggestrete, xx (*tit.* Cestria).
Brun, Henr. de, xx.
Brundrett, Mr., viii.
Brunghill, xiv.
Brunlay, xx; de capella, xx.
Brunlay, 𝔑, xx.
Bruno, Giordano: account of, xiii.
Brunsell, Mr., xiii.
Brunswick-street, Liverpool, xii.
Brus, 𝔑, xx, xxii.
Bruse *or* Braos, Giles de, bishop of Hereford: his tomb, i.
Brussels, ix.
Bryan, 𝔑. xxvii.
Brycall, Joh., viii.
Bryche, X'pofer, xxii.
Brydges, sir Egerton, bart., xxiv; his discussion of the Banbury peerage case, xiv; *Censura Literaria*, xxix.
Brydges' *Peers of James I.*, xiv.
Brydges, sir John, ix.
Bryer, rev. Thomas, of Marton, on the character of the Fylde people, xxii.
Bryges, *i.e.* Bruges: saynt Ethelburge now lyeth in, xv.
Bryn, sir Peter de, of Brynhill, xxii.
Bryn hall, Ashton-in-Makerfield: notices and description of, ii, xxii.
Brystowe, *i.e.* Bristol, xv.
Bubwith, Nicholas, bishop of Wells, i.
Buccleugh, dukes of, xiv, xix, xxii.
Bucer, portrait of, i.
Buchanan, xiii, xiv.
Buck, 𝔑, xiii, xix, xxvii.
Buckbridge *or* Bugbrook, deanery of Daventry, xv.
Buckden-Rake, xiv.
Buckflatt, xx (*tit.* Whalleye).
Buckingham, dukes of, ii, xiv, xix, xxii.
Buckingham, Mr., ix.
Bucklegh, 𝔑, xx.
Buckler's *Views of Endowed Schools*, xix.
Buckley, township of Malpas, viii.
Buckley hall, Rochdale: account of, xix.
Buckley hill, xviii.
Buckley, 𝔑, vii, xviii, xix, xxii.
Bucknall, sir William, knt., xii.
Bucknall, Mr., xxvii.
Bucksye, Nich., prebendary of Chester, viii.
Buckworth, Theophilus, bishop of Dromore, i.
Buddæus, xiii.
Budgell's *Memoirs of the Boyles*, xiii.
Budiford, Rob. de, xx.
Budle, 𝔑, xviii, xxvii.
Budworth magna, iv; account of, viii.
Budworth parva, account of, viii.
Buersell, George, xix.
Buhle (J. G.) on the Rosicrucians, xiii.
Buildwas, Rad. abbas de, xx.
Bukenham, Tho., xiii.
Bulches *for* bulges or projections, i.
Bulcock, 𝔑, vi.
Bulkeley *or* Bulkley, 𝔑, ii, viii, xii, xxii, xxvii.
Bullen, Anne: yellow mourning of, xiv.
Bulliadus, Ismael: account of, xiii.
Bullinger, portrait of, i.
Bullock, 𝔑, vi, xxii.

Bulloes, local name for wild plums, VI.
Bullough, Richard, "preacher of Langoe," XIV.
Bull's-Head inn, Manchester, XIV.
Bullynge, Henry: his tenancies in Warrington, XVII.
Bulstrode gardens, a Glastonbury thorn in, XIII.
Bulymer, Ric., XX.
Bunbury, co. Chester, XIII, XIV, XIX; offered to Henry Newcome, XVIII; general account of, VIII.
Bunbury monastery, suppression of, VIII.
Bunbury, ℞, I, VIII, IX, XIV.
Bunce, ℞, XX.
Bund, the, near Blackburn, XIV.
Bunebury, ℞, XX.
Buneuill, Alex, de, XX.
Bunhall, Mr., VIII.
Bunnion, Th., VIII.
Bunyan, John, boast of, XIV.
Burchelle, Edmundus de, XXX.
Burches, ℞, VIII.
Burd, William, chantry priest of Clitheroe, XXII.
Burd, Mr., XVIII.
Burdon, Rogerus, XX.
Burdredus, kynge of Mercelande: legendary notices of, XV.
Burdsell, Raph, XXVII.
Burgage rent, XII.
Burgagium, explanation of, XVII.
Burgersdicius's (Francis) *Institutiones Logicæ*, IV.
Burgess, ℞, VIII, XIII, XIX.
Burgess's *Spirituall Reviveing*, XVIII.
Burgh, ℞, VIII, XXII.
Burghall, Edward, vicar of Acton, molested by Quakers, VIII.
Burgher-soldiers at Rotterdam and Dort, I.
Burghill, John, bishop of Coventry and Lichfield, VIII.
Burgo, Hubertus de, XX.
Burgomasters in Holland, offices and dignities of, I.
Burgundy, duchess of, XXII.
Burhill, Robert: account of, XXIX.
Buri *or* Bury, ℞, XX.
Burial customs, IV, XIV.
Burial in churches the result of monkish avarice, VII.
Burie, co. Lanc., XIV; church of, XIX.
Burigny's *Memoir of Hugo Grotius*, XIII.
Burk, M., pastor of Weiltingen, XIII.
Burke, ℞, IX, XXVIII.
Burke's *Commoners*, XII, XVIII.
Burleigh, Robert lord, IX.
Burleigh, William lord, XIV, XXV, XXIX.
Burley, Francis, D.D., XIII.
Burleydam chapelry, Wrenbury, Cheshire: account of, VIII.
Burlington, William earl of, XIV, XXII.
Burn hall, Poulton-in-the-Fylde: account of, XXII.
Burn, Richard, of Garstang, XXII.
Burne, XIV; top of, XIV.
Burnedge near Manchester, XIX.
Burnehull, ℞, XX.
Burnell, ℞, VIII.
Burnet, Gilbert, bishop of Salisbury, IX, XIII, XVIII, XIX; notice of, IV; his *History of his own Times*, IX, criticisms of, XIII.
Burnet, Archibald, of Carlops, V.
Burnett, Ralph, IX.
Burney (Dr.) on Mace's *Musick's Monument*, XIII.
Burnley, VI, XIV; general account of, XXII; grammar school, XIV, XIX, account of, XXII.
Burnside, XIV.
Buron, Robert de, XIV.
Burrell, captain, governor of Mersey island, XII.
Burron, Edward (? John), XXII.
Burrough, John, XXIV.
Burrow, Robert, XXII.

Burry river, Caermarthenshire, i.
Burscough abbey, xxii; monastery, xix; priory, xxii; account of, viii; Willmus prior, xx.
Burscough, Peter, xxii.
Burscow hall, Ormskirk: notice of, iv.
Bursely's (Ann) case of casuistry, xxvii.
Burslam, captain, xxvii.
Burslem, viii.
Burton brok, xx (*tit.* Whelton).
Burton, co. Chester: account of, viii; its church given to Nesse hospital, viii.
Burton, township of Tarvin, Cheshire, viii.
Burton, co. Lanc., ix.
Burton, co. York, viii.
Burton on Trent stormed by Tyldesley, ii.
Burton, 𝔑, iv, viii, xviii, xx, xxii.
Burton's *Anatomy of Melancholy*, quotations from, xiv.
Burton's *Diary*, ix, xii, xviii.
Burtonwood, near Warrington, xvii; account of, xxii.
Burtonwood peramb., xx.
Burtonwood, John, preacher of Padiham, xiv.
Burwardesley, township of Bunbury, viii.
Burwell, xiii.
Burwell, Dr., chancellor of York, his virulent visitation speech, xviii.
Bury, co. Lanc., iv, ix, xiv; military proceedings at, ii; its "church style," xiv; general account of, xix. *See* Burie.
Bury classis, irregularities in, xviii.
Bury St. Edmund's, execution of witches at, xiii.
Bury, 𝔑, ix, xviii, xix, xxii. *See* Buri.
Burying the dead, Presbyterian irregularities at, xviii.
Buryngel, Petrus de, xx.
Busby, Dr., xiii.
Bushell, 𝔑, vii, viii, xii, xxii.
Busk *or* Stalling-Busk, in Wensleydale, xiv.
Busli, Roger de, xxii.
Busseburne, xx (*tit.* Bilyngton).
Bussell, 𝔑, viii, xxii, xxx.
Busses, Dutch herring-boats: their abundance, i.
Buth, le, xx (*tit.* Castelton).
Butiller, John, xvii.
Butler, 𝔑, i, v, viii, xii, xiii, xvii, xviii, xix, xxii, xxvii, xxviii.
Butler Papers, extract from, xvii.
Butley, township of Prestbury, viii.
Buttel, Alanus, xx.
Butter, 𝔑, xxvii.
Butterfield, Thomas, xxii.
Butterword, xx.
Butterword, 𝔑, xx.
Butterworth, township of Rochdale, xix.
Butterworth hall, Milnrow, Rochdale: notice of, xix.
Butterworth, 𝔑, ii, vii, xviii, xix, xxii, xxvii.
Button, William (? Edward), mayor of Chester, xiv.
Buttry, 𝔑, xxvii.
Butts for archery, description of, xiv.
Butts in Penwortham, xxx.
Butturlache, field in Warrington, xvii.
Butyller, William le, xvii.
Buxton, co. Derby, viii, xviii; its warm springs, vii.
Buxton, 𝔑, ii, v, xviii, xxvii.
Buxtorf, John: notice of, xiii.
Buylli, Alanus, xx.
Buys wife of Barrowford, vi.
Byfield, Mr., xxvii.
Byfield *On the Creed*, xviii.
Bygot, Rad., xx.
Byley grange, near Middlewich: notice of, viii.

Bymmecroft, XX (*tit.* Eccleshul).
Byng, Mr., XIII.
Byrne, sir John, of Timogue, bart, VIII.
Byrom, N, II, VIII, IX, XIII, XVIII, XIX, XXII, XXVII.
Byrom chapel in Manchester cathedral, XVIII.
Byrom hall, Winwick: account of, XXII.
Byrom-street, Liverpool, XII.
Byron, N, II, VIII, XIV, XVII, XIX.
Byset, Henr., XX.
Byton, Wm., IX.

CADESHWALLED, hamlet of Eccles, XIX.
Cadewalisset, XX.
Cadiz, wager respecting, IX. *See* Cales.
Cadock, Thomas: his Liverpool rent, XII.
Caen, death of Bochart at, XIII.
Caerleon, "where king Arthur kept his court," I; legendary notices of, XV.
Caermarthen, I. *See* Carmarthen.
Caeruska, or els called Caerleon, buylded by kyng Belinus, XV.
Caerwerid, "green city," the British name of Lancaster, XXII.
Cæsar, Julius, on British trees and mines, VII.
Cæsar, Dr. Julius, judge of the admiralty, XXIV.
Cæsar's (sir Julius) wife kept unburied five weeks, XIV.
Caghe *and* Caghe-meare, near Leyden, I.
Caillonet, Mr., IX.
Cain and Abel depaynted on arras, XV.
Cairne, Messrs., London correspondents of Richard Norris, IX.
Cairns, Mr., XXII.
Caithness, VII.
Caius college, Cambridge, XIII.
Cake, a groaning-, XIV.
Calamy, Dr., XII, XVIII, XIX; his dispute with the conforming clergy, VIII; praise of Tuckney and Cradock, XIII; imprisonment, XVIII.
Calandrine, Mr. VII.
Caldebrok, XX. *See in same volume* Eccles, Maunton, Swynton *and* Westewod.
Caldecot, township of Shocklach, Cheshire, VIII, XVIII; the living held by Henry Newcome's father, XVIII.
Calderwood, William, rebel quartermaster, V.
Calderwood's *Altare Damascenum:* notice of, I.
Caldey, great and little, co. Chester, VIII.
Caldicot, XIII.
Caldra *or* Calder abbey in Cumberland, account of, XXII.
Caldre, XX. *See in same volume* Reued.
Caldy island, I.
Calecot, Ido de, XX.
Calendar, reformation of the, XXIV.
Cales *or* Cadiz, expedition against by the earl of Essex, VII.
Caley, N, VIII, XIX, XXVII.
Callander, lord, II, XVIII.
Callixtines, the Moravians dissent from the, XIII.
Callott, serving-wench, VII.
Callys, Rob., VIII.
Calovius no match for Zwicker, XIII.
Calseys *i.e.* Causeways, directions for making, IX.
Calveley, township of Bunbury, VIII; hall; notice of, VIII.
Calveley hall, Handley, notice of, VIII.
Calveley, N, VIII, XXII, XXVII.
Calvert, N, XXII.
Calvin, XIV; on election of priest by people, XVIII; portrait of, I.

Calvinism, IV; its decline at the English universities, XIII.
Calwich abbey, co. Stafford, XIV.
Cambden, William, clarencieux, historian, XIII.
Cambrebok, Willmus, cler., XX.
Cambridge and its university, VIII, XII; sundry notices of, XIII; compact of a woman with the devil at, XVIII, XXVII.
Cambridge, Charles duke of: notice of, XIII.
Cambridgeshire, visit of Newcome to his relations in, XVIII.
Camden, **P**, VII, XIII, XIV, XIX.
Camden's *Britannia*, XIII; extract from, VII.
Camden's *Institutio Græcæ Grammaticis compendiaria*, IV.
Camelford, Gabriel, curate of Staveley, XXII.
Camera, Joh. de, XX.
Caméro *or* Caméron, his interview with James I. XIII.
Camoys, Thomas lord, XIX, XXII.
Campanella, Thomas, XIII.
Campano, Rob. de, XX.
Campbell's (lord) *Lives of the Chancellors*, XVIII, XXII; criticisms upon, XIII, XIX.
Campbell's (Dr.) *Life of Sir Kenelm Digby*, XIII.
Campeden, Walter de, rector of Wigan, XXII.
Camp-green, in Rosthorne, IV.
Campian, Mr., XXVII.
Campion, the jesuit, XXV.
Campsie, lord: notice of, I.
Can *or* Canne, John: account of, XIII.
Canal from Haerlem to Amsterdam, description of, I.
Canarie, a favorite wine of John Hales of Eton, XIII.
Cancefeld, J. de, XX.
Cancefield. **P**, XXII.
Cancia, Tho. de, XX.
Cancliffe, Abraham, of Salford: judgment upon, XXVII.
Candia, war of Venice against the Turk in, XVIII.
Canleschagh, XX (*tit.* Chaderton).
Canne, Mr. a Brownist minister at Amsterdam, I.
Canon-row house, Westminster, I.
Canons of 1603, XIV.
Cansfield, John, of Cansfield: notice of, II.
Cantelupe, Thomas de, bishop of Hereford: notice of, I.
Cantelupe, Willmus de, XX.
Canterbury, I: legendary notices of, XV; archbishops of, V, VIII, XIV, XX, XXII, XXIV.
Canterbury Tales by Chaucer: extract from, XIV.
Cantilupe, Milisent daughter of William de, VIII.
Cantire, mull of, I.
Canuilla, Willmus de, XX.
Canute, forest laws of, XIV.
Canwod abbay (*i.e.* Coldingham in Berwickshire) XV.
Cap justice, a masque character, XIV.
Cape de Verd islands, IX.
Capel, **P**, IX, XII, XIV, XVIII.
Capenhurst, XX (*tit.* Staneye).
Capes, **P**, XXX.
Capesthorne *or* Capeston, chapelry in Prestbury: account of, VIII.
Capgrave, John: account of, VII.
Capito, Joannes, medicus, XXIV.
Cappenhurst, township of Shotwick, VIII.
Capper, Ralph, XXVII.
Capusterne, Sarah daughter of Ranulphus de, VIII.
Caraites, a Jewish sect: account of, XIII.
Carberry, earl of, VIII.
Cardan, fanciful genius of, XIII.

Carden *or* Cawarden, township of Tilston, Cheshire, VIII: hall, notice of, VIII.
Carden *or* Cawarden family, notice of, VIII.
Cardiff, I.
Cardigan, earls of, XIV, XXII.
Cards (playing-), a Puritan's treatment of, XIV.
Cardun, Walterus, XX.
Cardwell, N, XXII.
Careless, John, "a wonderful weaver," XXVII.
Carew, George, earl of Totnes, VIII.
Carey, lady, XXVII.
Carick in Scotland, ringing rock and haunted cave at, I.
Carick in Ireland, account of, I.
Carincham, Cheshire, XVIII; notice of, I.
Cark hall, Flookborough, co. Lanc.: notice of, XXII.
Carleton, N, II, XIII, XX.
Carleton parva, XX.
Carlile family, XIX.
Carlinwark *now* Castle Douglas, Scotland, I.
Carlisle, I, XIV; founded by kynge Leil, XV; trials of Scottish prisoners at, V.
Carlisle, bishop of: his activity against the rebels, V.
Carlow, county of, I.
Carlton, N, XIII, XXII.
Carlton in Craven, XIV.
Carlton hall, Poulton in the Fylde: notice of, XXII.
Carlyle's (Thomas) *Life of Cromwell*, XII, XIII.
Carmarthen, marquis of, XXVIII.
Carne, Thomas, a papist delinquent, XXII.
Carnew, Ireland, I.
Carnwath (earl of) supports the earl of Mar and joins the rebels, V.
Caroll, sir James: his "stately house" in co. Wexford, I.
Carpentarius, Petrus, XX.
Carpenter, general: his military conduct, V.
Carr, N, XIV, XXII.
Carr hall, Blackburn: notice of, XXII.
Carre, N, IV, XII.
Carrickfergus, I, IX.
Carrington, township of Bowden, VIII: hall, notice of, VIII.
Carrington, N, VIII.
Carryer, N, XIV.
Cart, Dr., XXVII.
Carta de Foresta on the mutilation of dogs, XIV.
Cartegate, XX (*tit.* Croenton).
Carter, N, VIII, XII, XXII, XXVII.
Cartes, Réné des, IV. *See* Descartes.
Cartesian glasses, grinding of, XIII.
Cartesian princess, XIII.
Cartewright, Thomas, XVII.
Cartmell, co. Lanc., VIII, XIX: account of, XXII: battle of Lyndale in, II; episcopal leases in, VIII. *See* Kertmell.
Cartmell priory, account of, XXII.
Cartmell-fell chapelry, account of, XXII.
Cartwright, N, VIII, XII, XVIII, XIX, XXII, XXVII, XXVIII.
Cartwright's *Diary*, extracts from, IX.
Carus, N, V, XXII, XXVIII.
Carver, Ric., XXX.
Cary, Mr., of Cary, XXVIII.
Caryl, Joseph, II, XIII, XVIII: account of, IV.
Caryl, viscount Molyneux, IX.
Casaubon, Isaac, XIII.
Casaubon, Meric: account of, XIII; his views of witchcraft, VI.
Casbell, XX (*tit.* Whalleye).
Case, N, II, IX, XVIII, XIX, XXII, XXVII, XXIX.
Case street, Liverpool, XII.

Cassels, Robert, XXVIII.
Cassilis, John sixth earl of: notice of, I.
Castell, Dr. Edmund: account of, XIII.
Castello, ₦, XX.
Castelton, XX.
Castelton, ₦, XX.
Castle, Mr., XXVII.
Castle *for* (?) Newcastle-under-Lyne, XIV.
Castle-hill-car, Rochdale, XIV.
Castle hey, XII; Castle hill, XII; Castle street, IX, XII; Castle-street field, XII; all in Liverpool.
Castlemain, Roger earl of, XXII, XXVIII.
Castles and other fortifications in Lancashire at successive periods, II.
Castleton, Derbyshire, VIII.
Castleton church, Vale Royal, VIII.
Castleton, township of Rochdale, XIX; hall, XIV, XIX.
Castres, XIII.
Catalogue of Antiquities, &c. of the Soc. of Antiq. of London, by Way, XIV.
Catalogus Plantarum circa Cantabrigiam nascentium by Ray, extract from the preface, XIII.
Catcroft in Farington, XXX.
Caterallwyfes, XX (*tit.* Whalleye.)
Cateschagh, XX (*titt.* Spotlond, Whelton.)
Cateschaghsike, XX (*tit.* Whelton).
Catharine hall, Cambridge, XIII.
Catherick deanery, in Richmond, VIII.
Catholic soldiers, why better than others, XXV.
Cato, writings of, IV.
Caton chapelry, Lancaster: account of, XXII.
Caton, ₦, XXII, XXVII.
Cator, captain: wreck of the ship of, XII.
Catridge, John, bishop of Coventry and Lichfield, VIII.
Cattenburg's (Adrian van) *Life of Grotius*, XIII.
Cattenhall hall, Frodsham: notice of, VIII.
Cattenhall manor, account of, VIII.
Catteral, XIV.
Catterall, ₦, IX, XIV.
Catterick bridge, I.
Cattermole's *Literature of the Church of England*, XIII.
Catteschagh, XX (*tit.* Chadewyk).
Cattle, cheapness of in Ireland, I; wild cattle at Bishop's Auckland, I.
Catullus, Vossius's edition of, XIII.
Cavalier, Newcome accounted a, XVIII.
Cavanagh, ₦, I.
Cave, Jonathan, XXVIII.
Cavendish, ₦, VIII, XII, XXII.
Caves, haunted, in Scotland, I.
Cawarden family, notice of, VIII.
Cawdrey, Zachariah, rector of Barthomley, XVIII, XXVII; notice of, VIII.
Cawdwall, John, XVII.
Cawley, Th., VIII.
Cawood, VIII.
Cawson, ₦, XXII, XXVIII.
Cawthorne, ₦, XXII.
Cecil, Mr. secretary, lord treasurer, XXIV.
Cecill, Mr., IX.
Ced *or* Cedda, bysshop of Lychefelde: legendary notices of, XV. *See* Choddus.
Cedda (earl) gives name to Chadkirk, VIII.
Cera panis, a church due: account of its origin, XXII.
Cerdicus, fyrst kynge of West Saxons, XV.
Ceres, a nation on whose history Isaac Vossius builds, XIII.
Cesses, excavations, VII.
Cestria, XX. *See* Chester.
Cestria, Peter de, rector of Whalleye, XXII.
Cestrie abbates, camerarii, cancella-

rius (Petrus), comites, constab., justic., officiales, priores, vicecomites. archid., civ. maiores, civ. vicecomites, cives, xx.
Chadburn, gifts to the poor of, xiv.
Chadderton, township of Oldham, xix; hall, xiv, notice of, xix.
Chadderton in Tottington, xix.
Chadderton, 𝔉, xii, xix, xx.
Chaddesden, Henry de, canon of Lichfield, xxii.
Chaddock hall, Leigh: account of, xxii.
Chaddock, 𝔉, vi, viii, xix.
Chaderton, xx.
Chaderton, 𝔉, viii, xiii, xiv, xix, xxii.
Chadewyk, xx.
Chadewyk, 𝔉, xx.
Chadkirk, chapelry of Stockport, iv; account of, viii.
Chad's (St.), Saddleworth: ancient armour at, xiv.
Chadwick chapel, viii.
Chadwick hall, Rochdale, xix.
Chadwick, 𝔉, vii, ix, xiv, xviii, xix, xxii, xxvii.
Chadwykford, xx (*tit.* Chadewyk).
Chaffe sands, a North term for dry loose sands, vii.
Chalice and shepherd, a house in St. Botolph's, Bishopsgate, xxii.
Chalmers's *Biographical Dictionary*, vii.
Chalon, Robert, xvii.
Chaloner, 𝔉, i, xiii, xvii, xix, xxix.
Chalton, township of Backford, Cheshire, viii.
Chamber hall, Oldham: account of, xix.
Chamberlain 𝔉, xiv, xxii.
Chambers, 𝔉, i, xii, xiii, xxii.
Chamier, an eminent Protestant minister, xiii.
Chamney, 𝔉, xxii.
Champaigne, Rogerus, xx.
Champney, lady, viii.
Chancellor, Richard, "the incomparable," xxiv.
Chancellor Cottington (of the exchequer), xiv.
Chancellor Egerton (lord chancellor), xiv.
Chancellor of Chester, viii.
Chancellor of York (Dr. Burwell), xviii.
Chancellor of the duchy of Lancaster (sir John Dackombe), xiv.
Chancellor (vice-) of duchy of Lancaster (Christopher Banastre), xiv.
Chancey, Charles: account of, xiii.
Chandler, John: his extraordinary translation of Van Helmont, xiii.
Chandler, John, of Liverpool, xii.
Chandois, lord Gray, and his wife, xxix.
Chandos peerage, claim to the, xiv.
Chanon, 𝔉, xx.
Chantrell, captain (also called Chantwell and Channell), at Manchester siege, ii.
Chantrey, sir Francis: sculpture by in Bolton church, xix.
Chantry rentals, Liverpool, xii.
Chanu, 𝔉, xx.
Chapel, now called Stranraer, in Galloway, i.
Chapel (domestic) in Hoghton tower, xiv.
Chapel wage, origin of, xix.
Chapel-street, Liverpool: account of rentals and tenants in, xii.
Chapels do not qualify chaplains, xix.
Chapman, 𝔉, viii, xii, xiii, xxii.
Chappell, 𝔉, i, xiii.
Charge against Newcome, of willingness to conform, refuted, xviii.
Charity commissioners, *Nineteenth Report of* (1827), xix.

Charytas (saynt) purtrayed on arras, xv.
Charlemagne confederate with kyng Offa, xv.
Charleroi, wager respecting, ix.
Charles I., ix, xii, xiii, xiv, xviii; incidental notices of, ii; examination of witches by, vi; sadness in Cheshire at the death of, xxvii.
Charles II., xii, xiv; his military progress in Lancashire and Cheshire, ii; grant of a charter to Liverpool, ix; grant to the Moore family, xii; proclaimed in Manchester, xxvii; incidental notices of, xiii, xviii.
Charles V. (of Germany) and Dr. Dee, xxiv.
Charles Louis, prince Palatine, i; requests to be allowed to raise soldiers in England, xviii.
Charleton, sir Job, iv.
Charlton, Peter: criminal charge against, iv.
Charms used by witches, vi.
Charrier, Ben., D.D., xiii.
Charnley, 𝔑, xxii.
Charnock, 𝔑, ii, xiv, xxii.
Charnok, William, ix.
Charteris, 𝔑, v, xxii.
Chatham, co. Kent, i, xiii.
Chatteburn, xx.
Chatterton *or* Chadderton hall, xiv.
Chattox (old), a Pendle witch, vi.
Chaucer, xiii, xv.
Chaule (? jowl), a jaw or jaw-bone, xxiii.
Chaumberlyn, Thomas, xx.
Cheadle, co. Chester, xiii, xviii; account of, viii.
Cheadle family, account of, viii.
Cheadle-Bulkeley manor, viii.
Cheadle-Holme *or* Cheadle-Mosley, viii.
Cheapside, Liverpool, xii.
Cheapside cross demolished, xiii.
Cheapyn, viii.
Cheate, trick of a, xiv.
Check-stones, chuck-stones *or* duck-stones, a game, i.
Checke, sir Thomas, knt., xiii.
Checkley-cum-Wrinehill, township of Wibunbury, viii.
Chedle, 𝔑, xx.
Cheesemongers of London, their contest with the Liverpool corporation, ix.
Cheetham, 𝔑, xxvii.
Cheke, sir John, knt., xxiv; notice of, iv.
Chelford-cum-Withington chapelry, Cheshire, iv; account of, viii.
Chelmley family, viii.
Chelmundel, Hugo de, xx.
Chelsea, ix, xiii.
Chelsea college, account of, xiii.
Chepstow, co. Monmouth, i.
Chepyn manor, co. Lanc.: account of, xxii.
Chepyn family, xxii.
Chequer inns at Canterbury and London, xiv.
Chernok, Adam de, xxx; Ric. de, xx.
Cherr, Anne, xviii.
Cherry orchards at Gravesend and Wexford, i.
Chersey, Richard, xxvii.
Chesham, near Bury, xiv.
Cheshire, west part of ancient Mercia and praised for valour, xv; many settlers in Ireland from, i; its gentry, their excellent character, xxiii, and gallant spirit, xxix; sons of many of them apprenticed in Liverpool, xii; royal militia of; xiv (?); a peculiarity of the pronunciation of, xxix.
Cheshire *or* Chesshyre, 𝔑, viii, ix.
Chess, the game of, xiv; Dr. Thomas Hyde's learned work on, xiii.
Chester, i, ix, xii, xiii, xviii; full

and detailed ecclesiastical account of, VIII; sundry notices of, XIV; legendary notices of, III, XV; its walls, I; castle, IV; Roman remains, VII; notices of its garrison in 1643-6, II; account of the rejoicings at in 1610, III; imprisonment of Adam Martindale there, IV; and of the rebel prisoners of 1715, V; witch enquiry, VI; defeat of the Britons at, VII; its connexion with the Stanley family, XXIX. *See* Cestria.
Chester, earls of, VIII, XIX, XXII.
Chester, bishops of, VIII, IX, XIV, XVIII, XIX, XXII, XXVII.
Chester, archdeacons of, VIII, XXII.
Chester, deans of, VIII, XVIII.
Chester, 𝔄, II.
Chester-le-street, I.
Chesterfield, John Huntingdon's lands at, XIX.
Chesterfield, countess of, XII.
Chesterton, Dr. Worthington's estate at, XIII.
Chetaston, Stephen de, rector of Warrington, XXII.
Chetham, township of Manchester, XIX.
Chetham, 𝔄, II, VIII, XII, XIV, XVIII, XIX, XX, XXII.
Chetham society, IX, XVIII.
Chetham's hospital, formerly the collegiate house, XIX.
Chetham's college library, XII, XVII.
Chetham's English library, Manchester, XVIII.
Chetton, 𝔄, XXX.
Chetwin, Mr., XXVII.
Chetwode family, VIII.
Chetwynd, 𝔄, VII, XX.
Cheuerel, 𝔄, XX.
Chevalier St. George, V.
Cheverley-Butter-back lane in Huntington, township of Chester, VIII.
Cheveu, Mark, mayor of Wexford, and his wife, I.
Chevy Chase, earliest known MS. of, and supposed author, XXIX.
Chew, 𝔄, XXII.
Cheyle, Ric. de, XX.
Chicheley, 𝔄, XXII, XXVIII.
Chichester, IX.
Chichester, John Lake of Oldham nonjuring bishop of, XVIII.
Chichester, sir Edward, second baron and first viscount Chichester in Ireland: notice of, I.
Chidlow, township of Malpas, VIII.
Chief rents in Liverpool, XII.
Child, Mr., XIII.
Childbed gifts, custom of, XIV.
Childer-Thornton, Cheshire: account of the free school in, VIII.
Childers' wife bewitched to death, VI.
Childewal, XX.
Children (365 at one birth) of the countess of Henenburg, I.
Childrey, Joshua: account of, XIII.
Childwall, co. Lanc., VIII, IX, XII; general account of, XXII; bishop's rent in, XIX; race course, IX.
Childwall church, VIII, IX; extract from William Leigh's funeral sermon at, XIV.
Childwall church register, notices of the Norris family from, XII.
Childwall hall, account of, XXII.
Childwall, 𝔄, XX.
Chilinsky, Samuel Boguslaus: account of, XIII.
Chillingworth a latitudinarian leader, XIII.
Chimney stones *i.e.* painted Dutch tiles, description of, I.
Chipendall, 𝔄, XXII.
Chipping, co. Lanc., VIII; general account of, XXII; rectory, VIII.
Chirche, XX.
Chirche, 𝔄, XX.

Chircheschagh, XX (*tit.* Croenton).
Chirye de Baylegh, Rob., XX.
Chisenhale, 𝔑, II, VI, XXII, XXVIII.
Chisenhale hall, Coppul, co. Lanc.: notice of, XXII.
Cho, manerium de, co. Lanc., XX.
Cho ho!, a falconer's call, XXIII.
Chobank, XX (*tit.* Bilyngton).
Choddus (St.), bishop of Lichfield, VIII.
Choir service begun at Manchester, XXVII.
Cholmeley, 𝔑, II, XIII, XVIII, XIX.
Cholmondeley, 𝔑, IV, VIII, XIV, XXII, XXVIII.
Cholmondeley chapel, in Malpas: account of, VIII.
Choo, XX (*tit.* Wordull).
Chorley, in Croxton, co. Lanc., XVIII; general account of, XXII.
Chorley halls, higher and lower: notice of, XXII.
Chorley, township of Wilmslow, VIII.
Chorley, 𝔑, II, V, VIII, XII, XIV, XXII.
Chorlton, township of Wibunbury, VIII.
Chorlton, township of Malpas, VIII.
Chorlton, township of Manchester, XIX.
Chorlton-cum-Hardy chapelry, account of, XIX.
Chorlton hall, Manchester: notice of, XVIII; account of, XIX.
Chorlton Row, township of Manchester, XIX.
Chorlton, 𝔑, VIII, XVIII, XIX, XXVII.
Chowbent, Atherton, co. Lanc.: acaccount of, XXII; parliamentary successes at, II; loyal Presbyterian force raised there, V.
Chowley, township of Coddington, VIII.
Chrichley, a drunken curate, XXVII.
Chrisom, meaning of the word, VI.
Christianity, legendary notices of its progress in Britain, XV.
Christina, queen of Sweden: account of, XIII; wax image of, I.
Christleton, co. Chester: account of, VIII.
Christmas at Whalley, XIV.
Christopher (St.), gigantic figure of, and legend respecting, VII.
Christopherson, John, bishop of Chichester, XXIV.
Christophilus, Richard: account of, XIII.
Christ's college, Cambridge: its obligations to Worthington, XIII.
Christ's hospital, London, IX.
Chubb, Fr., VIII.
Church, 𝔑, XIII.
Church of England, XVIII; its liberal character, XIII; strong leaning of Grotius to, XIII.
Church interference at the election of king Ethelred, XV.
Church property, ceremonies and services in Holland and Scotland, I.
Church bells, XVIII.
Church dole, XIX.
Church land in Warrington, XVII.
Church built in Manchester for Henry Newcome, in which he lies buried, XVIII.
Church-en-heath, near Chester, VIII.
Church *or* Church-kirk, co. Lanc.: account of, XXII.
Churches, antiquity of the custom of dedicating, XIV; burial in a result of monastic avarice, VII.
Churches in Chester, legendary acaccount of their foundation, XV.
Churches in Dublin, account of, I.
Churchill, colonel, V.
Churchlop, township of Coppenhall, Cheshire, VIII.
Churchlowe, Mr., minister of Langho, Blackburn, XXII.
Churchman, Anne, VIII.
Churchyard's *True Discourse Histo-*

ricall of Governours in the Netherlands, XXIII.
Churton, township of Aldford, VIII.
Churton, township and hall, Farndon, VIII.
Churton heath, near Chester; tithes of, VIII.
Churton's *Life of Dean Nowell*, XIII, XIV, XIX, XXII.
Cicero *De Officiis*, IV; *De Republica*, XXV.
Cilly, Roger de, XX.
Cimento, accadémia del, of Florence: account of, XIII.
Cinnamon, medicinal virtues of, I.
Cirploise, dispute about the, XIV.
Cities in Holland, the five ancientest, I.
Cities in Scotland, the prime, I.
Civil war in England, period of the, IX.
Civil-War Tracts, XII, XIV, XVIII.
Clafehaye, XX (*tit.* Whalleye).
Claghaman, co. Wexford: notice of, I.
Claghtonfelde in Farington, XXX.
Claighton, township of Bidston-cum-Ford, Cheshire, VIII.
Claighton, township of Woodchurch, Cheshire, VIII.
Claiton, 𝔑, XXX.
Claneboys, a parliamentary commander XII.
Clapham, co. York, VIII.
Clare, earl of, XXVII.
Clare, 𝔑, XX, XXII.
Clare hall, Cambridge, XIII.
Claremont, co. Lanc., XIV.
Clarendon, sir Edward Hyde earl of: his impeachment, IX; conduct after the Restoration, XII; love for the Church of England, XVIII; charming portraiture of lord George Digby, XIII; *History of the Rebellion*, IX, XII, XVIII; *State Papers*, XIII.
Claret wine, port wine so called in the North, VII.
Clark, 𝔑, VIII, XIII, XXVIII.
Clarke, 𝔑, V, XII, XIII, XVIII, XIX, XXII, XXIV, XXVII.
Clarke's charities, Manchester: account of, XIX.
Clarkson, 𝔑, XIII, XXII, XXVIII.
Claudius, emperour, sends a legion of knyghtes to Chestre, XV.
Claughton, co. Lanc., XIX; account of, XXII.
Claughton hall, XIV; description of, XXII.
Clavell, R., bookseller, IV, XXIV.
Clawbacke, a backbiter or sycophant, XXIII.
Clay, 𝔑, XVIII.
Claycrofte, XX (*tit.* Whalleye).
Clayeakyr, land in Orford near Warrington, XVII.
Clayfelde, XX (*tit.* Whalleye).
Clayhanger hall, Barthomley: notice of, VIII.
Clayton hall, Manchester, XVII; account of, XIX.
Clayton hall, Leyland: account of, XXII.
Clayton, 𝔑, IV, IX, XII, XIV, XVIII, XIX, XX, XXII, XXVII, XXVIII.
Clayton street, Liverpool, XII.
Cleaves alley, Liverpool, XII.
Cleby in Handley, Cheshire, VIII.
Clederhow, Rob. de, parson of Wygan, XXII.
Cleg, Bernard, XVIII.
Clegg, 𝔑, VI, XIX, XX, XXII.
Clegg halls, great and little, Milnrow, Rochdale, XIV; account of, XIX.
Cleggswood hall, Littleborough: account of, XIX.
Clegton, Richard, XXVII.
Cleiveland, William, of Liverpool, IX.
Clement's (St.) church, Strand, London: Richard Towneley buried in, XIV.
Clenard, Nicholas: account of, IV.

Clergy, scarcity of, and how caused, VII.
Clergy, scandalous: proposed commission for punishment of, II.
Clerk, 𝔑, VIII, XIII, XVII, XXVIII.
Clerke, 𝔑, XIII, XIV.
Clerke's *Marrow of Ecclesiastical History*, XIV.
Clerkenwell, foot race from St. Alban's to, XIV.
Clerkson, Mr., XIII.
Cleveland, 𝔑, IX, XII, XVIII.
Cleveland-street, Liverpool, XII.
Cleves, John Dury's letters from, XIII.
Cleves, John William duke of: account of, I.
Cleworth hall, Tyldesley, XIX; account of, XXII.
Cleydon, 𝔑, XIX.
Cleyton, 𝔑, XVIII.
Cliderhou, XX; de capella, XX.
Cliderhow, 𝔑, XX, XXII.
Clieveland, John, of Birkenhead, M.P., VIII.
Clif (le), XX (*titt.* Castelton, Gerstan).
Cliffe, 𝔑, VIII, XIX.
Clifford, 𝔑, VIII. XIII, XIV, XXIX.
Clifton, hamlet of Eccles, XIX, XX.
Clifton hall, Eccles, XVIII; account of, XIX.
Clifton *or* Rock-savage, township of Runcorn, VIII.
Clifton, 𝔑, II, V, XIV, XX, XXII, XXVIII, XXX.
Climping, co. Sussex, IX.
Clince, Edward, of Rathmell, near Settle, XIV.
Clinton, Willmus de, XX.
Clitherall, 𝔑, XXII.
Clitheroe, co. Lanc., VI, XIV; account of, XXII; proceedings at during the Civil war, II; castle and free grammar-school, accounts of, XXII.
Clitherow, Margaret, IX.
Clive, township of Middlewich, VIII; hall, account of, VIII.
Clive, 𝔑, VIII, XVIII, XIX.
Cliviger, XIV; superstition in, VI.
Clodius, chemist: notice of, XIII.
Clogh, XX (*tit.* Wythenhull).
Clogh parua, XX (*tit.* Whiteword).
Clonmel, Ireland, I.
Clopton, Thomas, rector of Christleton, VIII.
Close, Anthony, VIII.
Cloth given away at funerals, temp. James I., XIV.
Cloth (housing-), description of, XIV.
Cloth or livery, custom of wearing, XIV.
Clotton-cum-Hoofield, township of Tarvin, VIII.
Cloud (the), mountain near Congleton, XXVII.
Clough, 𝔑, XIX, XX, XXVII.
Clough house, XXVII.
Cloutshoes, wooden clogs tipped with iron, XXIII.
Clowes, 𝔑, XIX, XXII.
Club, Th., VIII.
Clutton, township of Farndon, VIII.
Clyderhow, 𝔑, XXII.
Clyffe, William, VIII.
Cnoll, Ric. de, XX.
Coal-mines near Edinburgh, I.
Coat, judicial search for a, I.
Cocage *or* Cockhedge, a field in Warrington, XVII.
Cocceius, Johannes: notice of, XIII.
Cochede *or* Coelred, kynge of Merciens: solempne translacion of the glorious virgyn saint Werburge by, XV.
Cock, Anthony, XXVII.
Cockayne, sir Aston: poems of, XXIX.
Cockburne, John, grantee of Kepyear in Eyton, I.
Cocke, Walter, XXII.
Cockenskell, John, XXII.
Cockerham hall, co. Lanc., XXII.

Cockerham priory, account of, xxii.
Cockermouth *error for* Cockermore monastery, viii.
Cockersand abbey, co. Lanc., viii, xiv(?).
Cockett, Mr., servant to the earl of Derby, xxviii.
Cockey, chapelry of Middleton, xviii; account of, xix.
Cock-fighting, xiv; Newcome preaches against, xviii.
Cock-shooting at Manchester school, xviii, xxvii.
Cockley *for* Cockey chapel, xix.
Cockmore monastery, Cheshire, viii.
Cockshutt, 𝕹, ix, xxii.
Cocks, 𝕹, viii, xxix.
Cockson, 𝕹. xviii, xxvii.
Coco, Walterus, xx.
Coddington, Cheshire: account of, viii.
Coddington hall, notice of, viii.
Coddington, township of Coddington, viii.
Coddington family: account of, viii.
Codensure, Willmus, xx.
Codnor, lord Grey of, xvii.
Codyngton, Jac. de, xx.
Coelred, kynge. *See* Cochede.
Coffee, Edward Pocock's translation of an Arabic work on, xiii.
Coggan, Mrs., xiii.
Cogging, cheating, xxiii.
Coghall, township of Backford, Cheshire, iii, viii.
Coghill, Jo., xxvii.
Coins current in Scotland in 1635, their names and value, i.
Coke, lord chief justice, ix, xii; notice of his family, xix.
Cokersand abbey, co. Lanc., xix; account of, xxii; *Coucher Book* of, xxii. *See* Cockersand.
Cokersand, church of St. Mary of, xxii.
Cokersond, Henr. abbas de, xx.
Cokesay family, of Worcestershire, viii.
Cokeschagh, xx (*tit.* Dounom).
Cokewelbuttes, xx (*tit.* Cliderhou.)
Cokgreues, xx (*tit.* Whiteword).
Cokolles, xx (*tit.* Hanword).
Colborne, 𝕹, xviii, xxii, xxvii.
Colbrond the gyaunt slayne by Guy erle of Warwike, xv.
Colchester, chyef cytee of Estsex, xv; its salt works, i.
Colchester, the lords, ix, xii.
Colclough, sir Adam, i; Duffry hall a seat of the family, i.
Coldecotes, xx.
Coldecotes, 𝕹, xx.
Coldstream, muster of the Merse troop at, v.
Cole, 𝕹, xiii, xviii, xix, xxii, xxvii, xxviii.
Cole's MSS., xiv, xix, xxix.
Coleburne, John, xiv.
Colechurch, xiii.
Coleraine, i.
Coleraine, Henry lord, xix.
Coleridge's *Literary Remains*, xiii.
Colesnolesik, xx (*tit.* Bilyngton).
Colet, Dr. John, xviii; his portrait and *Sermon of Conforming and Reforming*, xiii.
Colleclogh, xx (*tit.* Whiteword).
Collector of customs at Liverpool, proposal to buy off the, ix.
College, Stephen, the Protestant joiner, xiii.
College, different plans for a philosophical: Evelyn's, Cowley's, sir William Petty's, Becher's psychosophic, xiii.
College, Nicholas Ferrar's Protestant, at Little Gidding: account of, xiii.
College, pontifical: kynge Kenred and bysshop Egwin afore the, xv.
College of arms, xiv, xix; its constitution and privileges, xxiv.

Colleges: Chelsea, Dulwich, Fotheringhay, accounts of, XIII; Gresham, XIII.
Colleges and halls in Cambridge: list of, with their contributions to the poor, XIII.
College garden, Manchester: Newcome plays at bowls in, XVIII.
Collegiate church, Manchester: fortunes of during the civil war, XVIII; story of a murder from the church register, XVIII.
Collen *for* Cologne, XIII.
Coller, Thomas, rector of Malpas, I.
Colley, ℞, I, VIII, XXVII.
Collier, ℞, XIII, XVIII, XXII, XXIII, XXVIII, XXIX.
Collier's *Annals of the Stage*, III.
Collier's *Historical Dictionary*, extracts from, XIII.
Collinge, ℞, XIV, XIX.
Collins, ℞, IV, IX, XIII, XIX, XXVII.
Collins's *Baronetage*, XIX.
Colloquies of Erasmus, XVIII.
Colly, Mr., a cousin of Henry Newcome, XXVII.
Collyhurst, Manchester, XVIII.
Colmar, Matthew, VII.
Colne, XX; de capella, XX; military proceedings near, II; general account of, XXII.
Colne-field, near Colne: a witch's malice at, VI.
Cologne, XIII.
Colomies's *Collection of Letters to and from G. J. Vossius*, XIII; *Mélanges Historiques*, extract from, XIII.
Colour of the high-priest's ephod: account of the fierce dispute between Ainsworth and Broughton on this subject, XIII.
Colquitt *or* Calquitt, Mr., IX.
Colstone, Francis, XIX.
Colt, sir Dutton, XXVIII.
Colty, ℞, XX.
Coluille, Thom. de, XX.
Columbers, Cicely daughter of Alan de, XXII.
Colunio, ancient name of Colne, XXII.
Colwick, co. Stafford, XIV.
Colwych, Humfry, XIX.
Colyngham, Joh. de, XX.
Comb, a large tub, I.
Combe-Martin, co. Devon, I.
Comberbach, township of Budworth, VIII.
Comberbach, rev. Mr., VIII.
Combermere abbey, account of, VIII.
Comberworth chapel, XIV.
Combination of the young men of Manchester, XVIII.
Combral juxta Longlegh, XX (*tit.* Croenton).
Comenius, John Amos: account of, with notices of his works, XIII; his *Physicæ ad Lumen divinum reformatæ Synopsis*, IV.
Comet of 1577 breeds great feare and doubt, XXIV; of 1664, described as dreadfull, IV.
Commander, Hercules, XXIV.
Commerse, XXX (*tit.* Hocwyk).
Commissions or committees in Lancashire during the Civil war, II.
Committee for plundered ministers, IV; of triers of ministers, IV.
Common Prayer (Book of), IV; bishop Moreton's opinion of, XXVII.
Commons' Journals, XII, XVIII.
Commonstable, XX (*tit.* Whalleye).
Commonwealth, sale of prisoners into slavery by the, XVIII.
Communion, bread of the: wanted by witches, VI.
Complaynte of Scotland, XXIX.
Compleat Ambassador, XVIII.
Complexion sellers, XIV.
Comprehensive bill of 1663, Clarendon's opposition to, XVIII.
Compton, ℞, VIII, XIV, XXII.

Comus, occasion of the masque of, i.
Comyn, Mary, xix.
Concordantiæ Sanctorum Patrum by James, vii.
Condé, prince de, xviii.
Conder, 𝔑, ix.
Coney-grees or rabbit warrens, i.
Confession, jugglery at, i.
Confessions of witches, their visionary character, vi.
Conformity not a question in 1660, xviii.
Conformity, Booke of Cases about, xviii.
Congleton, township of Astbury, viii, ix, xviii.
Congleton chapelry, account of, viii.
Congregationalists and Presbyterians, contests between, iv; heads of accommodation agreed upon, xxvii.
Coniers, J., bookseller, iv.
Coningshead *or* Conishead priory, near Ulverston: account of, xxii.
Coniston chapelry, Ulverston, xiv; account of, xxii.
Coniston Hall by Gresley, extract from, xxii.
Connought, major: his crime, ii; and sentence, xxvii.
Conringius, Herman: account of, xiii.
Conspiracy (Gowry), account of, i.
Constable, 𝔑, ii, xiv, xxvii.
Constable sands, on the Dee: legend of, xv.
Constantine, 𝔑, viii, xiii, xviii, xix, xxvii, xxx.
Constantinople, xiii.
Consterdine, Joseph, xix.
Contest in London between the French and Spanish ambassadors: account of, xviii.
Convention of witches at Malkin tower, vi.
Conway, 𝔑, i, iv, viii, xiii, xiv, xxvii.
Conyers, 𝔑, i, xxii.
Conyngton, marine fossil found at vii.
Conyngton, Richard de, vicar of Ormskirk, xxii.
Cook, 𝔑, viii, xii, xiii, xxii, xxiv.
Cooke, 𝔑, i, ix, xii, xiii, xviii, xix xxvii.
Cookson, Henry, xxvii.
Cool, Jos., viii.
Cool-lane, township of Audlem, viii.
Cooper, 𝔑, viii, xii, xiv, xxii, xxvii
Coote, sir Charles, xii, xiv.
Cope, 𝔑, i, xxvii.
Copeland deanery, viii.
Copes, (rich) in Durham minster, i when required to be worn, xiv.
Copimslone, xx (*tit.* Cestria).
Coplestone, xviii.
Copley, Stephen, vii.
Copp *or* Cop chapelry, St. Michael's upon-Wyre: account of, xxii.
Copp *or* Great-Eccleston school, St Michael's: account of, xxii.
Coppehull, Ric. de, xx.
Coppenhall, co. Chester: account of viii.
Coppenhall (Monks-), township o Coppenhall, viii.
Copper works at Dort, account of, i.
Copperas work "most ingenious" a Queenborough, i.
Copperode, xx (*tit.* Spotlond).
Coppidhurst, xx (*tit.* Spotlond).
Coppock, 𝔑, viii, xviii, xxvii.
Coppocke, Robt., xxvii.
Coppow, John, xii.
Coppul chapelry, Standish: account of, xxii.
Coppull, Rich., son of Thomas, xii.
Coptrod, in Rochdale, xix.
Coranto, a dance, xiv.
Corbet, 𝔑, viii, ix, xviii, xx.
Corbishley, Mr., xviii.
Cordier (Mathurin), *or* Corderius, iv.
Coriton, a parliamentarian, xii.

Cork, xii.
Cork, earls of, i.
Corker, 𝔑, viii, xviii.
Corles, 𝔑, xii.
Corn, fluctuations in price of, xxvii.
Corn-market, Liverpool: alteration of, ix.
Cornall, 𝔑, xii, xxii.
Cornelius, Peter, of Zurichsea, xiii.
Cornhull, William de, bishop of Coventry, viii.
Cornwall, Worthington's journal through, xiii.
Coroder of Leyland Church, viz. John de Farington, xxii.
Corona, Thomas de, of Adlington, viii.
Corona Regia, "a most venomous piece of irony" against James I., xiii.
Corporation of Liverpool, incidental notices of, ix.
Corporation of Preston entertain James I., xiv.
Corporation act, reflections on and fears from, xviii.
Corpus Christi college, Cambridge, subscribes towards relief of the protestants in Poland, xiii.
Corpwaldus, grandson of Tytylus kynge of Eest-England, xv.
Correspondence of sir George Radcliffe, extracts from, xiv.
Corser, Rev. Thomas: his MS. catalogue of John Webster's library, vi.
Cort, Thomas, xxii.
Corton, xiii.
Cosby, Arnold, xxv.
Cosins, bishop: notices of, xiii.
Cosney, Dorothy, xxii.
Costentyn (Geoffrey de) holds the castle of Stockport, viii.
Costumes, Irish and French, described, i.
Cotes, 𝔑, viii, xiii, xix, xx.
Cotgrave, co. Notts, viii.
Coton, Rogerus de, xvii.
Cotsall town, i.
Cotswold hills, i.
Cotta, John: notice of, vi.
Cottam, 𝔑, xiv, xxviii.
Cottenham, xiii.
Cottenham's (lord) judgment in the case of Manchester school, xix.
Cotterille, John: executors of, viii.
Cottingham, co. York: account of the rectory of, viii.
Cottington (colonel) prisoner near Ormskirk, ii.
Cotton, 𝔑, v. vii, viii, xiii.
Cotton-Abbots *and* Cotton-Edmunds, townships of Christleton, viii.
Cotton mill in ruins: Dr. Whitaker's satisfaction in seeing it, xiv.
Cotyngham, Johannes de, xvii.
Coucher Book of Whalley Abbey, xix.
Coudray, 𝔑, xx, xxx.
Couentry, episcopi, xx.
Coulborn, Mr. xviii.
Coulton, co. Lanc.: account of, xxii.
Coulton hall, notice of, xxii.
Council at York, xiv.
Council of the North: trial before, xiv.
Counseylls (generall) held by Kenrede kyng of Mercyens and Wylliam conquerour, xv.
Counscough *or* Cunscough hall, Halsall: notice of, xxii.
Countrey Almanacke and *Countrey-Survey-Book*, by Adam Martindale: notices of, iv.
Coupenura, Adam de, xx.
Coupland, deanery of, xix.
Coups, a dyer at Knutsford, xviii.
Courcy *or* Coucy, lords de, xxii.
Court and Character of James I., by Weldon: extracts from, xiv.
Court of King James, xviii.
Court of King Charles, xviii.
Courts of law at Edinburgh, description of, i.

Court rolls of Chatburn, Worston and Pendleton, XIV.
Courtmantell, a short mantle, VII.
Courtship at Delft, how conducted, I.
Cousin an indefinite term, I.
Cousins, marriage of, XIV.
Cousin's (Victor) edition of *Descartes*. XIII.
Cousin's *or* Cozen's *List*, IX, XII.
Couteau de chasse, XIV.
Covell, 𝔑, VI, XIII.
Covenant, incidental notices of the, II, IV, XVIII.
Coventry, XIII, XIV; erle Leofric founds the abbay in Couentre, and makes the cite free for loue of his countesse the lady Godith, XV.
Coventry, lord, XIII.
Coventry, 𝔑, XVIII, XXVII.
Coventry and Lichfield, diocese of, VIII; bishops of, VIII.
Coverley, sir Roger de: death-day of, XIV.
Cowell *or* Couel, Thomas, coroner, VI.
Cowkett, widow, IX.
Cowles, Joh.: bequests by the widow of, VIII.
Cowley, 𝔑, VIII, XIII.
Cowley's *Cutter of Coleman Street*, XVIII.
Cowp justice of peace, an ancient dance, XIV.
Cowpe-cum-Lenche, Bury, co. Lanc., XIX.
Cowper, 𝔑, XIII, XIV, XVII, XXII.
Cowperthwaite, Leonard, XXII.
Cowpland, 𝔑, XXII.
Cox, 𝔑, VII, XII, XIII.
Coxe's *Life of Marlborough*, IX.
Coxon, Mr., XVIII.
Coys for catching wild-fowl, I.
Crab, William, XIII.
Crabbe's portrait of a village pastor, XIV.
Crabhall, Chester, VIII.
Crabtree oxhey, XX (*tit.* Whalleye).
Crabtree, William, mathematician, XIII, XXVII.
Crabtree, Mr. curate of Todmorden, XIX.
Crabwall, township of St. Oswald's, Chester, VIII.
Cradock, 𝔑, IV, VIII, XIII, XXVII.
Cragge, Mr., curate of Satterthwaite, XXII.
Crakenthorp, Richard: notice of, IV; his *Defensio Ecclesiæ Anglicanæ*, XIII.
Crambo, old: a masque character, XIV.
Cranage, Susan, XXVII.
Cranburn, lord Ranelagh's seat at, IX.
Cranburn, trial and execution of, IX.
Crane, 𝔑, II, XXII.
Cranfield, 𝔑, IX, XII, XIV.
Cranmer, archbishop, XVIII; his management of church property in Lancashire, XIX, XXII.
Crantz's (David) *History of the United Brethren*: its character, XIII.
Cranwell, Mr., XXVII.
Craven, VI, XIV; Whitaker's *History* of, XIV.
Craven, William first baron and earl: account of, XIII.
Craven, 𝔑, XX, XXII, XXVII.
Crawford and Balcarres, earl of: his Blackrod estate, XIX.
Crawford, captain, XII.
Crawford's (Isabel) conduct at her execution for witchcraft, VI.
Creewood *or* Crew-wood hall, Frodsham, XII; notice of, VIII.
Creichley *or* Crechley, Mr., XVIII.
Cremona, wager respecting it, IX.
Creton, widow, XII.
Crew, township of Farndon, VIII.
Crew, township of Barthomley, VIII.
Crew *or* Crewe, 𝔑, VII, VIII, XIV, XXII, XXIV, XXVII.
Creyk, Walterus, XX.

Crineboys, William de, vicar of Leyland, XXII.
Criplegate, Morning Exercise at, XVIII.
Crisp, 𝔑, XIII, XXII.
Cristelton, Adam de, XX.
Critchloe, William, XXVIII.
Croenton, villa de, XX.
Croft, in Winwick, XIX; forms with Southworth a separate parish and rectory, XXII.
Croft, 𝔑, XXII.
Croft castle, co. Dorset, XIV.
Croftes, XX (*tit.* Butterword).
Crofthendis in Farington, XXX.
Crofton, 𝔑, IV, XVIII, XXVII.
Crofts, captain, XII.
Croice, Rob., XX.
Croipidraik, XX (*tit.* Whiteword).
Croke, Ralph, VIII.
Crokedlond, XX (*tit.* Castelton).
Crokeston, Rob. de, XX.
Crokyng, Joh., XXX.
Crollius, a seraphic doctor, VI.
Crombach, John, of Wiswall, XIV.
Crombleholm, 𝔑, XXII.
Crombock, Mr., XIV.
Crompton, township of Oldham, XIX; hall, account of, XIX.
Crompton, 𝔑, II, VIII, XIII, XIV, XVIII, XIX, XXII, XXVII.
Cromton, villa de, XX.
Cromton, 𝔑, XII.
Cromwell, Oliver, I, IX, XII, XIII, XVIII, XXIX; his letters on the battle of Preston, II; conduct of his army in Rosthorne parish, IV; grants Little St. John's to Chester city, VIII; charged with atheism, XXVII; notices of his family, VIII, IX.
Croncischagh, XX (*tit.* Croenton).
Cronckshaw, Anne, a Pendle witch, VI.
Cronkeford, XX.
Cronkiscar, XX (*tit.* Blakeburn).
Crook, 𝔑, XII, XIII, XIX, XXII.
Crook hall, in Leyland: account of, XXII.
Crooke, 𝔑, VI, XIV.
Croon, Mr. XIII.
Cropley, 𝔑, XXVII.
Crosby (great-), co. Lanc., XII; account of, XXII; its grammar-school, XXII.
Crosby, 𝔑, IV, XXVIII.
Crosby's *History of English Baptists*, XIII.
Crosdail *or* Crosedaile, Mr., XVIII, XXVII; death of his son Samuel, XVIII.
Crosdale, in Bowland, XIV.
Croslegh, John del, XIX.
Croslegh, Roger de, VIII.
Crosley, 𝔑. XIII, XIX.
Crosley's (David) *Triumph of Sovereign Grace*, VI.
Cross *or* Crosse, 𝔑, IV, IX, XII, XIII, XIV, XIX, XXII, XXVIII.
Cross (high-), Chester: notice of, III.
Cross (the), Manchester, XIV.
Cross (the), Preston: notice of, XIV.
Crossehul, XX (*tit.* Cliderhou).
Crossfelde, XX (*tit.* Whalleye).
Cross hall, in Chorley: notice of, XXII; in Liverpool, XII; in Ormskirk, notice of, XXII.
Cross lane, Liverpool, XII.
Cross street, Ashton-upon-Mersey: origin of its name, VIII.
Crossbank, township of Ashton-under-Line, XIX.
Crosseby, 𝔑, XX.
Crossefeld, XX (*tit.* Eccles).
Crosse ferry, on the Mersey, XVII.
Crosset, Edwd., XXVII.
Crosse-town, part of township of Over-Knutsford, Rosthorne, VIII.
Crosse-town, chapelry of Nether-Knutsford, Rosthorne, VIII.
Crossley, 𝔑, XII, XIV, XIX, XXV.
Croston, co. Lanc., XVIII; general ac-

count of, XXII; grammar-school, account of, XXII; hall, notice of, XXII.
Croston, ℞, IX, XX, XXII, XXX.
Crouch, Mr., XIII.
Crouchback, Edmund, earl of Lancaster, XIX.
Croughton, township of St. Oswald's, Chester, VIII.
Croukeshagh, William de, vicar of Poulton, XXII.
Croule, Ric. de, XX.
Croune, Dr. William, XIII.
Crow, Mr., an Aberdeen mathematician, executed at Lancaster, V.
Crowder, John, XXVII.
Crowehaue, XX (*tit.* Whelton).
Crowley, hamlet of Higher-Whitley, Cheshire, VIII.
Crown counsell at the Jacobite trials: names of the, XXVIII.
Crowparke, XX (*tit.* Whalleye).
Crowther, ℞, XII, XVIII, XXVII.
Crowton, XVII.
Croxstath preamb., XX.
Croxteth park, Walton, co. Lanc., IX; account of, XXII.
Croxton, township of Middlewich, VIII; hall, notice of, VIII.
Croxton, ℞, II, VIII, XII, XIX, XX, XXVII.
Croxton-Keyrial abbey, co. Leicester, XXII.
Croyden, Mr., of Trinity college, Cambridge, XXVII.
Croydon-head, near Waterford, I.
Croynton, Joh. de, XX.
Crue, ℞, XIV, XX.
Cruisers, bill for appointing, IX.
Crumpsall, township of Manchester, XIX.
Cruys, ℞, XIII.
Cryda, fyrste kynge of Merslande, ancestor of saynt Werburge, XV.
Crymbull (le), a croft in Warrington, XVII.
Cucking stool, account of the, XII.
Cuddington, township of Malpas, VIII.
Cudworth, ℞, VI, XIII, XIX, XXVII.
Cudworth chapel in Oldham church, notice of, XIX.
Cuerdale hall, Law chapelry, Blackburn, XIV; notice of, XXII.
Cuerden, John, of Cuerden, and Mary his daughter, XIX.
Cuerden hall in Leyland, XIV; notice of, XXII.
Cuhopeheued, XX (*tit.* Brendewod).
Culachemos, XX (*tit.* Stanword).
Culcheth, ℞, XIV, XIX, XX, XXII, XXVIII.
Culcheth hall, Newton, Manchester: account of, XIX.
Culcheth hall, Winwick: account of, XXII.
Culiford, ℞, IX.
Cullen *or* Colzean castle and its fairy-haunted caves, I.
Cullenberg, graf *or* count, I.
Culliton, co. Devon, XIII.
Culnefaltholme, XX (*tit.* Bilyngton).
Culverwell, Nath., XIII.
Cumba magna *et* parva, XX (*tit,* Whiteword).
Cumbebrok, XX (*titt.* Sadelword, Whiteword),
Cumbehop, XX (*tit.* Brendewod).
Cumberland, Henry earl of, and his daughter Margaret, XIV.
Cumberland militia, cowardice of, V.
Cumberland street, Liverpool, XII.
Cumbermere, abbas Joh. et monachi, XX.
Cumbray, Aluredus de, XX.
Cundecliue, Rob. de, XX.
Cundy, Patrick, XXV.
Cunliffe, ℞, II, IX, XIV, XVIII, XXII.
Cunliffe street, Liverpool, XII.
Cunney (Mr.) paints Newcome's portrait, XXVII.
Cunnington, XIII.

Cunscough hall, Halsall: notice of, XXII.
Cuntellan, I.
Cup: "To syt bytwene the cuppe and the wall," XV.
Currer, 𝔓, VIII, XIV.
Curtis, 𝔓, XVIII.
Curwen, 𝔓, II, XIII, XXII, XXVIII.
Curzon, 𝔓, XIV, XXII.
Custis, Mr., I.
Custom-house, Liverpool, IX; want of, XII.
Custom-house, London, IX.
Cutbertson, Robert, XXVII.
Cuthbertson, Robert, XIX.
Cutlane in Rochdale, XIX.
Cutter, Mr., XIII.
Cutter of Coleman Street, a play by Cowley, XVIII.
Cuvier's remarks on Ray as a zoologist, XIII.
Cuylli, Hugo, XX.
Cuyteruyding, XX (*tit.* Swynton).
Cycyly (saynt) brothered in hallynge, XV.
Cytharista, 𝔓, XX.

D'ACHERI, Luc: account of, XIII.
Dackombe family, account of, XIV.
Dacomb's castle, in Normandy, XIV.
Dacre, 𝔓, V, XX, XXII.
Dacres, colonel sir Thomas, II.
Daddefelde, in Warrington, XVII.
Daffy, Dr.: his elixir salutis, IV.
Dagenhale, Rad. de, XX.
Dagenham, co. Essex, XIV.
Dahl, Michael, the painter, XIV.
Daille, theologian, XIII; studied by Newcome, XVIII.
Daily service neglected *temp.* James I., XIV.
Dakins *or* Dakyns, 𝔓, VIII, XIV.
Dalcarr medo, Orford, near Warrington, XVII.
Dale, 𝔓, VIII, XIX, XXVII.
Dale-street, Liverpool: account of the tenements and tenants in, XII.
Dallaway's *Heraldic Enquiries*, XXIV; *Sussex*, IX.
Dalrymple, Charles, and his daughter Elizabeth, XXII.
Dalton in Furness, general account and various notices of, XXII.
Dalton, 𝔓, II, V, XIV, XXII, XXVIII.
Dalziel, captain James: incidental notices of, V.
Dam house in Tyldesley, account of, XXII.
Damietta, incident at the siege of, I.
Danby, 𝔓, II, XIX.
Danby orchard, XX (*tit.* Whalleye).
Dance, Robert, XIV.
Dancing, Hinde's comment upon, XIV.
Dand, Mr., XVIII.
Dandy, 𝔓, XVIII, XXII, XXVII, XXVIII.
Dandy, name of a familiar spirit, VI.
Dane *or* Daven river, in Cheshire, VIII.
Daneport, Willmus de, XX.
Danes, legendary notices of the invasions by, XV.
Danesius, XXIV.
Daniel *or* Daniell, 𝔓, III, VIII, XIII, XVII, XXII, XXVII.
Danks, John, XIII.
Danneuill, Colinus de, XX.
Danson, Thomas, under-sheriff of Lancashire, II.
Dantzig, appearance of seven suns together at, XIII.
Danuilla, 𝔓, XX.
Danvers, 𝔓, II, IX.
Danyell, 𝔓, II, XVII.
Danyers, 𝔓, VIII, XVII.
Darbie, my lord of (William sixth earl), XIV.
Darby, 𝔓, XIII, XVIII, XXVII.
Darcie, Abraham: notice of, XXIX.
D'Arcy, sir Francis, knt., XXII.
Darcy, 𝔓, VIII, XX.

Darcy-Lever, co. Lanc., xiv.
Daresbury, Runcorn: account of, viii.
Darley hall, Over, Cheshire: account of, viii.
Darlington, John, xxiv.
Darnelker, xx (*tit.* Bilyngton).
Darrell's (rev. John) version of the marvellous events at Cleworth hall, xxii.
Darrow, J., viii.
Dartmouth, co. Devon, xiii.
Darwell, 𝔑, xix.
Darwen (upper-), co. Lanc.: account of, xxii.
Datchet, co. Bucks., xiii.
Dati, Carlo, the friend of Milton, xxiv.
D'Aubigné's *Protector*, xix, xxii.
Dauson, Will., viii.
Dauyd (kynge) browdred on arras, xv.
Daven *or* Dane river, Cheshire, viii.
Davenant, 𝔑, xiii, xiv, xviii.
Davenham, co. Chester: account of, viii.
Davenport, township of Astbury, viii.
Davenport, 𝔑, i, viii, xiii, xiv, xviii, xix, xxvii, xxviii.
Davenports of Cheshire, proverb respecting, xxiii.
Davidis yorde, an orchard in Warrington, xvii.
Davidson, W., xxii.
Davies, 𝔑, iii, vi, viii, xiii, xxviii, xxix.
Davila's *History* studied by Newcome, xviii.
Davy, 𝔑, viii, xviii, xix.
Davyhulme, township of Eccles, xix; hall, account of, xix.
Davys, Thomas, xviii.
Dawbeny, sir Ralph, and his wife Katherine, xxii.
Dawes, 𝔑, viii, xix.
Dawes's (bishop) *Memorandum Book*, xxii.
Dawne, Thomas, xvii.
Dawney, 𝔑, i, viii, xiv.
Dawpool in Thurstaston, co. Chester, viii.
Daws, Jane, viii.
Dawson, 𝔑, xviii, xix, xxii, xxvii.
Day, 𝔑, viii, xiii.
Day of Judgment, meditation on, xviii.
Daykins, 𝔑. *See* Dakins.
Daylight gate, *i.e.* evening, vi.
Dayntrie, Daintry, Daventry, xiv.
Deacon, Dr. Thomas: incidental notices of his conduct and character, v; his tomb, xix.
Deacons and elders at Rotterdam, their duties, i.
Dean, co. Lanc.: general account of, xix; its church visited by Henry Newcome, xviii.
Dean of Chester, xviii.
Deans of Whalley in Early-English times, xxii.
Deans (rural), their ancient jurisdiction, viii.
Dean, 𝔑, ii, viii, ix.
Deane, 𝔑, vi, viii, xiv, xviii, xxviii.
Dean-row, township of Wilmslow, viii.
Deans, sir William, ix.
Dearden family, of Rochdale, viii, xiv, xix.
Dearnley, N., of Manchester, viii.
Death, supernatural prognostics of, i.
Death of Henry Newcome: account of, xviii.
Deborah the midwife, xiv.
Debrett corrected, xiv.
De Caus at the Bicêtre, xviii.
Declaration of Breda, xviii.
Declarations (Collection of) between the King [Charles II.] *and Parliament*, xviii.
Dedham, co. Essex, xiii.
Dee river, England: alteration of its

channel, I; boundary stones between it and the Mersey, XII; miraculous division of its waters, XV.
Dee, Dr. John, warden of Manchester college, VI, VIII, XXII, XXVII; incidental notices of, XIII; his *Diary*, XVIII; autobiographical tracts reprinted, XXIV.
Dee, Rowland, father of Dr. Dee, XXIV.
Deeping, XIV.
Deer (a wylde) by myracle retournes at the prayer of saynt Cead, XV.
Deeringe, sir Edw., XVIII.
De Feriol, XVIII.
De Flassan, XVIII.
Defoe, Daniel: his visit to Liverpool, IX, XII.
Deimer mere, Amsterdam: description of the drainage of, I.
Deiram, kyngedome of, XV.
Dekker, quotation from, XVIII.
Delamere forest and horn, VIII, XIV.
Delamere, the lords, IV, VIII, XVIII, XXVII.
De Lancre, VI.
De la Rue, Mr., XXVIII.
Delavall, sir Ralph, IV.
Delaware, the lords, XXII.
Delaware, 𝔑, XXVIII.
Delft, detailed account of, I.
Delfthaven, I.
Delille, M., XIII.
Delrio, VI.
Deluge, proofs of the, VII.
Delves, 𝔑, IV, VIII, XXII.
Demdike (old), a Pendle witch, XII; particulars of her trial, VI.
Demoniacal possession, stories of, I, XXII.
Demonology, XIV.
Dempster, Thomas, XIII.
Denby grange, XIV.
Dendarum chapel. *See* Dendron.
Dendermond, surrender of, IX.
Dendrological man, a masque character, XIV.
Dendron chapelry, Aldingham: account of, XXII.
Dene, 𝔑, XIX.
Denebrok, XX (*titt.* Eccles, Swynton, Westewod).
Denelonde, XX (*tit.* Reued).
Denesgreue, XX (*tit.* Brendewod).
Denesgrove, XX (*tit.* Whiteword).
Denham family, XIV.
Denison, Stephen, minister of Katherine Cree church, London, XIV.
Denmark, king of, XIII.
Denmark, queen Anne of, XIV.
Dennis, 𝔑, VIII.
Dennison, William, XXII.
Dent, John, XXII.
Denton, co. Lanc., IV, XIII, XVIII, XX; account of, XIX.
Denton, 𝔑, I, II, IX, XX, XXII.
Denwall, hamlet of Nesse in Neston, VIII; hospital, notice of, VIII.
Depedale, XX (*tit.* Childewal).
Depenbech *or* Malpas, VIII.
Derbie-cum-Thyngwall, co. Lanc.: assessment for a subsidy, IX.
Derby, earls of, I, II, VI, VIII, IX, XII, XIV, XVIII, XIX, XX, XXII, XXIII, XXV, XXVII, XXIX. *See* Darbie.
Derby, cives de, XX.
Derby, never a minister at, XVIII.
Derby-house committee, XII.
Derby-street, Liverpool, XII.
Derby (West-), Walton, co. Lanc.: account of, XXII.
Derbye, VIII.
Derbyshire: its trade connexion with Liverpool, IX, XII.
Derbyshire, 𝔑, XX, XXII.
Dere, to hurt, VI.
Derham's *Life of John Ray*, XIII.
Dering, sir Edward, II, XII.
Derisbury, Hugo de, XX.
Dermot, 𝔑, IX.

Derneley, Nicholas, and his wife, XVIII, XXVII.
Dernelowe, Thomas, XVII.
Derneluff, Thomas, XVII.
Dernhall, township of Whitegate: its hall a seat of the Corbetts, VIII.
Derodon, David: notice of, IV.
Derwent superior, XX.
Derwentwater (earl of) joins the Northumbrian insurrection: his conduct, trial and execution, V.
Desborough, J., XIII.
Descartes, Réné, IV; account of, XIII. *See* Cartes.
Des Maiseaux's *Life of John Hales*, XIII.
De Sola and Raphal's *Translations from the Mishna*, XIII.
Despenser family, VIII.
D'Estrades, the French ambassador: account of his contest with the Spanish ambassador for precedency, XVIII.
Dethick, Humphrey, of Longford and Newhall, co. Derby, XIX.
Deulacres *or* Pulton abbey: account of, VIII.
Deurden, Robert: his bequest to the church of Haslingden, XXII.
Deurest, Walterus, XXX.
Deusbury, Joh. de, XX.
Deuyas, Joh., XX.
Deventer, account of the surrender of, XXV.
Devereux, Nicholas: notice of, I.
Device family, trial of four of them for witchcraft, VI.
Device of the Biron family, now their crest, XIV.
Devil (the), his marks, VI; he is cloven-footed, VI.
Devonshire, duke of, XXVIII.
Devonshire, earl of, XXII, XXVIII.
D'Ewes, sir Simonds, bart.: his character of Richard James, VII; buys Dr. Stafford's *MSS.*, VIII.
Dewhurst, 𝔑, VIII, XXII.
D'Ewyas, 𝔑, XXII.
Dewyhurst, 𝔑, XX.
Dewyshurst, XX (*tit.* Heleye).
Deyne hall, Prestwich: account of, XIX.
Deynul, Willmus de, XX.
Diacinnamomum, a medicine, I.
Dialling instrument invented by Martindale, IV.
Diary (*Henry Newcome's MS.*), account of, XVIII; extract from, XIV.
Dibbley, excellent watch-clock made by, XXIV.
Dibdin, Dr.: extracts from his *Bibliomania*, XIII.
Dicconson, 𝔑, II, XXII, XXVIII.
Dickenson, 𝔑, VIII, XVIII, XIX, XXII, XXVII.
Dickie, David, I.
Dickin, George, XXVII.
Dickinson, Mr., XIII.
Dickonson, Frances, a Pendle witch, VI.
Dickson, 𝔑, XVIII, XXII.
Diconson, Wm., of Allerton, IX.
Didsbury, near Manchester: account of, XIX; Civil-war skirmish at, II; Worthington preaches at, XIII.
Dier, Mr., XIII.
Digby, the lords, I, II, XII, XVIII.
Digby, sir Kenelm, VII; account of, XIII; his rationale of a corpse bleeding at the murderer's touch, VI.
Digby, lady Venetia: eulogised by sir Kenelm, XIII; by Ben Jonson, XXIX.
Digby, 𝔑, IX, XIII.
Digby's *Letters*, XVIII.
Diggle, 𝔑, XIX, XXVIII.
Diggles, 𝔑, IX, XII, XVIII, XIX, XXVII.
Diggs, serjeant, XIV.
Dighull, XX (*tit.* Sadelword).
Dig-lane *now* Cheapside, Liverpool, XII.
Digles, 𝔑, XVIII.

Digrave (the), a Dutch officer: his jurisdiction, I.
Dike, David, minister of Irvine, I.
Dillenius's edition of Ray's *Synopsis Methodica*, XIII.
Dillingham, 𝔑, XIII.
Dilston, the Northumbrian force halts at, V.
Dimble, a hollow, XXIII.
Dimmock, 𝔑, XXVII.
Dinelay, Joh. de, XX.
Dingles, Job, advocate, VIII.
Dinkley hall, Langho: account of, XXII.
Dinner, supper and breakfast at Hoghton for James I.: details of, XIV.
Diot, Robert, VII.
Direckson, Gabriel, a rich Dutch boor: account of his farm and coy, I.
Discourse (trial) at Manchester of Henry Newcome, anecdote respecting it, XVIII.
Disley dene, Cheshire, XIII: account of, VIII; sir Piers Legh's foundation of the chapel, XVII.
Disney, 𝔑, XIII, XXIV.
Dispensarius, 𝔑, XX.
Dispensation granted for marriage of John Greenhalgh æt. 13, XIV.
Disraeli (the elder), notices of his criticisms, XIII, XIV.
Dissenters (*Declaration for Indulgence of*), Martindale's view of it, IV.
Ditchfield, Thomas, and Jane his wife, XIV.
Ditton, 𝔑, XX, XXII.
Ditton hall, Prescot, XII; account of, XXII.
Ditton (fenny-): connexion of Dr. Worthington with, XIII.
Dives, sir Lewis: account of, II.
Divines (character of great contemporary) in a *MS.* of Glanville's, XIII.
Divining rod, account of trial of, XIII.
Divinity Knots unbound, a tract by Martindale, IV.
Dixon, 𝔑, VIII, XIV, XIX, XXII.
Dixwells, sir Basil, XXVIII.
Dobbs, Joh., VIII.
Dobson, 𝔑, XXII.
Dochesbury, Hunardus de, XXX.
Dockwray, Mr., XXVIII.
Doctours four (the), *viz.* Athanasius, Basil, Gregory Nazianzen and Chrysostom, XV.
Dod, 𝔑, I, VIII, IX, XIII, XXVII.
Dodcoat-cum-Wilksley, township of Audlem, VIII.
Dodd, 𝔑, XII, XXVII, XXIX.
Dodding, 𝔑, II, XXII.
Doddington, township of Wibunbury, VIII; hall, account of, VIII.
Doddleston, co. Chester: account of, VIII; hall, VIII.
Doddridge, sir John, XIV.
Dodemon, Adam, XX.
Dodgson, 𝔑, VI, IX, XXII.
Dodswell, Richard, XXVIII.
Dodsworth, 𝔑, XXII, XXVIII.
Dodsworth's *Collections*, XXIV.
Dodsworth's plot, XXVIII.
Doe, John, XVIII, XXVII.
Doesborg, capture of, XXV.
Doewife (old) of Samlesbury, a witch, VI.
Dog-guage of Bowland forest still kept at Browsholme, XIV.
Doghton, John, and Johanna his wife, XVII.
Dogwall, XX (*tit.* Chadewyk).
Dogwalleclogh, XX (*tit.* Spotlond).
Dokesbury, 𝔑, XVII, XX.
Dolben, archbishop, of York, XXII.
Doles at funerals, XXII.
Doleman's *Conference*, authorship of, XXV.
Domesday survey of Bowland, XIV.
Dominis, Marcus Antonius de: notice of, XIII.

Domveve, a ladye of the royall blode of Kent, maryed vnto Merwalde of Mercyens, XV.
Domville, moiety of Lymm, Cheshire: account of, VIII.
Domville, 𝔑, VIII, XVIII, XXII.
Donaghadee, I.
Donatus, heresiarch, XII.
Doncaster, IX, XIV.
Done, 𝔑, VIII, IX, XIV, XVII, XXIV.
Done bridge, description of, I.
Donegal, Arthur earl of: account of, I.
Donegal, countess of: Newcome's residence with, XXVII.
Donne, Dr.: Izaac Walton's remark on, XIV.
Donneuille, Rog. de, XX.
Donyngbothe, XX (*tit.* Spotlond).
Donynton, 𝔑, XX.
Doole-houses (town-halls) in Holland: descriptions of, I.
Doolittle's (Rev. Mr.) meeting-place, XIV.
Dopping (bishop of Meath)'s character of archbishop Marsh, XIII.
Dopping's *Tract. de Visitat. de Episc.*, XIX.
Dorchester, XIII; bysshopric of Mercyens, XV; epithalamium by Howell on the marriage of Henry marquis of, XXIX.
Dore abbey, VIII.
Dormer, brigadier: account of his attack on the Windmill barricade, Preston, V.
Dorning, 𝔑, XXII.
Dorpe, *i.e.* a village, I.
Dorset, duke of, IX.
Dorset, marquises of, XXII.
Dorset, Pembroke and Montgomery: Ann Clifford countess of, XIV.
Dorsetshire, XIV; heraldic visitation of in 1623, XIV.
Dort, description of, I; synod of, XIII.
Doson, 𝔑, XVIII.
Douay college, XXV.
Doughty, 𝔑, II, XIV.
Douglas, in Parbold, co. Lanc.: account of, XXII.
Douglas, 𝔑, IV, V.
Dounes, 𝔑, XX.
Dounom, XX; de capella, XX.
Dounom, 𝔑, XX.
Dove, miracles worked by a, XV.
Dove, Henry, D.D.: account of, VIII.
Dove bridge, near Uttoxeter: dangerous adventure at, IV.
Dover destroied by a great hoost of Pagans, XV.
Dover, lord, IX, XII, XVIII.
Dowbell, Mr., XXVIII.
Dower, custom of London with respect to, XXIV.
Dowling's *Notitia Scriptorum SS. Patrum*, XIII.
Downe-house medo, Warrington, XVII.
Downes, township of Macclesfield, VIII.
Downes, 𝔑, II, VIII, XII, XIV, XVIII, XIX, XXII, XXVII.
Downham, co. Lanc., XII, XIV: account of, XXII; notices of the manor, XIV.
Downham, 𝔑, VIII.
Downside, near Bristol, XIII.
Dowresses in 1465, large number of, XVII.
Dowsing, Sa., XIII.
D'Oyley's *Life of Archbishop Sandcroft*, XIII.
Drabicius, Nicholas: account of, XIII.
Draclo. *See* Drakelow.
Drage's (William) *Treatise of Diseases from Witchcraft*: comment upon, VI.
Dragons fleynge in the ayre forebode the comyng of Danes, XV.
Dragons (artificial) in ancient pageants, notice of, III.
Draining mills in Holland, description of, I.

Drake, ℞, VIII, XII, XXII, XXIII.
Drake's *Shakspere and his Times*, extract from, XXIX.
Drakelow, township of Davenham, VIII; hall, account of, VIII.
Drakes, guns so called, I.
Drawbridges in Holland, I.
Draw-well in Liverpool, XII.
Draycott, ℞, XX, XXVIII.
Drayton, co. Salop, VIII.
Drayton, Adam de, VIII.
Drayton, Willmus persona de, XX.
Drayton's *Polyolbion*, extracts from, XIII, XVII.
Dreams and apparitions, IV, XXVII.
Dress, peculiarities of, I; exhortation against the vanity of women in, XV.
Driffield, ℞, VIII.
Drinkhall, Mr., curate of Tatham fell, XXII.
Drinkwater ℞, XIX, XXVII, XXVIII.
Drogheda, description of, I.
Droman, David, XIV.
Dromedaries in Holland, I.
Dromore, I; bishops of, I, XIII, XXII; bishop Jeremy Taylor's tomb at, XIII.
Dronfield, co. Derby, XIV.
Drought in 1635, I.
Droylsden, township of Manchester, XIX.
Druestclogh, XX (*tit.* Spotlond).
Drum and ancient, with a scarf, belonging to Manchester, XIV.
Drummond, ℞, V.
Drunken Barnaby, extract from, XIV.
Drunmer castle taken by major Stanley, XII.
Drury, ℞, IX, XXV.
Drury-lane, London, XIV.
Dryden's (John) *Works*, references to, XII, XIV, XVIII.
Du Bartas, Sylvester's, XVIII.
Dubhall in Arlecden, VIII.
Dubleday, ℞, XX.
Dublerose, Annabel, XVII.
Dublin, VIII, IX, XII; description of, I; educational progress at, XIII; Newcome invited to settle in, XVIII.
Dubois, John, M.P. for Liverpool, IX, XII.
Du Cange, *voce* officium, XIV.
Ducarel's *Repertory*, XIX.
Duchy of Lancaster, officers of the, XIV; seal forcibly taken away by the royalists, II.
Ducie, the lords, XIX.
Duck and dog, XIV.
Ducks in Holland, price of, I.
Duckenfield, co. Chester: account of, VIII; church troubles at, IV.
Duckenfield, ℞, VIII, XII, XIX, XXVII.
Ducket, ℞, XIV, XXVIII.
Duckfield, Mr., XIII.
Duckington, township of Malpas, VIII.
Duckworth, a seat of the Holdens, XIV.
Duckworth, John, a victim of witchcraft, VI.
Duddon, township of Tarvin, VIII.
Dudley, ℞, VII, VIII, XIV, XXII, XXVII.
Duerden, Geo., XXVIII.
Dufferie (the), an ancient Irish district, I.
Duffry hall, Templeshanbo, co. Wexford, I.
Dugard, ℞, VIII, XIII, XIX.
Dugdale, ℞, VIII, XIV, XVIII, XXII, XXIV, XXIX.
Dugdale's visitations of Lancashire, XIV, XIX, XXIV.
Dugdale's *Monasticon*, XIX.
Dukedale, John, chantry priest of Clitheroe, XXII.
Duke-street, Liverpool, XII.
Dukinfield, ℞, II, XXII.
Dulwich college, XXIX; accouut of, XIII.
Dumbarton, I.
Dumfries, I; menaced by the rebels, V.

Dumplington, hamlet of Eccles, XIX.
Dumplinton, William de, vicar of Rochdale, XIX, XX.
Dunbar, description of, I.
Dunbar, George Hume earl of: notice of, I.
Duncombe *for* Dackombe, sir John: an error of Whitaker's, XIV.
Dundalk, XII; description of, I.
Dunfermline abbey, notice of, I.
Dungan, battle of, XII.
Dunglass castle, account of, I.
Dunham, near Chester, VIII.
Dunham-Agden, township of Bowden, VIII.
Dunham-Massey, IV, VIII; notice of the hall, VIII; Newcome's visits to, XVIII.
Dunkannon fort, Waterford, I.
Dunken, sir Francis, knt., IX.
Dunkenhalgh hall, Church, XIV; notice of, XXII; occupied by the parliamentary forces, II.
Dunkirk privateers, I, IX.
Dunlop's *History of Fiction*. XIII.
Dunmow flitch, poetical allusion to, VII.
Dunn, William, a diligent preacher, XXII.
Dunne, Thomas, first *emperor* of Trinity college, Cambridge, XXIV.
Dunnishope hall, Accrington: notice of, XXII.
Dunnoe *or* Dunnow hall, near Sladeburn: notice of, XIV.
Duns Scotus's nose, effigy of, XII.
Dunse, arrival of the Highlanders at, V.
Dunskey castle, I.
Dunstable, IV, XIV; local proverb respecting, XXIII.
Dunstan (the blessed) herde angels singe in the natuite of kynge Edgar, XV.
Dunstan *or* Dunster, ℞, XVIII.
Dunstarr, Henry, minister of Northenden, VIII.
Dunster, ℞, XIX, XXVII.
Dunster castle, I.
Dunton, honest John, XIV.
Dunyngesbothes, XX (*tit.* Whiteword).
Dunyngesboth rode, XX (*tit.* Whiteword).
Dupiter (Rob.) restores to God the church of St. Mary of Bruera, VIII.
Duport, Dr.: account of, XIII.
Durdent, Walter, bishop of Lichfield, excommunicates Randle fourth earl of Chester, VIII.
Durel's writings studied by Newcome, XVIII.
Durem, Hugo de, XX.
D'Urfey, ℞, XVIII.
Durham, description of, I.
Durham, Hugo de, XX.
Durham's *Commentary on Revelation*, XVIII.
Durie *or* Dury, John, a Scotch divine: account of, IV; incidental notices of, XIII.
Dury, Mr., of Manchester, XVIII.
Dutch, their venality, XXV; service unpopular, XXV; fire the English ships at Chatham, XXVII.
Dutton, township of Budworth, VIII.
Dutton's chapel, in Budworth: notice of, VIII.
Dutton manor, near Ribchester, VIII: account of, XXII; notice of the hall, XXII.
Dutton, ℞, VIII, XIV, XVII, XVIII, XX, XXII, XXVII.
Dutton-Chedle, Geoffrey de: notice of, VIII.
Du Vaix's *Moral Philosophy of the Stoicks*, VII.
Duxbury, Nicholas, XIV.
Duxbury hall, Standish: account of, XXII.
Duyna (afterwards bishop of Lichfield) brought to preche in Mercia, XV; notice of, VIII.

Dwerrihouse, Ann: her charities, XXII.
Dwerryhouse, William, mayor of Liverpool, XII.
Dwight, ꝑ, VIII.
Dwina. *See* Duyna.
Dyar, Hugh, VIII.
Dyce, rev. Alexander, XXIX; his edition of Webster, VI.
Dychefeld, ꝑ, XVII.
Dychefield, ꝑ, XXII.
Dyke, ꝑ, XIII, XIV.
Dykes, ꝑ, XVIII, XXVII.
Dynelay, Joh. de, XX.
Dyneley, ꝑ, XIV, XXII.
Dynkedlegh, ꝑ, XX.
Dynkley orchard, XX (*tit.* Whalleye).
Dysart, earls of, VIII, XXIV.
Dysart, Grace countess of, XXIV.

EADBALDE, kynge of Kent, XV.
Eadburg of Kent, sainte, doughter of kynge Ethelbryc, XV.
Eadfryde, sone of Edwyn kynge of Northumberlande, XV.
Eagida, a matrone thries restored to helth by saynt Werburge, XV.
Eagle at Leyden fifty years old, I.
Eagle tower, I.
Eagle and Child inns, XIV.
Earle, ꝑ, IV, IX, XII, XIII, XXVIII.
Earle-street, Liverpool, XII.
Earnslow grange, Whitegate, Cheshire: notice of, VIII.
Easington woods, XIV.
Easingwold, co. York, VIII.
East-England, fyfth kyngdome of the Saxons, XV.
East-Gilling, Yorkshire, XIV.
East hall, Rosthorne: notice of, VIII.
East-India company, IX.
East- *or* Market-Lavington, XIII.
East-Retford, XIV; parliamentary election at, IX.
East sea (*i.e.* the German ocean) mesureth the Eest parte of Mercyens, XV.
Eastgate-street, Chester, VIII.
Eastham, co. Chester: account of, VIII.
Easton, Mr., XXVII.
Easton-Mauduit, co. Northampton, VIII.
Eaton, township of Astbury, VIII.
Eaton, township of Davenham, VIII.
Eaton hall, near Chester: account of, VIII.
Eaton *or* Ayton hall, Davenham: notice of, VIII.
Eaton manor, near Tarporley, VIII.
Eaton, ꝑ, IV, VIII, IX, XIV, XVIII, XXVII.
Eatonfield *or* Edenfield, near Bury, XIV; account of, XIX.
Eawood, Mr., XXVII.
Ebba (saynt), abbesse of Canwod, XV.
Ebranke, king: notice of, III.
Ebrulf's (St.) abbey: notice of, VIII.
Ecclefechan, proceedings of the insurgents at, V.
Eccles, co. Lanc., XVIII, XX; account of, XIX; vicarii de, XX.
Eccles church, XIX, XX; account of the chantry of St. Mary in, XIX.
Eccles, hamlet of Barton in Eccles, XIX.
Eccles, ꝑ, XX, XXII, XXVII.
Eccleshall, ꝑ, XX.
Eccleshull, XX.
Eccleston, co. Chester: account of, VIII; Eccleston-cum-Belgrave, a township of, VIII.
Eccleston, co. Lanc.: account of, XXII.
Eccleston (great-) school, St. Michael's-upon-Wyre: account of, XXII.
Eccleston hall, Prescot: notice of, XXII.
Eccleston, ꝑ, XII, XVIII, XX, XXII, XXVII, XXVIII.

Eccos, 𝔑, XII.
Echard, historian, XII, XVIII.
Ecton's *Thesaurus*, XIX.
Eddleston, 𝔑, XXII.
Edelfled, doughter of kynge Oswy: legendary notice of, XV.
Eden, Dr., master of Trinity hall, Cambridge, XIII.
Edenfield *or* Eatonfield chapelry, Bury, co. Lanc.: account of, XIX.
Edenfield, township of Tottington in Bury, XIX.
Edensor, Richard, XIX.
Edesford, 𝔑, XX.
Edesford, XX (*tit.* Cliderhou).
Edgar, king of the Mercians, founds St. Werburge's abbey, VIII; legendary notices of, XV.
Edge, township of Malpas, VIII.
Edge, 𝔑, II, XVIII, XIX, XXVII, XXVIII.
Edge-hill, battle of, IX.
Edgeley, Mr., XXVII.
Edgerley, township of Aldford, VIII.
Edgworth, township of Bolton, XIX.
Edgworth, hamlet of Turton in Bolton, XIX.
Edinburgh, V, IX; description of, I.
Edinburgh Review, XVIII.
Edington, co. Wilts, XIII.
Edisbury, edified of newe by Elflede doughter to kynge Alurede, XV.
Edmonds, a cook of Queen's college, Cambridge, XIII.
Edmondson, 𝔑, XVIII, XXII.
Edmunde (saint) kyng of Estenglande, slayne by kyngs Hingware and Hubba, XV.
Edmunde, kynge of England, regned fyue yeres hauing great victory, XV.
Edmund's (St.) church, Salisbury: wilful destruction of its painted window, XIV.
Edred. *See* Elred.
Education, viscountess Ranelagh's remarks on, XIII.
Edwarde, kynge, senyor: legendary account of, XV.
Edwarde (saynt), kyng and confessour, XV.
Edward II., monument to in Gloucester cathedral, I.
Edward IV., obligations of the Stanleys to, XXIX.
Edward VI. gives a pension to Dr. Dee, XXIV.
Edwards, 𝔑, I, VIII, XXII, XXVIII.
Edwin, earl, VIII.
Edwin, 𝔑, XXII.
Edwyn, kynge of England, XV.
Edwyn (saynt), kynge of Northumberlande: subdued by prince Penda, XV.
Edwyne, kyng of North, XV.
Effingham, William lord, and Elizabeth his daughter, XIV.
Egbryct, kynge of Kent, XV.
Egbryct *or* Egfryde, kynge of the North parte, XV.
Egergath in Halsall, XXII.
Egerton, township of Malpas, VIII.
Egerton, 𝔑, I, II, IV, VIII, XIV, XVIII, XIX, XXII, XXIII, XXV, XXVII, XXVIII, XXIX,
Egerton Papers, IX.
Egfryde. *See* Egbryct.
Egham, XIII.
Eglinton, sir Alexander Seton sixth earl of: notice of, I.
Egnicius, martyre, kynge of Eest-England, XV.
Egton-with-Newland chapelry, notice of, XXII.
Egwyn, bysshop of Worcester: legendary notices of, XV.
Egypt, the ten plages of, embost on arras, XV.
Eires, Mrs., XXVII.
Eland, 𝔑, XIX, XX.
Elcock, Ephraim, IV.
Elcocke, Dr., XVIII.

Elde, Richard, VIII.
Eldon (lord) on the Banbury peerage case, XIV.
Election Papers, 1780, IX.
Elentherius (pope) sends II doctours to converte Britayne by desire of kyng Lucius, XV.
Elephant at the Hague, I.
Elerius, St.: account of, VII.
Elflede, doughter of kynge Alurede, wife to duke Ethelrede, builds churches at Chester, VIII; legendary notices of, XV.
Elflede, wyfe to prynce Peada, slays him by treason, XV.
Elijah *or* Hely, prophet, refuged by a rauen, XV.
Eliot, 𝔑, XII, XIII.
Elizabeth, queen, VIII, IX, XIV, XXIII, XXV, XXIX; personal notices of, I, XXIV.
Elizabeth, daughter of James I.: her marriage, XIV; as widowed queen of Bohemia, I; account of her daughter Elizabeth princess Palatine, XIII.
Elizabeth, princess, daughter of Charles I.: her birth, XIII.
Elizabeth, Mrs.: her evidence at the Jacobite trials, XXVIII.
Ella, kynge of Southsex, XV.
Ellale, Grimbaldus de, XX.
Elland, sir Richard de, XXII.
Ellell chapelry and grange, Cockerham: account of, XXII.
Ellell, Grimbold de, XXII.
Ellen's (St.)-in-Windle chapelry: account of, XXII.
Ellenbrook chapelry, Eccles: account of, XIX; Newcome's connexion with, XVIII.
Ellenthorpe, co. York, I.
Eller, Dick, XVIII.
Ellers, elder-trees, I.
Ellesmere, lord chancellor, XIV, XXIX.
Ellesmere, earl of, XIX.
Elliot *or* Elliott, 𝔑, XXVII, XXVIII.
Elliotson, Daniel, XXII.
Ellis, 𝔑, XIII, XIX, XXVIII.
Ellis, a writer studied by Newcome, XVIII.
Ellis's (sir H.) *Letters of Eminent Literary Men*, XXII.
Ellison, 𝔑, VIII, XVIII, XIX, XXII.
Elliston, Mathew, XIII.
Ellker, XX (*tit.* Whalleye).
Elm, Mr., of Barnewell, XXVII.
Elphinstone, sir George, I.
Elred, kynge, XV.
Elseley, Gregory, VIII.
Elsen, an awl, VI.
Elsner's *Brevis Conspectus Doctrinæ Fratrum Bohemorum*, XIII.
Elston *or* Ethelstan hall, Preston: account of, XXII.
Elswick chapelry, St. Michael's-upon-Wyre: account of, XXII.
Eltoftes, Edmund, XXII.
Elton, township of Bury, co. Lanc., XIX.
Elton, township of Warmingham, Cheshire, VIII.
Elton hall, Thornton, Cheshire, VIII.
Eltonhed, Wil., prior of y[e] hermit-friers of St. Aug. at Warrington, VIII.
Eltonheued, Alanus de, XX.
Ely, legendary notices of, XV.
Elyott, sir Jhon, VII.
Elyseclogh, XX (*tit.* Chadewyk).
Elzevir, printer: notices of, XIII.
Embroiderers and embroidery, XIV.
Emigration from Scotland to Ireland, I.
Emma of Fraunce, maryed to Eadbalde kynge of Kent, XV.
Emmanuel college, Cambridge: notices of, XIII.
Emmanuel-lane, Cambridge, XIII.

Emmeakyr, land in Orford, near Warrington, XVII.
Emmot, parson, XIV.
Emmott hall, Colne: account of, XXII.
Emot, ꝶ, XIV, XXII.
Empereur, Constantinus: professor of Hebrew at Leyden, I.
Empson, Tho., VIII.
Encœnia et vigiliæ the analogues of modern wakes, XIV.
Enckhuysen, beast-market at, I.
Engagement (the) of 1649, disputation at Warrington concerning it, IV; signed by Newcome, XVIII.
England after the Restoration, XVIII.
England, kings of, viz: Ethelred, Henry III., Edward I., Henry VII., Henry VIII., Elizabeth, James I., James II., VIII.
English, Anne, XII.
English Annotations, XVIII.
English atheism, XXV.
English catholics, loyalty of, XXV.
English college in Rome, disunion in, XXV.
English library, *i.e.* Chetham college library: early notices of, XVIII.
English refugees, their miserable condition, XXV.
English troops in Dutch garrison service, I.
Ennis, colonel: taken prisoner at Wigan, II.
Enniscorthy, description of, I.
Enoch ap Evan, a murderer, I.
Enswyde (saynt), sone of kynge Eadbalde of Kent, XV.
Ent, Dr. George, XIII.
Entwisle, township of Turton near Bolton, XIX; sale of in 1657, XIX; its poor-tax in 1707, XIX.
Entwisle hall, Bolton: account of, XIX.
Entwisle, ꝶ, IX, XIX, XXII.
Epicharmus, his good counsel, XIII.
Epictetus, edition of, in 1655, XIII.
Epigram on a fat prior by Clement Marrot, VII.
Episcopalians and presbyterians, their mutual relations, XVIII.
Episcopius, the great, XIII.
Epithalamium (a pastoral) on the marriage of Dr. Worthington, XIII.
Epsom-Wells, death of Roger Downes at, XIV.
Erard, Edward: petition in favour of, XII.
Erasmus, XXII; his statue at Rotterdam, I; his *Life of Dr. Colet*, XIII; critical notices of his *Colloquies* and *Paraphrase*, XIII; the former studied by Newcome, XVIII.
Erastus, Thomas: his high rank as a writer, VI.
Erbury (William) disputes in a church in Lombard-street, VI; his *Great Earthquake*, VI.
Ercall parva, VIII.
Erchenwyn, fyrste kynge of Estsex, by the kynge of Merselande brought ofte to ruyne, XV.
Ercombert, kynge of Kent: legendary notices of, XV.
Erdbury priory, co. Warwick, XXII.
Erdswick hall, Middlewich: account of, VIII.
Erestan, old hundred of, VIII.
Erfurt, birthplace of Job Ludolf, XIII.
Ergar *for* Edgar, kyng, XV.
Ericson (*Gustavus*), *Life of*, XVIII.
Erkengode (saynt), doughter of kynge Lothary of Kent, XV.
Ermenberge, Ermenburge and Ermengyde (saynts), doughters of prynce Ermenred of Kent, XV.
Ermenred, prynce, sone of kynge Eadbalde of Kent, XV.
Ermenrycus, kynge of Kent, XV.
Ermenylde (saynt), mother of saynt

Werburge: legendary account of, xv.
Erneshalgh in Farington, xxx.
Ernesti on Erasmus's *Paraphrase*, xiii.
Erneys, ℞, xx.
Ernle (sir Michael) lands at Mostyn, xii.
Errington, ℞, i, v.
Erskine, lord, xiv.
Erskine, ensign: trial and execution of, v.
Erynach, Bello-Becco and Arkel: three cells in Ireland subject to Furness abbey, xxii.
Escheator of the duchy of Lancaster, xiv.
Escoyd, co. Flint, a township of Malpas, viii.
Eshton hall, in Craven: extracts from Hopkinson's *MSS.* at, xiv.
Eskrigge, George, of Over Kellet: his charity, xxii.
Esmond, lord, i.
Esmond, sir Thomas, i.
Essebe, Rob. de, xx.
Esseby, villa de, xx.
Essencyals of relygyon thre, viz., obedyence, chastyte and wylfull pouerte, xv.
Essex *or* Estsex, fourth realme of Saxons in Englande: legendary notice of, xv.
Essex, earls of, xii, xiv, xviii, xxv, xxvii.
Estcourt, Fran., viii.
Estgate strete, xx (*tit.* Cestria).
Esthed, John, ix.
Estoft, Christopher: account of, viii.
Eston, villa de, xx.
Eston, Ric. de, xx.
Etchells, township of Northenden, viii.
Ethelbryct *or* Ethelbert, fyrst chrysten kynge of Saxons: legendary account of, xv; his costly tomb, xviii.
Ethelbryct of Kent, prynce and martyr, xv.
Ethelburge (sainte) doughter of kynge Ethebryct, xv.
Ethelburge (saynt) doughter of kynge Anna of Eest-Englande: legendary notices of, xv.
Etheldrede of Kent, prynce and martyr, xv.
Etheleswyk, villa de, xx.
Etheleswyk, ℞, xx.
Ethelfleda *or* Elflida, relict of Ethelred duke of Mercia, builds Runcorn town and castle, viii.
Ethelfride, kynge of Northumberlande: his acts at Chester and Bangor, xv.
Ethelred, kynge of Mercelande: legendary account of, xv; builds St. John's church, Chester, viii.
Ethelrede, duke of Merciens: his piety, xv.
Ethelstan, kynge, sonne of Edwarde seniour: legendary account of, xv.
Ethelston, Simon, of Hadley, viii.
Ethelwod, prynce, of Eest-England, xv.
Ethics, Martindale's study of, iv.
Eton, co. Bucks.: Newcome visits, xviii.; Dr. Worthington's frequent preachings at, xiii.
Eton, villa de, xx.
Eton, ℞, viii, xvii, xx, xxii.
Eucheston, xxx.
Eueryk, Rob. de, xx.
Eueshalgh *error for* Erneshalgh, in Farington, xxx.
Eueswall, xx (*tit.* Bilyngton).
Eugène (prince) raises the siege of Turin, ix.
Eugenius (pope) and Lytham priory, xxii.
Eukestone, Willmus de, xxx.
Eure, ℞, xviii, xxx.

Eure, William lord, and Elizabeth his daughter, XIV.
Eusam, XV.
Eusebius *De vitâ Constantini*, Valesius's edition of, XIII.
Eustace, ℞, XXII.
Eustace *or* Eustach (saynt), legend of, XV.
Eustachius, Francis: notice of, IV.
Euxton chapelry, Leyland: account of, XXII.
Euxton hall, account of, XXII; visited by Charles II., II.
Euxton manor, account of, XXII; rental of in 1694, XXVIII.
Evans, ℞, VIII, XIII, XIV, XVIII, XXVII.
Evelyn, John, XII, XVIII; account of, XIII; his remark on Mrs. Godolphin, XIV; John, his son, translator of Plutarch, XIII.
Everard, ℞, VIII, XIII, XXII.
Evers, John, XII.
Everton-cause, Liverpool, XII.
Every, ℞, XXII.
Evesham monastery, co. Worcester, VIII, XXII; legendary account of, XV; list of abbots and bailiffs, XXX.
Evidence for the crown at the Jacobite trials at Manchester: its character by an eye-witness, XXVIII.
Evyn-poole in Penwortham, XXX.
Ewod, Ric. de, XX.
Ewyas, Joh. de, XX.
Exchanges at Amsterdam and London compared, I.
Exchange-buildings and Exchange-street, Liverpool, XII.
Exclusion bill, XVIII.
Excommunicated sovereigns, miserable condition of, XXV.
Executioners, their sanguinary circuit through Lancashire, V.
Exercises of religion, XIV.
Exeter, XIII; entry of William III. into, IX.
Exeter, Margaret duchess of, XXII.
Exeter, Elizabeth countess of: her trial, XIV.
Exmoor to Exford in Devonshire, a terra incognita inhabitabilis, XIII.
Exmynge in Suffolke, birth-place of blessed Audry, XV.
Exon, Ran. de, camerarius Cestrie, XX.
Extempory fooles, performances of, XIV.
Extwisle hall, Burnley: notices of, XIV, XXII.
Eyes, Anne, widow, IX.
Eynoldesdale, ℞, XX.
Eyntre, Willmus de, XX.
Eyre, ℞, VIII, XXVIII.
Eyres, Robert, IX.
Eyrick, ℞, XVIII.
Eyves, Thomas, IX.

FABER, Albertus Otto: account of, XIII: his test for angels, XIII.
Fabricius, J. A., XIII.
Fadeschaghbrok, XX (*titt.* Whelton, Wythenhull).
Fage, Edward, mathematical-instrument maker, IV.
Fagh-side, XX (*tit.* Whiteword).
Failsworth, township of Newton, Manchester, XIX.
Faire of saynt Werburge, Chester: its special privilege, XV.
Fairbank, ℞, XXII.
Fairclogh, ℞, XIII.
Fairclough, Dr. James, XXII.
Fairfax, Ferdinand lord, XIX; notice of, I.
Fairfax, sir Thomas, XII, XIV, XVIII, XIX; his military conduct in Lancashire, II.
Fairfax, Edward, the poet: his witch prosecution and *MS. Discourse of Witchcraft*, VI.
Fairfax, ℞, XIX, XXII, XXIV, XXVII.
Fairfax Correspondence, XIX.
Fair-head *or* Marble-head in Ireland, I.

Fairhurst hall, Eccleston: notice of, XXII.
Fairhurst's chantry rent, dispute respecting, XII.
Fairies, an orchard guarded by, I.
Fair-oak house *anciently* Fair-delholme, account of, XIV.
Fairsnape in Bleasdale, XIV.
Faithorne's portrait of Dr. Henry More, XIII.
Falconberg, Mr., XIII.
Falconbridge, 𝔑, XIII.
Faldo, Mr., XXVII.
Faldworthinges, Joh. de, XXX.
Falengesik, XX (*tit.* Heleye).
Falingbrome. *See* Fallibroom,
Falkirk, I; battle of, I.
Falkland, Henry Cary viscount, XII; notice of, I.
Falkland, Lettice viscountess: her character by Grainger, XIII.
Fallibroom, township of Prestbury, VIII.
Fallowfield, township of Stretford, Manchester, XIX.
Fallows, Richard, XVIII, XXVII.
Fallows, William, VIII.
Fallows hall, Alderley: notice of, VIII.
Fall-wall well, Liverpool, XII.
Falwitz (le) family, VIII.
Falmouth, XIII.
Falselydyates, XX (*tit.* Whiteword).
Falstaff, sir John, XIV; why the name was employed by Shakespeare, VII.
Falyes, XX (*tit.* Merton).
Falyngtrekar, XX (*tit.* Bilyngton).
Familiar spirits, their names, nature, arts and special peculiarity, VI.
Family of Henry Newcome, XVIII.
Fancie, name of a familiar spirit, VI.
Fane, sir Francis, knt.: notice of, XIV.
Fanshaw, 𝔑, II, VIII, XIV.
Farber, Ralph, VIII.
Fardanclogh, XX (*tit.* Spotlond).
Farenden, church of, VIII.
Farewell Sermons by the London Ministers, XVIII.
Farindon's (Anthony) account of John Hales, XIII.
Faringdon, co. Berks: furniture at, XIV.
Farington and its subdivisions, XXX.
Farington church given to Penwortham monastery, VIII.
Farington hall in Penwortham: notice of, XXII.
Farington, 𝔑, II, VIII, XIX, XXII, XXVIII, XXX.
Farm at Delft, description of, I.
Farmer, 𝔑, II, VIII.
Farnaby, Thomas, grammarian: notice of, IV.
Farndon, co. Chester: account of, VIII.
Farnham, co. Surrey, XIII.
Farnworth chapelry, Prescot: account of, XXII.
Farnworth, township of Dean, co. Lanc., XIX; account of its school, XIX; hall, notice of, XIX.
Farnworth, John, of Little Hilton: his bequest, XIX.
Farquharson, lieut.-col. John, V.
Farquharson, captain Peter: his death, V.
Farrall, lady, XXVII.
Farrall, W.: his charitable bequests, VIII.
Farrandly *or* farrantly, meaning of, VI.
Farrant, 𝔑, XIII, XXVII.
Farren, Richard, XXII.
Farrer, 𝔑, VII, XIV, XXII, XXVIII.
Farrington, Henry, XXVIII.
Fast-day for the persecutions in Piedmont, XIII.
Fast- and festival-days, XVIII; disregard of *temp.* James I., XIV.
Fasting maid of Bern, account of, I.
Fat man at Amsterdam, description of, I.

Fauconberg, earls of, viii, xix.
Fauconberg, viscounts, xix, xxii.
Faukner, a poor woman, xxvii.
Fauldingham, xiv.
Faulkners of Liverpool, xii.
Faunt, Mr., xxix.
Favour, Dr. John, vicar of Halifax, xiv.
Fawcett, Thomas, minister of Overton, xxii.
Fawkener, Ralph, xvii.
Fawkes, F. H., of Farnley, xiv.
Fawkes, Guy, xxv.
Fawre-akyr and Fawre-akyr lane, Orford, near Warrington, xvii.
Fayrehurstsik, xx (*tit.* Bilyngton).
Fazakerley, 𝔑, ix, xii, xxii, xxviii.
Fazakerley-street, Liverpool, xii.
Fear, to frighten, vi.
Fearnehead, Peter, iv.
Fearnside, Adam: notice of, iv.
Fearnside, Henry, xxii.
Feathers inn, Chester: Adam Martindale's imprisonment at, iv.
Featly, Dr. Daniel, xiii, xxii.
Feeilden. *See* Feilding.
Feilden, 𝔑, xxii.
Feilding, James, of Street, and Alexander his son, xix.
Felgenhaver's *Postilion*, xiii.
Fell, 𝔑, ii, xiii, xiv, xviii, xxii, xxvii.
Fellgate, Mr., minister of Bradshaw chapel, xix.
Fellowes, R. G., of Edmonton, xxii.
Fellowship of collegiate church, Manchester: proceedings at an election, xviii.
Fellowship of Emmanuel college, Cambridge: particulars of a disputed election, xiii.
Fells, 𝔑, ix, xii.
Felton, Dr., bishop of Ely, xxii.
Felton-bridge, Merse troop placed at, v.
Fence (the) in Pendle, vi, xiv.
Fennam, co. Northumberland, i.
Fenner *On Willfull Impenitency*, xviii.
Fenney, Mr., incumbent of Stalmine, xxii.
Fenton, 𝔑, v, viii, xiii, xix, xxii, xxvii.
Fenwick, 𝔑, viii, ix, xii, xxii, xxviii.
Fenwick hall, Liverpool, xii.
Fenwick alley *and* Fenwick-street, Liverpool: descriptions of, xii.
Fere, a companion, husband, vii.
Ferguson, Robert: account of, xxviii; his visit and letter to Newcome, xxvii.
Fermanheye in Penwortham, xxx.
Fermery garthes, xx (*tit.* Whalleye).
Ferne islands, i.
Ferne, Henry, bishop of Chester: account of, viii; notices of, xiii, xviii.
Fernelius seeks Dr. Dee's acquaintance, xxiv.
Ferneside, 𝔑, xxvii.
Fernylegh, xx (*tit.* Spotlond).
Ferrand, 𝔑, xix.
Ferrar, Nicholas, of Little Gidding, viii; account of, xiii. *See* Gidding.
Ferrers, earls of Derby, xix, xxii.
Ferrers, earls, xiv, xix, xxii.
Ferrers *or* Ferrars, 𝔑, xiv, xix, xxii.
Ferriar *On Popular Illusions*, extract from, vi.
Ferrie, *i.e.* Littleborough on Trent: notice of, xiv.
Ferror, sir Henry, preste, xix.
Ferry at Warrington, feud respecting, xvii.
Ferrys (George) accuses Dr. Dee of treasonable enchantments, xxiv.
Ferthings, xx (*tit.* Aluetham).
Festival on saynt Werburge's profession, legendary account of, xv.
Fetherston, Mr., parson of Bentham, xiv.

Fever at Manchester, xxvii; singular remedy for a, xxvii.
ffalenge, 𝔑, xx.
ffalenges, villa de, xx.
ffarington, 𝔑, xiv, xviii.
ffarneword, Adam de, xx.
ffarneworth, Birchehalgh in, xx.
ffarrant, Mr., xviii.
ffearneside, Mr., xviii.
ffeld family, xx.
ffenre, Ric., xx. *See* ffeure.
fferneside, xx.
fferrers, 𝔑, xx.
fferthyng, xx (*tit.* Gerstan).
ffetherstan family, xx.
ffeure, Ricardus fil. Willi de, xx.
ffilyngham, Radulphus de, xx.
ffisburn, Thom. de, xx.
ffisher, Mr., xviii.
ffitton, 𝔑, xx.
ffleitcroft, Robert, xviii.
fflekho, Thom. capellanus de, xx.
ffleynesburgh, Robertus de, xx.
ffog, 𝔑, xviii.
ffolrig, xx.
fford, 𝔑, xviii, xx.
fforesta, 𝔑, xx.
ffornace, Mrs., xviii.
fforneby, xx.
fforneby, 𝔑, xx.
ffouk, Hugo, xx.
ffoune, Oliverus de, xx.
ffrance, 𝔑, xxii.
ffreckelton, Ric. de, xx.
ffrodesham, Petrus de, xx.
ffryston, ecclesia de: Ricardus de Moselaye, rector, xx.
ffulwood, peramb., xx.
ffytton, 𝔑, xxii.
Fiddlers' ferry, near Warrington, xvii.
Field, 𝔑, xiii.
Field house *or* Overth' fields, Bury, xix.
Fielden, John, xxii.
Fielding, John, xix.
Fiennes, 𝔑, xxii.
Fifth-monarchy men, iv.
Figulus, Petrus: account of, xiii.
Filmer, sir Robert: character of his writings, vi.
Filthy habits of the Scotch, i.
Finanus, bishop: legendary notices of, xv.
Finch, 𝔑, iv, ix, xii, xiii, xiv, xxii, xxvii.
Finch house, Liverpool, xii.
Finett, sir John, author of *Finetti Philoxenis:* notice of, xiv.
Fininden, xx (*tit.* Stanword).
Finlow, 𝔑, viii, xii, xxvii.
Finmore, William, xxvii.
Finney family, xix.
Finsthwaite chapelry, co. Lanc.: account of, xxii.
Fire of London, notices of, xxvii.
Fires in Manchester, frequency of, xviii.
First-fruits, historical account of, viii.
Firth, Thomas, xxii.
Fish, management of, in Holland, i.
Fish-ponds in York, i.
Fish-wears in the Mersey, injurious effect of, ix.
Fisher, 𝔑, iv, xii, xiii, xviii, xxii, xxvii, xxix.
Fisherbuttes, xx (*tit.* Cliderhou).
Fishwyck, Mr., viii.
Fitches, Reuben, a Cambridge cook, xiii.
Fittleton, co. Wilts., xix.
Fitton, 𝔑, ii, viii, xviii, xxvii.
Fitz-Alured, Roger, and Alice his daughter, viii.
Fitzgerald, sir Luke, and his wife "colonel Mary," xii.
Fitz-Gilmuth, Robert. *See* Gilmuth.
Fitz-Henry (Robert) founds Burscough priory, viii.
Fitzherbert, 𝔑, viii, xix, xxv, xxviii.
Fitz-Hugh, Robert, baron of Malpas, and his daughter Letitia, viii.

Fitzmaurice, John, of Ireland, and his wife Joanna, XXV.
Fitz-Nigel, William, baron of Halton, founder of Norton priory, VIII.
Fitz-Norman, Hugh and Ralf, VIII.
Fitz-Roger (Richard) founds Lytham priory, XXII.
Fitz-Siward, Henry, XIX.
Fitz-Swayn, (Adam) founds Monk-Breton priory, VIII.
Fitz-Tezzon, Osbern, ancestor of the Boydells of Doddleston, VIII.
Fitzwalter (Robert baron) created earl of Sussex, XIX.
Five-miles act, its operation in Lancashire, IV, XVIII.
Flagellum, a book so called, XVIII.
Flanders, IX.
Flandrensis (Michael) *or* Le Fleming, *otherwise* Michael de Furness: notice of, XXII.
Flanner, Phil., VIII.
Flats near the isle of Thanet: passage of, I.
Flaxpughull, XX (*tit.* Butterword).
Fledde (*or* Sledde), kynge of Estsex and Mydylsex, XV.
Fleere, to mock, gibe, flout, VII.
Fleetwood, 𝔑, II, IV, VIII, IX, XII, XIV, XXII, XXVIII.
Fleetwood pedigree, XXX.
Fleitcroft, Robert, XXVII.
Fleming, 𝔑, I, VII, XXII.
Flesher, R.: his bequest to the poor of Chester, VIII.
Fletcher, 𝔑, VIII, IX, XII, XIV, XVII, XXII.
Fletewoode, John, XXX.
Flintshire, VIII.
Flitcroft, 𝔑, XIX, XXVII.
Flixton, co. Lanc., VIII; account of, XIX.
Flodden, battle of, VII, IX, XIV, XVII; ballads on, XXIX.
Flodden Field, in Nine Fits, a poem: extracts from, VII.
Flood, 𝔑, XIII.
Floods at Dort and Rotterdam, I; at Manchester, XVIII.
Flookborough chapelry, co. Lanc.: account of, XXII.
Flookersbrook, near Chester, VIII.
Florence, *MSS.* of Scioppius in the Laurentian library at, XIII; notice of the grand-duke Ferdinand II. of, XIII.
Florentine, a special kind of cross-bow, XIV.
Florentius, Dr., author of *De Peste*, I.
Flotes, XX (*tit.* Kyuerdale).
Flower, 𝔑, I, XII, XXIV.
Floyd, Mr., IX.
Flud, John, servant to sir William Stanley: his depositions and execution, XXV.
Fludd, Robert, the rosicrucian, VI; notices of, XIII.
Flushing, I.
Flyndal, XX (*tit.* Staneye).
Foden, John, VIII.
Fog, 𝔑, II, IV, XIII.
Fogg, 𝔑, VIII, XIII, XIV, XIX.
Fogge, 𝔑, II, XIII.
Foing, cleansing, VII.
Foldes, near Rivington, XIX.
Foldestidde (the), Warrington, XVII.
Folds, Mr., XXII.
Foldgreue, XX (*tit.* Bilyngton).
Foley, 𝔑, IV, XXVII.
Fontenoy-street, Liverpool, XII.
Foot-races a royal amusement, XIV.
Forbes, 𝔑, I, V.
Ford over the Mersey at Warrington, XVII.
Ford, township of Sefton, XII.
Ford, co. Sussex, IX.
Ford's *Perkin Warbeck*, XXIX; *Witch of Edmonton*, extract from, VI.
Fordham, XIII.

Foreness in Kent, I.
Forest of Bowland, extirpation of deer from, XIV.
Forests, decay of, in Lancashire and Cheshire, VII.
Forester (master-) of Wensleydale and Raydale: royal grant of the office of, XIV.
Forms or benches admitted into churches before the Reformation, XIV.
Formby, chapelry of Walton (account of, pp. 227–8), XXII; assessment of a fifteenth in, IX.
Formby, 𝔣𝔣, IX, XII, XXII.
Forme, Mr., XXII.
Fornace, 𝔣𝔣, XXVII.
Fornby *or* Forneby, 𝔣𝔣, XXII, XXVII.
Forrester, lord: account of his successful attack at Preston, V.
Forshall, 𝔣𝔣, VIII.
Forshaw *or* fforshagh, 𝔣𝔣, XXX.
Forster, 𝔣𝔣, V, VIII, XIII, XIX.
Fort, 𝔣𝔣, XXII.
Fortalitium Fidei contra Judæos, *Fortalitium Fidei contra Judæos*, &c., by Alphonsus de Spina: notice of, XIII.
Fortescue, 𝔣𝔣, I, XXVIII.
Forth river, character of its shores, I; passage of by the Highlanders, V.
Forth, Mr., XXVII.
Fortune's fickleness, lines on, XXIII.
Fossard, Richard de, VIII.
Foster, 𝔣𝔣, XIII, XIX, XXII, XXIV.
Fotherby, Martin, D.D., XIII.
Fothergill, Dr., VIII.
Fotheringhay college, account of, XIII.
Fouch, Mrs., XXVII.
Fouden, fox-hunting at, XIV.
Foul-women (? nurses) at Leyden, I.
Foulds, near Rivington, XIX.
Foulds, Anne, killed by witchcraft, VI.
Foulhurst, Foulshurst, *or* Fulleshurst family, of Crewe, VII, VIII, XIX.
Foulrig, XIV.
Foulk-Stapleford, near Tarvin: origin of the name, VIII.
Fountain, Mr., XIII.
Fowke, 𝔣𝔣, IX.
Fowler, 𝔣𝔣, II, IV, XXVIII. *See* Scoler.
Fox 𝔣𝔣, VIII, XIII, XXII, XXVII, XXVIII.
Foxe, 𝔣𝔣, II, XIV.
Foxes, fees paid for destroying, XIV.
Foxcroft, 𝔣𝔣, XIII.
Foxdenton hall, Oldham: account of, XIX.
Fox hall, Blackpool: notice of, IX.
Foxholes, Rochdale: account of, XIX.
Foxhunting, *temp.* James I.: character of, XIV.
Foxlowe, Henry, XVII.
Foxwist in Whitegate, Cheshire, VIII.
Fozzi (the) at Venice, XVIII.
France, IX; arms of, XIV; Henry III. king of, XIV; Mary queen-dowager of, XIV; history of, studied by Newcome, XVIII.
France family, VIII.
Francis, John, IX.
Franeker, in Friesland, XIII.
Frankby *or* Franceby, township of West-Kirby, VIII.
Frankfort, XIII; *Catalogue of*, XIII.
Frankland, sir Thomas, bart., M.P.: account of, VIII.
Franklin, Chaucer's description of a, VII.
Franklyn, 𝔣𝔣, XIII.
Frantzius, author, XIII.
Freckleton, co. Lanc., XXX.
Frederick II. king of Denmark, XIV.
Free-school at Liverpool, notice of, XII.
French and Spanish ambassadors, fight at London between, XVIII.
French fashions prevail at the Hague, I.
French, Peter, B.D., XIII.
Frere-medo, Warrington, XVII.
Frewen, archbishop of York, XIII.
Friburg bell, Müller's poetical account of, XVIII.

Friend, Jo., XIII.
Friend-makers in Holland, their office and powers, I,
Friesland, political description of, I; account of a remarkable native of, XIII.
Frisius, Gemma, mathematician, XXIV.
Frith river. *See* Forth.
Frobisher *or* Forbisher, sir Martin: account of, XXIII.
Frodsham, co. Chester, XII; account of, VIII; church belongs to Vale-Royal abbey, VIII; rent paid by rural-dean to bishop, VIII; gaol at, XVII; Newcome commences his ministry at, XVIII.
Frodsham, ℜ, VIII.
Frog, Mary, VIII.
Frog-lane, Liverpool, XII.
Froggatt, T. Sutton Mort, XXII.
Frogmore, XIII.
Frome, co. Somerset, XIII.
Fromonds, ℜ, XXIV.
Frost, ℜ, XIII, XXII, XXVII, XXVIII.
Fuente, Spanish ambassador: haughty speech of, XVIII.
Fulache, XX (*tit.* Bilyngton).
Fulebachehope, XX (*tit.* Brendewod).
Fulford, ℜ, XXVII.
Fulginio, Angela de: full title of the book so called, XIII.
Fullbrough in Cartmell, VIII.
Fuller, ℜ, VIII, XIII, XVIII, XIX, XXII, XXVII.
Fuller's pretended plot, XXVIII.
Fuller's *Church History*, XIV; *Worthies*, XIV, XIX.
Fulleshurst, ℜ, VIII. *See* Foulhurst.
Fulshagh, John, of Warrington, XVII.
Fulshaw, township of Wilmslow, VIII.
Fulthorpe, sir Roger, knt., XXII.
Fulwood, near Preston, XII.
Funeral ceremonies *temp.* James I., XIV; at the Hague, I; over the body of saynt Werburge, XV.
Funeral sermons, custom of, XIV.
Furafta, XX (*tit.* Spotlond).
Furness deanery, VIII, XIX; account of, XXII; rent paid by rural-dean to bishop, VIII.
Furness abbey, account of, XXII.
Furness, ℜ, VIII, XIV, XIX, XXII.
Furnifall, John, IV.
Furniture, inventory and valuation of, VII.
Fyfe *or* Fyffe, ℜ, XIV, XXII.
Fyld (William) endows Great-Eccleston school, XXII.
Fyssher, Henry, and his wife Catherine, XVII.
Fytcheakyr *and* Fytchelande, in Warrington, XVII.
Fyton, ℜ, VIII.
Fytton, ℜ, XXVII.

GABEL, in Bohemia, birth-place of P. Figulus, XIII.
Gadsden, co. Bucks.: earl of Bridgwater's monument at, VIII.
Gage, sir John, bart., and Mary his daughter, XIV,
Gaignères, Monsieur, intendant de Madame de Lorraine, XIII.
Gaitskill (Richard) founds Bowbridge hospital, XXII.
Gale *or* Gavill, hamlet of Whitegate, VIII.
Gale, ℜ, XXII.
Gale-crofte, Gale-parrok *and* Gale-sperthe: lands in Orford, near Warrington, XVII.
Galeway, Willmus de, XX.
Galey, ℜ, XIX.
Galfridus *or* Gaufridus, capellanus, XXX.
Gallaw, Thomas, XII.
Galliard (lieut.-col.) taken prisoner at Wigan, II.
Galliards and corantos, XIV.
Galloway, moor of, I.

Galloway, Thomas, bailiff of Liverpool: his character sketched, XII.
Gallows in Holland, dainty and curious, I.
Galtree forest, VIII.
Galva'h, a spirit: her dialogue with Dr. Dee, XIII.
Galway, viscount, IX.
Gamelscroft, XX (*tit*, Wythenhull).
Gamigès, birth-day feast at, XIV.
Gamul, ꝑ, II, IV, VIII, XXX.
Gangrene, terrible case of, I.
Garden, Philip, VIII.
Gardens (account of) at the Hague, Leyden, Allifein, York, Carrickfergus, Drogheda, I.
Gardiner, ꝑ, IX, XII, XIII, XIV, XXII, XXVII.
Gardner, ꝑ, XII, XVIII, XXII, XXVII.
Garecloghes, XX (*tit*. Whalleye).
Gargape in Penwortham, XXX.
Garice, John, and Elizabeth his daughter, XII.
Garner, William, minister of Farnworth, XXII.
Garnet, ꝑ, XVII, XX.
Garnett, ꝑ, XII, XXII.
Garnstone near Weobley, residence and burial-place of colonel John Birch, XVIII.
Garrard, ꝑ, XIV, XXIX.
Garratt hall, Manchester, XVIII; account of, XIX.
Garroway, ꝑ, IX, XXII.
Garside *or* Garsett, ꝑ, VIII.
Garstang, co. Lanc.: account of, XXII; high-awlter at, XXII; brasses in the church, XIV; rebels and executions at, V.
Garstang market-town chapel, account of, XXII.
Garstang-side, XVIII.
Garston, co. Lanc., VIII, IX, XII; account of, XXII; hall, notice of, XXII.
Garston leet jury, extract from order of, IX.
Garston *or* Gerstan, ꝑ, XX.
Garswood hall, Ashton-in-Makerfield: notice of, XXII.
Gartesiche, XX (*tit*. Cromton).
Garteside, ꝑ, XX.
Garthwayte, Mr., XIII.
Garton, Richard, XXII.
Gartside, ꝑ, XIV, XIX, XXII, XXVII, XXVIII.
Gartside hall and manor, XX; account of, XIX.
Gartsyde, rev. Thomas, XXII.
Garway, ꝑ, IX, XII.
Gascall (Mr.) founds a school at Newton, Manchester, XIX.
Gascoigne *or* Gascoyne, ꝑ, V, IX, XXII.
Gaskell, ꝑ, II, XVIII, XIX, XXII, XXVII.
Gassendus *or* Gassendi, Peter: account of, XIII.
Gastrell, ꝑ, VIII, XIX, XXII.
Gastrell's *Notitia Cestriensis*, XIX.
Gataker, ꝑ, XIII, XIV, XVIII, XXVII.
Gate, street or way, XVII.
Gatecroft in Farington, XXX.
Gathorne *or* Gaythorn, Edward, a "bloody Anabaptist," rescued by Newcome from prison, XVIII, XXVII.
Gauden, Dr., XIII.
Gaule, John: notice of, VI.
Gaunt, John of, XXII; insignia of, XIV.
Gauntes, wild-geese: their merueylous obedyence to saynt Werburge, XV.
Gavil *or* Gale, township of Whitegate, VIII.
Gawsworth, co. Chester: account of, VIII; Newcome's connexion with, XVIII: hall, account of, VIII.
Gawthorp hall, Padiham, XIV; account of, XXII.
Gay, quotation from, XIV.
Gayrestang, ꝑ, XX, XXX.

Gaysworth *for* Gawsworth, VIII.
Gaythorn. *See* Gathorn.
Gayton hall, Heswall, Cheshire: notice of, VIII.
Gazette, story of naval engagement in the, XXVII.
Geaf "in Saxons tongue," XV.
Geaton, ꝑ, VIII.
Gee, ꝑ, II, IV, XXII, XXVII.
Geere, Mons[r] de, XIII.
Geering, Mr., XVIII.
Geese, wild. *See* Gauntes.
Geez, XX (*tit.* Whalleye).
Gell, Mr. and Mrs., XVIII, XXVII.
Gellebrand, Rich., XVIII.
Genebrard's character of Johannes Lasitius, XIII.
Geneva, praise of the English liturgy in, IX; John Pell's residence there, XIII.
Gent, Mrs., XIII.
Gentleman's Magazine, XIV, XVIII.
Gentleman's Recreation, XIV.
Gentyl, Joh. le, XX.
Geoffrey *or* Jeffery of Monmouth, notice of, VII.
Geoffrey, bishop of Coventry: notice of, VIII.
Geoffreys, Robert: his dispute with Henry Norris, IX.
Geohegan's accusation against the Roundheads, XII.
George I., political conduct of, V.
George II., rustic ignorance in Raydale in the time of, XIV.
George, David, the famous enthusiast, XIII.
George *or* Gorge, sir Thomas, knt., XXIV.
George (St.) sir Richard, knt., Norroy, XIV.
George inn, Lichfield, XIV.
Gerard, ꝑ, I, II, VI, VIII, IX, XII, XIII, XIV, XVII, XVIII, XIX, XX, XXII, XXVII, XXVIII.
Gerbier, sir Balthazar, XIII.
Gerdes's *Miscellanea Groningiana*, XIII.
Gerlaffr *or* Gulaffr, Willus, XX.
Germaine, lady Betty, IX.
German landsknechte's march against Rome, XVIII.
German, Thomas, mayor of Preston, XXII.
Gernet, ꝑ, XX, XXII.
Gerneth, Roger: notices of, XXII.
Gerrard, ꝑ, XXVIII.
Gerstan and its subdivisions, XX.
Gesselius's (Timannus) *Ecclesiastical History*, notice of, XIII.
Gey, Stephen, vicar of Whalley: notice of, XXII.
Gfrorer, A. F., editor of Bruno, XIII.
Ghisnes *or* Ghynes, Ingelram de, and his wife Christiana, XXII.
Ghosts at Berlin and Weimar, I.
Guesthouses in Holland: description of, I.
Giants in Holland, I.
Gibbets in Holland, I. *See* Gallows.
Gibbon, Mr., XXVII.
Gibbons (J.) elected mayor of Liverpool, IX.
Gibbs, sir Vicary, attorney-general, XIV.
Gibraltar, straits of, IX.
Gibs, Rebecca, IX.
Gibson, ꝑ, VIII, XII, XIII, XIV, XXII, XXVII.
Gibson's *Codex* and *Concilia*, XIX.
Gidding (little-), XIV. *See* Ferrar.
Giffard's (George) *Dialogues concerning Witches and Witchcraft*: critical notice of, VI.
Gifford, ꝑ, XXVIII.
Gifford, William: his critical opinions quoted, XII, XIV, XVIII, XXIX.
Gilbert, Mr., XXVII.
Gilbody, ꝑ, XIX, XXII.
Gilds *for* Guilds of St. Anne and St. Ursula, Chester: accounts of, VIII.

Gildart, Richard, M.P. for Liverpool, and his wife Ann, XII.
Gildart-street, Liverpool, XII.
Gilden-Sutton, Cheshire: account of, VIII.
Giles, Anna, XVIII.
Gill, William, of Speke, IX.
Gille, Cecilia, XVII.
Gillefylde *and* Gille-lande in Warrington, XVII.
Gilliam, 𝔉, XIX, XXVII.
Gillibourne, Mr., XXVIII.
Gillibrand, 𝔉, II, XXII.
Gillibrand hall *or* Lower-Chorley hall, XXII.
Gilling (east-), co. York, XIV.
Gillingham rectory, Kent, vested in Brasenose college for Middleton school, XIX.
Gillow, Robert, XXII.
Gilmuth, Robert Fitz-, XXII.
Gilpin, 𝔉, IV, XIII, XXII.
Gilsburgh, XIII.
Gipps, rev. Thomas, rectory of Bury, XIX, XXII.
Giraldus Cambrensis, XV; notice of, VII.
Girlington, 𝔉, II, XIV, XXII, XXVIII.
Girona, wager respecting, IX.
Girton, XIII.
Gisburne in Craven, VI, XIV, XIX.
Gisburne, Mr., mayor of Derby, XXVII.
Gisthill, a writer, XIII.
Glamorgan, 𝔉, XII.
Glanville, Joseph: account of, XIII; notices of him and his works, VI, XIII.
Glasgow, description of, I; notices of the university, I, IV.
Glasier, 𝔉, II, VIII, XXV.
Glass of skill, probably the beryl, XXIII. *See* Dee (Dr.), XXIV.
Glass-works at Dort, I.
Glassbrook, 𝔉, XXII.
Glasse-house, township of St. Oswald's, Chester, VIII.
Glasseure, Thomas, VIII.
Glastonbury, description of, I; notices of its holy thorn, I, XIII; Hearne's *Antiquities of Glastonbury*, XXII.
Gleast, Eleanor, XXII.
Gleaston castle, description of, XXII.
Gleave, 𝔉, VIII.
Glebedekar, XX (*tit.* Bilyngton).
Glegg *or* Glegge, 𝔉, VIII, XIV.
Gleides *or* gledes, red-hot coals, XXIII.
Glen, George, IV.
Glendole, John, XIII.
Glisson, Dr. Francis, XIII.
Glossaries. *See* vols. XV, XX.
Gloucester, XVIII; description of, I; Elfleda doughter of kynge Alured edifies a noble monastery at, XV.
Gloucester, Henry duke of, XIII, XXVII.
Glouerstone, XX (*tit.* Cestria).
Glover, 𝔉, VIII, XII, XVIII, XXII.
Glyd, Jeffrey, IX.
Glyn, 𝔉, XII.
Goad, 𝔉, VII, XIII. *See* Good.
Goch, Robertus, XX.
Goddard, 𝔉, XIII, XXVIII.
Godderícke, sir Henry, IX.
Goddersyde in Cartmell, VIII.
Godelegh *or* Godley manor in Longdendale, VIII.
Godericheclogh, XX (*tit.* Riblecestria).
Godewayt, Ad., XX.
Godfathers in Anglo-Saxon times, XV.
Godfrey, sir Edmundbury, XIII.
Godith *or* Godiva, wife of duke Leofric, obtains the freedom of Couentre from her husband, XV.
Godley, township of Mottram, VIII. *See* Godelegh.
Godolphin, 𝔉, XIV, XXII.
Godwin's *Life of Milton*, XXIV.
Goet, a native of Gothland or Jutland, XV.
Gogava, Antonius, mathematician, XXIV.
Gogney, 𝔉, XII.

Golborn-Bellow, township of Tattenhall, VIII.
Golborn-David, township of Handley, notice of, VIII.
Golborne in Winwick, XVII; constituted a parish, XXII.
Golborne, Mr., XVIII.
Goldacher, XX (*tit.* Gerstan).
Goldbourn, War. de, XXX.
Goldehord, XX (*tit.* Staneye).
Golden, Lawrence, IX.
Golden Mirrour, account of, XXIII.
Goldsborough, incident of the great storm at, I.
Goldsborough, bishop of Gloucester, I.
Goldshaw, Goldshaw-Booth *or* Gouldshey, in Pendle, VI.
Goldwell, Thomas, bishop of St. Asaph: notice of, VII.
Golyn, John son of Nicholas, of Golynrode, XIX.
Gonolfemore, XX. *See in same volume* Whelton.
Gonville and Caius college, Cambridge, XIII.
Good (*properly* Goad), Dr., head-master of Merchant-tailors' school, IV.
Goodacre, 𝔑, VIII.
Goodall, John, IX.
Good counsel, poems of, XXIII.
Good-Friday a day for witch-meetings, VI.
Goodfellow, Robin, a character in a masque, XIV.
Goodier, Mr., minister of English church at Leyden, I.
Goodman, 𝔑, IX, XIII, XXVIII.
Goodrich court, ancient armour at, XIV.
Goodricke, sir Henry, knt.: notice of, I.
Goodridge *or* Gotherick (sir John) taken prisoner, II.
Goods of deceased persons in Holland, distribution of, I.
Goodshaw, co. Lanc: account of, XXII.
Goodwin, 𝔑, IV, XIII, XVIII, XIX, XXVII.
Goodwyn, Dr., XXVII.
Goolden, Edm., XIX.
Gooseberries, receipt for a tansy of, I.
Gooselane grange, Rochdale: account of, XIX.
Goosetree, chapelry of Sandbach, IV; account of, VIII; Newcome officiates at, XVIII.
Goosnargh, co. Lanc., XIV; account of, XXII.
Goosnargh *or* Gosnell, James, vicar of Bolton, XIX.
Goostrey family, VIII.
Gorbals (the), a suburb of Glasgow: notice of, I.
Gordon, a Scotch conspirator, XXVIII.
Gore, Thomas, XXII.
Gore's *Liverpool Directory*, 1790: list of names from, XII.
Goree in Holland, I.
Gorges, Mr., XIII.
Goring, 𝔑, I, II, XIII, XIV.
Gorse-acre hey *and* Gorsey heys, Liverpool, XII.
Gorsichelache, XX (*titt.* Brendewod, Whiteword).
Gorstelow, Richard, vicar of Rochdale, XIX.
Gorsty-akyr, Orford, near Warrington, XVII.
Gorsty-croft, Warrington, XVII.
Gorsuch, James, IX.
Gorton, near Manchester: account of, XIX; Martindale's connexion with, IV.
Gorton, James, XIX.
Goselone, XX (*tit.* Cestria).
Gosenargh, Randulphus de, XX.
Gosnall *or* Gosnell, 𝔑, VIII, XIX, XXVII. *See* Goosnargh.
Gostlin, Jo., XIII.
Gottingen, Royal society of, XIII.
Gouet, Lodowycus, XX.

Gouge, 𝔑, XVIII, XXVII.
Goulborn, co. Chester, VIII.
Goulbourn's (J.) letter on the Manchester riots, XXVIII.
Gould, 𝔑, XIII, XXVIII.
Goulden, Ja., XXVII.
Goupylus (Jacobus) desires Dr. Dee's acquaintance, XXIV.
Gousehouse, XX (*tit.* Whalleye).
Gout (the), Liverpool, XII.
Government of Ireland, extract from, XXV.
Gower, 𝔑, VIII, IX, XIX, XXVII.
Gower, the poet: Latin verses by, VII.
Gowre, captain, XXVIII.
Gowry conspiracy, account of, I.
Goydwin, Mr., XIII.
Grace, Joseph, XIII.
Gradill, Mr., of Barbers-moor XXVIII.
Grævius's edition of Martinez's *Lexicon*, XIII.
Grafton, hamlet of Tilston, Cheshire, VIII; hall, account of, VIII.
Graham, 𝔑, I, V, XIV.
Graham's dyke, description of, I.
Graisdale *or* Grizedale village and hall in Satterthwaite, notices of, XXII.
Graisty, Joh., VIII.
Graithwaite chapelry and halls, Hawskshead: notices of, XXII.
Grampound, co. Cornwall, XIII.
Grand jury at Jacobite trials in Manchester: list of, XXVIII.
Grandison, Otho de, XIX; sir Otto de, XXII.
Grange (the) in Ince-Blundell, XXII.
Grange hall, West Kirby: notice of, VIII.
Granger, Margaret, XII.
Granger's *Biographical History* XII, XIII, XIV.
Grant, 𝔑, XVIII, XIX, XXVII.
Grantham, 𝔑, VIII, XIV.
Granville, George, duke of Sutherland, XIX.
Grappenhall, co. Chester, XIX; account of, VIII. *See* Gropenhall.
Grass-day, XIV.
Graveley, XIII.
Gravelines in Flanders, I, XIV.
Graves, XX (*tit.* Whalleye).
Gravescende in Holland, I.
Gravesend, co. Kent, I, XIII.
Gray, 𝔑, I, VI, XIII, XVII, XX, XXII.
Graysbrook, co. York, IV.
Grays-Inn, London, IX, XIV.
Greasby, townships of Thurstaston, West-Kirby and Wibunbury, VIII.
Great Britaines Great Deliverance, a sermon by Leigh of Standish, XIV.
Great-Carlton, XII.
Great-Crosby, XII.
Great-Lamford, XIII.
Great-Sankey, XVII.
Greatraks, Valentine, XIII.
Greaves, 𝔑, VII, XVIII, XIX, XXVII, XXVIII.
Gredley *or* Gredle, 𝔑, XIV, XIX.
Greek, grammars and pronunciation of, IV.
Green, 𝔑, II, VIII, XII, XIX, XXII, XXVIII.
Greene, 𝔑, II, VIII, IX, XIV, XVIII, XXII, XXVII, XXIX.
Green-acres, Sacheverell mob at, V.
Greenacres, 𝔑, XIV, XXII.
Greenall, 𝔑, VIII, XXII.
Green-castle, Newry: notice of, I.
Greenfield, sir Christopher, XXVIII.
Greenhalgh, 𝔑, II, IV, XIV, XVIII, XIX, XXII, XXVIII.
Greenhalgh castle: account of, XXII; siege and surrender of, II.
Greenhalgh hall, Bury: notice of, XXII.
Greenhead in Pendle, notice of, VI.
Greenhead hall, Poulton: account of, XXII.
Greenloes tenement, Walmsley near Bolton, XIX.

Green-men, characters in pageants: notice of, III.
Greenvil, sir Richard, XII.
Greenwich (east-), manor of, VIII, XIX.
Greenwood, 𝔑, I, XXII.
Greese (turn) in Eccles church, XIX.
Gregg, 𝔑, XIX, XXVIII.
Gregge, 𝔑, II, VIII.
Grégoire, abbé: his notice of quakers, XVIII.
Gregory, 𝔑, VIII, XVIII, XX, XXII.
Gregorye, saynt, sendeth Austyn to England, XV.
Gregson, 𝔑, IX, XII, XIV, XXVII.
Grelley *or* Grelle, 𝔑, XIX, XX, XXII.
Grenacr, Ric de, XX.
Grene (Barthlet) burnt in queen Mary's reign, XXIV.
Grenecroft, XX (*tit.* Bilyngton).
Grenegate, XX (*tit.* Aluetham).
Grenegore, Thoma de le, XX.
Grenehalgh, 𝔑, XIX.
Grenehou, XX (*tit.* Dounom).
Grenehou, Willielmus de, XX.
Grenehough, 𝔑, XIX.
Greneridding XX (*tit.* Bilyngton).
Greneruydyng, XX (*tit.* Workedelegh).
Greneruydyngsike, XX (*tit.* Bilyngton).
Greneschagh, XX (*tit.* Wythenhull).
Gresendale, XX (*tit.* Gerstan).
Gresford, co. Denbigh, VIII.
Gresham, sir Thomas, I.
Gresham college, XIII.
Gresley, 𝔑, VIII, XIX, XXII. *See* Gredley *and* Grelley.
Gressingham, chapelry of Lancaster: account of, XXII.
Gressingham, Thomas de, XXII.
Gresyerde, XX (*tit.* Whalleye).
Gretser, James, jesuit, VII.
Gretton, 𝔑, XII.
Greue, XX (*tit.* Spotlond).
Greues, Thomas, IX.
Grey, 𝔑, II, IV, VIII, XII, XIV, XVII, XX, XXV, XXVII.
Greyhounds and hare, a witch-story, VI.
Griffin, 𝔑, VIII, XXVIII.
Griffinus, kyng of the Walshemen: legendary account of his siege of Chester, XV.
Griffith, 𝔑, VIII, XIX, XXVIII.
Griffiths, 𝔑, XII, XIII, XXV.
Grimbalston, John, XXVIII.
Grime, John, of Baxenden, XIX.
Grimm, quotations from, XII.
Grimsargh, co. Lanc., XIV; account of, XXII.
Grimsdich hall, Budworth-magna: notice of, VIII.
Grimsdich John, VIII.
Grimshaw, 𝔑, XIX, XXII.
Grimstone, 𝔑, XVIII, XIX.
Grindleton in Craven, XIV.
Grindletonians, account of the, XIV.
Grisedale, Mr., XXII.
Grislehurst hall, Middleton: account of, XIX.
Gristwayth, Johannes de, vicar of Blackburn, XX.
Grizedale hall, Satterthwaite: notice of, XXII.
Groaning-cake, XIV.
Groats, corn so called, XXII.
Groningen, cities of, I; victory of, XXV.
Gronovius, James: character of, XIII.
Gronovius, John Frederick: notices of, XIII.
Groole, burgomasters of, IX.
Gropenhall, XVII.
Gross, Mr., XIII.
Grossus-venator, Robertus, XX.
Grosvenor, 𝔑, VIII, IX, XII, XX, XXVII, XXVIII.
Grotius, Hugo: critical account of and notices of his writings, XIII.
Grover, Mr., XXVII.
Gruffyth, Dauid ap, IX.
Grundles, XX (*tit.* Staneye).

Grundy, 𝔫, xix, xxii.
Grunshaw's widow, xviii.
Gryme, John, xxii.
Grymeschagh, 𝔫, xx.
Grymesley, xx. (*tit.* Spotlond).
Grymesleyker, xx (*tit.* Spotlond).
Grymesleysik, xx (*tit*, Spotlond).
Grymmeslee, xx (*tit.* Chadewyk).
Guelderland, towns of, i.
Guérard *or* Gérard, Balthazar de: his murder of William of Nassau, i.
Guest, 𝔫, xix, xxii.
Guilds. *See* Gilds.
Guild-merchant of Preston, notice of, xxii.
Guildford (lord) and the brothers North, xiii.
Guildhall, trial at, *in re* Yeamond Robinson, xiv.
Guillam, John, xix.
Guilleragues, 𝔫, xviii.
Guizot on Ben Jonson, xxix.
Guldenaleford xx (*tit.* Eccles).
Guldeneleford, xx (*tit.* Westewood).
Gulliford *or* Gullyford, 𝔫, xviii, xxvii.
Gunn-ferrie, xiv.
Gunning, 𝔫, xiii, xviii, xxii.
Gunpowder-plot, xiv, xxv.
Gunter, Thomas, and his daughter Margaret, xii.
Gurnall, Mr., xiii.
Gurney, 𝔫, ix.
Guy earle of Warwike slays Colbrond the gyaunt, xv.
Guy, Rob., apparitor-general, viii.
Guyse, sir John, xxviii.
Gwillym, R. Atherton, and his daughter Henrietta, xxii.
Gwynne, Matthew, M.D.: account of, xxix.
Gynoue, 𝔫, xx.
Gyrarde (? Giraldus Cambrensis), xv.
Gysors, Willus le, xx.

H. (T.), his unsuccessful contest with Worthington for a vacant fellowship, xiii.
Haak, Theodore: account of, xiii.
Haberdashers' company, viii.
Habergham, 𝔫, xxii.
Habergham hall, Burnley: account of, xxii.
Habington. *See* Abington.
Habringeham, 𝔫, xx.
Hackensall hall, account of, xxii.
Hacker, colonel, xii.
Hacket *or* Hackett, 𝔫, viii, xiii, xix, xxiv.
Hackforth, xiv.
Hacking, 𝔫, xii, xxii.
Hacking's hall, Langho: account of, xxii.
Hacking-hey *and* Hacking-house, Liverpool, xii.
Hackness near Scarborough, xiv.
Hacquet's-town, Ireland: account of, i.
Hacus (Mathias), mathematician, visits Dr. Dee, xxiv.
Hadelond, xx (*tit.* Aluetham).
Haddington, highlanders arrive at, v.
Haddock *or* Haddocke, 𝔫, ii, xxvii.
Haddon, 𝔫, ix, xix.
Haddon hall, xiv.
Hadfield, Tho., viii.
Hadley in Blackburn, xxii.
Haerlem, description of, i.
Haggehouse, xx (*tit.* Whalleye).
Hague, the, xiii; description of, i.
Hague, John, xviii.
Hai Ebn Yokdhan, an Arabic romance: account of, xiii.
Haigh, 𝔫, xix.
Haigh hall, near Wigan. *See* Hough hall.
Hailes, lord: his edition of John Hales's *Sermons*, xiii.
Hainault, the admiral of, xxix.
Haine, to hinder, vii.

Hair, how worn by English soldiers at Flodden, VII.
Hakeford, Joh. de, clericus, XX.
Hakkyng, 𝔑, XX.
Hakonschou, Joh. de, XX.
Hakynsall, John: account of his Warrington tenancy, XVII.
Halce, Mr., XIII.
Hale, township of Bowden, VIII.
Hale in Childwall, IX; account of, XXII; perambulation of, XX; painted east window at, VII; hall, account of, XXII.
Hale, sir Matthew, XII, XIV; character of, VI.
Hale, 𝔑, IX, XX.
Hale's *or* Hales's *Sermons*, XVIII.
Hales, Dr., his claim to the Fen-Ditton tithes, XIII.
Hales, John, of Bath: account of, XIII.
Halesworth, co. Suffolk, XIV.
Halewood-cum-Halebouke, Childwall: particulars of a subsidy at, IX.
Haley, 𝔑, XXIV, XXVIII.
Half-acre, in Rochdale, XIX.
Halgh, XX (*tit.* Bilyngton).
Halgh, Roger, of Halgh, divorces his wife, VIII.
Halghes (le) given to Stanlawe abbey, XX. *See in same volume* Whiteword.
Halghton, villa de, XX.
Halghton parva, XX.
Halghton, 𝔑, XX.
Halifax, XIV; levy of ship-money on, I.
Halifax, marquis of, XXVIII.
Halilands in Wilmslow, VIII.
Hall 𝔑, I, IV, V, VIII, IX, XII, XIII, XVIII, XXII, XXVII, XXVIII.
Hall's *Baronial Halls*, view of Turton tower in, XIX.
Hall (old), Ashton-under-Line, XIX.
Hall-i'-th'-wood, Bolton: account of, XIX.
Hall-o'-th'-hill, in Heath-Charnock, XIX.
Hall-o'-heath, Bartomley: account of, VIII.
Hall-o'-wood, Bartomley, VIII.
Hall-street, Liverpool, XII.
Hall-Whittle in Sankey, XVII; notice of, XXII.
Hallam, Henry, historian: critical remarks on his writings, VI, IX, XIII, XIV, XVIII.
Hallamore-heath, township of Barrow, VIII.
Halleclyf, XX (*tit.* Whalleye).
Halle, 𝔑, XXIX.
Haller, 𝔑, XIII.
Halliwallebrok, XX (*tit.* Croenton).
Halliwell, township of Dean, XIX.
Halliwell, 𝔑, VII, XIV, XVIII, XIX, XXVII, XXIX.
Hallmote kept at Clitheroe, XIV.
Hallowes *or* Hallows, 𝔑, XIII, XIX, XXVII.
Halls, Edward, XXVII.
Hallested *or* Hallstudes, Willmus del, XX.
Hallestudes XX (*tit.* Whiteword).
Hallstudes *or* Hallestedes, XX. *See in same volume* Merton *and* Wordull.
Hallum, Johannes de, XX.
Hallums-lane in Warrington, XVII.
Hallums-walle, a fountain in Warrington, XVII.
Hallwood in Halsall, XII, XXII.
Hallywell, 𝔑, XIII, XIV.
Halsall, co. Lanc., IX; account of, XXII; hall, notice of, XXII.
Halsall, 𝔑, II, IX, XII, XIV, XVII, XX, XXII.
Halesworths *or* Houldsworth, a wiseman, VI.
Halsey *for* Halsall, sir Cuthbert, XIV.
Halsgrave, Mr., VIII.
Halsnead park, Prescot: account of, XXII.
Halsted, co. Suffolk, XIV.

Halsted *or* Halstead, 𝔑, VIII, XIV, XXII, XXVII.
Halt, township of Aldford, VIII.
Halton, co. Chester: account of, VIII; barons of, VIII; notices of its castle, VIII, XXIII; praise of its ale, XXIX.
Halton, co. Lanc.: account of, XXII; hall, notice of, XXII.
Halwerdeword *or* Hawerldword, villa de, XX.
Halwood, 𝔑, VIII.
Halydoms, sanctuaries or tombs, VII.
Hambleton, co. Lanc.: account of, XXII.
Hambleton (colonel) taken prisoner, XII.
Hamburg, XIII.
Hamburg in Offlow, co. Stafford: connexion of saynt Werburge with, XV.
Hamby, Eliz., XXII.
Hamelius (Paschasius) courts Dr. Dee's acquaintance, XXIV.
Hamer, 𝔑, XIX.
Hamer hall, Rochdale: account of, XIX.
Hamersley, Mr., XXVII.
Hamerton, 𝔑, XIV, XX, XXII.
Hameston hundred, VIII.
Hamelstansike, XX (*tit.* Whiteword).
Hamilton, dukes of, II, V, IX, XXII.
Hamilton, marquises of, I, XIV.
Hamilton, 𝔑, II, V, VIII, XII, XIX.
Hamilton's expedition, fate of the Scotch prisoners after, XVIII.
Hamilton's *New Account*, IX.
Hammond, 𝔑, II, VIII, XIII, XIV, XXII, XXVII.
Hamond, 𝔑, XIV, XXVIII.
Hamor, Robert, XIX.
Hampden, lord, XII.
Hampden, John, XII; released from the tower, XXVII.
Hampole's (Richard) *Pricke of Conscience*, XVII.
Hampson, 𝔑, VII, XXII.
Hampton, township of Malpas, VIII.
Hampton, 𝔑, I, XIII, XX, XXII.
Hampton court, XII; conference at, XIII; death of queen Anne at, XIV; visit of Newcome to, XVIII, XXVII.
Hamundisholme in Hollay, Warrington, XVII.
Hanbridge, Chester, VIII.
Hanck, origin of the word, VI.
Hancock, 𝔑, XIV, XXII.
Hand, alderman of Chester, VIII.
Handford, township of Cheadle, VIII; residence of sir William Brereton, I.
Handford chapel in Cheadle church, account of, VIII.
Handford, William, of Handford, VIII.
Handley, co. Chester: account of, VIII.
Handlo family, notice of, VIII.
Hands, in Rochdale, XIX.
Hanepol, 𝔑, XX.
Hanewal, 𝔑, XX.
Haney, Mr., of Chester, VIII.
Hanging-ditch, Manchester, XVIII.
Hangmansbanck in Penwortham, XXX.
Hank, "the moss is good hanking," I.
Hankelow, township of Audlem, VIII.
Hankeye, a field in Orford, Warrington, XVII.
Hankinson, 𝔑, XXII.
Hankinson house, near Myerscough, XIV.
Hanley, in Macclesfield forest, VIII.
Hanlowe, sir John de, VIII.
Hanmer, 𝔑, VIII, XXVII.
Hannecroft, XX (*tit.* Aluetham).
Hanover, IX.
Hanover-street, Liverpool, XII.
Hansby, lady: her benefaction to Cheadle, VIII.
Hanson, 𝔑, XIII, XXVII.
Hapsford hall, Thornton: notice of, VIII.
Hapton tower, Padiham, XIV; account of, XXII.

Harald, 𝔑, xx.
Harbert, 𝔑, i.
Harcourt, 𝔑, viii, xviii. *See* Harwecurt.
Harden in Bowland, xiv.
Harden, Thomas, surgeon, of Tattenhall, viii.
Hardewar, John: his tenancies in Warrington, xvii.
Harding's great work, xiii.
Hardinge (Mr. justice), a line from the pen of, xiv.
Hardman, 𝔑, ix, xii, xviii, xxii, xxvii.
Hardshaw in Prescot: property of the Martindales at, iv.
Hardwar *or* Hardware, 𝔑, viii, xiv, xvii.
Hardwick, Worthington preaches at, xiii.
Hardwick Papers, ix.
Hardy, 𝔑, i, viii, xvii, xxvii.
Harebroune, 𝔑, ix.
Harefield; Milton's *Arcades* performed at, xxix.
Hareschagh, xx (*tit.* Dounom).
Harewell, John, bishop of Wells, i.
Harewythnes, xx (*tit.* Whiteword).
Hargrave chapelry, Tarvin: account of, viii.
Hargrave in Neston, viii.
Hargreave, 𝔑, xxii.
Hargreaves, 𝔑, vi, xiv, xix, xxii.
Harison, 𝔑, xviii.
Haristanden, aqua de, xx.
Harland, John, xiv.
Harleian MSS., xiv, xxix.
Harley, 𝔑, ix, xii.
Harmar, Mr., constable of Manchester, xxvii.
Harmer, Samuel, xxvii.
Harmon, Mr., xviii.
Harmonious Consent, 1648, signed by Hollinworth, xviii.
Harne panne, *i.e.* cranium, vi.
Harnesse (Mrs.) gives a house to the minister of Knutsford, viii.
Harold, earl and king: defeated at Hastings, xv; retires to the "Anchorite's cell," Chester, viii.
Harold, kyng of Danes, with others, besieges Chestre and is repelled by the shryne of saynt Werburge, xv.
Harper, 𝔑, ii, viii, xix, xx, xxii.
Harper-heigh, township of Manchester, xix.
Harpur, 𝔑, xiv.
Harrant, Mr., xviii.
Harre, *i.e.* higher, xxiii.
Harre, Alex., xx.
Harrington, 𝔑, viii, ix, xii, xiv, xix, xxii, xxviii, xxix.
Harrington-street, Liverpool, xii.
Harris, 𝔑, viii, ix, xiv, xviii, xix, xxvii, xxviii.
Harrison, 𝔑, ii, iv, viii, xii, xiv, xviii, xix, xxii, xxiv, xxvii.
Harrock hall, Eccleston, co. Lancaster: account of, xxii.
Harrogate, Thomas Norris dies at, ix.
Harrop *or* Arrope fells, xiv.
Harropwell, xiv.
Harsnape, 𝔑, xiv.
Harsnet, Samuel, archbishop of York, xxii; his *Declaration of Popish Impostures*, vi.
Harstancroft, xx (*tit.* Whiteword).
Harstandenbrok, xx (*tit.* Whiteword).
Harstandenheued, xx (*tit.* Whiteword).
Hart, 𝔑, ii, xiv, xxii.
Hartford, co. Chester, viii.
Hartford, earl of, xxii.
Hartgraves, master of Burnley School, xxii.
Harthill, co. Chester: account of, viii.
Harthill, co. Lanc., xiv.
Hartland point, near Barnstable, i.
Hartley, 𝔑, ii, vi, ix, xiv, xviii, xix, xxii, xxvii.

Hartlib, Samuel: detailed notices of, XIII.
Hartop, Mr., XXVII.
Hartshead, township of Ashton-under-Line, XIX.
Harts-horn inn, XXII.
Hartshorne, rev. C. H., XIV.
Harvard college, New-England, XIII.
Harvey, 𝔓, XIII, XXIX.
Harvie, 𝔓, I, XXVII.
Harwecurt *or* Harcourt, Iuon de, XX.
Harwod and its subdivisions, XX.
Harwod, 𝔓, XX.
Harwood, (Joh.) gives 5*l.* to Thornton school, VIII.
Harwood, township of Bolton, XIX.
Harwood-magna, chapelry of Blackburn: account of, XXII.
Harwood (little-) hall, Blackburn: account of, XXII.
Harwood orchard, XX (*tit.* Whalleye).
Haryngton, 𝔓, IX, XVII.
Hasaliswallehurst, boundaries of, XX.
Haselwall, 𝔓, XX.
Haselum, Hug. de, XX.
Haslam, 𝔓, IX, XIX, XXII.
Haslam hey, XIX.
Hasland hall, Derbyshire, VI.
Haslbanck in Childwall, VIII.
Haslewall *or* Heswall, co. Chester: account of, VIII.
Haslewall, 𝔓, VIII.
Haslewood, Mr., XXIII.
Haslingden, co. Lanc., XIV, XX; account of, XXII; de capella, XX; Newcome preaches at, XVIII.
Haslingden, 𝔓, XIX, XXII.
Haslington in Barthomley, account of, VIII; hall, VIII.
Haslington, Thomas de, de le Ermites, VIII.
Haslome, Ann, of Bury: anecdotes of, XXVII.
Hasponwalsiche, XX.
Hassall, township of Sandbach, VIII.
Hassall, 𝔓, VIII, XXVII.
Hastings (colonel) intercepts pistols sent to Manchester, II.
Hatch, John, of Preston: his bequest to Fulwood school, XXII.
Hatfield, John, XIX.
Hatherton, township of Wibunbury, VIII; hall, notice of, VIII.
Hathfeld, Willus, XX.
Hatley, George, XIII.
Hattersley, township of Mottram, VIII.
Hattersley family, VIII.
Hattock of corn, XXII.
Hatton, township of Waverton, VIII; hall, description of, VIII.
Hatton in Daresbury, near Runcorn, VIII.
Hatton, religious conversion of four gentlewomen of, XIV.
Hatton garden, London, IX.
Hatton 𝔓, VIII, XVII, XIX, XX, XXIV, XXV, XXVIII.
Haudley, Hawdley *or* Audley hall, Blackburn: notice of, XXII.
Haueryngton, Robert de, XX.
Haugh, Mrs., XVIII.
Haughton, township of Bunbury, VIII.
Haughton, 𝔓, IV, XXVIII.
Haukeford, XX (*tit.* Sadelword).
Haukeschagh, 𝔓, XX.
Haukesherd XX (*tit.* Bilyngton).
Haulgh hall, Bolton: notice of, XIX.
Haunton, Roger de, XXII.
Haut (the), a hall in Childwall: description of, XXII.
Haverbeck, XIX.
Haveringge, Richard de, archdeacon of Chester, XXII.
Haverington, 𝔓, XXII. *See* Haueryngton.
Haversege, Matthew de, XIX.
Haversham, lord, XXII.
Haverthwaite in Coulton, co. Lanc., XXII.
Havorbro, XIII.

Haward, ℞, XIX.
Hawarden, co. Flint, VIII, XII.
Hawarden, ℞, VI, XVII.
Hawes, Dr., XXVII.
Hawet *or* Hawett, ℞, II, XVIII, XXII.
Hawick, united rebel forces at, V.
Hawkes, Thomas, M.P., XXII.
Hawkesegh, Agnes, XVII.
Hawkeston, ℞, VIII.
Hawking, XIV.
Hawkins, ℞, XXIII, XXIX.
Hawks, Chr. of Born, XIII.
Hawkshead, co. Lanc.: account of, XXII; notices of the hall and grammar-school, XXII.
Haword, ℞, XX.
Haworth, ℞, II, VII, VIII, IX, XIV, XVIII, XIX, XXII, XXVII. *See* Howarth.
Haworth hall, Rochdale: account of, XIX.
Haworthyn, Willmus de, vicecomes Cestrieshir, XX.
Hawrobyn, Henry, XVII.
Hawrydynge, in Warrington, XVII.
Hawtyn, Mr., XIII.
Hawys, Mr., XVIII, XXVII.
Hay, lord, ambassador to France, XIV.
Hay, ℞, VI.
Hay stacked for deer, XIV.
Hay *or* haye, a hedge, VII; derivation of, XVII.
Haya, Rob. de, XX.
Haybonk, XX (*tit.* Plesyngton).
Haycocks, rev. Mr., II.
Haydoc, John, XIII.
Haydock orchard, XX (*tit.* Whalleye).
Haydock chauntry, last "resting place" of sir Peter Legh, XVII.
Haydock lodge, Winwick: notice of, XXII.
Haydock, ℞, XVII, XXII, XXV.
Haydok, ℞, IX, XX.
Hayes, ℞, XXVII.
Hayford, Dennis, VIII.
Hayhurst, ℞, XVIII, XXII, XXVII.
Hayley's *Life of Milton*, XXIV.
Haymer, ℞, XIII.
Haynes, G., XIII.
Hayward, ℞, VIII, XIX, XX, XXII.
Haywood, John, XIII.
Hayworth, John, II.
Hazlehurst in Bleasdale, XIV.
Hazlehurst, township of Ashton-under-Line. *See* Hurst.
Hazlehurst, ℞, VIII.
Heald, William, XIII.
Heale, Mr., I.
Health-drinking, puritanical aversion to, XVIII.
Healey hall, Burnley: account of, XXII.
Healey hall, Rochdale: notices of, VII, XIX.
Healey dene, description of, VII.
Heap, hamlet near Bury, XIX.
Heap *or* Heape, ℞, II, XIX, XXVIII.
Heapy, co. Lanc.: account of, XXII.
Heapy, ℞, XII, XXII.
Hearne, Thomas, VII, XII, XIII, XXIX.
Hearon, Cuthbert, XIV.
Hearst, Elizabeth: affidavit of, XXVIII.
Heasantforth, Hesandforth *or* Phesantford hall: notice of, XXII.
Heath, ℞, I, VIII, XIV, XIX, XXVII.
Heath's *Survey of Rochdale Manor*, XIV.
Heath *or* Hethe street, Warrington. XVII.
Heath cocks, XIV.
Heathcote, ℞, XII, XIX, XXII.
Heaton, ℞, VIII, XXII.
Heaton, XVIII; township of Dean, XIX; townships of Prestwich, XIX.
Heaton hall, notice of, XIX.
Heaton-Norris, XIV, XIX.
Heaveningham, ℞, XII.
Heawood, William, XXVII.
Heber, ℞, VI, XIII, XIV, XXIII.
Hebrew language, study of, IV.

Hector of Troy slayne by fals treason, pycture of on arras, XV.
Hedda *or* Headda, bysshop of Lichefeld, XV.
Heden, riv., XX.
Hedges, sir C., secretary of state, IX.
Hee, XX (*tit.* Wythenhull).
Hefferston grange, Whitegate: notice of, VIII.
Heghe-Hadeland, in Warrington, XVII.
Hem, Peter, Dutch admiral: notice of, I.
Heinsius, Daniel and Nicholas, XIII.
Helbree, Helburghee *or* Hildeburgey island, VIII; the constable of Chestre by myracle goes thence into Wales upon the drye sondes, XV.
Helen, daughter of Llewellyn prince of Wales, poisons John Scot earl of Chester, VIII.
Heley, Thomas de, and his daughter Avicia, XIX.
Heleyden, XX (*tit.* Spotlond).
Heleye and its subdivisions, XX.
Heleye, ℞, XX.
Heleysclogh, XX (*tit.* Spotlond).
Helinsrode, XX (*tit.* Heleye).
Helker, XX (*tit.* Whalleye).
Hellehole, a field in Warrington, XVII.
✓Hellesby, ℞, XX.
Hellier, William, archdeacon of Barnstaple, XIII.
Hellifield, XIV.
Hellifield peel, XIV.
Helme, ℞, XXII.
Helmont. *See* Van Helmont.
Helmshawes in Rivington, XIX.
✓Helsby, township of Frodsham, VIII.
Hemflete, in Holland, XII.
Henbury Pexhall, township of Prestbury, VIII.
Henchman, Rev. Charles: extracts from his letters to Bishop Gastrell, VIII.
Henderson (colonel) killed, XII.
Hendon, XIII, XX.
Henenberg, countess of, and her 365 children, I.
Henese in Balschagh, XX (*tit.* Heleye).
Hengendebank, XX (*tit.* Eccles.).
Hengyst, duke, by vyctory kynge of Kent, XV.
Henhall, ℞, XX.
Henley upon Thames, XIII.
Hennehouse, XX (*tit.* Whalleye).
Henrisiche, XX (*tit.* Spotlond).
Henry III. gives a merchant-guild to Liverpool, XII.
Henry VII., XXIX; visits Lathom house, XIV.
Henry VIII. wore white mourning, XIV; compared to Divine Providence, XVIII: license of companies of players customary in his reign, XXIX.
Henry, prince of Wales, son of James I.: account of, III; incidental notices of, XIII, XIV.
Henry ℞, VIII, XXVII.
Henry, Robert Fitz-, founder of Burscough priory: notice of, XXII.
Henshaw, ℞, XIII, XXIV, XXVII.
Henslowe, XXIX; value of his *Diary* to the history of the drama, XIII.
Henthorn, Henr. de, XX.
Hepay, ℞, XX.
Heppal, ℞, XX,
Heppewell, ℞, XXII.
Heptarchy, description of the, XV.
Heraldic visitations, various: account of, XXIV.
Herbert, George, XIII, XIV.
Herberts (the), satirical rhyme on, XIV.
Hereboord, Adr., of Leyden: notice of, IV.
Hereford, description of, I; capture of, XVIII; Hulmian exhibitions of, XIX.
Hereford, Humphry Bohun earl of: his tomb, I.

Hereford, Rob. de, XX.
Hereford Ridding in Penwortham, XXX.
Hererye kynge of Deiram, father of saynt Hylde the abbesse, XV.
Hereswyth, wife of Anna kynge of Eest-England, XV.
Heresy maketh infamous, XXV.
Hereticarmies always overthrown, XXV.
Herford, Nicholaus, prior of Evesham, XXX.
Herice, ℟, XX.
Heries-house (? hearse-house), I.
Heriot's hospital, Edinburgh: notice of, I.
Herle, ℟, II, XII, XX, XXII, XXVII.
Herleshall, *See* Halsall, XXII.
Hermetic school, philosophers of the, VI.
Hermitage (le), a chapel in Tarporley, VIII.
Herne, ℟, XXVII.
Herneys, Robertus, XX.
Herod *or* Heyrod hall, Ashton-under-Line: notice of, XIX.
Heron, ℟, VIII, XXVII.
Herons or storks at Dort, I.
Herrick. *See* Heyrick.
Herring, Mr., XXVII.
Herring fishery, busses and nets, I.
Hersey, Mr., XXVII.
Herstelgreve, XX (*tit.* Aluetham).
Hertford, Worthington preaches at, XIII.
Hertford, Robert de, XX.
Hescham. *See* Heysham.
Hesewall. *See* Haslewall.
Hesiod, IV.
Hesket, Mr., XXVIII.
Hesketh, ℟, V, VIII, IX, XIV, XIX, XX, XXII, XXV, XXVIII.
Heskin, township of Eccleston, co. Lanc., XXII; notices of Old and New halls in, XXII.
Heskin, ℟, XXII.
Heskyn, ℟, XXX.
Hespias *for* Hesperus *or* Hesperides, XXIII.
Hesse, landgrave of, I.
Hessewort *or* Assheworth, ℟, XIX.
Hesswall. *See* Haslewall.
Hesteham, ecclesia de, XX.
Hesychius, XIII.
Hethecellar, XX (*tit.* Bilyngton).
Hethediche, XX (*tit.* Bacford).
Heton in Waverton, VIII.
Heton, ℟, VIII, XIX, XXII.
Heuedlond, XX (*titt.* Bacford, Etheleswyk).
Hevelius, Johannes: account of, XIII.
Hevilands, in Liverpool, XII.
Hewitt, Katherine, witch of Colne: her trial, VI.
Hewley, sir John, knt.: notice of, VIII; his wife's charities and will, VIII, XVIII.
Hewod, ℟, XX.
Hewson, Mr., XXVII.
Hewston, Mr., IX.
Hexham, Northumbrian insurgents at, V.
Hextal, Robertus de, XX.
Hexte, highest, XXIII.
Hey, ℟, IV, XII, XIV, XVIII, XIX, XXII.
Heyes, ℟, XII, XXII, XXVIII.
Heyhurst, Mr., XXVII.
Heylin, Dr. Peter, XIII, XVIII; account of, VII.
Heylin's *Life of Laud*, XIV.
Heynolesdal, Ada de, XX.
Heyrick, Richard, warden of the collegiate church of Manchester: account of, II; incidental notices of, II, IV, XXVII.
Heyrick *or* Heyricke, ℟, XVIII, XXVII.
Heys, ℟, VIII, XII, XX.
Heysam *or* Heysham, William, M.P. for Lancaster, VIII, IX, XXII.
Heysham, ℟, XXII.
Heysham, co. Lanc.: account of, XXII.
Heyton, ℟, XXII.

Heyward, 𝔉, xx, xxvii, xxviii.
Heywood, near Bury: account of, xix; its marvellous growth, vii; etymology of the name, vii.
Heywood hall, Heap, near Bury: description of and poetical eulogium on, vii; notice of, xix.
Heywood hall, Alderley: notice of, viii.
Heywood, 𝔉, ii, iv, vii, viii, xiii, xiv, xviii, xix, xxii, xxvii, xxviii.
Heywood's *Four Apprentices*, ix.
Heywood and Broome's *Last Lancashire Witches*, extracts from, vi.
Hezekiah *or* Esechyas pyctured on arras, xv.
Hiat. *See* Hiet.
Hibbert, 𝔉, viii, xviii, xxvii.
Hibernia, John de, xxii.
Hickling, Robert de, xxii.
Hickman, 𝔉, iv, viii.
Hickson, 𝔉, xxvii.
Hide, 𝔉, ii, xiv.
Hierarchies *or* Ierarchyses, the thre angelycall, xv.
Hieron, Mr., xxvii.
Hiet, James, B.D. and his wife, xviii; account of, xxii.
Higden, 𝔉, viii.
Higginson *or* Higinson, 𝔉, viii, xii, xxii, xxvii.
Higgison, 𝔉, viii, xii.
Higgs, John, viii.
Higham, 𝔉, xviii, xxii, xxvii.
High-Bulhaugh, in Anglezargh, xix.
High-church tories: history, conduct and character of, v.
High-cross, Liverpool, ix, xii.
Highgate, Worthington preaches at, xiii.
High-gill, near Aysgarth, xiv.
High-heyes, birth-place of Adam Martindale, iv.
Highlanders, dress of, i, v; their conduct in the rebellion under the earl of Mar, v.
Highland clans, a detachment of under brigadier Mackintosh of Borlum: detailed account of their proceedings, v.
Highland war-signal, *i.e.* the fiery cross: the clans summoned by, v.
High-Legh, co. Chester, iv; account of, viii; notice of the hall, viii.
High lynge, xx (*tit.* Whalleye).
High-street, Liverpool, xii.
Hightonhull, xx.
Highways in West-Derby, wretched state of, ix.
Higinbotham, 𝔉, xviii, xxvii.
Higmought, 𝔉, xii.
Hignet, 𝔉, viii.
Higson, Mr., xiii.
Hilbert, Henry, minister of Mottram, viii.
Hildebrighthop, xx. *See in same volume* Sadelword.
Hildersam, Samuel, "a noble friend," xxvii.
Hill, 𝔉, i, iv, viii, xiii, xviii, xix, xxii, xxvii.
Hille, 𝔉, xvii.
Hilliard (major) taken prisoner, ii.
Hillingdon, co. Middlesex, viii.
Hilton, 𝔉, v, ix, xviii, xix, xxii, xxvii, xxviii.
Hilton spa, Newcome's visit to, xxvii.
Hinchman, bishop: notice of, xiii.
Hinckly, i.
Hind and Panther by Dryden, extract from, xviii.
Hind, 𝔉, viii, xxii, xxvii.
Hinde, 𝔉, xiv, xix, xxvii.
Hindele, 𝔉, xxii.
Hinderwell's *History of Scarborough*, xiv.
Hindle, John, xxii.
Hindley, near Wigan, xix; account of, xxii; notice of the hall, xxii;

outrages of the cavaliers in the chapel, ii.
Hindley, 𝔑, xix, xxii.
Hinfield moor, skirmish of, ii.
Hingwar, kyng, invades England, xv.
Hipperholme, 𝔑, xix.
History, Newcome's readings in, xviii.
History of the Grand Rebellion, xxix.
History of the Sevarites, xiii.
Historical "novelists," xiv.
Historical Register, xii.
Hoadly, Mr., viii.
Hoare, G. M., xix.
Hoarstones in Pendle, vi, vii.
Hobart, Mr., xiii.
Hobbeakyr, land in Warrington, xvii.
Hobbes, Thomas, of Malmesbury, vi, xiii; character of his writings, xiii.
Hobson, Francis, xxvii.
Hoccleve, Thomas: notice of a poem by, vii.
Hoch, Willus de, xx.
Hockenhall, 𝔑, xii.
Hockenhall alley, Liverpool, xii.
Hockenhull, township of Tarvin, viii.
Hockenhull, 𝔑, viii.
Hocknell, 𝔑, xxv.
Hocton, Adam de, xiv, xxii.
Hocwyk, villa de, xxx.
Hocwyk, 𝔑, xxx.
Hodder, river, xiv.
Hoddisdenebrok, xx (*tit.* Eccleshul).
Hoderod, Joh. de, xx.
Hodges, Owen, viii.
Hodgkinson, 𝔑, xxii, xxviii.
Hodgson, 𝔑, ii, v, viii, ix, xii, xiv, xxii.
Hodgson's *Account of Queen Anne's Bounty*, xix.
Hodson, 𝔑, xxii.
Hoe *or* how, a hill: etymology of, vii.
Hogarth's "Rake's Progress," xviii.
Hogg, John, minister of Liverpool, xxii.
Hoggekynson, Gilbert, xvii.
Hoghe, Richard del, viii.
Hoghton, xx (*tit.* Aluetham).
Hoghton, 𝔑, ii, viii, xiv, xviii, xix, xx, xxii, xxvii.
Hoghton broke, Orford, near Warrington, xvii.
Hoghton common, success of royalists at, ii.
Hoghton tower, descriptions of, xiv, xxii; royal entertainment at, xiv; taken by the parliament, ii. *See* Houghton tower.
Hoghwyk, 𝔑, xx.
Hogill, 𝔑, xviii, xxvii.
Hogs-hey *alias* Town's commons, Liverpool, xii.
Hokenby, Rob. de, xx.
Hokenrod, Alex. de, xx.
Hokerod, xx (*tit.* Spotlond).
Hokesiche, xx (*tit.* Spotlond).
Holand, 𝔑, xvii, xxx.
Holbech, Mr., xiii.
Holbroke, 𝔑, xvii.
Holbrook *or* Holbrooke, 𝔑, xviii, xxvii.
Holclogh, xx (*tit.* Bilyngton).
Holcloghheued, xx (*tit.* Bilyngton).
Holcomb, near Bury: account of, xix
Holcroft, 𝔑, ii, vii, viii, ix, xii, xvii xix, xxii, xxiii.
Holcroft hall, Winwick: notice of, xxii; sale of, ix.
Holdebrok, xx (*tit.* Acton).
Holden, 𝔑, xiii, xiv, xviii, xix, xx xxii, xxvii, xxviii.
Holden hall, Haslingden, xxii; hunting at, xiv.
Holderness, earl of, xii.
Holdsworth, 𝔑, xiii, xiv.
Holdsworthy, co. Devon, xiii.
Hole, 𝔑, xx, xxx.
Hole (le), a field in Warrington, xvii
Holeakyr, land in Orford near Warrington, xvii.
Holewetlon, xx (*tit.* Bilyngton).

Holford, 𝔑, VIII, IX, XIV.
Holford hall in Plumley, co. Chester: account of, VIII.
Holgate, 𝔑, VI, XXII.
Holiday, Dr. Barten: judgment upon, XIII.
Holinshead, *or* Hollinshead, 𝔑, VIII, XXII.
Holished, 𝔑, XVIII.
Holker, 𝔑, XIV, XX.
Holker hall, Cartmell: account of, XIV, XXII.
Holland, *i.e.* the Dutch provinces, IV, IX; account of, I.
Holland, near Wigan, IV; its castle, XXII; priory, VIII, XXII; estates, rental of, XVIII.
Holland, earl of, XIII.
Holland, 𝔑, II, VIII, IX, XII, XVII, XVIII, XIX, XX, XXII, XXVII, XXVIII.
Hollinfare *alias* Hollinferry, chapelry of Warrington: account of, XXII; passage of fugitive royalists at, II.
Hollingworth, township of Mottram, VIII; hall, notice of, VIII.
Hollins, 𝔑, XVIII, XXIV.
Hollins hall, Accrington: account of, XXII.
Hollinshead hall, Tockholes, co. Lanc.: notice of, XXII.
Hollinworth, Richard, author of *Mancuniensis*, II, IV, XIX, XXVII; account of, IV.
Hollinworth, *or* Hollingworth, 𝔑, VIII, XVIII, XXVII.
Hollis, 𝔑, XII, XXVIII.
Hollywell, Richard, II.
Holman, colonel, XXVIII.
Holme, in Cliviger, near Burnley: account of, XXII; notice of its hall, XXII.
Holme *for* Hulme, near Manchester: tragedy acted at, XIII.
Holme, 𝔑, IV, VIII, XIV, XVII, XIX, XXII, XXIV, XXIX.
Holmelake, XX (*tit.* Staneye).
Holmes, 𝔑, XIII, XIX.
Holmes-chapel, co. Chester: account of, VIII.
Holmhouse in Plemondstall, VIII.
Holmhouse in Stoke, VIII.
Holms, flat and steep, in the Severn, I.
Holpul, XX (*tit.* Staneye).
Holreton, Ric. de, XX.
Holrys, Rog. de, XX.
Holstein, duke of: his ambassador's *Travels*, XVIII.
Holsworth *for* Halsworth, Thomas, XXII.
Holt, a woody enclosure, VII.
Holt (the), Blackburn: notice of, XIV.
Holt castle, co. Worcester, XIV.
Holt, 𝔑, II, VII, IX, XII, XIV, XVIII, XIX, XX, XXII, XXV, XXVIII.
Holte, 𝔑, VIII, XIV, XVII, XIX, XXII.
Holteschagh, XX (*tit.* Acton).
Holy Ghost, simulated descent of, at Gloucester, I.
Holyhead and Whitehaven, coasts between, XII.
Holyhurst, in Whitchurch, VIII.
Holy isle, miraculous tides at, I; taken and retaken, V; spoiled and destroied by the Danes, XV.
Holyne-grene. *See* Hollinfare.
Holyrood palace despoiled by sir William Norres, XXII.
Holywell, legendary account and description of, VII; visited by Worthington, XIII.
Holzt, sir Thomas, of Grizzlehurste, XIV.
Homer, study of, by Martindale, IV.
Homes, 𝔑, XIII.
Homstalclogh, XX (*tit.* Whiteword).
Homur plokke, meadow in Orford near Warrington, XVII.
Hondford, 𝔑, VIII.
Hone's *Every-Day Book*, XVIII.

Honeycomb, a petrified, VII.
Honey-dew on oak leaves, I.
Honeywood (brigadier) assaults and takes Preston, V.
Honiton, co. Devon, XIII.
Honorius, archdeacon of Richmond, XXII.
Honorius III., pope, XXII.
Hoods and surplices not used by the puritans, XIV.
Hoofield, co. Chester, VIII.
Hoo-heath, township of St. Oswald's, Chester, VIII.
Hoo St. Werburgh, Kent: myracle of the oke tree at, XV.
Hooke, 𝔑, IX, XIII.
Hooker, Richard, XXII; his *Ecclesiastical Polity*, XII, XVIII.
Hoole, co. Lanc.: account of, XXII.
Hoole hall, Plemondstall: notice of, VIII.
Hoole heth, barbarike nacions attack Chestre from, XV.
Hoole, Mr., VIII.
Hoolmore, Edward, minister of Flixton, XIX.
Hoop, Jos., XXVIII.
Hooper, 𝔑, XXVII.
Hoornbeckius, 𝔑, XIII.
Hoose (great-), co. Chester, VIII.
Hooton, township of Eastham, co. Chester, VIII; destruction of the hall, VIII; origin of the Stanleys of, XXIX.
Hope, co. Flint., XII.
Hope, XX. *See in same vol.* Swynton.
Hopehey, XX (*tit.* Swynton).
Hopkin, Mr., VIII.
Hopkins, 𝔑, V, VI, XIII, XXII, XXVII, XXVIII.
Hopkinson, 𝔑, XIV, XXII.
Hoppe, Robert, VIII.
Hoppewod, Willmus de, XX.
Hopton, Ralph, XII.
Hopwood, township of Middleton, XIX; hall, IX, notice of, XIX.
Hopwood, 𝔑, II, VIII, IX, XII, XIV, XVIII, XIX, XXII, XXVII, XXVIII.
Hopyndore, Nich., XX.
Horace, IV; illustration of witchcraft from, VI.
Horax, 𝔑, XIX.
Hordern, XX.
Horehaghe, XX (*tit.* Whiteword).
Horelowe, XX (*tit.* Bilyngton).
Horeston, XX (*tit.* Wlipshire).
Horewythnes, XX (*tit.* Whiteword).
Hornby, 𝔑, IX, XIX, XXII.
Hornby castle, surrender and description of, II; visited by the rebels, V.
Horne, 𝔑, XIII, XVIII.
Horneck, Dr., XIII.
Horner, Hen., advocate, VIII.
Horobin, 𝔑, XII.
Horreby, 𝔑, XX.
Horrobin lane, near Whalley, XIV.
Horrocks *or* Horrox, 𝔑, II, XIII, XIX, XXII.
Horsecroft, major *and* minor, XX (*tit.* Whiteword).
Horses, horse-dealing, horse-doctoring, I.
Horse-market, Warrington, XVII.
Horse-mill at Dort, I; at Liverpool, XII.
Horse races, XIV.
Horsemanship of H. Newcome, XVIII.
Horsedge hall, Oldham: account of, XIX.
Horselip sands, near Waterford, I.
Horseman, William, priest, VIII.
Horsey, Mr., XXVII.
Horton, township of Tilston, co. Chester, VIII.
Horton, co. Dorset, XIV.
Horton, 𝔑, IX, XII, XIII, XIX, XXVIII.
Horton chapel, in Oldham church: notice of, XIX.
Horwich, co. Lanc.: account of, XIX.

Hospitallers, knights: notice of, VIII.
Hospitals, officers of the, at Rotterdam, I.
Hotham, ℞, I, II, V, XXII, XXVII.
Hothersall, ℞, XIV.
Hothersall hall, Longridge: notice of, XXII.
Hotoker, Ric. de, XX.
Hoton, Willus de, XX.
Hottinger, J. H.: account of, XIII.
Hotuna, lands in, XXX.
Hough, township of Barrow, VIII; of Wibunbury, VIII; of Wilmslow, VIII; all in Cheshire.
Hough, ℞, VIII, XIII, XVIII, XXII, XXVII.
Hough hall (*should be* Haigh hall) near Wigan: account of, XXII.
Hough hall, Didsbury: notice of, XIX.
Hough heath, Martindale's residence at, IV.
Hough's-end, a seat of the Mosleys, XVIII; description of, XIX.
Houghton, IV.
Houghton, township of Denton, near Manchester, XIX.
Houghton common, XVIII.
Houghton-street, Liverpool, XII.
Houghton tower, IV, XXII.
Houghton, ℞, IV, V, VI, IX, XII, XIV, XVIII, XIX, XXII, XXVII, XXX.
Houlden, ℞, VI, XIV.
Houlgh, Mrs., and her son Robert, XVIII.
Hount, John, a Franciscan priest, XII.
House-in-the-wood (Huis in't bosch), a royal palace at the Hague: description of, I.
House of commons, accounts of proceedings in, IX, XXVIII; conference with the lords, IX.
Houses of the hill, in Spotland, XIX.
Household gods, poetical address by, XIV.
Housing cloth, description of, XIV.
Hovenden, captain, XXV.
Howard, ℞, I, VIII, XII, XIV, XVIII, XIX, XXII, XXIV, XXVIII, XXIX. *See* Heywood, ℞, XXVIII.
Howarth, Howorth *or* Haworth, ℞, IV, VII, XIX, XXVII.
Howe, IX, XIV, XXII, XXVII, XXVIII.
Howell, James, XVIII, XXIX; account of, XIII.
Howell's *State Trials*, XIV.
Howgate, Christopher, of witch fame, and Elizabeth his wife, VI.
Howgrave hall. *See* Hulgreve.
Howker stable, XX (*tit.* Whalleye).
Howley *or* Hollay field and lane, Warrington, XVII.
Howroben, Edward, XII.
Howson, John, D.D., XIII.
Howth, hill of, I.
Hoyle, Joshua, D.D.: account of, I.
Hubba (kyng) slays saint Edmunde kyng of Estenglande, XV.
Hubbapella, steward of Durham cathedral: legend respecting, I.
Hubbert *alias* Forges, Robert: notice of, VII.
Hubberthorne, Richard: notice of, IV.
Hubbul, Henry, XXVII.
Huber's *English Universities*, XVIII.
Huckler, Bill, a masque charater, XIV.
Huckler, dancing the, XIV.
Hudleston *or* Huddleston, ℞, II, XX, XXII.
Hudibras, Newcome's criticism on, XVIII.
Hudson, ℞, IV, XXII, XXIV.
Huet *or* Huetius, incidental notices of, XIII.
Hueys, Rob., XX.
Hugh Lupus erle of Chester, legendary account of, XV.
Hughes, ℞, XXVII.
Hughlocpighil, XX (*tit.* Bilyngton).
Hughs, Mr., XIII,
Huhelocheheued, XX (*tit.* Stanword).

Huish, Mr., xiii.
Huite, 𝔑, xviii.
Hulgreve hall, Middlewich: notice of, viii.
Hulileye, xx (*titt.* Riblecestria, Spotlond).
Hull, co. York, ix.
Hull *or* Hulle, 𝔑, xx, xxii.
Hulm, township of Astbury, viii.
Hulm, township of Middlewich, viii.
Hulm, 𝔑, viii, xx.
Hulm MSS., xix.
Hulme *now* Holmes-chapel, viii.
Hulme, near Warrington, xvii.
Hulme, near Manchester, xviii, xix; account of the hall, xix.
Hulme hall, in Reddish, Manchester: account of, xix.
Hulme, 𝔑, xix, xxii, xxvii, xxviii.
Hulse, in Witton chapelry, co. Chester, viii.
Hulse, 𝔑, viii, xviii, xxvii.
Hulton, xx.
Hulton, over-, middle-, and little-, in Dean, co. Lanc., xix.
Hulton park, notice of, xix.
Hulton, 𝔑, viii, ix, xiv, xviii, xix, xx, xxii, xxvii, xxviii.
Humber, William and John, of Preston, xiv.
Humbre and Mersee, waters of, dyuyde Mersee from Northumberlande, xv.
Hume, 𝔑, ii, v.
Humfrauille, Ric. de, xx.
Humfryes, a great divine, xii.
Humphrey *or* Humphreys, 𝔑, xiii, xviii, xxvii.
Humylyte, the xii degrees of, xv.
Hundersfield *or* Hunresfeld, township of Rochdale, xix, xx.
Hunecote, xx.
Hunecotes, Ada de, xx.
Hunewyn, Ricardus, xx.
Hungate, Raph, horse-dealer: his recipe for a strain, i.
Hungrehulfeld, xx (*tit.* Plesyngton).
Hunresfeld, Thom. de, xx.
Hunsdon, lord chamberlain: anecdote concerning, i.
Hunslow-dike, Hague, i.
Hunsterton, township of Wibunbury, viii.
Hunt, 𝔑, ii, iv, viii, xii, xiii, xiv, xviii, xix, xxvii.
Hunter, 𝔑, v, xii, xviii, xix, xxii, xxvii.
Hunter's *Life of O. Heywood*, xii, xix; *Sheaf of Gleanings*, xxiv.
Hunting and hawking, reflections upon, xiv.
Hunting match, dream of a, xxiii.
Huntingdon, xiii, xiv; church given to Penwortham monastery, viii.
Huntingdon, Henry earl of, xiv.
Huntingdon, lord, xxv.
Huntingdon, lady, xxix.
Huntingdon, 𝔑, xiv, xxii.
Huntington, township of Bruera, near Chester, viii.
Huntington hall, Stidd, Ribchester: notice of, xxii.
Huntington, John: account of, xix.
Huntroyd hall, Padiham, xiv; account of, xxii.
Hunts, colonel, ix.
Hunt's-bank, Manchester, xviii.
Hurd's *Cowley*, xiii.
Hurdey, John, xxvii.
Hurdsfield, township of Prestbury and Macclesfield, viii.
Hurel, Alexander, and Margaret his wife, xx.
Hurlers (the), Cornwall, xiii.
Hurleston, 𝔑, viii.
Hurry, colonel, ii.
Hurst, xx (*tit.* Acton).
Hurst *and* Hazlehurst, townships of Ashton-under-Line, xix.
Hurst, 𝔑, ix, xx.
Hurstebrok, xx (*tit.* Acton).

Hurstwood hall, Burnley: account of, XXII.
Husband, "negatur that he may beat his wife," XIII.
Husband, ℞, XII, XVIII, XXVIII.
Huss, John: portrait of, I.
Hussey, John, warden of Battelfylde college, XXII.
Hutchins, Mr., incumbent of Gawsworth, XXVII.
Hutchinson, ℞, VI, VIII, IX, XII, XVIII, XIX, XXVII.
Huthersall, ℞, XIV.
Hutlone, XX (*tit.* Eccleshul).
Hutte *or* Haut (the), hall in Childwall: account of, XXII.
Hutton, ℞, I, XIV, XXII, XXVII.
Huxelegh, Rob. de, XX.
Huxley, township and hall in Waverton, VIII.
Huxley, Mrs., VIII.
Huyton, co. Lanc., IV, IX; account of, XXII; church given to Burscough priory, VIII.
Huyton, ℞, XX.
Huyton-hey hall, XII; notice of, XXII.
Hwithul, Rob. de, XXX.
Hyat *or* Hyet, James, rector of Croston, II, XVIII, XXII, XXVII. *See* Hiet.
Hybernia, ℞, XX.
Hyde, ℞, II, IV, VIII, XIII, XVIII, XIX, XX, XXVII, XXVIII. *See* Hide.
Hylde, saynt, abbesse of Whytbye, XV.
Hyll orchard, XX (*tit.* Whalleye).
Hylton, John: account of, II.
Hymen with the Barriers, masque by Ben Jonson, XIV.
Hynd, ℞, XXII.
Hyndebranceis, XX (*tit.* Reued).
Hyndele, Ric. de, XX.
Hyndeley, ℞, XVII.
Hyrlond, Rogerus de, XX.

IALLE, Willmus, XX.
Ibbetson, ℞, XIX.
Ida, kynge of Northumberlande, XV.
Idenshaw, bounds of, VIII.
Idolatry chaunged into chrysten relygyon, XV.
Ignatius, *Latin MS.* of, at Cambridge, XIII.
Ilbree monastery, suppression of, VIII.
Ilfracombe, haven of, I.
Illidge, R., VIII.
Illingworth, ℞, XIII, XVIII, XXVII.
Imbarne, to enclose or shut up, III.
Immortality of the Soul by Henry More: critical account of, XIII (p. 121).
Impartial Scout, XII (p. xlv).
Impeachment of lord Strange for high treason, II.
Imperialists, victory and defeats of, I.
Impyerde, XX (*tit.* Whalleye).
Ince, co. Chester, XIX; account of, VIII.
Ince, ℞, VIII, IX, XVII.
Ince hall, Wigan: account of, XXII; when acquired by the Gerards, XVII.
Ince-Blundell hall, Sefton: account of, XXII.
Ince land in Arpeley, Warrington, XVII.
Ince medo, Warrington, XVII.
Inchequin, ℞, XII.
Incomes of Henry Newcome and the fellows of collegiate church of Manchester, XVIII.
Indemnity, general: act of, V.
Independents, their struggle with the presbyterians, IV; lampoon by, V; notices of, XVIII, XXVII.
Indians, public collection ordered for, XXVII.
Indictment for high treason, form in English and Latin, XXVIII.
Indulgences, address of the house of commons concerning, XVIII.
Ines, XX.
Infants' corpses, magical use of, VI.

Ingelo, Dr. Nathaniel: account of, XIII.
Ingham, 𝔑, XIX, XXII.
Ingleby, 𝔑, VIII, XIV.
Ingoldsby, 𝔑, XII.
Ingoll, Rog. fil. Ric. de, XX (?).
Ingram, sir Arthur: notice of, I.
Inman, Thomas, XXII.
Innerwick castle, notice of, I.
Inquisition post mortem 21 Eliz., XIV.
Inquisition at Warrington, XXVIII.
Inskipp school, St. Michael's-upon-Wyre, XXII.
Intake, le, XX (*tit.* Whalleye).
Inundation at Cambridge, XXVII.
Inverness, I.
Ipres, wager respecting, IX.
Irby, co. Chester, manor and hall, VIII; commandery of knights-hospitallers at, VIII.
Irby-millhill, township of Thurstaston, co. Chester, VIII.
Ireland, IX, XII, XIII.
Ireland, 𝔑, II, VII, IX, XII, XIV, XVII, XXII.
Ireland's office, a post mortem inquisition, XIV.
Ireton, major-general, II, XII, XVIII.
Irewell, XX (*tit.* Brendewod).
Irifford, XX (*titt.* Chadewyk, Spotlond).
Iriffordheghes, XX (*tit.* Chadewyk).
Irish customs &c.: description of, I.
Irish papists and their proceedings, II.
Irish rebellion, and the Latin prayer at Cambridge in consequence, XIII.
Irish soldiers, XXVIII; description of, XXV.
Irish territories and alleged title-deeds of them, XXIV.
Irlam, in Eccles, XIX; hall, account of, XIX.
Irland, John, of Lydeat, IX.
Iron works in Carnew and Clanmullen, Ireland, I.
Irpul's Erthe, Orford, near Warrington, XVII.
Irvine (*styled* Erwin) in Scotland: description of, I.
Irvine, William, nonjuror, preaches at Kelso, V.
Irwell, river, IX, XX.
Irwelham, in Eccles, XIX.
Isaac, Mr., XIII.
Isherwood, 𝔑, VIII, XIX, XXII.
Israel, Manasses Ben, XIII.
Iter Boreale, by Robert Wild, XVIII.
Iter Lancastrense, XVIII; critical account of, VII. *See* James.
Ivel *or* Inhel, sir, priest of Tattenhall, VIII.
Ivimey's *Life of Milton*, XXIV.
Ivy, lady, XXVII.

JABLONSKY, 𝔑, XIII.
Jacchæus, Gilbertus: his *Institutiones Physicæ*, IV.
Jack, meaning of the word, III.
Jacks, 𝔑, VI.
Jackson, 𝔑, II, VII, VIII, XIII, XVIII, XIX, XXII, XXV, XXVII, XXVIII.
Jacob, 𝔑, XIII, XXVII, XXVIII.
Jacobite plot, discovery of, XXVII.
Jacobites, IX.
Jacobites, English and Scottish: history and notices of, V.
Jacobitism the object of toryism, V.
Jacomb, 𝔑, XIII, XXVII.
Jacque for jacket, XIV.
Jacques, John, vicar of Bolton-le-sands, XXII.
Jacson, 𝔑, XIV, XXII.
Jager's (Robert) *Decimal Arithmetic*, IV.
Jalousie, a hidden watching, I.
Jamaica, IX, XII.
James I., IX, XII, XIII, XXIX; his *Dæmonologie*, VI; taste in dress, XIV killing wit, XIX; *Regulations* for the king's preachers, XXII.
James II., IX, XVIII.
James the Third of England and

Eighth of Scotland proclaimed and prayed for, v; his arrival and departure, v.
James IV. of Scotland, ix, xii; supposed to have been slain at Flodden by sir Edward Stanley, xxix.
James, 𝔑, vi, vii, xii, xiv, xxv.
James's *Iter Lancastrense*, xiii, xiv, xix. *See* Iter.
James-street, Liverpool, xii.
James's (St.) day at Whalley, xiv.
Jameson, William, ix.
Jamesson, Roger, xvii.
Janny, 𝔑, viii.
Jansonius, xiii.
Jaques, 𝔑, viii, xix, xxv.
Jarrerd, Mr., mayor of Stockport, xviii.
Jedburgh, arrival of the rebels at, v.
Jefferies's (Dr.) edition of Whichcote's *Aphorisms*, xiii.
Jefferson, serjeant, viii.
Jehuda, rabbi, xiii.
Jeinson, Mr., xxvii.
Jenkins, co. Essex, xiv.
Jenkins, John, musician: account of, xiii.
Jenkinson, 𝔑, xix, xxii, xxiv.
Jenks, William, rector of Gravely, xiii.
Jenkyns, Mr., xxvii.
Jenyns, Mrs. Eliza, xix, xxii.
Jermie, colonel, ii.
Jermyn *or* Jermin, 𝔑, ii, ix, xii, xiii.
Jerom, Mr., of Dublin, i.
Jerome, Mr., iv.
Jerome of Prague, portrait of, i.
Jerome, saynt, embrodred in ryche tysshewe, xv; his sanction of hunting and fishing, xiv.
Jerrom, James, mayor of Liverpool, xix.
Jerrumannus byshop of Lychfelde, legendary notices of, xv.
Jerusalem (St. John of) rent, xix.
Jervaux abbey, xiv.
Jervis, sir Thomas, xiv.
Jesse's *Memoirs*, xiii.
Jessey *or* Jessie, Henry: account of, xiii.
Jests and jesters, i. *See* Armstrong.
Jesuits, ix; store of in Lancashire, vi; Scioppius's crusade against, xiii; notices of, xxv.
Jesuits' church, Dublin, i.
Jesuits' Downefall, by James, vii.
Jesuitisme, Mystery of (*i.e.* Pascal's *Lettres Provinciales*), xviii.
Jesus college, Cambridge, xiii.
Jewell, 𝔑, i, xii, xiii.
Jews, notices of the, i, xiii; visit to a synagogue, xxvii.
Joanes, 𝔑, i, ix.
Joanna countess of Kent, xxii.
Jocularia, xviii.
Jodrell, 𝔑, viii, xiv.
John of Gaunt, xii.
Johnes, 𝔑, xii.
Johnian fellows, Cambridge: expulsion of, xviii.
Johnson, 𝔑, ii, iv, vi, viii, ix, xii, xiii, xiv, xviii, xxii, xxiii, xxvii, xxviii.
Johnson's (Dr.) defence of Laud, xiv; his *Lives of the Poets*, ix, xxiv.
Johnson-street, Liverpool, xii.
Johnston, George, xxii.
Joliffe, Rebecca daughter of sir William, xix. *See* Moyer.
Jolly *or* Jollie, 𝔑, ii, iv, viii, xviii, xix, xxii, xxvii.
Jones, 𝔑, vii, viii, ix, xii, xiii, xiv, xviii, xix, xxii, xxvii, xxviii.
Jonquet's (Denys) *Hortus sive Index Plantarum*, notice of, xiii.
Jonson, Ben, xiii, xviii; notices of, vii, xiv, xxix; extracts from, vi.
Jordan, a cook, xiii.
Joseph, history of, in purtrayture, xv.
Josephus, xiii.

Joshua ledynge the Isrehelytes, in pycture, XV.
Journals: Nicholas Assheton's, XIV; Henry Newcome's, XVIII; House of Commons', XVIII.
Joyce, cornet, XVIII.
Jube the Sane, XXIX.
Judges, censure upon, VII.
Judges at the Jacobite trials at Manchester, names of the, XXVIII.
Judgments and visitations, stories of, XXVII.
Judith, a barrayne woman: her miraculous cure, XV.
Jugges, 𝔑, VIII.
Juggler-street, Liverpool, XII.
Jugglers, XIV.
Julius Cæsar sendes a legion of knyghtes to Chestre for to subdue Irelande, XV.
Jumpe, 𝔑, XII.
Jumps, coats so named, XXII; shifts, expedients, XXIII.
Jungius, Dr. Joachim: account of, XIII.
Juries (London), their unwillingness to convict, V.
Jurieu's book on Comenius's three prophets, XIII.
Jurwyne of eest England, saynt and martyr, XV.
Jury at Jacobite trials at Manchester, list of, XXVIII.
Justice (cowp) of peace, a masque character, XIV.
Jutes descend linyally fro Woden, XV.
Juxon, archbishop, XIII, XIX, XXII.

KABAHIK'S (Martin) *In Palestinam et Ægyptum Peregrinatio*, XIII.
Kapenhurst, Thoma de, XX.
Kar, Ric. del, XX.
Karleton, 𝔑, XX.
Karmingham *or* Kermincham, township of Swettenham, and hall, VIII.
Karruyding, XX (*tit.* Bilyngton).
Kateford, 𝔑, XX.
Katharine hall, Cambridge, XIII.
Katheryne, saynt, on arras, XV; altar of at Eccles, XIX; her festival day kept by a puritan, XIV.
Kaufmann, Nicholas: account of, XIII.
Kavenagh. *See* Cavanagh.
Kay *or* Kaye, 𝔑, II, XII, XIV, XIX, XXII.
Kaye's *Guide Book of Liverpool*, IX.
Keale-bones, nine-pins, I.
Keck, 𝔑, XXII.
Keckerman, Bartholomew: notice of, IV.
Keckwick, near Runcorn, VIII.
Keeling, 𝔑, VIII, XXVII.
Keene, bishop, XXII.
Keeve *or* keere, a brewing vessel, I.
Kegesworth, 𝔑, XX.
Keighley, Mr., XIII.
Keirmes *or* kermes, fairs in Holland, I.
Kellesay, Willmus de, XX.
Kellet, 𝔑, XX, XXII.
Kellet (over-), Bolton-le-Sands, XXII; chapel of, XXII.
Kellurmargh, Ralph, XVII.
Kelly, John, XXVIII.
Kelsall, township of Tarvin, VIII.
Kelsall, 𝔑, VIII, XXVII.
Kelso, proceedings of insurgents at, V.
Kelston, sir John Harrington of, XIV.
Kemp *or* Kempe, 𝔑, XII, XIII, XXII.
Kempis, Thomas à, XVIII; translated by Worthington, XIII.
Kempnall, Kempnough *or* Kempenhalgh hall, Worsley: account of, XIX.
Kempsay house, co. Worcester, XIX.
Kendal, co. Westmoreland, XIV; proceedings of rebels at, V; strange story of a woman at, XIII; barony, VIII; deanery, VIII, XIX, XXII.
Kendall, 𝔑, XVIII, XXII.
Keneburge *and* Keneswyde, saynts,

doughters of Penda: legendary notices of, xv.
Kenion hall, Winwick: account of, xxii.
Kenion, ℞. *See* Kenyon.
Kenmore, earl of, taken near Lancaster, ii.
Kenmure, viscount: his character and conduct, v.
Kennerley, ℞, viii.
Kennet, Dr. White, xiii, xxii; his *Case of Impropriations*, xix; *Par. Antiq. Gloss.*, xix; *Register*, xiii, xviii.
Kenrede, kynge of Mercyens: legendary account of, xv.
Kenrick, ℞, i, xxii.
Kensington, Worthington preaches at, xiii.
Kent, realme of: legendary account of, xv.
Kent, Thomas earl of, xix.
Kent, ℞, viii, xiii, xxii.
Kenuherus of eest England, a noble man of fame, xv.
Kenwalcus, kynge of West Saxons, conquered in batayle by Wulfer, xv.
Kenwolmersh, William, treasurer and chancellor of England, xxii.
Kenyon *and* Kenion, ℞, viii, ix, xii, xiv, xvii, xviii, xix, xx, xxii, xxvii.
Keppel, F. Walpole, xxii.
Ker, ix.
Kerby, Mr., xviii.
Kerns, xxv.
Kersall, William Lever of, xix.
Kersall cell: notice of, xix; description of Byrom's library at, xiii.
Kershaw, ℞, xix, xxii.
Kersley, township of Dean, xix.
Kertmell, xxii. *See* Cartmell.
Kerton, Mr., a jesuit, xii.
Ketelisholmwathra, xx (*tit.* Merton).
Ketelishurst, xx (*tit.* Salebury).
Ketelisworth, xx (*tit.* Merton).
Kettlesholm, township of Macclesfield, viii.
Kettleshulm, township of Prestbury, viii.
Kettlewell, xiv.
Keverdale, ℞, xix, xx.
Key, ℞, ii, ix, xviii, xxvii.
Keye *or* Keyes, Mrs., of York, i.
Keykewyc, Johannes, ii.
Kidd, ℞, ix, xxii.
Kidder, Mr., xviii.
Kidson, ℞, xxii, xxviii.
Kildare, George sixteenth earl of: notice of, i.
Kildwick in Craven, vi.
Killum Mack Caricke, xii.
Kilmorey, lord, ii, viii.
Kilnekar, xx (*tit.* Wythenhull).
Kiln-hey, Liverpool, xii.
Kilsyth, viscount of, i.
Kilwardecroft, xx (*tit.* Castelton).
Kilwining, abbey of, i.
Kinaston, Mr., xxvii.
Kinderton-cum-Hulm, township of Middlewich, viii; hall and lodge, notices of, viii.
Kinderton, barons of, iv, viii, xiv.
Kinerton, higher and lower, townships of Doddleston, viii.
King, ℞, viii, xii, xiii, xiv, xxii, xxiv, xxvii, xxix.
King's *Vale Royal*, viii.
King's college, Cambridge, xiii.
Kings-preachers for Lancashire, xxii.
King's Rentaly, xii.
King's-Walden, ix.
Kings-head, Waterford, i.
Kingroad, near Bristol, i.
Kingsley, co. Chester, viii.
Kingsley, Mr., xxviii.
Kingston, meke Edgar coronate at, xv.
Kingston's *True History*; account of the author, xxviii.
Kington magna, near Shaftesbury, xix.

Kinnersley church, co. Salop: bishop Bridgeman buried at, VIII.
Kinsale, in Ireland, prince Rupert's harbour, XII.
Kinsey, 𝔑, VIII, XXVII.
Kinsman, rev. Arthur, XXII.
Kippax, 𝔑, XVIII, XXII.
Kirby, 𝔑, IX, XXII, XXVIII.
Kirby in Wallesey, co. Chester, VIII.
Kirby (west-): account of, VIII; Grange hall in: notice of, VIII.
Kirby-chapel, co. York, VIII.
Kirby-grange, co. Chester, VIII.
Kirby *or* Kirkby Irelith, co. Lanc.: account of, XXII.
Kirby-Irelith, chapelry of Dalton: account of, XXII.
Kirby-Ravensworth, co. York, VIII.
Kircher, Athanasius: account of, XIII.
Kircudbright, burning of, XXIX.
Kirden, Henr. de, XXX.
Kirk *or* Kyrke street, Warrington, XVII.
Kirkby, 𝔑, II, XIX, XXII.
Kirkby in Cleveland, XIV.
Kirkby hall *or* cross: description of, XXII.
Kirkby in Walton, account of, XXII.
Kirkby-Lonsdale, arrival of rebels at, V.
Kirkby-Malghdale, XIV.
Kirkdale, near Liverpool, XII; subsidy at, IX.
Kirke *or* King, Edward, XIII.
Kirkham, account of, XXII; church, VIII, XXII.
Kirkham, 𝔑, VIII, XXVII.
Kirkhoven, John, of Hemflete, XII.
Kirkland hall and school, Garstang, XXII.
Kirkland-how in Arlecden, VIII.
Kirkmanshulme, township of Manchester, XIX.
Kirkmichael, Scotland, rebel standard first set up at, V.
Kirknowles in Arlecden, VIII.
Kirkyng henhurst, XX (*tit.* Whalleye).
Kitchen *or* Kitchin, 𝔑, XII, XXII.
Knail, Dr., head-master of Rugby school, XII.
Knapesheued, Robertus de, XXX.
Knaresborough, IX, XIV.
Knight, 𝔑, VIII, XIII.
Knights' grange, in Whitegate: notice of, VIII.
Knighthood, commonness of *temp.* James I., XIV.
Knightley, Devereux, VIII.
Knip *or* Knype, William, II.
Knockfergus, I.
Knocktorum, township of Woodchurch, VIII.
Knoilyn, Ricardus, XX.
Knolle, 𝔑, IX, XXII.
Knolls, *error for* Knotts, vicar of Bolton-le-sands, XXII.
Knollys, 𝔑, XIV.
Knot *or* Knott, 𝔑, XII, XVIII, XIX, XX, XXII.
Knot mill, Manchester, XVIII.
Knouthall, XX (*tit.* Sadelword).
Knowes, James, XIX.
Knowles, 𝔑, VIII, IX, XXII, XXVIII, XXIX.
Knowsley, II, XXII; subsidy at, IX; connexion of Chester actors and singers with, XXIX.
Knowsley *or* Knouslegh, 𝔑, XX, XXII.
Knubb *or* knobber, a stag of the second year, XIV.
Knutsford, II, IV, XVII, XVIII; over- and nether-, account of, VIII.
Knyvet *or* Knivet, sir Thomas; account of, VI.
Kobold, the drudging goblin, XII.
Kocshutelegh, XX (*tit.* Croenton).
Kohlius, J. P., XIII.
Kokerdene in Hoton, XXX.
Kor lacus, XX (*tit.* Whiteword).
Kotgreues, XX (*tit.* Whiteword).

Kotterus, Christopher, a famous prophet, XIII.
Kuerden, Dr., XIV, XXII; original letter from him to Randle Holme, XXIV.
Kulnekarsik, XX (*tit.* Wythenhull).
Kumbebrok, XX (*tit.* Whiteword).
Kyghel, ℞, XX.
Kyghley, ℞, XVII, XX, XXII.
Kylne, XX (*tit.* Whalleye).
Kylnefeld in Farington, XXX.
Kylne-house, Warrington, XVII.
Kylnepitt, XX (*tit.* Whiteword).
Kyme, barony of, XIV.
Kyneswith *or* Keneswith, quene of Mercyens, XV.
Kyneyers, Robert de, XXII.
Kyngesley *or* Kyngeley, ℞, XVII, XX.
Kynton, Philippus de, XX.
Kyrkebrok, XX (*tit.* Saynte mariden).
Kyrkeby, monastery of, XX.
Kyrkeby, Willmus de, XX.
Kyrkegate, XX (*titt.* Bilyngton, Cliderhou).
Kyrkehalgh, XX (*tit.* Westewod).
Kyrkestall, Turgisius abbas de, XX.
Kyrkshagh, ℞, XIX.
Kytchin garthe, XX (*tit.* Whalleye).
Kyuerdale, XX.
Kyuerdale, Alex. de, XX.

LA BARRE'S edition of Dacherius's *or* D'Acheri's *Spicilegium*, XIII.
Laborer, Robert, XIX.
Labourne, bishop, IX, XIX.
Lacey, ℞, VIII.
Lach *or* Lench, William de, vicar of Blackburn, XXII.
Lache, St. Mary's, Chester, VIII.
Lache, ℞, XVII.
Lachedennys, village near Budworth, VIII.
Lacheford *or* Lacheforth, near Warrington, XX; chief rent in, XVII.
Lacheforthe, Henry, XVII.
Lachegard piscaria, XX (*tit.* Gerstan).
Lachemersche, XX (*tit.* Cliderhou).
Lacy, ℞, XIV, XIX, XXII; arms of, XIV.
Lady, Jo., IX.
Lady Bessy, the "pleasant song of," XXIX.
Ladyes, saynt Werburge an example for, XV.
La Force, monsieur, I.
Laithwayte, William, alderman of Wigan, XXII.
Laitus, Anthony, XXII.
Lake, XX (*tit.* Gerstan).
Lake, ℞, XIV, XVIII, XIX.
Lamaire's *Life of Salmasius*, XIII.
Lamb (Charles) on book-borrowers, XIII.
Lambe, dream of a, XXIII.
Lambe, ℞, XIII, XXIII.
Lambehith, manor of, XXII.
Lambert, ℞, II, IV, XII, XIV, XVIII, XXII, XXVII.
Lambeth, IX; *MSS.* at, XIV, XIX.
Lambton (Ralph) murders his two wives, I.
Lamp, perpetual, I.
Lamp-light, an old tenure, XXII.
Lamplugh, ℞, VIII, XIII.
Lamport, co. Somerset, XIII.
Lancashire, state of religion in, XXV; military conduct and sufferings during the Civil war, II, XII; state of parties in *circa* 1715, V; description of in 1756, XIX.
Lancashire bowmen at Flodden, VII; dances, XIV; dialect, specimens of, VI; forests, decay of, VII; funeral custom, XIV; militia, II; palatinate, XXII; pedigrees, XIV; plot of 1694, XXVIII; presbyterians, IV, XVIII; roads, badness of, IX; spelling, XXIX; warlike spirit, XXIX.
Lancashire MSS., XIV, XIX.
Lancashire, ℞, XVIII, XIX, XXVII.
Lancashire's *Valley of Achor*, XII.

Lancaster, XII; account of, XXII; political state of, in 1642–51, II; in 1715, V; assizes at, XIII, XIV; castle, II, VI, XXII; chartulary, XXII; hospital, XXII; members of parliament, VIII; priory and priors, VIII, XX, XXII; receptor, XX; recorder, XIV; St. Mary's church, XXII.
Lancaster, *History of the Duchy of*, by Fleetwood, XXII.
Lancaster, dukes of, XIX, XXII; earls and vicecomites, XIX, XX, XXII, XXX.
Lancaster, 𝔑, VIII, XXII, XXVII.
Lancastria, 𝔑, XX; pedigree, XX.
Lancel, Willmus, XX.
Lancelot, 𝔑, XII.
Lancelot's hey, Liverpool, XII.
Lancelyn, 𝔑, VIII.
Land, value of, in Ireland, I.
Landaff, earls of, XIV.
Land bank, failure of the, IX.
Land's-end, Cornwall, XIII.
Landell, Thomas, XII.
Landican, township of Woodchurch, VIII.
Lane, 𝔑, VIII, IX, XXVII.
Lanes, township of Ashton-under-Line, XIX.
Langale, XX (*tit.* Bilyngton).
Langbaine, XVIII, XXIX.
Langdale, Marmaduke second lord, XXII.
Langdale, sir Marmaduke: account of, II.
Langfield in Rochdale, XIX.
Langeland, XX (*tit.* Reued).
Langelond, XX (*tit.* Rauensmeles).
Langford, 𝔑, VIII, XXVII.
Langho, near Blackburn: account of, XXII.
Langholm, arrival of the rebel forces at, V.
Langley hall, Middleton: account of, XIX.
Langley hall, co. York, XIV.
Langley, 𝔑, I, IV, VIII, XIV, XVIII, XIX, XXII, XXVII, XXVIII.
Langley's *Polydore Vergil*, XIV.
Langton, manor of, co. Leicester, XXII.
Langton, 𝔑, IX, XIV, XVII, XIX, XX, XXII, XXVIII, XXX.
Langtree, Mr., of Scarbrick, XXII.
Langworth, Mr., XXVII.
Lankester's (Dr. Edwin) *Memorials of John Ray*, XIII.
Lanlydrock, co. Cornwall, XIII.
La Noue, Francis de: account of, VII.
Lany, bishop, XIII; his *Sermon on the Liturgy*, XVIII.
Lappage, Edward, minister of Newchurch in Pendle, XXII.
L'Arbalastier *or* Balistarius, Galfrid, XX, XXII. *See* Balistarius.
Large, Mr., VIII.
Larton, township of Malpas, VIII.
Lascales, Umfridus de, XX.
Lascelles, 𝔑, II, VIII.
Lascy, 𝔑, XIX, XX, XXII.
Lasitius, Johannes: account of, XIII.
Laskey, lord, XXIV.
Latchford, near Warrington, XVII. *See* Lacheford.
Lathbury's *History of the Nonjurors*, XIII.
Latham *and* Lathum. *See* Lathom.
Lathom chapelry, Ormskirk: account of, XXII.
Lathom house, IX, XII, XIX, XXIX; notices of, XIV, XXII; sieges of, II, IV, XII, XIV; marvellous screen at, XXIX.
Lathom spa, IX.
Lathom, 𝔑, II, VIII, IX, XIV, XIX, XX, XXII, XXVII.
Latimer, William lord, XXII.
Laton parva, XX.
Laton, 𝔑, XX.
La Tremouille, the spread eagle the cognizance of, XXIX.

La Trobe's edition of Crantz's *History*, XIII.
Latus, 𝔑, XVIII, XXII.
Latymer, Willus de, XX.
Laud, archbishop, I, IV, XII, XIII, XIV, XIX, XXII.
Lauder, John, IX.
Lauderdale (earl of) taken prisoner, II.
Lauedileye, XX (*tit.* Riblecestria).
Lauedileyeclogh, XX (*tit.* Riblecestria).
Lauerokhull, XX (*tit.* Bilyngton).
Launceston, co. Cornwall, XIII.
Laund (the) in Pendle, VI.
Laund, priory of, co. Leicester, VIII, XXII.
Laurence, 𝔑, XXII.
Laurence (saynt) purtrayed in arras, XV.
Laveering, a nautical term, I.
Lavenham, co. Suffolk, XIII.
Law and lawyers, lady Ranelagh's attempt to reform, XIII; popular saying respecting, XVII.
Law, 𝔑, VI, XIII, XXII, XXVII.
Lawe, 𝔑, XIV, XVII, XX, XXIX.
Lawne, Thomas, alderman of York, XIV.
Lawrence, 𝔑, XIII, XVIII, XXVII.
Lawrenson, Pet., VIII.
Lawrinson, Nicholas, XXII.
Lawson, 𝔑, IX, XIX, XXII, XXVIII.
Lawsyng stede, XX (*tit.* Whalleye).
Lawton *alias* Church-Lawton, co. Chester: account of, VIII; hall, notice of, VIII.
Lawton, 𝔑, VIII, IX, XVIII, XXII, XXVII, XXVIII.
Laybourn *and* Layburn, 𝔑, XXII.
Layfield, 𝔑, XIII, XXII.
Laylond, 𝔑, XX.
Layrebrek, XX.
Lays and duties (parochial), unwillingness to pay, XIV.
Layton *for* Leighton-Buzzard, co. Bedford, XIII.
Layton, sufferings of, IV.
Lazarus *or* leper-house, description of, I.
Lazarus-klap, explanation of, I.
Lea, township of Backford, co. Chester, VIII.
Lea, township and hall, Bruera chapelry near Chester, VIII.
Lea, township and hall, Wibunbury, VIII.
Lea, township and hall, Preston, XXII.
Lea hall, Middlewich: notice of, VIII.
Lea (*in text* Lee) hall, Lawton, co. Chester: notice of, VIII.
Lea-Green hall, Minshull, co. Chester: notice of, VIII.
Lea-Newbald, township of Bruera chapelry, VIII.
Lea, 𝔑, VIII, XX, XXII.
Lead works near Bristol, I.
Leadbeater, 𝔑, XVIII, XXII, XXVII.
Leadbetter, Hen., IX.
Leaguer, assembly of leigers, *i.e.* ambassadors or agents, I.
Leake, John, vicar of Tunstall, XXII.
Leaver, John, II.
Leavers *for* Levens hall, XIV.
Leber, Ameilhon, XII, XVIII.
Leblay, XX.
Lebbeleye, XX (*tit.* Sunderland).
Lecayle, island of, Ulster, XII.
Leche, 𝔑, VIII.
Lechres, Nich. de, XX.
Leck *alias* Overleke, in Tunstall: account of, XXII.
Leckhamton, Amaricus de, XX.
Ledsham, township of Neston, VIII.
Lee in Childwall, VIII.
Lee, 𝔑, VIII, IX, XIII, XX, XXII, XXVII, XXVIII, XXX.
Leech, 𝔑, VIII, XVIII, XXVII.
Leeds, I, IX; batell in the regyon of, XV.
Leeds, 𝔑, XVIII.
Leeming lane, I.

Lees, ℟, XVIII, XIX, XXVII.
Lees hall, Oldham, XIV; account of, XIX.
Lees-kirk, VIII.
Leet court, XIV.
Leftwich, township of Davenham, VIII; hall, notice of, VIII.
Leftwych, ℟, VIII.
Le Fyche, ℟, XVII.
Lega, H. de, XX (?).
Legacies, XIV, XVIII.
Legay, Samuel, IX, XXII.
Legendary, the swete, XV.
Legende, the true, XV.
Legends, how composed, VII.
Legge (colonel Richard) taken at Wigan, II.
Legh, ℟, I, II, VIII, IX, XII, XVII, XVIII, XIX, XX, XXII, XXIII, XXVIII, XXIX.
Legh's chapel in Rosthorne church, VIII.
Legh (high-), Rosthorne: account of, VIII.
Legh (little-), Budworth: account of, VIII.
Legh (west-) in Legh, VIII.
Legions, two cites of, *viz.* Caeruska or els Caerleon in south Wales, and Caerlleon after named Chestre, XV.
Leibnitz, XIII.
Leicester, XIII; its likeness to Hereford, I.
Leicester *for* Leinster, Robert Cholmondeley earl of, VIII.
Leicester, Robert Dudley earl of, XXII, XXIV, XXV, XXIX.
Leicester, lord, XII.
Leicester, ℟, IV, VIII, XIX, XXII, XXVII.
Leicestershire, Nichols's *History of*, XIV.
Leigh, co. Essex, I.
Leigh, co. Lanc., IV, IX, XIX; account of, XXII; parliamentary successes at, II.
Leigh, ℟, I, II, IV, VI, VIII, IX, XII, XIII, XIV, XVIII, XIX, XXII, XXIII, XXVII.
Leigh's *Observations*, XVIII.
Leighton, township of Neston, VIII; hall, notice of, VIII.
Leighton hall, in Warton: notice of, XXII.
Leighton-Conyers, XXII.
Leil, kynge, founder of Chestre and Caerleil, XV.
Leilond, ecclesia, XXX.
Leilond, Thom. de, XXX.
Leisin et filii ejus, XXX.
Leith, description of, I; taken and occupied by the Highlanders, V; siege of, XIV.
Leland, church of, VIII; rent paid by rural deans of, VIII.
Leland and Adderton families, XIV.
Leland's *Encomia*, XXIX; *Itinerary*, XIV.
Lely, sir Peter, XIV.
Lench *or* Lenches, William de, vicar of Blackburn, XXII.
Le Neve, XVIII.
Lennow, lean, feeble, XXIII.
Lennoy, Mr., XIV.
Lenox, duke of, I.
Lenox, earl of, XXIX.
Lent *or* Lenton, Ercombert commaunds all his realme to kepe the fast of, XV.
Lenthall, speaker, XII.
Lenton priory, co. Notts., VIII, XIX.
Leofric, erle of Chestre and duke of Merciens: legendary notices of, XV; styled count, VIII.
Leoffwin, duke, father of Leofric, XV.
Leominster, I, IX, XVIII.
Leonard, ℟, VI, VIII.
Leonence monastery founded by earl Leofric, XV.
Leoni, Giacomo, architect, VIII, XXII.
Lepers, treatment of, I.
Lescard *for* Liskeard, co. Cornwall, XIII.

Lesh *i.e.* leash, three, VII.
Lesley, general David: his flight and capture, II.
Lesna, fire of, XIII.
Lester, Willm., mayor of Chester, III.
Lestithill *for* Lostwithiel, co. Cornwall, XIII.
L'Estrange, XIII.
Letchmore, Edmund, XXVIII.
Lets, hindrances, III.
Leufrihebrugge, XX (*tit.* Whiteword).
Leusden and Villemandy's edition of *Bochart*, XIII.
Levant company, IX.
Leven, XVIII.
Levens hall, near Kendal: account of, XIV.
Levenshulme, township of Manchester, XIX.
Lever (Darcy-) hall, Bolton: account of, XIX.
Lever (great-), co. Lanc., II, VIII, XIV; account of, XIX.
Lever (little-), XIX.
Lever, 𝔉, VIII, XIV, XVIII, XIX, XX, XXII, XXVII, XXVIII.
Leveson, 𝔉, IV.
Leveston (lady) sees a ghost, I.
Lewes, a scrivener, IX.
Lewis, 𝔉, VI, XXII, XXV.
Lex, Rex, a tract, IV.
Ley, Mr., XVIII, XXVII.
Leybourn, John, account of, XXVIII.
Leyburn *and* Leyburne, V, XX, XXII.
Leycester, 𝔉, VIII, XII, XVII, XX, XXIV.
Leyden, XIII; description of, I.
Leye, XX (*tit.* Wythenhull).
Leyland, co. Lanc., XIX; account of, XXII.
Leyland, 𝔉, XIV, XXII.
Leylondeschir, Petrus de, XX.
Leys (the), near Weobley, IX.
Libavius, VI.
Liber Ecclesiæ de Whalley, XXII.
Library, *MS. Catalogue* of John Webster's, VI.
Libraries, parochial and lending, in Lancashire, VIII.
Licenses of non-residence, XXII.
Lichfield, surrender of, II; see of Canterbury removed to, XV. *See* Litchfield.
Lichfield (see of) removed to Chester, XV.
Lichfield, bishops of, XV, XXII, XXX.
Liddeyate, Simon de, XX.
Lidiate abbey, XXII.
Lidiate hall, Halsall: account of, XXII.
Lidiate, 𝔉, IX, XXII.
Lidyate, XX (*tit.* Croenton).
Lieutenants (deputy-), parliamentary appointment of, II.
Liffy river, I.
Lightbourn *or* Lightbowne, 𝔉, II. XVIII, XXVII, XXVIII.
Lightfoot, 𝔉, VIII, XIII, XVIII, XIX, XXVII.
Lightheseles, XX (*tit.* Heleye).
Light horse, XII.
Light-horseman, a small boat, I.
Lightolres, 𝔉, XX.
Lilborne *or* Lilburne, 𝔉, II, IV, XVIII, XXVII.
Lilford, lords, XXII.
Lily, vyrgyns are crowned with the, XV.
Lilly *and* Lilye, 𝔉, XIII, XVIII.
Lilly's *Grammar*, IV; *Midas*, XXV.
Limborch, XIII.
Limbottis XX (*tit.* Meluer).
Lime *and* lime-kiln, I.
Lime, Jane, XXVII.
Limerick, I.
Limme, co. Chester, IV.
Lincock, Rich., VIII.
Lincoln, incidental notices of, XIV, XV.
Lincoln, earls of, VIII, XIX, XX, XXII.
Lincoln, William Barlow bishop of, XIV.

Lincolnshire, Newcome fails to obtain a grammar-school in, xviii.
Lindale in Cartmel, account of, xxii.
Lindley, 𝔑, ix, xxii.
Lindsey, earl of, xiii.
Lindsey *or* Lindsay, 𝔑, i, xxii.
Lingard, Mr., viii.
Lingard's *History of England*, ix, xii, xviii.
Linlithgow, description of, i.
Linnacre's (James) ghost appears to a gentlewoman, xxvii.
Linney, 𝔑, xiv, xix.
Linsley-Garven, Ireland: description of, i.
Linton in Craven, xiv.
Lion, 𝔑, xii, xxii.
Lisbon, ix.
Lisle *for* Lille in Flanders, wager respecting, ix.
Lisle, the lords, xii, xiv, xxii.
Lisle, William, xiii.
Lister, 𝔑, vi, viii, xiv, xix, xxii, xxvii.
Litanie daies, xiv.
Litche, John, xvii (?).
Litchfield, xiv; St. John's hospital in, viii; bishops, dean and chapter, and vicars choral of, viii.
Litchford, Robert: notice of, xix.
Litelchadewyk, xx (*tit.* Chadewyk).
Litellegh, Willmus de, xx.
Litel pughull, xx (*tit.* Whiteword).
Literary labour, payment of, vii.
Literature and learning, praise of, xv.
Litherland, in Aughton, xiv; notice of, xxii.
Litherland, 𝔑, xii.
Litherland-street, Liverpool, xii.
Littel eighes, xx (*tit.* Aluetham).
Littleborough, near Rochdale, xiv; account of, xix.
Little-Dalby, co. Leicester, xviii.
Little-Gidding, Isaac Walton's account of, xiii.
Little-Hole. *See* Hoole.
Little-meadow, Liverpool, xii.
Little-moss, township of Ashton-under-Line, xix.
Little Sankey, near Liverpool, xvii.
Littleton, 𝔑, i, v. ix, xxvii.
Littleton, co. Middlesex, ix.
Littleton hall, Chrisleton: notice of, viii.
Littlewood hall, Croston: account of, xxii.
Liturgy, English, xviii; praise of, ix; conference respecting, xiii.
Liulfus, progenitor of the Howick family, xxx.
Liverpool, ix, xiv, xviii, xix, xxix: account of, xxii; its state during the Civil wars, ii, iv, xii; during the rebellion of 1715, v; castle, ii, ix, xii, xxii; charters, ix, xii; corporation, xii, xxii; elections, ix; ferry, viii; heath, xii.
Liverpool, John de, xxii.
Liversage *or* Liuersegge, 𝔑, viii, xx.
Livesay *or* Livesey, 𝔑, iv, xii, xix, xx, xxii, xxviii.
Livesay, township of Blackburn, xx, xxii.
Livesay hall, notice of, xxii.
Livingston, sir William, of Kilsyth; notice of, i.
Lizours, Albreda daughter of Robert de, xxii.
Llandaff, earls of, xiv.
Llangathen, co. Caermarthen, viii.
Llanyhernian, church or chapel of, viii.
Llanpeplick, co. Caernarvon: revenues of, viii.
Lleon Gauer, a myghty stronge gyaunt, foundeth Chestre, xv.
Lloyd, 𝔑, i, viii, xix, xxviii.
Lloyd's *Memoirs*, ix, xviii.
Lobkowitz, Jo. Caramuel, xiii.
Loccenius, Johannes: account of, xiii.

Loch in Estgate-street, xx (*tit.* Cestria).
Lochaber, trade from Liverpool to, xii.
Lochlomond, in Perthshire: floating islands in, i.
Lochmaben, rebel standard set up at, v.
Locke, John, vi, xiii, xiv.
Locket, nurse, xxvii.
Lockey, Dr. Thomas, xiii.
Lockhart, captain Philip: his trial and execution, v.
Lockyer, Margaret, xiv.
Lodge, Edmund, xix.
Lodge's *Illustrations of English History*, xiv, xxix; *Pedigree*, xii; *Portraits*, xiii.
Loe, ℞, xiii, xviii.
Loftus, ℞, xxiv, xxvii.
Lofwic, William son of Robert de, xxii.
Logan *or* Loggan, Mr., "the graver," xiii.
Logic, study of, iv.
Lok's *Christian Passions*, extract from, xxix.
Lomax, tithes of, xix.
Lomax, ℞, ii, xiv, xviii, xix, xxii, xxvii.
Lomshawe, widow, of Burnley, vi.
Lomylache, xx (*tit.* Whiteword).
London, i, iv, viii, ix, xii, xiii, xiv, xv, xviii; apprentices, ix; bishop of, xviii; chief archbishop's see at, xv; fire of, xii; plague of, iv, xii.
London, ℞, xx,
Long, Dr., of Burscow hall, and his widow, iv.
Longacre, xx (*tit.* Whiteword).
Long causeway (the), xiv.
Longden *or* Tintwistle, township of Mottram in Longdendale, viii.
Longeforth, near Warrington, xvii; bridge of, xvii.
Longehey, Warrington, xvii.
Longehurst, xx (*tit.* Bilyngton).
Longelandes, xx (*tit.* Merton).
Longerung, xx (*titt.* Chadewyk, Spotlond).
Longe-shote, meadow near Warrington, xvii.
Longespé, Roger de, xix.
Longfield, James, curate of Downham, xxii.
Longformacus, the Highlanders arrive at, v.
Long-green, township of Barrow, viii.
Longlegh, xx (*tit.* Samlesbury).
Longley, ℞, xix.
Longley, xx (*tit.* Whalleye).
Longman, ejectment of, from Aynhoe, xviii.
Longo-campo, ℞, xx.
Long parliament (the), ix, xii, xviii.
Longridge in Ribchester, account of, xxii.
Longridge-bottom, xiv.
Longstainfeld in Farington, xxx.
Longton *or* Longtown, v, xxx.
Longton, ℞, xxx.
Longtre, ℞, xvii, xxx.
Longuevilliers *or* Longuillers, ℞, xx, xxii.
Longworth, ℞, xix, xxii, xxviii.
Longworth, township of Turton near Bolton, xix; hall, notice of, xix.
Lonsdale, xx; deanery of, viii, xxii; rent paid by rural dean of, viii.
Lonsdale (lord) driven back by the rebels, v.
Lonsdale, ℞, xix, xxii.
Loosdruenen, in Holland: singular tomb and legend at, i.
Lord-street, Liverpool, xii.
Lord's (captain) dainty cherry orchard, i.
Lord's-day, act for observance of, iv.
Lord's-supper, terms of admittance to the, iv.
Lords' Journals, xii.

Lordeshull, xx (*tit.* Aluetham).
Lorrington, Mr., xxvii.
Lort, 𝔑, xiii, xviii.
Lorting, 𝔑, xii.
Lostock, near Budworth, viii.
Lostock, near Eccles, xix.
Lostock hall, Bolton, xiv; account of, xix.
Lostock river, xx.
Lostock, 𝔑, xx, xxii.
Lostok, xx (*tit.* Wythenhull).
Lothary, kynge of Kent, xv.
Lothiam, Mr., xiii.
Lothian (east-), the rebels recruited from, v.
Loudham, Walterus de, xx.
Loueproud, Rogerus, xx.
Loueshurst, xx (*tit.* Bilyngton).
Louis XIV. of France, ix, xviii.
Loungate, xx (*tit.* Bilyngton).
Louthre, Johannes de, xx.
Love, 𝔑, xiii, xviii, xxvii.
Lovell, 𝔑, viii, xiii, xxii, xxvii.
Low *or* Lowe, 𝔑, viii, xviii, xxii, xxvii, xxviii.
Lowchurch *or* Law, near Blackburn: account of, xxii.
Low church, its distinguishing principles, v.
Low-Countries, injustice of English wars in the, xxv.
Lowe hall, Hindley, near Wigan: account of, xxii.
Lower's *Curiosities of Heraldry*, extracts from, xiv.
Lowick, trial of, ix.
Lowick, near Ulverston: account of, xxii; hall, notice of, xxii.
Lowlane, township of St. Oswald's, Chester, viii.
Lowndes, 𝔑, viii, ix, xviii, xxviii.
Lowndes's *Bibliographical Manual*, character of, xiii.
Lowry, 𝔑, xiii, xviii.
Lowten, Thomas, viii.
Lowther, 𝔑, ii, viii, xiv, xxii.
Lowther hall visited by insurgents, v.
Lowthier, Mrs., of Chester, xxvii.
Lowton and Golborne constituted a rectory, xxii.
Loxam *or* Loxham, 𝔑, xxii, xxviii.
Loy, Margaret, a confessed witch, xii.
Loynd wife, her witch practices, vi.
Lueas, Robert lord, xxviii.
Lucas, 𝔑, ii, xiii.
Lucius kynge of Britayne requires his realme to be baptized, xv.
Lucretius *or* Ritterhusius, a translation of, vii.
Lucy, 𝔑, xiii, xviii, xx, xxii.
Lucy, daughter of Randle earl of Chester, second prioress of St. Mary's, Chester, viii.
Lucye, saynt, brothered in ryche tysshewe, xv.
Luddelow, Willmus de, xx.
Luddenden, co. York, xiv.
Luddington, Dr., archdeacon of Stow, viii.
Ludlow, i, xxix; castle, i.
Ludlow, republican general, xii.
Ludolf *or* Ludolphus, Job: account of, xiii.
Lully, Raymond, and the "Ars Lulliana," xiii.
Lumley, 𝔑, i, xxii.
Lumley castle, i.
Lumm hall, Edenfield, Bury: notice of, xix.
Lund chapel, in Kirkham: account of, xxii.
Lund *alias* Crags, Richard, xxii (?).
Lundy island, xii; description of, i.
Lune river, early defences of, ii.
Lunguillers, 𝔑, xx.
Lunt, near Bury, xix.
Lunt or Lunte, 𝔑, viii, ix, xxviii.
Lupton, Thomas, xxix.
Lupus, Hugh, erle of Chestre, xv. *See* Hugh Lupus.

Lurtin *or* Lurting, ℞, XII.
Lusley, township of Ashton-under-Line, XIX.
Luther's advice on intramural burial, VII; toleration, XIII; portrait, I; *Mensalia*, XVIII.
Lutheran church, Amsterdam: description of, I.
Lutley, Phil., of Ludlow, VIII.
Lutterworth, I.
Luttrel family, I.
Lutwich, ℞, XIX, XXVIII.
Lux in Tenebris, account of, XIII.
Lydgate, "sententious," XV.
Lydiat, XIII.
Lye, Mr., of Fairclough, XXVII.
Lyme, near Disley, XIII; park, account of, VIII; chapel, VIII.
Lyme, co. Dorset, XIII.
Lyme, Oliver, mayor of Liverpool, XII; his alms-house, XXII.
Lyme-Hanley, township of Prestbury, VIII.
Lymm, co. Chester, account of, VIII. *See* Limme.
Lymme, ℞, VIII, XX.
Lymme's Hobbeakyr, Warrington, XVII.
Lynacre, Thomas, M.D., XXII.
Lynch, sir Thomas, knt., XVII.
Lyncoln, Thom. de, XX.
Lyndesy, prouynce of, ny unto Lyncolne, XV.
Lyndesey *and* Lyndsey, ℞, XXII.
Lyndhurst's (lord-chancellor) decision respecting Manchester school, XIX.
Lyndwood's *Provinciale*: notice of the author, XXII.
Lynford, ℞, XIII, XXVII.
Lynn, XIII.
Lynnet, ℞, XIII.
Lynton, William, junr., IX.
Lyolfesik, XX (*tit.* Bilyngton).
Lyon, ℞, VI, IX, XII, XIX, XXII, XXVII.
Lysons, XXIX.
Lyster, Mrs. Doll., XIV.
Lytham: account of, XXII; hall, XXII; priory, XXII.
Lythgoe, Matthew, XXII.
Lytill Walton hey, XVII.
Lyttelmore in Farington, XXX.
Lyverpul, Ricardus de, XX.

MAAS river, I.
Macaria, a projected society: notice of, XIII.
Maccabees, storye of, rychely done on arras, XV.
Macclesfield, IX; account of, VIII; forest, VIII, XXIII; priory, VIII; rent paid by rural dean of, VIII.
Macclesfield, earls of, IX, XIV, XXII; XXVIII.
Maccovius, XIII.
Mace, author of *Musick's Monument*, XIII.
Macefen, township of Malpas, VIII.
Machel and Ulf, XXII.
Machell, ℞, XXII.
Machiavelli, XII; his *Principe* not original, XIII.
Machin, ℞, XIII, XVIII, XXVII.
Mackay, ℞, IX.
Mackerell, Robert, chantry priest, XXII.
Mackintosh, ℞, V, IX, XIII, XXIV.
Mackworth, ℞, II, XXVII.
Maclean (captain) and his volunteers, V.
Madden, sir Frederick, XXIII.
Madderer, Robert, B.C.L., XXII.
Madeira, account of a visit to, IX.
Maden, Roger, of Hopwood, XIV.
Mader, John, II.
Madhouses, Brown's work on, XVIII.
Madock, ℞, VIII, XXVII.
Madox's *Formulare*, XIX.
Madrid, wager respecting, IX.
Madur, Gilbert: his tenements in Warrington, XVII.

Mael, Mr., XIII.
Magazines, seizures of, during the Civil war, II.
Magdalen college, Cambridge, XIII.
Maghersone, Ric. de, XXX.
Maghull, in Halsall: account of, XXII; hall, notice of, XXII.
Maghull, 𝔓, XII, XXII.
Magistrates, parliamentary appointment and removal of, II.
Magna mara, XX (*tit.* Steynynges).
Magnionus (Jo.) courts Dr. Dee's acquaintance, XXIV.
Magu island, Ireland, I.
Mahomet, History of, by Henry Stubbe: critical notice of, XIII.
Maiden city, why Dort is so named, I.
Maiden lands *and* Maiden's green, Liverpool, XII.
Maillardus, Willus, XX.
Main-Amber, Cornwall: description of, XIII.
Mainwaring, 𝔓, I, II, IV, VIII, IX, XII, XIII, XIV, XVIII, XIX, XXVIII. *See* Manwaring.
Maisterson *or* Masterton, John, XXVII.
Maitland, John, duke of Lauderdale, XIII.
Maitland's *Dark Ages*, notice of, VIII.
Makay's (captain) *Memoirs*, VIII.
Malbank, 𝔓, VIII.
Malbeding, 𝔓, VIII.
Malbon, 𝔓, VIII.
Malbranche, XIII.
Malby, Chr., VIII.
Male, 𝔓, IX, XIII.
Malet, Walterus, XX.
Malham, Francis son of Henry, XXII.
Malkin, Mr., XXVII.
Malkin tower, in Pendle forest: notices of, VI, VII.
Mallet, Dr., XXIV.
Mallinson, 𝔓, IV, XXII.
Mallison, Mr., XVIII.
Malliston, Mr., XVIII.
Mallory, 𝔓, VIII, XVIII, XXVII.
Malone, XXIX; his *History of the English Stage*, XIV.
Malo passu, David de, XX.
Malorre, Petrus de, XX.
Malpas, co. Chester: account of, VIII; barony, VIII; rent paid by rural dean of, VIII.
Malpas old hall, notice of, VIII.
Malpas, 𝔓, VIII.
Malt act, passing of the, IX.
Malt liquor at funerals, XIV.
Malton, Thomas earl of, XIX.
Malueysgate, XX (*tit.* Cliderhou).
Malvern, death of colonel Parker at, XIV.
Malyn, Robert, of Nottingham, M.D., VIII.
Mamecestre, ballivi, receptor, senesc., XX.
Mamilian, name of a familiar spirit, VI.
Man, isle of, IX, XII; proceedings in during the Civil wars, II; bishops of, VIII, XXII; John Greenhalgh, governor of, XIV; Olave, lord of, founds St. Mary's abbey at Rushen, XXII.
Man, 𝔓, VIII, XXIV.
Mancetter (co. Warwick), sir Guy de, XIX.
Manchester, IX, XII, XIII, XIV, XIX, XXII; proceedings at during the Civil wars, II, IV, VII, XVIII; and during the Jacobite rebellion, V; pestilence, IV; presbyterian proceedings, IV; popular anger against the crown witnesses, XXVIII; rural deanery of, VIII, XIX; manor of, XIX. *See* Mamecestre.
Manchester collegiate church, IV, VIII, XIV, XVIII; account of, XIX.
Manchester grammar school, IV; account of, XIX.
Manchester, earls of, II, IX, XVIII.
Manchester Recorder, error in, XXVIII.

Mancknolls family, XXII.
Mandeslo. *See* Olearius.
Mandillion, a jacket, VII.
Manley, township of Frodsham, VIII; hall, notice of, VIII.
Manley *or* Manly, ℞, VIII, IX.
Manners, lady Elizabeth, countess of Sunderland: notice of, VIII.
Manners, lord John, XIV.
Mansell, father, XXVIII.
Mansergh, ℞, XXII.
Mansfeldt, Agnes de, XXV.
Mansfield, earl of, VIII.
Mantle and ring, symbolical meaning of, XXII.
Manton, Dr., XIII, XVIII, XXVII; notice of, IV.
Mantua, wager respecting, IX.
Mantua, duke of, XXIV.
Mantuan. *See* Spagnoli.
Manuscript (Latin) of a Greek work, its advantage, XIII.
Manuscripts (Islandian) sent to Loccenius, XIII.
Manwaring, ℞, II, XXVII.
Manx ale, IX.
Manx arms at Myerscough lodge, XIV.
Maplesden, Mr., XXVII.
Mapletoft, John: notice of, VIII.
Mar, earl of: his conduct in the Jacobite rebellion, V.
Marbadæus' *De Gemmarum Lapidumque Viribus*, punning extract from, I.
Marblehead, Ireland, I.
Marbury, in Whitchurch: account of, VIII.
Marbury, township of Budworth, VIII.
Marbury, ℞, IV, VIII, XVII, XXVII.
Marceyl *or* Mersellyn, kynge and saynt, XV.
March, ℞, XII, XXVII.
Marchbanke *or* Marshbanke, Thomas, I.
Marchden, Mr., minister of Neston, VIII.
Marchia, William de, bishop of Wells, I.
Marcke, co. Somerset, I.
Marckius, XIII.
Mardestan, Rad. de, XX (?).
Mardyke fort, Liverpool, XII.
Mare, ℞, XX.
Mare, XX (*tit.* Wynlaton).
Mareschal, ℞, XXII.
Marets (des) *or* Maresius, his tracts against Comenius, XIII.
Marfield *or* Macclesfield forest, XXIII.
Margarete, saynt, brothered on arras, XV.
Margaryte, epithet applied to saynt Werburge, XV.
Margate, I.
Maridene, saynte, capella de, XX.
Marie's St. (Pembroke hall), Cambridge, XIX.
Marius (kyng), a bryton, fortifies Chestre, XV.
Marjoribanks, sir John, bart., and Janet his daughter, XXII.
Markets in Holland, description of, I; in Liverpool, IX, XII.
Market place, Warrington, XVII.
Market-Jew, co. Cornwall, XIII.
Market- *or* East-Lavington, co. Wilts., XIII.
Markethe yate (le), Warrington, XVII.
Markethestrete, XX (*tit.* Cliderhou).
Markham, bishop, XXII.
Markland, ℞, II, III, IX, XIX, XXII, XXIX.
Marland in Castleton near Rochdale, XIV, XIX; notice of the mill at, XIV.
Marland, ℞, XIX.
Marlborough, XIII, XIV; school, XIX.
Marlborough, John Churchill duke of, IX; his conduct in the Jacobite rebellion, V; Sarah his duchess, IX.
Marler, ℞, II, XIX, XXVII.
Marlet hey (le), Warrington, XVII.
Marlorat, Augustina: notice of, IV.
Marlow, Ashton, XXVII.
Marlowe, Kit, XII, XXIX.

Marlpton cum Lache, township of St. Mary's, Chester, VIII,
Marmion, Shakerley, VIII.
Marmoset, etymology of, III.
Marnhall, co. Dorset, XIX.
Marot's (Clement) epigramme uppon a fat priour, VII.
Marple, near Stockport: account of, VIII.
Marresley *or* Marrick priory, co. York, XIX.
Marrett *or* Marsede *or* Marset, XIV.
Marriage at Amsterdam, I; instances of early marriages, XIV; royal argument in favour of, XV. *See* Matches.
Marring of cards and dice by a puritan, XIV.
Marrow, colonel: defeat and death of, II.
Mars, dream respecting, XXIII.
Marsden within Colne, VI; account of, XXII; hall, account of, XXII.
Marsden, ℞, IV, IX, XIX, XXII, XXVII, XXVIII.
Marsh, ℞, II, VIII, IX, XII, XIII, XVIII, XIX, XXII, XXVII.
Marshall, ℞, VIII, XIII, XVIII, XIX, XXII,
Marston, township of Budworth, VIII.
Marston, John: extracts from masque by, XXIX.
Marston moor, battle of, II, XII, XIV, XVIII.
Marston orchard, XX (*tit.* Whalleye).
Martha p^t^., township of Rosthorne, VIII.
Marthall cum Little-Werford, township of Over-Peover, VIII.
Martholme hall, in Harwood magna: notice of, XXII.
Martial, extract from, XVIII.
Martin, ℞, XIII, XIV, XXII.
Martin Marprelate produced on the stage, XXIX.
Martindale, Adam, IV, VIII, IX, XII, XVIII, XXVII; his family and relations, IV,
Martindale, J., XVIII.
Martinez *or* Martinius, Matthew: account of, XIII.
Martinius, Martinus: account of, XIII.
Martinscroft, ℞, IV, VIII, XVIII.
Marton, in Prestbury: account of, VIII.
Marton in Gawsworth, VIII.
Marton, ℞, XXII.
Marton-sands cum Foxwist and Villaview, township of Whitegate, VIII.
Martyne, saynt, embrodred in ryche tysshewe, XV.
Martyrs, Booke of, XVIII.
Marvel, Andrew, XII; his skill in controversy, XIII.
Marwalde *or* Merwalde, kynge and saynt, XV.
Mary, queen, XXIV; her proclamation for redresse of preachars, pryntars and players, XXIX.
Mary, queen, wife of William III., IX.
Mary queen of Scots, XII, XXIII.
Mary's (St.) abbey, York, XIX.
Maryborough, viscount, XIV.
Maryons, Wyon de, XXII.
Mascy *or* Mascie, ℞, VIII, XIX, XX, XXII.
Masey, Mary, IX.
Masham, Elizabeth daughter of John lord Scrope of, XIV.
Masks, masking, masquerades, XIV.
Mason, ℞, I, VII, IX, XII, XIII, XVII, XX, XXII.
Masons lodge, XX (*tit.* Whalleye).
Mass, bold attendance at, in Ireland, I.
Massam, Ralph, mayor of Liverpool, XII.
Massey, ℞, II, VIII, IX, XIV, XVII, XVIII, XXII, XXV, XXVII, XXVIII.
Massie, Dr., rector of Wigan, XXII.
Massinger, extract from, IX.
Master, ℞, VIII, XXII.
Masters, Mr., XXVIII.

Masulipatam, IX.
Matches and marriages, mercenary: homily upon, XIV.
Mather, ff, VIII, XIII, XXII.
Mathews, Toby, XIV.
Matild (the lady), nece to the first kynge Henry: her conduct and fate, XV.
Matley, township and manor of Mottram in Longdendale, VIII.
Matley, Dorothy: dreadful judgment upon, XIII.
Mattaynsmere, XX (*tit.* Steynynges).
Matthew, ff, XIII, XIV.
Matthews, ff, XIV, XIX, XXII.
Maubanc, Alda, XX.
Maucolyn of Scotland comes to spoyle Chestre, XV.
Maud, Robert, XXVIII.
Maude, T. Holme, and Elizabeth his wife, XXII.
Maudesley *or* Maudesly, ff, II, VIII, IX, XXII.
Maudit, Jasper, mayor of Liverpool, and M.P., IX, XII, XXVIII.
Maudlin day, XIV.
Maudsley, William, XVIII.
Maudsley *versus* Leigh, case of, XIX.
Mauliverer, sir Richard, and his daughter Isabel, XXII.
Maunsel, John, rector of Wigan and chancellor of England, XXII.
Maunton, XX.
Maunton, ff, XIV, XX.
Maupas, Willmus de, XX.
Mauricaceston, XX (*tit.* Staneye).
Mauricas- *vel* Mauriches-Eston, villa, XX.
Maurice, prince, XIII.
Maurice *or* Morres, John, vicar of Blackburn, XIV.
Mauritius, the, IX.
Mavkischius, XIII.
Mawdesley *or* Mawdsley, ff, XIX, XXII.
Mawhood, Mr., XIII.
Maxfield monastery. *See* Mayfield.
Maxicroft, XX (*tit.* Whiteword).
Maxicroftschore, XX (*tit.* Whiteword).
Maximilian II. of Germany, XXIV.
Maxwell, ff, I.
May, isle of, Scotland, I.
May, chevalier Louis du, XIII.
May, Thomas, M.P., for Liverpool, IX, XII, XXIX.
Maydenston, R. de, archid. Salop., XX.
Mayer, Mr., XXVIII.
Mayes *or* Maire, Edward, XIX.
Mayfield *error for* Maxfield monastery, co. Chester, VIII.
Mayfield, John, of Staining hall, XXII.
May-games, XIV.
Maylin *or* Malyn, Dr. Massey, rector of Ashton-upon-Mersey, VIII.
Maynard, ff, XIII, XVIII, XIX, XXIV.
Mayne, Jasper: extract from, IX.
Maynilwarin *or* Menylwar, ff, XX.
Maynwareng, Carolus, IX.
Mayor, Robert, XXII.
Maypoles, XIV, XVIII, XXVII; contention respecting, IV.
Mead's *Letters*, extract from, VII; *Works*, XXVII.
Meadowcroft, ff, XII, XIX, XXVIII.
Meaker, Mat., VIII.
Meakin, ff, XXIV, XXVII.
Meales, ff, XXII.
Mear *or* Meare, ff, XVIII, XXVII.
Mearley, great-, XIV, XXII (?); little-, XIV.
Mears, Peter, XII (?).
Measures, *i.e.* dances, XIV.
Meath, Edward Brabazon second earl of, I, XII.
Meautis, Mr., XIII.
Medcalfe *or* Metcalfe, sir Thomas, XIV.
Meddowcroft, Mr., XVIII.
Mede, Joseph, "the incomparable," XIII. *See* Mead.
Medical practice and receipts, I, IV.
Medici, cardinal Leopold di, XIII.

Medina Celi, duke of, XXIV.
Mediolanum *and* Milaine, ancient names of Lancaster, XXII.
Meditations on various subjects by Henry Newcome, XVIII.
Mediterranean sea, IX.
Medo heye, in Orford near Warrington, XVII.
Meek *or* Meeke, 𝔑, XVIII, XIX, XXVII.
Meeles, le, XX.
Megh, Alex. filius Alexandri le, XX.
Meibomius, an ague cured by conversation with, XIII.
Meir, township of Rosthorne, IV, VIII; hall, notice of, VIII.
Mekehurst, XX (*tit.* Baylegh).
Mel, 𝔑, XXX.
Meland, Roger, bishop of Coventry and Lichfield, VIII.
Melcombe I.
Melcombe Regis, XIII.
Meldon hall, co. Northumberland, XII.
Meldresiche, XX (*titt.* Bretharue, Wolueton).
Meldrum, sir John, XII; his conduct in the Civil war, II.
Meles, 𝔑, XX, XXII.
Melford *or* Milfort, lord, XXVIII.
Melhuish, Ja., XIII.
Melinge. *See* Melling.
Mellier, Richard, XXII.
Melling in Lonsdale, account of, XXII; its church given to Lancaster priory, XXII.
Melling, chapelry in Halsall: account of, XXII.
Mells, near Frome, co. Somerset, XIII.
Meluer, villa de, XX.
Meluer, 𝔑, XX.
Melvin, lord, XXVII.
Members (the secluded) sitting as a house of commons, XIII.
Memgate, XX (*tit.* Bilyngton).
Memnonites *or* Mennonites, an anabaptist sect, I, XIII.
Men of Manchester, hospitality of, XIV.
Menage's account of Bochart, XIII.
Menefeld, XX (*tit.* Bilyngton).
Menegate, XX (*tit.* Whiteword).
Menill, El., VIII.
Meningways, XX (*tit.* Bacford).
Mentz, elector of, XIII.
Menyl, Rob. de, XX.
Menzies, James, of Culdare: his trial, V.
Meoles, 𝔑, VIII.
Meols, great-, little- and Kirkby-, VIII; derivation of the word, VII.
Meols, north-, VIII; account of, XXII; hall, notice of, XXII.
Meols stocks (the), explanation of, VII.
Merbury, 𝔑, VIII, XVII.
Merbury's house and lande, Warrington, XVII.
Mercator, 𝔑, XIII, XXIV.
Mercer, 𝔑, II, XII, XIII, XX, XXII.
Merchant-tailors' school, London, IV, VIII.
Mercia, bishops of, VIII. *See* Mercyens.
Mercies vouchsafed to Newcome, XVIII.
Merclesden *now* Marsden, XX, XXII. *See* Marsden.
Merclesden, 𝔑, XX, XXII.
Mercurius Politicus, notice of, XIII; posting advertisement in, XII.
Mercurius Pragmaticus, XVIII.
Mercurius Rusticus, XVIII.
Mercyens, legendary history and description of, XV.
Mere, 𝔑, XXII.
Mereclogh, XX (*tit.* Whiteword).
Meredith, 𝔑, VIII, XII.
Meresheia, Roger de, XIX.
Meretun, villa de, XXX.
Mereum, cousin to saynt Werburge, taken by myracle expresse to the blys of heven, XV.
Merian, Mrs., XXIV.
Merillum, Willus, XX.

Meriton, ff, XVIII, XXVII.
Merivale abbey, co. Warwick, IX, XXII.
Merland, XX.
Merland, ff, XX.
Merlaya, magna et parva, XX.
Merret, Christopher, M.D., XIII.
"Merrie blades," a favourite phrase of James I, XIV.
Merriman, captain, XVIII, XXVII.
Mersapeltre, XX (*tit.* Croenton).
Merse, XX (*tit.* Bilyngton).
Merse officer, extracts from the journal of a, V.
Mersey river, VIII, IX, XII, XX; early defences of, II; gave name to Mercia, XV; styled the sea, XVII.
Mersey island, fort on, XII.
Merton in Whitegate, co. Chester, VIII.
Merton, villa de, co. Lanc., XX.
Merton magna, XX.
Merton, ff, XX.
Merula, merle, the blackbird, XXIII.
Meschines (Ranulph) founds Cokersand and Calder abbeys, XXII.
Messes, forty: explanation of, XIV.
Messiah, Jewish expectation of, I.
Metaphysics, value of to a divine, IV.
Metcalf, ff, XIV.
Methley, IX.
Methrocschaghheuil, XX (*tit.* Whiteword).
Methuen, lord chancellor, IX.
Metyngham, Joh. de, XX.
Meuland, Roger de, bishop of Lichfield and Coventry, XIX, XXII.
Meure, maid of: her wonderful abstinence, I.
Meynilwarin, ff, XX.
Meyrick *or* Meyricke, ff, VIII, XIV, XVIII, XXVII.
Michael's (St.) upon Wyre, account of, XXII.
Michell, Chris., VIII.
Micrœlius, XVIII.
Middleburgh, Holland, I.
Middleforth, XXX.
Middleham, co. York, XII, XIV.
Middleham, ff, XIV.
Middlehurst, Hugh, his tenancy in Warrington, XVII.
Middlemore, William de, and Margery his wife, XXII.
Middlesex, IX.
Middleton, co. Lanc., IV, XII, XIII, XIV, XVIII; account of, XIX; church, VII, XIV, XIX; grammar school, account of, XIX; hall, notices of, VII, XIV, XIX.
Middleton, ff, II, XII, XIII, XIX, XXII, XXVII, XXVIII.
Middleton chapel, Runcorn: notice of, VIII.
Middleton hall, Kirkham: notice of, XXII.
Middleton's *Witch*, extracts from, VI.
Middle-walks, hamlet of Higher-Whitley, Budworth, VIII.
Middlewich, co. Chester, IV; account of, VIII; battle at, II; rent paid by rural dean of, VIII.
Middlome, Adam, XIV.
Mide, Ric. de, XX.
Midelhole, XX (*tit.* Gerstan).
Midelword, XX (*tit.* Workedelegh).
Midgley, ff, VIII, XIV, XIX, XXIX.
Midhope, XIV.
Midhope, Joh. de, XX.
Midilclogh, XX (*tit.* Spotlond).
Midleton, ff, XIV, XX.
Mierscough lodge, notice of, II.
Mikelbrok, XX (*tit.* Bilyngton).
Mikel coumbebrok, XX (*tit.* Whiteword).
Mikel pughul, XX (*tit.* Whiteword).
Milan, wager respecting, IX.
Mildmay, ff, XII, XXII.
Miles, ff, VI, XIII.
Milford haven, I.
Milington, ff, XX.
Militia, training of, at Manchester, II.

Mill's *India*, ix.
Millar, antagonist of Bentley, xiii.
Millard, Mr., minister of St. Helen's, xiii.
Mill-croft, Liverpool, xii.
Mill-end, Gawsworth, viii.
Mill-lane, Liverpool, xii.
Millenaries, Amyrault's book against, xiii.
Miller, 𝔑, v, xiv.
Millgate, Manchester, fire in, xviii.
Millicent's (sir John) notable fooling, xiv.
Milling *and* Millinge, 𝔑, xii.
Millington, township of Rosthorne, iv, viii; hall, notice of, viii.
Millington, 𝔑, viii, xviii, xix, xxvii.
Mills in Holland, i; in Liverpool, xii.
Mills, 𝔑, xiv, xviii, xxvii.
Millward, judge, iv.
Milne, 𝔑, xix, xxii.
Milnebrok, xx (*titt.* Croenton, Dounom).
Milnecroft, xx (*tit.* Aluetham).
Milnefurlong, xx (*tit.* Cliderhou).
Milne-hey, Liverpool, xii.
Milne-street, Liverpool, xii.
Milnehouses, 𝔑, xx.
Milner, 𝔑, xx, xxii.
Milnes, 𝔑, xii.
Milnrow, in Butterworth, Rochdale, xiv; account of, xix.
Milton, co. Camb., xiii.
Milton, John, iv, xiii, xviii, xxix; notices of himself, widow and family, xxiv.
Milton, 𝔑, xxiv.
Milton green, Handley, co. Chester, viii.
Mimms, xiv.
Minehead, description of, i.
Mineries, the, co. Somerset, xiii.
Minibole, i.
Ministerial duties of Newcome, xviii.
Minmore, near Carnew, Ireland, i.
Minne, John, vii.
Minshul *or* Minshull, 𝔑, viii, xiii, xviii, xxiv, xxvii, xxviii.
Minshull *or* Church-Minshull, account of, viii.
Minshull-Vernon, township of Middlewich, viii.
Minster at Chester, building and endowment of, xv.
Minstrel all other ferre passynge, lofty song of a, xv.
Minstrels, xiv, xv.
Mint at Dort, description of the, i.
Miracles by saynt Werburge and others, account of, xv.
Miralache, xx (*tit.* Wordelword).
Mirica, Gaspar à, mathematician, xxiv.
Mirror, xiv.
Mirrour for Magistrates, extract from, xxix.
Mishna, the: notice of, xiii.
Misrule, lords of, xiv.
Misson's account of ducking machines, xii.
Mist's *Weekly Journal*, xxiv.
Mitchell, Mr., of Heptonstall, xxii.
Mitford, rev. John, xiii.
Mitton, xiv.
Mitton, little-, xiv, xx.
Mitton, 𝔑, ii, xx.
Mizaldus courts Dr. Dee's acquaintance, xxiv.
Moated houses, prevalence of, xvii.
Mobberley, co. Chester: account of, viii; priory, account of, viii.
Mobberley, 𝔑, viii.
Modena, Leo of, xiii.
Moderate Messenger, xii.
Modern history, Newcomes's readings in, xviii.
Modie, Richard, first protestant rector of Standish, xxii.
Moeles, capella de, xxx.
Moffat, muster of south-country Scots at, v.

Mohaut, Rogerus senesc. de, XX.
Mohun, the lords, VIII, IX, XXII.
Moil, Christopher, XIII.
Moire, co. Chester, IV. *See* Meir.
Mokenes, XX (*tit.* Workedelegh).
Molaes, abortions: etymology of the word, VII.
Mold, co. Flint, XII.
Moldenhall, *error for* Moldeworth, Robertus de, XX.
Molesworth, rev. Dr., vicar of Rochdale, XIX.
Molesworth's (sir William) edition of *Hobbes*, XIII.
Molewarps *i.e.* moles, VII.
Molines, ff, XXII.
Molineux, ff, II, IX, XXVIII.
Mollenexe, widow, IX.
Mollineux, ff, IX.
Molyneus, ff, XX.
Molyneux, ff, VIII, IX, XII, XIV, XVII, XIX, XXII, XXV, XXVIII.
Mollington, St. Mary's, Chester, VIII.
Mollington, township of Backford, VIII.
Molynton, XX.
Monaldeschi, murder of, XIII.
Monasteries and religious houses, foundation of, XV; favourite places of custody for valuables, XVII; vices and corruptions of, VII.
Moncaster, Roger. *See* Muncaster.
Moneley *or* Monely, ff, XII.
Moniphornes, terra de, XX.
Monithornes, terra de, XX.
Monk, ff, XIII, XVIII, XXII, XXVII.
Monk's *Life of Bentley*, XIX.
Monk's hall, Eccles: account of, XIX.
Monkbretton *alias* Landa, chartulary of the monastery of, VIII.
Monkedik, XX (*tit.* Dounom).
Monkeshulles, XX (*titt.* Stanword, Whelton).
Monkton, Mr., XXVII.
Monlewler, Mr., XXVII.
Monluc, monsieur de, ambassadour to the Great Turk, XXIV.
Monmouth, James duke of: his intrigues and rebellion, IV, IX, XXVII, XXVIII.
Monroe *or* Monerott, Mr., minister of West Kirby, VIII.
Mons, wager respecting, IX.
Monson, punishment of, XII.
Montacute, ff, VIII, XIV.
Montagu, ff, I, IX, XIII, XIV, XXII, XXVIII.
Montaigne, XIII.
Montalt, barony of, VIII.
Montalt, ff, VIII, XX.
Montaureus (Petrus) courts Dr. Dee's acquaintance, XXIV.
Montbegon, ff, XIX, XXII.
Monteagle, lords, VIII, XXII, XXIX.
Monte forti, Alex. de, XX.
Montford, pedigree of Bromley baron, XIV.
Montgomery, Herberts earls of, XIV.
Montgomery family, earls Mount-Alexander: notice of, I.
Monton, Manchester, XIX; Sacheverell mob pulls down the presbyterian meeting-house in, V.
Monuments and tombs, notices of, I.
Moody, Sa., XIII.
Moor *or* Moore, township of Daresbury, Runcorn, VIII.
Moor, ff, XXII.
Moor hall, Aughton: notice of, XXII.
Moorcroft, Sylvester, mayor of Liverpool, IX.
Moore, ff, I, II, IV, VI, VIII, IX, XII, XVIII, XXVII, XXVIII.
Moore fields and hall, Liverpool, XII.
Moore Rental, XVIII, XXII.
Moorgame, XIV.
Moot hall, Wigan, XXII.
Mora, ff, XII, XX.
Morant, XIII (?).
Moravian brethren, account of, XIII.

Moray, 𝔑, xiii.
Mordaunt, 𝔑, viii, xiv, xxii.
More *or* Mora, xx.
More, 𝔑, vi, viii, ix, xii, xiii, xiv, xvii, xviii, xx, xxii, xxvii.
More crofts, Liverpool, xii.
More street, Liverpool: detailed account of, xii.
Morehey, xx (*tit.* Whalleye).
Morehouses, xx (*titt.* Rauensmeles, Ynes).
Moremersch in Roncore, xx.
Morent *error for* Morcut, Mr., xxvii.
Moreri, xviii (?).
Moresbarrow cum Parme, township of Middlewich, viii.
Mores orchard, xx (*tit.* Whalleye).
Morethwayth, Willmus de, xx.
Moreton, township of Bidston cum Ford, co. Chester, viii; chapelry, account of, viii.
Moreton, earl of, afterwards king John, xxii, xxiv.
Moreton, 𝔑, i, viii, xiv, xx, xxii, xxvii. *See* Morton.
Moreton-Alcomlow, township of Astbury, viii; great and little halls, notices of, viii.
Morewood, Mr., of Norton, xxvii.
Morgan, 𝔑, i, ii, xxv.
Morgate, xx (*tit.* Whiteword).
Morgell, 𝔑, viii.
Morhof on the comparative merits of Vossius and Martinius, xiii.
Morice, co. Chester, iv.
Morisco, Peter, xxviii.
Morison, 𝔑, xiii.
Morison's (Fynes) *Itinerary*, xiv.
Morison's *Poems*, extract from, vi.
Morland, sir Samuel, xiii.
Morlay, township of Barrow, viii.
Morley, viii; township of Wilmslow, viii.
Morley, 𝔑, xiii, xviii, xxii.
Morleys, xiv.
Mornay, xiii.
Morneing Exercise at Criplegate, xviii.
Morpeth, notice of, i; Northumbrian insurgents arrive at, v.
Morrall, Thomas, vicar of Bolton, xix.
Morres, Henry, minister of Burnley, xxii.
Morrice, 𝔑, xviii, xxvii.
Morris, 𝔑, ix, xiii, xiv, xxii.
Morris and Phillips, grantees of church estates, xix.
Morris dance, xxvii.
Morritt, 𝔑, xxii.
Morslande (le), Warrington, xvii.
Mort, a musical hunting-call, xxiii.
Mort *or* Morte, 𝔑, ii, ix, xix, xxii, xxvii.
Mortlake, account of Dr. Dee's library at, xxiv.
Morton *error for* Worton in Wensleydale, xiv.
Morton, 𝔑, i, vi, xiii, xviii, xxvii. *See* Moreton.
Mortuaries, value of, viii.
Moseley, township of Ashton-under-Line, xix.
Moseley, 𝔑, ii, iv, viii, xiii, xx, xxviii.
Moses, history of, depaynted on arras, xv.
Moses, Mr., master of Pembroke college, Cambridge, xiii.
Mosheim's *Ecclesiastical History*, xiii.
Mosier, W., xix.
Mosiley, in Spotlond, xx. *See* Spotlond *in same volume.*
Mosley, 𝔑, xiv, xviii, xix, xxii, xxvii.
Mosok *or* Mossok, 𝔑, ix.
Moss *or* Mosse, 𝔑, iv, ix, xii, xix, xx, xxii, xxviii.
Moss-lake fields, Liverpool, xii.
Mosslanes *for* Moshems in Farington, xxx.
Mossock, Mossocke *or* Mossoke, 𝔑, xxii.

Moss-side, in Halton, Runcorn, VIII.
Moss-side, in Manchester, XIX.
Moston, township of Warmingham, VIII.
Moston, manor of, near Chester, VIII.
Moston, near Manchester, XIX.
Moston, ꝑ, XX, XXVIII.
Mostyn, ꝑ, VIII.
Mostyn, co. Flint, IX, XII.
Mostyn, St. Mary's, Chester, VIII.
Mostyn hall, near Manchester, XIV.
Moton, ꝑ, XX, XXII.
Motteville, XVIII.
Mottram in Longdendale, account of, VIII; sudden death at, XVIII.
Mottram-Andrew, township of Prestbury, VIII.
Moudsley, Rogerus fil. Hugonis de, XXX.
Mouldheeles, wife of, VI.
Mouldsworth, great- and little-, townships of Tarvin, VIII.
Moulest, forest of, VIII.
Moulin, Peter du, XIII.
Moulins, in Bourbonnais, France, XXII.
Moulson (sir Thomas, bart., lord-mayor of London) builds Hargrave chapel, VIII.
Moulton, township of Davenham, VIII.
Moulton, near Newmarket, XIII.
Moulton, Roger, VIII.
Mounson *or* Monson, sir John, K.B. and M.P., II.
Mounston, William lord, XIII.
Mountague, ꝑ, II, XIII.
Mountebanks, presbyterian visits to, XVIII.
Mountfichet, Rad. de, XX.
Mountgarret, Edmund second lord, I.
Mountgay, Robertus de, XX.
Mountjoy, Charles lord: employments of, XIV.
Mounton, hamlet in Eccles, XIX.
Mount Pleasant, Liverpool: bowling-green on, IX.
Mourning *and* mourning rings, XIV.
Moville, Alan de, XIV.
Moxon, ꝑ, IV, VIII, XVIII, XXVII.
Moyer, lady, XXII; some account of, XIX. *See* Joliffe.
Muchelbrok, XX (*tit.* Saynte mariden).
Much Hoole. *See* Hoole.
Much Woolton, IX.
Muckelt, George, XXII.
Mukedlandes, XX (*tit.* Cliderhou).
Mukelbrok, XX (*tit.* Westewod).
Mulachehalls, XX (*tit.* Wythenhull).
Mulchurst, VIII.
Mulecornhirst, XX (*tit.* Bilyngton).
Mulgrave, Constantine Phipps baron, XXII.
Mulint, Eitrop de, XX.
Müller's *Friburg Bell*, extract from, XVIII.
Mullineux, hon. W., IX.
Mulneplace and Mustarplace, in Faryngton, XXX.
Multon, ꝑ, XIX, XX, XXII.
Mulyngton, William, of Warrington, XVII.
Mummers *and* mumming, origin and etymology of, XIV.
Mummies at Leyden, I.
Muncaster, barons, XXII.
Muncaster, Roger, of Garstang, executed for rebellion, V.
Munchulf, VIII.
Munday, major, II.
Munden, brigadier, V.
Mundy, Edward Millar, M.P., XIX.
Munechene Wro, an ancient name of Vale Royal, VIII.
Mungay, Robertus de, XX.
Munke, ꝑ, XVII.
Munkegate, XX (*tit.* Bilyngton).
Munro, sir George, II, XII.
Munster, Ireland: forfeited estates in, XXV.
Munster's edition of St. Matthew's Gospel in Hebrew, XIII.

Muratori, XIII.
Murcot, Mr., XXVII.
Murdat, Adam, XX.
Murders, account of, I.
Murdering inn near Stralsund, I.
Murderer, discovery of by touching the corpse, VI.
Muriel, 𝔑, XIII.
Murr's *History of the Origin of the Rosicrucians*, XIII.
Murray, 𝔑, V, VIII, IX, XIX, XXII, XXVII.
Murryer, John, XIV.
Musæum Wormianum, notice of, XIII.
Musæus, IV.
Musberry, in Tottington, Bury, XIX.
Muschamp, Geoffrey, bishop of Lichfield and Coventry, VIII.
Musgrave, 𝔑, II, IX.
Music invented by Tuball and Tubalcain, XV.
Muskerry, lord, VIII.
Musselburgh, proverb respecting, I; arrival of Highlanders at, V; death of sir William Norris at, IX, XII.
Mussen, Mr., XXVII.
Muthom, XX (*tit.* Aluetham).
Mutlaw in Gawsworth, VIII.
Myddleton church, XIX.
Myels, Johannes, IX.
Myerscough lodge, account and description of, XIV.
Mylburge, saynt and vyrgyn, XV.
Myldred, saynt and vyrgyn, XV.
Mylgyde, saynt and vyrgyn, XV.
Mylne, Henry, XIX.
Mynne, colonel, defeated and taken, II.
Mynshall *or* Mynshull, 𝔑, XIX, XXVII.
Myrefeld, Radulphus de, XX.
Myrescogh, Walterus de, XX.
Mystery and Misery of Lending and Borrowing, XIV.
Mystery of Jesuitisme, XVIII.
Mytton, Henrie, of the Rough-Lee, bewitched to death, VI.

NABB'S tenement, in Bury, XIX.
Nabbe, Richard, XIX.
Nairn, lord, and his regiment, V.
Nairn, major, trial and execution of, V
Names of residents and places in an-cient Warrington, XVII.
Namptwych, account of, VIII; rent paid by rural dean of, VIII; St Nicholas' hospital, VIII: priory VIII.
Namur, wagers respecting, IX.
Nantwich, IV; battle of, XII; relieved by Fairfax, II; regulations of brine pits, I; presentment of Warrington bridge, XVII; traditions of Milton XXIV. *See* Namptwych.
Nappy ale, use of the term, IV.
Naps, Mr., XXVIII.
Narbonensis (Moses) translates *Ha-Ebn Yokdhan* into Hebrew, XIII.
Narbury, 𝔑, XII.
Nar crook hey, in Wallesey, VIII.
Nares, archdeacon, XIV.
Narweoutlone, XX (*tit.* Croenton).
Nash, 𝔑, IX, XXIX.
Nash's *Worcestershire*, XXIX.
Nassau (colonel) treats with the in-surgents, V.
Naude's (Gabriel) *Instruction sur la Vérité de l'Histoire des Frères de la Rosecroix*, XIII.
Naueden *now* Naden water, in Spot-land, XX. *See in same volume* Chade-wyk *and* Spotlond.
Navy, bill for manning the, IX.
Navy of Holland, extent of the, I.
Naylor, 𝔑, IX, XIII, XVII, XVIII.
Naylour, Mr., XXII.
Neal *or* Neale, 𝔑, XIII, XXVIII.
Neal's *History of the Puritans*, XIII.
Neath, Glamorganshire, I.
Nedrelebrok, XX (*tit.* Chaderton).
Needham, 𝔑, I, VIII, XIII, XXVII.
Needwood park, IV.
Neighbour-row *or* House-row, church

wardens of Warton returned by, XXII.
Neild, 𝔑, XVIII, XXVII.
Neile, Dr., bishop of Durham, XIII, XIV.
Nelson, R, VIII,
Nesh, soft, VII.
Nesh, Richard, XXVII.
Nesse, township of Neston: account of hospital in, VIII.
Neston, account of, VIII.
Nether eye, in Penwortham, XXX.
Netherestfeld, XX (*tit.* Aluetham.)
Netherlands, retirement of sir William Babthorp to, XIV.
Netherpool, township of Eastham, VIII.
Nethersole's (sir Francis) kindness to Newcome, XXVII.
Netherton, township of Frodsham, VIII.
Nets, Dutch method of seasoning, I.
Nett (*Fr.* nettoyer), to clean, I.
Netterville, viscount, I.
Neuham, Germanus de, XX.
Neuham, XX (*tit.* Westewod).
Neuton, XX.
Neuton, Willmus de, XX.
Neve, le, XII.
Neville, 𝔑, VIII, XX, XXII.
Newall, Newhall *or* Nual, township and manor of Davenham, VIII.
Newall, 𝔑, XIX.
New Atlantis: critical notice of the continuation of, XIII.
New Barns hall, XIX.
Newbold, township of Astbury, VIII.
Newbold (hamlet of) pays tithes to St. Oswald's, Chester, VIII.
Newbold, in Rochdale, XX; hall, ac-account of, XIX.
Newbold, 𝔑, XIX, XX.
Newborough school, in Lathom, Ormskirk: account of, XXII.
Newbrenner, Conradus Justus, XXIV.
Newbruches, XX (*tit.* Bacford.)
Newburgh, Edward lord, chancellor of the duchy of Lancaster, II.
Newcastle-on-Tyne, description and account of, I; threatened attack and defence of, V; Newcome's visit to, XVIII.
Newcastle, earl of: his conduct in the Civil war, II, XII.
Newchurch, in Pendle: account of, XXII.
Newchurch, in Rossendale: account of, XXII.
Newchurch, in Winwick, VIII; account of, XXII.
Newchurch, in Whitegate, VIII.
New close, in Penwortham, XXX.
Newcome, Henry, M.A., IV, XII, XIV; his *Autobiography*, XXVII, XXVIII; *Diary*, XIII, XIV, XVIII.
Newcome, 𝔑, VIII, XIII, XVIII, XIX, XXVII.
Newcomen, 𝔑, I, XVIII (XXVII, preface, p. vi).
Newcroft hall, Flixton: account of, XIX.
Newcrofte, near Warrington, XVII.
Newdigate, John, M.P. for Liverpool, XII.
Newefelde, XX (*tit.* Whalleye).
Newehous, XX (*tit.* Whalleye).
New Fleet prison, Manchester, XXVIII.
New Forest, Hampshire, XIII; story of Christmas-budding oak in, XIII.
Newgate, a street in Warrington, XVII.
New hall, Tottington, Bury, XIV; account of, XIX.
New hey, Liverpool, XII.
Newlands *or* Newlaunds, XIV.
Newport, co. Monmouth, I.
Newport, battle and treaty of, XVIII.
Newport *for* Nieuport, Belgium: wager respecting, IX.
Newport, earl of, XIII.
Newry, Ireland, I, XII.
Newsham, XIV.

Newsome, Edmund, stipendiary priest of Over-Peover, VIII.
Newton, in Manchester, IV, XVIII; account of, XIX.
Newton in Makerfeld, chapelry of Winwick, IX, XII; account of, XXII; hall, notice of, XXII.
Newton, near Downham, co. Lanc., XIV.
Newton, in Frodsham, VIII.
Newton, township of Malpas, VIII.
Newton, township of Middlewich, VIII.
Newton, township of Mottram in Longdendale, VIII; hall, notice of, VIII.
Newton, chapelry of Prestbury, VIII.
Newton, in Runcorn: tithes of, VIII.
Newton, township of St. Oswald's, Chester, VIII.
Newton, township of Tattenhall, VIII.
Newton, in West Kirby, VIII.
Newton, co. Durham, I.
Newton de Clanyboyes, Ireland, I.
Newton, 𝔑, II, VIII, XIII, XIX, XXIV, XXIX.
Nice, council of: its decree respecting Christian soldiers, XXV.
Nicholas, saynt, embrodred in ryche tysshewe, XV; statue of at Liverpool, XII; chantry of in Manchester church, XIX.
Nicholas III., pope: valor or taxation of, VIII, XIX.
Nicholas, secretary, XXVII.
Nicholas, Henry: his religious tenets, XIII.
Nichols or Nicholls, 𝔑, VIII, IX, XII, XIII, XIV.
Nichols's *Collectanea*, XIX; *Literary Anecdotes*, XIX; *Progresses of James I.*, IX, XII, XIV; *Progresses of Queen Elizabeth*, XXIX; *Topographer and Genealogist*, XIV.
Nicholson, 𝔑, I, XIII, XVIII, XXII, XXVII.
Nicol, Richard, XXVII.
Nicolai, Nicholaus Grudius, XXIV.
Nicolas, lieut.-colonel, of Gaunt castle, XII.
Nicolas, Sir Harris, XIV, XXIX; *Life of sir Kenelm Digby*, XIII; *List of Heraldic Visitations*, XXIV.
Nicols or Nicolls, 𝔑, VIII, XIII.
Nigellus, XIX.
Nismes, in Languedoc, XIII.
Nithsdale, (earl of) joins the rebellion: his condemnation and escape, V.
Nixon, 𝔑, VIII, XII.
Noble, 𝔑, VIII, XII, XXVII.
Noblemen, report of a robbery by, XVIII.
Noblemen of the court of James I, list of, XIV.
Noch, Hamo, XX (?).
Nocton, co. Lincoln, XIV.
Nodbury *for* Modbury, co. Devon, XIII.
Noe and his shyppe depaynted in arras, XV.
Noel, 𝔑, XX.
Nonant, Hugh de, bishop of Lichfield, XXII.
Nonconformists, position of, IV, XVIII.
None but Christ by Dr. Tuckney, XVIII.
Nonjurors, principles and position of, V; their church in Manchester, V.
Nonsuch, queen Elizabeth's court at, XXIV.
Norbrek, 𝔑, XX.
Norbury, 𝔑, VIII, XII, XIX, XXVII.
Norbury, near Stockport, XVIII; account of, VIII.
Norbury, township of Marbury, Whitchurch, VIII.
Norbury-Booths, in Knutsford, VIII.
Norcet, hamlet of Over-Whitley, Great Budworth, VIII.
Norcros or Norcross, 𝔑, XX, XXII.
Nordlingen, battle of, I.
Nore, the, I.
Norfolk, Offa fyrst kynge over, XV.

Norfolk, dukes of, xxv, xxix.
Northampton, Henr. de, xx.
Norlegh, Thurstanus de, xx.
Norley, in Frodsham, viii.
Norman, Thomas, xxii.
Normoles *for* North-Meols, xxii.
Norreis, John, of Warrington, xvii.
Norres, ℞, ix, xxii.
Norrese, ℞, xx.
Norreys, ℞, viii, xix, xxii.
Norris, ℞, ii, vii, viii, ix, xii, xiii, xix, xxii, xxv, xxviii.
Norris bond, xii.
Norris property in Warrington, xvii.
Norris-street, Liverpool, xii.
Norris Papers, xii.
Norrise, Will., xii.
Norroy, sir Richard St. George, xiv.
Norten, Edm., viii.
North, ℞, vi, vii, ix, xiii, xxii.
North's *Examen*, ix.
Northampton, xiii, xiv.
Northampton, Charles marquis of, xiv.
Northampton, lady marquess of, xxiv.
Northampton, (*Ancient Charters of*) by Rev. C. H. Hartshorne, xiv.
Northburgh, diocese of Lincoln, viii.
Northburgh, sir Hugh de, clericus, viii.
Northbury, Gregory de, first abbot of Whalley, viii.
North Cadbury, co. Somerset, xii.
Northcotes, Hug. de, xx.
Northcott, Mr., minister of Derby chapel, xxii.
Northenden, xiii, xviii; account of, viii.
Northerne Subscribers Plea, iv.
Northfleet, i.
Northgate-street, township of St. Oswald's, Chester, viii.
North Meols, ix; account of, xxii; hall, notice of, xxii. *See* Meols.
Northscawe, Thom. de, *error for* Northessawe, Rogerus de, xx.
North sea *for* Bristol channel, xiii.
North side, township of St. Oswald's, Chester, viii.
Northumberland, rebellion of the earl of, i.
Northumberlande, seventh realme of Saxons: account of its princes, xv.
Northumbrians, account of their rising in the Jacobite rebellion, v.
Northwich, township of Witton, Great Budworth, iv, viii, xviii; battle of, xxvii; Witton school at, notice of, iv.
Northwyco, xx.
Northwyco, ℞, xx.
Northwood, in High-Legh, Rosthorne, viii.
Norton, in Runcorn: tythes of, viii.
Norton priory, xvii; founded by Wyllyam constable of Chestre, xv; account of, viii; gigantic figure of St. Christopher at, vii; priors of, xx.
Norton, ℞, iv, xxvii.
Norwich, sir George Goring earl of, i.
Norwordine, ancient form of Northenden, viii.
Nostell priory, near Doncaster, xiv.
Note books, value of, xviii.
Noteschawe, ℞, xxx.
Noteschaweheued, xxx.
Notitia Cestriensis, xiv, xix.
Notogh, ℞, xix.
Nott, Joh., xiii.
Nottingham, earls of, ix, xiii, xiv, xxviii.
Nottingham, lord chancellor, xiii.
Notton, ℞, xix, xx.
Nottun, Gilbertus de, senescallus de Penwortham, xxx.
Nouant, Rob. de, xx.
Nouvelles Ordinaires de Londres, ix.
Novatian, xii.
Novo campo, ℞, xx.
Novo mercato, ℞, xx.
Nowell, ℞, ii, vi, vii, xiii, xiv, xix, xxii, xxviii.

Noy, Mr., xiv.
Nugent, Walter son of Richard, xix.
Nun, derivation of the word, viii.
Nuncio (the) in Ireland, xii.
Nuny, Wilmus de, xx (?).
Nuremberg, printing at, xiii.
Nuteschagh, xx (*tit.* Dounom).
Nuthall family, viii.
Nuthurst, xiv.
Nuttall, 𝔑, xix, xxii.
Nuttall hall, Bury: account of, xix.
Nutter, 𝔑, vi, xiv.
Nuttow, John, xxii.
Nye, 𝔑, xiii, xxvii.

OAK, winter-blooming, in New forest, i.
Oak at Hoo, which by miracle preserved saynt Werburge: its marvellous properties, xv.
Oak bedsteads, carved: description of, xiv.
Oak carving at Myerscough, xiv.
Oak, Stable-, xiv.
Oakenrod hall, Rochdale: account of, xix.
Oakes, Elizabeth, xxii.
Oakham, xviii. *See* Morris-dance.
Oakhanger hall, Barthomley: notice of, viii.
Ordshall *or* Ordsall, xviii.
Oates (Titus) only a tool in the hands of Dr. Esrael Tongue, xiii.
Oaths and exclamations, a puritan's trouble at, xxvii.
Obituary window in Bolton church, description of, xix.
Oblacions to saynt Werburge, miraculous virtue of, xv.
Oblation money at Bolton, scale of, xix.
Obsession, narrative of a case of, xviii. *See* Cambridge.
Occleston, township of Middlewich, viii.
Ockley's (Simon) translation of *Hai Ebn Yokdhan*, xiii.
Ocly, Robert, xvii.
Oculus Sydereus, a Latin treatise, xiii
Odcroft, John, preacher of God's word at Stretford, xix.
Odd-Rhode, township of Astbury, viii.
Ode (Latin) on Pococke by Smith, critical estimate of, xiii.
Odell, Mr., of Carnew, i.
Odyssey, οὔτις pun in the, xviii.
Offa, kynge of eest-Englande, legendary account of, xv.
Offerbeake, lord: description of his house at Allifein, Holland, i.
Offerton, township of Rosthorne, viii.
Offhuysen, Joannes Franciscus van: his foule iniury to Dr. Dee, xxiv.
Office, a gamekeeper's walk, xiv.
Offley, 𝔑, viii, xiv, xxvii.
Offryde (? Egfryde), kynge of Northumberlande, xv.
Ogden, 𝔑, xii, xviii, xix, xxvii.
Ogilby, John: account of, xiii.
Ogilvie (captain) wounded at Preston, v.
Ogle, 𝔑, ii, ix, xxii.
Ogleby (Ogilvie, lord) defeated near Preston, ii.
Ogles, Mr., ix.
Okeden, 𝔑, xix.
Okell, James, viii.
Okenrode, 𝔑, xix, xx.
Okeside, xx (*tit* Wythenhull).
Okey, 𝔑, xviii, xix.
Okey hole, near Wells: curiosities of, xiii.
Okill's map of Liverpool, xii.
Okkel, Joh., xx.
Olbia, notices and critical account of, xiii.
Old-Cambus, a Scotch village, i.
Oldcastel, sir John: notices and defence of, vii.
Oldcastle, township of Malpas, viii.

Old-dock *or* pool, Liverpool, XII.
Oldefelde, XX (*tit.* Cliderhou).
Oldenburg, Henry: account of, XIII.
Oldenburgh, earl of, XXIV.
Oldfeild, Mrs., XVIII.
Oldfield, ꝶ, VIII, XVIII, XIX, XXII, XXVII.
Oldfield hall, Heswall: account of, VIII.
Old hall, Mottram: notice of, VIII.
Old hall in Pilkington. *See* Pilkington hall.
Old *or* Moore hall, Liverpool, XII.
Old-hall street, Liverpool: tenancies in, XII.
Oldham, XIII, XIV, XVIII; account of, XIX.
Oldham ꝶ, XVIII, XIX, XXII, XXVIII.
Oldhaugh family, VIII.
Oldheld, Richard de, VIII.
Old-man house, Haerlem: description of, I.
Old-women houses, Haerlem, I.
Oldmixon's *Hist. of England*, XXVIII.
Old stable, XX (*tit.* Whalleye).
Old-yordes (le), Warrington, XVII.
Oldys's *British Librarian*, VII.
Olearius, Sandy's, XIII.
Olearius and Mandeslo's *Travels and Voyages*, XIII.
Oley, Barnabas, XIII, XIX.
Olhoff, J. E., XIII.
Olivarez, count-duke of, I.
Oliver, John, vicar of Audlem, VIII.
Olives, ꝶ, XII.
Ollerhead, Mr., VIII.
Ollers, alder trees, I; a field so called, VI.
Ollerton, in Knutsford, VIII; school, account of, VIII.
Ollort, manor of, co. Wexford, I.
Ollyffe, Mr., VIII.
Olreton, ꝶ, XX.
Ominous appearances in the sky, XIII.
Onely, Mary, XIII.
Onslow, sir Richard, speaker to the house of commons, IX.
Openshaw, near Manchester, XVIII, XIX.
Optatus, preface to Meric Casaubon's edition of, XIII.
Opton, Rogerus de, XVII.
Optone, VIII.
Orange, princes of, I, XIII.
Orchard feld, in Penwortham, XXX.
Orchards, Dr. John Beal's zeal for the plantation of, XIII.
Ordericus Vitalis, XIV.
Ordinances and resolutions, presbyterian, XVIII.
Ordinations, presbyterian, XVIII.
Ordsall hall, Manchester: account of, XIX; meeting of townsmen at, II.
Orel *or* Orell, ꝶ, XVII, XX.
Orford. *See* Overforthe.
Origen (*a Letter of Resolution concerning*): critical account of the tract, XIII.
Origines Sacræ, XVIII.
Orion's coy, near Bridgewater: description of, I.
Orm Fitz-Eward *or* -Ailward, notices of, XIX.
Orme, ꝶ, IX, XIX, XXVII.
Ormerod, ꝶ, XIV, XIX, XXII.
Ormerod, George, D.C.L., VI, VIII, XIV, XIX, XXII; his *History of Cheshire*, III, VIII, XII, XIII, XIV, XVIII, XXIV, XXIX; *Civil War Tracts*, IX; *Stanley Legend*, XIX.
Ormerod house, Burnley: account of, XXII.
Ormond, dukes of, I, V, IX, XII, XIV, XVIII.
Ormond, marquis of, XIII.
Ormond, earl of, I.
Ormskirk, VIII, IX, XII, XIX; account of, XXII; military proceedings at, II; presbyterian ministers imprisoned at, IV.
Ormus, ꝶ, XXX.
O'Roghan's (Dennis) evidence against Sir John Perrot, XXV.

Orontius desires Dr. Dee's acquaintance, XXIV.
Orphans, treatment of, in Holland, I.
Orreby, 𝔑, VIII, XX.
Orrell, 𝔑, XIX, XXII.
Osbaldeston in Balderston, Blackburn, VI; hall, account of, XXII.
Osbaldeston, 𝔑, XX, XXII.
Osbernus, 𝔑, XXX.
Osborne, Peter, remembrancer of the exchequer, XXIV.
Oscroft, in Tarvin, VIII.
Osmer, Saxon proprietor of Davenham manor, VIII.
Ossava, wife of prynce Ermenred of Kent, XV.
Osseburn, Robertus de, XX.
Ostend, IX, XIV.
Ostryde, queen of Mercia, moost cruelly slayne, XV.
Osun, co. Devon, XIII.
Oswald, kynge of Northùmberlande, sainte and martyr, XV.
Oswaldwisle *or* Osewaldtwysel (manor of), Church, Whalley, XX; account of, XXII.
Oswaldwisle, Philip de, XXII.
Oswolde, saynt, brother of Ebba abbesse of Canwod, XV.
Oswy, kynge of Northùmberlande: legendary notices of, XV.
Otefeild *or* Otfeild, Mr., XVIII, XXVII.
Oter, Willmus, XX (?).
Otirpul, XX.
Otterburne, XIV.
Otter-hunting in the Ribble and Hodder, XIV.
Ottiwell, Mr., minister of Chelford, XXVII.
Otty, 𝔑, VIII.
Otway, 𝔑, XXII.
Otwell, Joseph, XIII.
Ouera, Robertus de, clericus, XX.
Oufle *or* Ouffle, Thomas, VIII.
Oughton, Richard, merchant at Leverpool, XXII.
Ouldham, J., VIII.
Oulton, Rog., citizen of London, VIII.
Oulton-low, township of Over, VIII.
Ousey, Ralph, XIX.
Ousle, water, XIV.
Outlone, XX (*tit* Croenton).
Outlone in Farington, XXX.
Outwood in Prestwich, XIX.
Over, co. Chester: account of, VIII.
Over, co. Cambridge, ancient font at, XIX.
Overall, John, dean of St. Paul's, XIII.
Overburrow, the ancient Bremetonacæ, XXII.
Overbury, 𝔑, I, XIV.
Overchurch, account of, VIII.
Over-eye, in Penwortham, annual value of, XXX.
Overforthe *or* Orford, near Warrington, XVII; lands and tenements in, XVII; chief rent of, XVII.
Overforthe-fylde, XVII; heath, XVII; lane, XVII.
Overleke. *See* Leck.
Overpool, township of Eastham, VIII.
Over th'fields *or* Oversfield, in Bury, XIX.
Overthorpe, in Thornhill, near Wakefield, XIV.
Overton, township of Frodsham, VIII.
Overton, township of Malpas, VIII.
Overton *or* Waterville, chapelry of, near Lancaster: account of, XXII.
Overton hall, Taxall, co. Chester: notice of, VIII.
Overton, Adam de, clericus, XX.
Ovid's *Epistles* studied by Martindale, IV.
Ovid's *Metamorph.*, extract from, XVIII.
Owen, 𝔑, II, XII, XIII, XVIII, XXII, XXVIII.
Oxburgh, colonel: his proceedings in the Jacobite rebellion, trial and execution, V.

Oxehouse, XX (*tit.* Whalleye).
Oxford, parliament at, VII; convocation at, VII, XIII.
Oxford university, IV, XIV; expenses at, XII; Christchurch college, IV, VIII; library, XIII.
Oxford act (the) against nonconformists, IV.
Oxford, earls of, V, XIV, XXIV.
Oxford's (Wilberforce bishop of) *Church in America*, XVIII.
Oxford Reasons about the Covenant, XVIII.
Oxheye woode, XX (*tit.* Whalleye).
Ox-houses and market in Holland, I.
Oxton, township of Woodchurch, VIII.

PACKE of old Puritans, a tract, IV.
Pack horses, conveyance by, IX.
Paddescroft, XX (*tit.* Spotlond).
Padiham, near Whalley, XIV; account of, XXII; punishment of witches at, VI.
Pagans, *viz.* Danes, Gotes, Norwayes, Scottes, Pictes and Wandels entre Englande to punysshe the decay of religion, XV.
Page, 𝔑, VIII, XVIII, XXVII.
Pageants, occasion of, III.
Paget, 𝔑, I, VIII, XVIII, XXII, XXIV, XXVII.
Paget's *Heresiography*, XIII.
Pagius, P. Franciscus: notice of, I.
Pagius *error for* Fagius, reformer: portrait of, I.
Pagnall, colonel, I.
Pagnell, Mr., XIII.
Painter, W., VIII.
Palatinate, princes of the, I.
Palatine Anthology, XXIX.
Paler, Mr., XXVII.
Palmer, 𝔑, II, VIII, XVIII.
Palsgrave (prince-elector) the, visits Cambridge, XIII.
Paman, 𝔑, XIII.
Pandish, pentice, XIV.
Panelling, napkin, XIV.
Pansophia and its philosophy, XIII.
Pantop, Willmus, XX.
Papæ (of Rome), XX, XXX.
Papes-milk (? poppy-juice), I.
Papillon, 𝔑, IX.
Papists, IV, XXIII; their condition at Amsterdam, I; number in Lancashire, II; dread of, II, IX, XXVII; literary forgeries and secret *Index Expurgatorius*, VII; premium on informations against, XXVIII.
Papworth and Papworth-Agnes, XIII.
Par, 𝔑, IX, XXVII.
Paracelsus, VI; his writings in the Byrom library, XIII.
Paradise-street, Liverpool, XII.
Paræus, XIII.
Parbold hall, Eccleston: notice of, XXII.
Parcival, Richard, slain at Manchester, II.
Parenesis by Dr. H[ammond], XVIII.
Pares, 𝔑, XXVII.
Parhelia seen at Bolton and Manchester, excitement caused by, II.
Paris, literary activity of, XIII.
Parishes and parish churches in diocese of Chester, XIX.
Park, Catharine wife of Richard, XXII.
Park, township of Ashton-under-Line, XIX.
Park (the), a farm near Wexford, I.
Parke, 𝔑, XVIII, XXIX.
Parkefylde, Orford near Warrington, XVII.
Parker, 𝔑, VI, VII, VIII, XIII, XIV, XIX, XX, XXII, XXVII, XXVIII, XXIX.
Parkes, William, XIV.
Park hall, in Barrow, VIII.
Park hall, in Blackrod, XIX.
Park house *or* The Parks, Alderley: account of, VIII.

Parkhead, XIII.
Park-head gate, Myerscough, XIV.
Parkhurst, Mr., XXVII.
Parkins, Edward, XXII.
Parkinson, 𝔑, VI, VIII, XII, XIV, XXII, XXVIII.
Parks, widow, IX.
Parliament (the long) in connexion with Lancashire, II, XIII; devastation committed by their troops, XIII.
Parliamentary History, IX, XVIII.
Parlor-hey, Liverpool, XII.
Parma (duke of) in the Low Countries, XXV.
Parme in Middlewich, VIII.
Parnas *or* Parnasim, a Jewish council, I.
Parnell, 𝔑, VIII, XXVII.
Parnella, Mogul camp at, IX.
Parr, 𝔑, VII, IX, XVII, XIX, XXII.
Parr's *Life of Ussher*, VII, XIII.
Parr hall, Prescot, XII; notice of, XXII.
Parre, 𝔑, VI, XVIII.
Parren, Mr., XVIII.
Parrok, a piece of land, XVII.
Parry, 𝔑, XIV, XXIV.
Parrys orchard, XX (*tit.* Whalleye).
Parsons, 𝔑, VII, XVIII, XXV, XXVII, XXVIII.
Parsons (country), low moral state of many, XIV.
Parson's-lane, VIII.
Parson-wages, XIX.
Partington, 𝔑, IV, VIII, XIX, XXVII.
Partington, township of Bowden, VIII; hall, notice of, VIII.
Partivants, Richard, XXII.
Partridge, Mr., IX.
Parvular, a Latin grammar, IV.
Parvyng, Robertus, cancellarius Edwardi III., XX.
Parysrod, XX (*titt.* Chadewyk, Spotlond).
Pascal, Blaise, XIII.
Paschal *or* Paschall, 𝔑, XIII, XVIII.
Pascy, Hugo de, XX.
Pask, R., XIII.
Paslew, 𝔑, XIX, XX, XXII.
Pasmethe *or* Pasmythe, 𝔑, IX, XVII.
Pasor's (George) *Syllabus*, IV.
Passage on Severn, I; on Waterford river, I; from England to Holland, I; Scotland to Ireland, I; Ireland to England I; over Waterford river, I.
Passelows, in Dagenham, co. Essex, XIV.
Passion, remedies against, XVIII.
Passmore, Mr., XXVII.
Passyonary, a boke wherin saynt Werburge's holy lyfe wryten is, XV.
Pate, 𝔑, XIII.
Patric, Robert, VIII.
Patricius *or* Patrik, 𝔑, XX.
Patrick, bishop: account of, XIII; his *Jewish Caveat*, &c., XVIII.
Patrick-Brompton, co. York: bishop's leases in, VIII.
Patrickson, 𝔑, VIII.
Patronage, church, XIV.
Patten, 𝔑, V, VIII, IX, XVII, XXII, XXVIII.
Patun, Richard, and his wife, XVII.
Paul, rev. William: account of, V.
Paul's (St.), cross, London, XIV.
Paulet, 𝔑, VIII, XXV.
Paulinus' crosses at Whalley, VI, XXII; at Burnley, XXII.
Paunell, Tho., incumbent of Cottingham, VIII.
Paunton, Panter, Pantous, Normannus de, XX.
Paviser and cross-bow man, XIV.
Paw, Jacob: his house and grounds, I.
Paybody, Geo., apparitor-general, VIII.
Paying up at Portfield, XIV.
Payments by and to H. Newcome, XVIII.
Payn, Hug., XX.
Paynsfylde, in Orford, near Warington, XVII.

Paytesin, Rad., xx.
Paytesingis, xx (*tit.* Whiteword).
Peace between England and Scotland, public thanksgiving for, xiii.
Peacock, 𝔉, iv, xxvii.
Peada, prynce of Mercyens, xv.
Peak, wonders of the, vii.
Peak, James, of Warrington, and his wife Katharine, xiii.
Peake, George, xxvii.
Pearce, Richard, xxvii.
Pearcyall, Fran., viii.
Pearson, 𝔉, vi, viii, xiii, xiv, xix, xxii.
Peasholme green, York, xiv.
Peaseley crosse, vi.
Peast, Robert, of Caldicot, xiii.
Pecham, Edm., viii.
Peche, 𝔉, bishops of Lichfield and Coventry, viii.
Pechlinus's *Observationes Physico-medicæ*, xiii.
Peck's *Desid. Cur.*, xii; *Memoirs*, xxiv.
Peckards' *Memoirs of Nicholas Ferrar*, xiii.
Peckforton, township of Bunbury, viii; hall, notice of, viii.
Peckforton, George, viii.
Peckham, xiii.
Pedder, James, vicar of Garstang, xxii.
Pede, Mr., xiii.
Peden, Alexander, imprisoned on Bass island, i.
Pedigrees of two witch families, vi.
Peel, 𝔉, viii, xxii.
Peel castle, in Walney: notice of, xxii.
Peel hall, Dean: notice of, xix.
Peel hall, Winwick: account of, xxii.
Peele, 𝔉, ix, xiv.
Peele hall, in Tarvin: notice of, viii.
Peers, election of kynge Ethelrede by, xv.
Pegge, Edward, of Ashburne, viii.
Peghteshulle, xx (*tit.* Croenton).
Peirce, 𝔉, viii, xiii.
Peiresc, Nicholas Claude Fabri de: account of, xiii.
Peirse, Dr., xviii.
Pekko, Robertus de, xx.
Pele, the, a family mansion of the Rixtons in Great Sankey, xvii.
Pelham, 𝔉, ix, xxv.
Pell, 𝔉, xiii, xxvii.
Pellstarts, water fowl, i.
Pemberton, 𝔉, ix, xii, xiii, xxii.
Pemberton-street, Liverpool, xii.
Pembroke, earls of, xiii, xiv, xxii, xxiv.
Pembroke hall, Cambridge, xiii, xix.
Pena, Johannes à, courts Dr. Dee's acquaintance, xxiv.
Penance, form of, in Scotland, i.
Penda, kynge of Mercyens: legendary account of, xv.
Pendennis castle, Cornwall, xiii.
Pendice *or* Pentice, the, Chester, viii.
Pendle cross, Newchurch, xxii.
Pendle forest, xiv, xxii; account of its inhabitants, vi.
Pendle hall, Padiham, xiv; notice of, xxii.
Pendle hill, xiii, xiv, xxii; description of, vii.
Pendlebury *or* Penhulbury, in Eccles, xix, xx.
Pendlebury *or* Penhulbury, 𝔉, xix, xx, xxvii.
Pendleton, 𝔉, xix, xxvii.
Pendleton, township of Eccles, xix; hall, notice of, xix.
Pendleton hall, Clitheroe, xiv, xxii.
Penhulton, in Eccles, xx.
Penigent, proverbial rhyme on, vii.
Penket, Mr., viii.
Penketh, 𝔉, ii, xvii, xx, xxii, xxx.
Penketh hall, Prescot: account of, xxii.
Penn, William: anecdote of, xxviii; his *Tracts*, xiii.

Pennant, 𝔓, XII, XXVIII.
Pennant's remark on the Done family, XIV; *Journey*, extract from, XXIV; *Tour to Alston moor*, XXIX.
Pennart Point, near Cardiff, I,
Penniless Pilgrimage by Taylor the water-poet, extract from, XIV.
Pennington, 𝔓, IV, VIII, IX, XII, XXII.
Pennington, account of, XXII; castle, notice of, XXII.
Pennington hall, Leigh: account of, XXII.
Penniston, co. York, IV.
Penny, 𝔓, XXII, XXVIII.
Penny-bridge hall, Ulverston: notice of, XXII.
Penny-come-quick *or* Smythick, co. Cornwall, XIII.
Penrhyn, co. Cornwall, XIII, XVIII.
Penrith, conduct of the insurgents at, V.
Penrith fell, cowardly behaviour of the militia at, V.
Pensby, township of Woodchurch, VIII.
Pensions offered to Rosworm by Manchester townsmen, XVIII.
Penwerdham, 𝔓, XXX.
Penwortham, XIV, XXX; account of, XXII; hall, notice of, XXII; church, XXII, XXX; priory, notices of, VIII, XXII.
Penyplokke, le, meadow in Orford near Warrington, XVII.
Penzance, XIII.
Peover, great- *and* little-, townships of lower Peover, VIII.
Peover, higher-, township of Rosthorn, VIII; hall, notice of, VIII.
Peover, lower-, IV; account of, VIII.
Peover, over-, XIV; account of, VIII.
Pepir, Thomas, XVII.
Peploe, 𝔓, V, XVIII, XIX, XXII.
Peppard, Henry, XXII.
Pepper, Mr., of Dover, XXVIII.
Pepys's *Diary*, XII, XIII, XVIII.
Percival *or* Percivall, 𝔓, VIII, IX, XII, XIII, XVIII, XIX, XXII, XXVII, XXVIII.
Percy, 𝔓, I, XIX, XX, XXIX.
Percy society, XXIX.
Perfect Diurnall, IX, XII.
Perfect Occurrences, IX.
Perfect Weekly Account, XII.
Perfit, a term of chase, XXIII.
Perkins, 𝔓, I, XIII, XXVIII.
Perkins's *Workes*, XVIII.
Perle, Reginaldus, XX.
Perpoint *or* Perpount, 𝔓, XIX, XX.
Perrin, J., VIII.
Perrot, 𝔓, VIII, XXV, XXVII.
Perry, 𝔓, VIII, XXII, XXVII.
Perry's *Map of Liverpool*, XII.
Pershall, 𝔓, VIII.
Pershull, Robertus, XXX.
Personelone, XX (*tit.* Cestria).
Persons, F. R., jesuit: sundry notices of, XXV.
Perth, I.
Perusson, 𝔓, XVII.
Perynsfylde in Warrington, XVII.
Pesfurlong hall, Winwick: notice of, XXII.
Petavius, XIII.
Petchora, town and river in Russia, VII.
Peter, bishop of Lichfield, removes the see to Chester, VIII, XV.
Peter's (abbot) *Account of Vale Royal Abbey*, anno 1336, VIII.
Peter, brother of Henry Newcome, XXVII.
Peter house, Cambridge, XIII.
Peter's pence fyrst given by Offa kynge of Mercyens, XV.
Peterborough, abbey of, founded by Wulfer kynge of Mercyens, XV.
Peterborough, bishop of: his interview with Newcome, XXVII.
Peterborough, earls of, IX, XIV.
Peters, 𝔓, I, IX, XII, XIII, XXVII.
Petit *or* Petitus, Samuel: his *Josephus* and *Collectanea*, XIII.

Petitions: from county of Lancaster to the king and to the commons, II; from recusants to the king, II; from lord Derby to Cromwell and to parliament, II.
Petræus, Theodorus, Oriental scholar: notice of, XIII.
Petre, 𝔑, XXII, XXVIII.
Pett, sir Peter, XIII; his *Remains of Dr. Thomas Barlow*, XIII.
Petty, 𝔑, XIII.
Peveril of the Peak, XIV.
Pezelius, Dr. Christopher: his verses to Dr. Dee, XXIV.
Philemon, XVIII.
Philip clericus, VIII.
Philipps, Peter, "one of the greatest masters of musick in Europe," XXV.
Philippus sacerdos, filius Baldwini, XXX.
Philips, Will., VIII.
Philips's (Edward) *Life of Milton*, XXIV.
Phillips, Francis, XIV.
Philobiblon Richardi Dunelmensis, notice of, VII.
Philosophical Transactions, particulars relating to, XIII.
Philpot, 𝔑, I, XXVII.
Phinlow, Mr., XXVII.
Phiton, Ric., XX.
Phœnix alley *and* street, Liverpool, XII.
Piccope, John, M.A., incumbent of Farndon, XIV, XIX.
Piccup, J. *See* Picup.
Pichot, 𝔑, VIII.
Pickering, 𝔑, VIII, XXII.
Pickersall, Thomas, and Ellen his wife, XIV.
Pickford, 𝔑, VIII, XVIII, XIX.
Pickthank, a flatterer or tale-bearer, XXIII.
Picmere *or* Pickmere, township of Budworth, VIII.
Picroft, Mr., XXVII.
Pictavensis, Rogerus, grants Childwall church to abbey of Sies, XXII; and Hocwike to Evesham monastery, XXX.
Picton hall, Plemondstall: notice of, VIII.
Pictor, 𝔑, XX.
Picts' wall (wall of Agricola), I.
Pictures in wax at Amsterdam, I.
Pictures of clay (witch spells), VI.
Picup *for* Piccup, J., XXII.
Piedmont, fast-day for the persecution of the protestants in, XIII.
Pierce, a surgeon, XIII.
Pierce bridge, over the Tees, I.
Pierrepont, Elizabeth, wife of William Pierrepont, M.P.: notice of, VIII.
Pierson, 𝔑, IV, VIII, XXVIII.
Piers Plowman, notice of, VII.
Pierucci, count, XIII.
Piggin, a sort of pail, VI.
Pighells, Daniel, of Marsden, clerke: his contract with the inhabitants of Todmorden, XIX.
Pigot, 𝔑, VIII, XIV, XVII, XIX, XXII.
Pigs and pig-eating, XIV.
Pike, Mr., XXVII.
Pike house, XIX; *Evidences*, XIX.
Pikeryng, Robertus de: his decree respecting Steyninges tithes, XX.
Pile of Fouldrey. *See* Peel castle.
Pile foundations at Amsterdam, description of, I.
Pilkington, 𝔑, VIII, IX, XVIII, XIX, XX, XXII, XXIX.
Pilkington hall, tower and park, XIX.
Pilling chapelry, Garstang: account of, XXII.
Pilot hull, Warrington, XVII.
Pilsworth, township of Middleton, XIX.
Pimlett, Michael, XXVII.
Pimlot, 𝔑, XXII.
Pincel, 𝔑, XX.
Pincerna, 𝔑, VIII, XVII, XX, XXII.

Pindar, extract from, with translation, XIV.
Pindar, ℞, VIII, XIII.
Pingmunfosgate in Farington, XXX.
Pinkey, battle of, IX.
Pinkney, Mr., XXVII.
Pinners, John, of Manchester, XIV.
Pipers, XIV.
Pirates or Turks between England and Ireland, dread of, I.
Pitcairne's *Criminal Trials*, extracts from, VI.
Pit hey, Liverpool, XII.
Pitman's edition of Lightfoot's *Works*, XIII.
Pits, Rochdale, XIX.
Pitsey hall, Essex, XIX (?).
Pitt, colonel, V.
Place, ℞, XIII, XXII.
Placita Coronæ, VI.
Plague (the) in London in 1625, IV; in 1665, IV, XXVII; — in Cambridge in 1637 and 1647, XIII; — in Manchester in 1645, II, IV, XVIII; in 1661, XVIII; — in Lancashire in 1648–49, II.
Plague, Kircher's theory of, XIII.
Plainfield, muster of the Northumbrian rebels at, V.
Plat, ℞, XVIII, XXVII.
Plat, XX (*tit.* Whalleye).
Platt, township of Manchester, XIX.
Platt, Gabriel: his *Discovery of Subterraneal Treasures*, XIII.
Players at Rotterdam, I; licensed companies of, attached to the Derby family, XXIX.
Playford, John, printer, IV.
Pleadings (Calendar of), in court of duchy of Lancaster, XIV.
Pleasington *or* Plesyngton, Blackburn, XX; hall *or* priory, notice of, XXII.
Pleasington *or* Plesyngton, ℞, XX, XXII.
Plemondstall *or* Plemstow, account of, VIII; the church belongs to St John's college, Chester, VIII.
Plempius, Vopiscus Fortunatus, physician: notice of, XIII.
Plewes, Thomas, of Tunstall, VIII.
Plomb *or* Plombe, ℞, IX, XXII.
Plome, ℞, XII.
Plompton, Robert, of Hale, IX.
Plot, popish *or* Oates's, XXVII; wh[o] was at the bottom of it, XIII.
Pluckington bank, Liverpool: fort on XII.
Plumbe, ℞, IX, XXII.
Plumley, township of lower Peover i[n] Budworth, VIII.
Plummer *or* Plummers, Andrew, I.
Plumpton, ℞, XIX, XXII.
Plumpton hall, Ulverston: notice o[f] XXII.
Plumtre, sir Wyllyam, clerke, XVII.
Plungeon, ℞, XVIII, XXVII.
Plunket, Henr., XXX (?).
Plunkney, Edw., VIII.
Plutarch's *Lives*, XIII.
Plymouth, XII, XIII; Kirby shot at IX; prisoners sent up to house o[f] commons from, XVIII.
Plymyard, township of Eastham, VIII
Pockett clocke, XIV.
Pococke, ℞, XIII, XXVII.
Podmore, Tho., XXVII.
Poictiers *or* Poictou, Roger earl of sundry notices of, XIX, XXII.
Point island, near Newcastle, I.
Pointon, co. Chester, XVIII.
Pointon, Richard, XXVII.
Poiret, Peter, XIII.
Poisonous herbs and tree, I.
Poland, IX; rebellion in, XIII; protestants of, *see* Cambridge, XIII.
Polimanteia, XXIX.
Pollard, Mr., and Margaret his wife, XIV
Pollexfen, Nicholas, M.P. for Bedwin IX.
Pollit, ℞, XIX.

Polyander, Johannes, professor of divinity at Leyden, I.
Polycronicon by Ralph Higden, notice of, XV.
Pomfret *or* Pontefract castle, capture of, IV.
Poniatovia *or* Poniatowski, Christina, a famous prophet, XIII.
Pont, Alice, wife of Dean Parker, XIV.
Ponte, Philippus de, XX.
Pontecardonis, Johannes fil. Ricardi de, XX.
Pontefract, Oliverus constabularius de, XX; priory of St. John of, VIII, XXII. *See* Pomfret.
Ponteleysing, XX (*tit.* Merland).
Pontewyk, Rob. de, XX.
Pool, 𝔑, VIII, XIII, XXII.
Pool (the), Liverpool, XII.
Pool bridge *and* house, Liverpool, XII.
Pool lane, Liverpool, IX; tenancies in, XII.
Pool *or* Poole hall, Eastham: notice of, VIII.
Poole, 𝔑, VIII, IX, XII, XVIII, XIX, XXV, XXVII, XXVIII.
Poole, co. York: dangerous ford near, IV.
Poole, nether- *and* over-, townships of Eastham, VIII.
Pooley, captain Richard, XXII.
Poolton, township of Pulford, co. Chester, VIII.
Poolton in the Fylde, account of, XXII.
Poor, relief of, in Holland, I.
Poor Knight's Palace of Pleasures, probable author of, XXIII.
Poore, 𝔑, VII, XX.
Poosey, chapelry of Runcorn: account of, VIII.
Pope, 𝔑, VIII, XIII, XIV.
Pope, infallibility of the, I.
Pope Joan, Blondel's able tract on, XIII.
Popes of Rome. *See* Papæ.
Popery in Ireland, I.
Popish impostures in Gloucester cathedral, I.
Porden, Mr., of Chester, designs Eccleston church, VIII.
Port, sir John, of Etwall, and Elizabeth his daughter, XXII.
Portefeylde, XX (*tit.* Whalleye).
Portents in England of the Danish invasion, XV.
Porter, 𝔑, IX, XIII, XVIII, XIX, XXII, XXVII, XXVIII.
Portfield, near Whalley, XIV.
Portland, XIII.
Portland, lord, XXVIII.
Portpatrick, I.
Portraits of the reformers at Bishop's Auckland, I; various, XIV.
Portugal, IX; Don Emanuel prince of, I; Catherine infanta of, XIII.
Portway, XX (*tit.* Staneye).
Posset, a drink, XIV.
Possevine, Antonie, jesuit, VII.
Postellus, Gulielmus, courts Dr. Dee's acquaintance, XXIV.
Post-horses and posting, XII.
Postlethwaite, Will., XXII.
Pot Shrigley, township of Macclesfield, VIII.
Pots, Thomas, XXVII.
Pott, Thomas, master of the hunt to James I.: his fee, XIV.
Pott chapelry, Macclesfield: account of, VIII.
Potter, 𝔑, II, XIII, XVIII.
Potter's *Discourse of the Number* 666, XVIII.
Potterruydyng, XX (*tit.* Bilyngton).
Pottinger hey, Liverpool, XII.
Potto, Mr., XIII.
Potts, Thomas, VI; his *Discoverie of Witches*, VI, XIII, XIV.
Poulton. *See* Poolton *and* Pulton.
Poulton, Andrew: notice of, XXVIII.
Poulton-cum-Spittell, VIII.

Pountchardon, Ricardus de, xx.
Povey, Ch., viii.
Powell, 𝔑, viii, xiv, xix, xxiv, xxviii.
Powis, 𝔑, viii, xxviii, xxix.
Pownall, 𝔑, viii.
Pownall-fee, in Wilmslow, viii.
Powney, Mrs., xiii.
Poynton, chapelry of Prestbury, xiv; account of, viii.
Pracer, Mr., xxviii.
Praers, 𝔑, viii.
Pranck, to dress ostentatiously, xxiii.
Pratellis, Joh. de, xx.
Prat rowe, Warrington, xvii.
Prayer to get drink, form of, vi.
Prayer and praying, presbyterian, xviii.
Prayer Book, preface to, xiv.
Prayers "priores et posteriores in comitiis" at Cambridge, xiii.
Preachars, pryntars and players: proclamation for redresse of, xxix.
Preedy, 𝔑, xxii.
Prees, William de, xx, xxii.
Prees hall, Kirkham: notice of, xxii.
Prees *or* Pratis, abbey of St. Mary de, xxii.
Preeson *or* Preison, 𝔑, ix, xii.
Preeson-street, Liverpool, xii.
Preestesplattford, xx (*tit.* Eccles).
Preket, 𝔑, ix.
Prendergrasse, Simon, an Irish rebel captain, i.
Prenton, township of Woodchurch, viii; hall, notice of, viii.
Prenton in Wirrall, xii.
Prenton, Robert; his conduct to Edward Moore of Bank hall, xii.
Presbyterians, their conduct and system, ii, iv, v, xii, xviii; Henry Stubbe's reasons for hating, xiii.
Prescot, co. Lanc., ii, iv, ix, xiv, xix; account of, xxii.
Prescot *or* Prescott, 𝔑, viii, xii, xix, xxii.
Prescott's *Journal*, xix.
Presenting, a child-birth custom, xiv
President of the Marches of Wales, i
President (lord) of the North, xiv.
Prestbury, account of, viii; remain of an ancient priory at, viii.
Prestecot, 𝔑, xx.
Prestland family, ancient seat of the, viii
Presto-lee, in Prestwich, xix.
Preston, iv, vi, ix, xii, xviii, xx, xxx condition of during the Civil war ii; siege and capture of, v; genera account of, xxii; corporation of xiv; Magdalen hospital and Greyfriars' convent, notice of, xxii.
Preston, History of, xiv.
Preston moor, royalist meeting on, ii.
Preston on the hill, township of Daresbury, co. Chester, viii.
Preston, 𝔑, ii, v, vi, viii, ix, xii, xiv, xviii, xx, xxii, xxvii, xxviii, xxx.
Prestwich, near Manchester, xiii, xviii; account of, xix.
Prestwich, 𝔑, ii, xiv, xix, xx.
Price, 𝔑, viii, xxii, xxiv.
Pricker, a huntsman's attendant, xiv.
Pride, colonel, ii, xii, xviii.
Prideaux, 𝔑, xiii, xxiv.
Priest, Jo., xiii.
Priests and jesuits, their ordinary character, vi.
Priestley, Henry, vi.
Priket, Johannes fil. Roberti, de Pontefracto, xx.
Prikkeschagh, rivulus de, xx.
Primate, Rich., viii.
Prince, Charles Edward, xiv.
Prince, Mary, xviii.
Pringall, Mr., xxvii.
Prior, 𝔑, ix, xii, xxvii.
Priors orchard, xx (*tit.* Whalleye).
Priorshays, township of Tarvin, viii.
Prisly, 𝔑, xiii.
Prisoners at the Jacobite trials, list of, xxviii.

Prisoners, political: treatment of, V, XXVIII.
Private Intelligence, XXVII.
Probert, J., VIII.
Proby, alderman, IX.
Proclamation against conventicles, IV.
Proctor *or* Proctour, 𝔑, XXII, XXIII.
Proctors orchard, XX (*tit.* Whalleye).
Proctors stable, (*tit.* Whalleye).
Procurations, origin of, XIX.
Professyon of saynt Werburge, XV.
Promises of critics and philologers, XIII.
Protestants in Ireland, massacre of, XII; in Piedmont, persecutions of, XIII; in Poland and Germany, collections for, XIII.
Proudlove, George, XXVII.
Proverbs, XV, XXIII; rhyming, VII; collections of, XIII.
Providence, remarkable instances of trust in, XXVII.
Provincial assembly, meeting of the, at Preston, XXVII.
Provost, Mr., XIII.
Prowde, Joseph, XXVII.
Prudhom, Willmus, XX.
Prynne, William, XXVII; account of, IV.
Prytanæum a desideratum in England, XIII.
Psalms, XXIII.
Psalm-singing, XIV.
Puckeridge, co. Herts., XIV.
Pudsay, 𝔑, XIV.
Puenton, manor of, VIII.
Pues *or* pews in churches before the Reformation, XIV.
Pugh, Mr., XXVIII.
Pughull, litel *and* mikel, XX (*tit.* Whiteword).
Pugin, (A. W.) improves Scarisbrick hall, XXII.
Pul, XX (*tit.* Ynes).
Puleston, 𝔑, VIII.
Pulford, co. Chester; account of, VIII; Pulton abbey in, VIII.
Pulford *or* Pulforthe, 𝔑, VIII, XVII, XX.
Pulle, 𝔑. XX.
Pullen, Mr., XIII.
Puller, Mr., XIII.
Pulley, Richard, XXII.
Pulpit Conceptions, XVIII.
Pulpit-cushion grievance, XXVII.
Pultney, Daniel, M.P., XXII (?).
Pulton chapel, Pulford: account of, VIII.
Pulton parish, XX, XXII.
Pulton, 𝔑, XX.
Pun, to pound, I.
Puncerline, Hubertus, XX.
Punishment of petty larceners at Delft, I.
Punterlynk, Wrenous, XX.
Purcell, Hug., XX.
Purgatory, saynt Werburge releashed from peynes of, XV.
Puritans and puritanism, XII, XIV, XVIII; poetical satire upon, XIV.
Pursel *or* Pursell, 𝔑, XXVII, XXVIII.
Purser, William, I.
Pursle, pursy, fat, I.
Purvey, serjeant-major, prisoner at Preston storm, II.
Putington, Adam de, XX.
Pye, 𝔑, IX, XIII, XXII.
Pyghull, origin and meaning of the word, XVII.
Pyghyll, XX (*tit.* Whalleye).
Pygmæi, meaning of, in the Vulgate, XIII.
Pygott, John, XVII.
Pyke, 𝔑, XIII, XVIII, XIX, XXVII.
Pykering, sir William, knt., XXIV.
Pyketakyr, in Warrington, XVII.
Pykton, Ellen, XVII.
Pym, John, IX, XII.
Pyncel, Walterus, XX.
Pyngernun, Willus, XX.
Pynson, Willmus, XX.

Pynynton, Rob., xxx.
Pyrites, I.

QUADRYBURGE, wyfe of Edwyn kynge of Northumberlande, xv.
Quails kept in cages, I.
Quakers, IV, XVIII, XXVII.
Qualleye *for* Whalley, XXII.
Quarlton, township of Turton, XIX.
Quarterly Review, XIV.
Quarterly (British) Review, XIV.
Quatremares, Colinus de, XX.
Quaue, XX (*tit.* Liuesay).
Queen Henrietta Maria's political conduct, II.
Queen's college, Cambridge, and its obligations to Dr. Worthington, XIII.
Queen-street, Liverpool, XII.
Queenborough castle, notice of, I.
Quelot, Rich., and his wife: monument of, in Sandbach church, VIII.
Querela Cantabrigiensis, XII.
Quernmore foresta, peramb., XX.
Quetenne Halewes, an ancient name of Vale Royal, VIII.
Quicke, Robert, IX.
Quikleswyk, ℞, XX.
Quinquatria, feasts of Pallas, give origin to Christmas mummers, XIV.
Quirry, *i.e.* quarry, a square enclosure for slaughtered game, XXIII.
Quityngton, Henricus de, XX.
Quoisley in Marbury, Whitchurch, VIII.
Quyke, ℞, XX.
Qwyteakyr (le), in Orford near Warrington, XVII.

RABY, township of Neston, VIII.
Race, meaning and etymology of, VII.
Rachdale, church of, VIII; rectory and vicarage, XIV.
Rache, fluv., XX.
Rachedale, XX; ecclesia de, XX.
Rachedale, capellani, vicarii et persona de, XX.
Racing matches, XIV.
Racoczi, the princes, XIII.
Radcliffe, account of, XIX; tower, notice of, XIX.
Radcliffe *or* Radeclyf, ℞, II, V, VIII, IX, XIII, XIV, XVIII, XIX, XX, XXII, XXVII, XXVIII, XXX.
Raddeswell, Robertus de, archidiaconus Cestrie, XX.
Raddeswoth *error for* Reddewoth, Liulphus, XX.
Radford, ℞, IV, VIII.
Radley, ℞, II, XXII.
Radulfus, capellanus, XXX.
Radyche, Thomas, XVII.
Ragotzi and his army, XIII.
Raikes, Henry, chancellor of Chester, VIII.
Rakediche, XX (*tit.* Bacford).
Raines *or* Rayner, Thomas, VIII.
Rainford, near Prescot: account of, XXII; school, IV.
Rainford, Edward, XXII.
Rainford-street, Liverpool, XII.
Rainow, township of Prestbury, VIII.
Rairke, John, XIV.
Raleia, XXX.
Raleigh, sir Walter, XIII, XXV, XXIX; his belief in witchcraft, VI.
Ralph's *Other Side the Question*, IX.
Ramillies, battle of, IX.
Ramists, writings of the, XIII.
Ramkellecroft, villa de, XXX.
Ramsay *or* Ramsey, ℞, XIV, XIX.
Ramsbottom, James, XIX.
Ramsden, ℞, VI, XIV, XIX, XXVII.
Ramside *alias* Ramstead, chapelry of Dalton: account of, XXII.
Ramus, Peter, mathematician, XXIV; notice of, IV.
Ranconetus, XXIV.
Rand's (Dr. W.) translation of Gassendi's *Life of Peiresc*, XIII.

Randall, Mrs., xxvii.
Rands, Mr., xxvii.
Ranelagh, lord, ix.
Ranelagh, Catherine viscountess: account of, xiii.
Ranicars, John, of Atherton, xxii.
Ranke's *Reformation*, xviii.
Ranow, township of Macclesfield, viii. *See* Rainow.
Rant, Roger, xxii.
Ranulphus, clericus, xxx.
Ranulphus *or* Radulphus Higden, author of the *Polycronycon*, xv.
Rape mills at Swammerdam and Bristol, i.
Rappahannock river, Virginia, ix.
Raphal (M. J.) and De Sola's translations from the *Mishna*, xiii.
Rasbotham's (Dorning) *MSS.*, xix, xxii.
Raskelf, co. York, viii.
Ratchdale, account of, xix.
Ratchdalle, xiv.
Ratcliff *for* Redcliffe, near Bristol, xiii.
Ratcliff *or* Ratcliffe, 𝔉, iv, ix, xii, xiv, xviii, xxii, xxv.
Rathband, 𝔉, xiii, xviii, xxvii.
Rathbande, 𝔉, xix.
Rathbone, Mrs., xviii.
Rathmell house, near Settle, xiv.
Ratio Disciplinæ Fratrum Bohemorum, best edition of, xiii.
Rauenesmeles, villa de, xx.
Rauensholme, xx (*tit.* Dounom).
Raufflat, xx (*tit.* Cliderhou).
Raufhe, Mr., a preacher, xiv.
Raughrick *or* Rathlin, sound of, i.
Rauil, Willmus de, xx.
Ravald, 𝔉, xix.
Ravenscroft, township of Middlewich, viii; hall, account of, viii.
Ravenscroft, 𝔉, viii.
Rawcliffe, out- *and* upper-, townships of St. Michael's-upon-Wyre, xxii; halls, account of, xxii; school, account of, xxii.
Rawlins, 𝔉, ix, xxvii.
Rawlinson, 𝔉, xxii, xxvii.
Rawlinson MSS., xxix.
Raworth, Fr., xiii.
Rawrydinge, in Warrington, xvii.
Rawsthorne, 𝔉, xiv, xix.
Rawstone, Mrs., xxvii.
Rawstorne, 𝔉, ii, xxii, xxviii.
Ray, John: account of, xiii.
Raydale *or* Rydale, co. York, xiv.
Raydale house, Wensleydale: attack upon by sir Thomas Metcalfe, xiv.
Raydale side, tradition at, xiv.
Raynaud, Theophilus: his learned disquisition whether good angels can appear in woman's shape, xiii.
Raynford, 𝔉, ix.
Read, 𝔉, ii, xxvii.
Read hall, Padiham: account of, xxii.
Reade, co. Lanc., vi.
Reade, Roger, xxvii.
Reader, office of, xiv. *See* Reading wages.
Reader, alderman Enoch, xxvii.
Reading, co. Berks., xiii.
Reading wages, explanation of, viii.
Ready, John, viii.
Rebel officers, list of, xxviii.
Rebels or banditti in Ireland, i.
Rechat, a musical hunting call, xxiii.
Record, Robert, arithmetician, iv.
Recreation, honest: Lancashire specimens of, xiv.
Rectorship of Liverpool, contest for, ix.
Recusants' (popish) petition for restoration of arms, ii.
Redcliffe church, Bristol, i (p. 178). *See* Ratcliff.
Reddish, 𝔉, viii, xviii, xix, xxvii.
Reddish, township of Manchester, xix; hall, account of, xix.

Reddish hall, Grappenhall: notice of, VIII.
Redebrok, le, XX. *See in same volume* Chadewyk *and* Spotlond.
Rede-erthe, Orford, near Warrington, XVII.
Redeferne, XX (*tit.* Spotlond).
Redesdale, lord, XIV.
Redfern, in Rochdale: notice of, XX.
Redfern family, VI; trial of Ann Redfern for witchcraft, VI.
Rediche, Rob. de, XX.
Redish, captain, XXVIII.
Redkar, XX (*tit.* Merton).
Redman, 𝔑, XIV, XXVIII.
Redmayn, 𝔑, XXII.
Red stones near Liverpool, marking the bounds between Mersey and Dee, XII.
Redwald of eest England, a Chrysten prynce, XV.
Reed, Isaac, XIII.
Reet, Richard, XXII.
Reeve, 𝔑, IX, XIII.
Reeves, Richard, a trowman of Shrewsbury, I.
Reeves's *Ecclesiastical Antiquities of Down, Connor and Dromore*, XIX.
Regency bill, IX.
Regeneration by baptism, XV.
Regge (? Leghe) John, VIII.
Regicides, Speeches and *Booke of the*, XVIII.
Register (old) at collegiate church, Manchester: extract from, XVIII.
Registrars to rural deaneries, VIII.
Reimmannus, incorrect judgment of, XIII.
Reinberke, Holland, I.
Reinfrid, Gilbert Fitz-, and Helewise his wife, XXII.
Reinolds, Mary, XXVII.
Reio, W. de, prior Lancastrie, XX.
Religious ceremonies in Holland and Scotland, I.
Religious dramas, notice of, III.
Religious houses, VIII.
Religious (early) impressions of Henry Newcome, XVIII.
Relique of St. Laurence's head in Croston church, XXII.
Reliques of saynt Werburge, myracles worked by the, XV.
Reliquiæ Bodleianæ, VII.
Remarks on English Churches by J. H. Markland, XXII.
Remi, father, XIII.
Remigius, VI.
Remonstrance to the King by the ministers of London, XVIII.
Renaudot's *Conférences Publiques*, XIII.
Renouvier's (Ch.) *Manuel de la Philosophie Moderne*, XIII.
Rent in Ireland, I.
Rental of the Holland estates, XVIII.
Repton abbay, legendary notices of, XV.
Resbury, Mr., XXVII.
Resolutions and ordinances of 1641–49, XVIII.
Respublica by sir John Prestwich, XIX.
Restoration Sermon by H. Newcome, XVIII.
Retchless, reckless, XXIII.
Retrospect of mercies vouchsafed to Newcome, XVIII.
Retrospective Review, essay on health-drinking in, XVIII.
Reued, villa de, XX.
Reued, 𝔑, XX.
Revels at Hoghton, description of, XIV.
Reyneford, Radulphus de, XX.
Reyner, Will., XXVII.
Reyneuill, Thom. de, XX.
Reynolds, 𝔑, VI, IX, XII, XIII, XIX, XXVII.
"Rheum the chancellor," writes letters to John Bruen, XIV.
Rhodes, in Outwood, Prestwich, XIX.
Rhodes, 𝔑, XVIII, XXVII.
Ribbelhill, XX (*tit.* Cliderhou).

Ribble bridge abandoned by the rebels, V.
Ribble, river, VIII, XVII; early defences of, II; decrease of otters in, XIV.
Ribble, water of, VI.
Ribblesdale, Lister lord, XIV.
Ribblechester, ancient designation of Ribchester, XXII.
Ribchester, II; account of, XXII; bishop's leases in, VIII.
Riblecestre, XX.
Riblecestria, 𝔑, XX.
Ribs: women have one more than men, I.
Ribstone moor, loss of life upon, I.
Rical, Henr. de, XX.
Ricardus, 𝔑, XXX.
Rice, James, XXII.
Rich, 𝔑, I, IX, XIII, XXV.
Rich Treasure, XVIII.
Richard III., XIV; his promise to lord Stanley, XXIX.
Richard, second earl of Chester: legendary account of, XV.
Richard, monk of Bec, first abbot of St. Werburge, VIII, XV.
Richard, the hermit of Warrington, XVII.
Richards, Catherine, of Strangeways: her will and charities, XIX.
Richardson, 𝔑, I, IV, XIII, XIV, XVIII, XIX, XXII, XXVII.
Richardson's *Life of Milton*, XXIV.
Richelieu, cardinal, XIII.
Richemundie, Henricus, archidiaconus, XX.
Richerop, John, XVII.
Richmond, archdeaconry of, XXII; its extent, VIII, XXII; manor of, XIV.
Richmond, co. Surrey, XXIV; palace built upon the plan of Lathom house, XIV.
Richmond, Ludovic earl and duke of, XIV.
Richmond, Margaret countess of, XXII.
Richmond, 𝔑, VIII, IX, XII, XXII.
Richmond-street, Liverpool, XII.
Richmondshire, Whitaker's *History of*, XIV.
Rickmansworth, co. Herts., XIII.
Ricula of Kent, maried to Fledde kynge of Estsex and Mydylsex, XV.
Riddell, Edward, of Swinburne castle, and Dorothy his wife, XXII.
Rideng, Petrus, IX.
Rider, Rich., dep. reg., Lichfield, VIII.
Ridge, Mr., XVIII, XXVII.
Ridge hall, notice of, XXIII.
Ridge-hill, township of Ashton-under-Line, XIX.
Ridges, Mr., XVIII.
Ridgway, 𝔑, VIII, XIX.
Riding, 𝔑, XII.
Ridley, township of Bunbury, VIII; hall, account of, VIII.
Ridley pool *or* mere, XXIII.
Ridley, 𝔑, I, XXII, XXVII.
Rigby *or* Rigbye, 𝔑, II, VII, IX, XII, XIII, XIV, XVIII, XIX, XXII, XXVIII.
Rigby- *or* Ribby-cum-Wray, chapelry of Kirkham: account of, XXII.
Rigby street, Liverpool, XII.
Rigley, John, IX.
Rigmayden, 𝔑, XXII.
Riley *or* Ryley, 𝔑, XIII, XIV.
Rimbault's (Dr.) edition of Roger North's *Memoirs of Music*, XIII.
Rimer, Mr., XII.
Rimmer, 𝔑, XII.
Rimmer street, Liverpool, XII.
Rimour, Ric. le, XX.
Ringey, in Hale, Bowden, VIII.
Ringley, chapelry of Prestwich: account of, XIX.
Ringsend point, Dublin bay: description of, I.
Ringwood, co. Hants., XIII.
Rinuccini, XII.
Ripley, Simon, twenty-third abbot of St. Werburge: notice of, VIII.

Ripon, diocese of, VIII; consecration of monastery and church of, XXII.
Rippon, John, XXII.
Rischeflat, XX (*tit.* Aluetham).
Risenhalgh, XX (*tit.* Spotlond).
Rishton, 𝔑, XIX, XXII.
Rising of sir George Booth, XVIII.
Risley, 𝔑, IX, XXII.
Risley hall, Winwick: notice of, XXII.
Rissilache, XX (*tit.* Bilyngton).
Rither, Mr., of Wapping, IV.
Ritson's *Bibliotheca Poetica*, XXIX.
Riveley, Mr., XIII.
Rivers, earls, II, VIII, IX, XII.
Rivers *or* Ripariis, John, dominus Aungre, VIII.
Rivington, chapelry of Bolton: account of, XIX; hall, notice of, XIX.
Rivington, 𝔑, XIX.
Rixton, township of Warrington, XXII; chapel, XXII; hall, account of, XXII.
Rixton, 𝔑, XVII, XX, XXII.
Ro, a field in Penwortham, XXX.
Road *and* North Road, in Prestbury, VIII.
Roades, Frances, XXII.
Roads in Lancashire, bad state of, IX.
Robberies, XIII.
Robelogh, XX (*tit.* Wythenhull).
Robert duke of Normandy, tomb of, I.
Robert, old, servant of John Bruen: his perfect character, XIV.
Roberte feylde, XX (*tit.* Whalleye).
Roberts, 𝔑, IX, XIII, XIX, XXVIII.
Robertson, 𝔑, XIII, XXII.
Robertus, frater: notice of, XIII.
Robertus Pincerna, notice of, VIII.
Robey, Isobel, tried for witchcraft, VI.
Robin Hood well, XIV.
Robinson, 𝔑, II, VI, VIII, XII, XIII, XIV, XVIII, XIX, XXII, XXIII, XXIV, XXVII, XXVIII.
Roboas wrought in arras, XV.
Roby, 𝔑, XVII, XXVIII.
Roby's *Traditions of Lancashire*, XIX; sir Walter Scott's inaccurate reference to, VI.
Rochdale, IX, XIV, XVIII; general account of, XIX; garrisoned by the Manchesterians, II; arrest of sir John Bland at, XVIII; woollen trade of, IV, VII; "rectory" of, XVIII. *See* Rachdale *and* Ratchdale.
Rochdale Manor, Heath's *Survey of*, XIV.
Roche family, I.
Rocherake, XX (*tit.* Gerstan).
Roches croft, in Backford, VIII.
Rochester, XIII.
Rochester, lords, IX, XVIII.
Rochester, bishop of, XXVII.
Rochets, puritanical dislike to, XIV.
Rocks, ringing and deaf, I.
Rock-Savage, duke of Monmouth comes to, IV.
Rodbertus, 𝔑, XXX.
Rodd, Mr., bookseller: his curious purchase of a rare volume, XXIII.
Rode, 𝔑, VIII, XIX.
Rodelent, 𝔑, VIII.
Rodes, sir Edward, II.
Rodney Stoke, co. Somerset, I.
Roe, 𝔑, I, XIV, XXII.
Roelent, Matthew de: notice of, VIII.
Roger, bishop of Lichfield, XIX.
Rogerashes, XX (*tit.* Whalleye).
Rogers, 𝔑, I, III, VIII, XIII, XVIII, XXIX.
Rogerson, 𝔑, II, XII.
Rogertson, 𝔑, XXII.
Rogerus, 𝔑, XXX.
Rohan, monsieur de, XXIV.
Rokeby, Thomas, justice K.B., XXVIII.
Rokedene chapel, Winwick, XXII.
Rolleston, co. Stafford, XIV, XVIII.
Rollins, 𝔑, IX.
Rollock, Robert: account of, I.
Rolls, Dr., XXVII.
Rolls, searching the, IX.

Rolt, 𝔑, XIII, XXVII.
Roman catholics *and* Romanists, XIV, XVIII; their condition and conduct during the Jacobite rebellion, V. *See* Papists.
Roman encampment at Whalley, XIV.
Roman history songe by a mynstrell, XV.
Roman roads, notices of, VII.
Roman wall. *See* Picts' wall.
Romanus, John, archdeacon of Richmond, XXII.
Rome, XIII.
Romely manor, Stockport, VIII.
Romilly, sir Samuel, XIV.
Romilly's *or* Rumbles moor, in Craven, VI.
Romish church, errors and corruptions of, VII.
Romney, lord, IX.
Romsey, XIII.
Romswinckel, Joh. Hermannus, XIII.
Ronconer *or* Roncore, XX.
Rood, chapel de, Tarporley, VIII.
Roodee *or* Rood-eye, Chester: etymology of the name, III.
Rooke, 𝔑, VIII, IX, XIII.
Rooks, John, of Scotton, VIII.
Rooksby, Mrs., XXVII.
Rookwood, trial of, IX, XXVIII.
Roomer, Frische, wife of twenty-four husbands, I.
Roontry, John son of Elizabeth, VIII.
Roos, William lord: accusation of incest against, XIV.
Root, 𝔑, I, XVIII.
Roote, 𝔑, IV, XXII.
Rootes, 𝔑, XVIII, XIX, XXVII.
Roots, John, XVIII.
Rope, township of Wibunbury, VIII.
Rope, Laurence de, VIII.
Roper, Robert, IX.
Ros, William de, of Ingmanthorpe, XXII.
Roscarick, lieut.-colonel, governor of Appleby, II.
Roscoe, 𝔑, IX, XVII, XXII, XXVIII.
Roscow, James, shorthand writer at the earl of Derby's execution, II.
Roscow family, of Great Lever near Bolton, II.
Rose, 𝔑, XII, XIII.
Rose theatre held by Lord Strange's company, XXIX.
Rosemary lane, Liverpool, XII.
Rosas, in Catalonia: wager respecting, IX.
Roses, emblems of spiritual victory, XV.
Rosicrucians, account of the, XIII.
Ross, Ireland, I; sagacious procedure of the mayor of, I.
Ross, 𝔑, XIII, XXII.
Rossall hall, Poulton in the Fylde: account of, XXII.
Rosse hall, Bispham, XXII.
Rossendale, forest and chace of, XXII; license to hawk in, XX.
Rostern *or* Rosterne, 𝔑, XVIII, XXVII.
Rosthorne, co. Chester: account of, VIII; Adam Martindale's connexion with, IV.
Rosworm, lieut.-colonel John, XVIII; his conduct during the Civil war, II; extract from his *Complaint*, VII.
Roter, Peter and Randle le, VIII.
Rothbury, Northumbrians and Scots assemble at, V.
Rothelisden, XX (*tit.* Stanword).
Rotheram, co. York, IV.
Rotheram, Thomas, archbishop of York, I, VIII, XXII; his college, VIII, XXII.
Rotheram, 𝔑, I.
Rotherstone. *See* Rosthorne.
Rothstern *or* Rawsthorne, colonel, IV.
Rothwell, 𝔑, VIII, XIV, XIX, XXII, XXVIII.
Rotterdam, XIII; description of, I.
Roucester, priory of St. Mary at, VIII.
Roudestorn, Ricardus de, clericus, XX.
Roughcloghhull, XX (*tit.* Whiteword).
Rougheye, XX (*tit.* Whalleye).

Rough Lee in Pendle, description of, VI.
Roughlee, XIV (?).
Roughslakhull, XX (*tit.* Whiteword).
Roule, sir Richard, reader of Coniston, XIV, XXII.
Rouleghclogh, XX (*tit.* Harwod).
Roundhead, a weapon so called, II.
Rous, ℜ, IV, XXII, XXX.
Rous's *Northerne Subscribers' Plea*, IV.
Rouse, John, keeper of the Bodleian library, VII.
Routandeclogheued, XX (*tit.* Stanword).
Routhelesden, XX.
Routhescroft, XX (*tit.* Bacford).
Row, ℜ, IX, XII, XVIII.
Rowcroft, J., VIII.
Rowe, ℜ, VIII, XXII, XXVII.
Rowe moor, XIV.
Rowles, Francis, XIII.
Rowleson, John, XXVII.
Rowley, ℜ, I, XXIV.
Rowley hall, Burnley: account of, XXII.
Rowse, John, alderman of London, II.
Rowson, ℜ, XXVII.
Rowton, township of Chrisleton, VIII; heath, XVIII.
Rowyngton, Cecilia de, XX.
Rowyscroft, XX (*titt.* Bacford, Staneye).
Roxburgh, sir Robert Ker earl of: notice of, I.
Roxburgh club, XXIX.
Royal-oak list, XII.
Royal society, notices of and account of its origin, XIII.
Royds, ℜ, VIII, XIX, XXII.
Royle, Mr., VIII.
Royle hall, Burnley, XIV; notice of, XXII.
Royston, co. Herts., XIII, XIV.
Royton *or* Ryton, township of Oldham, IX, XIX; hall, account of XIX.
Ruacre, Willus de, XX.
Ruarus's (Martin) *Correspondence*, XIII.
Rubric, violation of the, XIV.
Ruddeby, Petrus de, XX.
Ruddegate, XX (*tit.* Croenton).
Rudheath, sanctuary at, VIII.
Rudyard, Anth., XVIII.
Ruelent *or* Roelent, Matthew de: notice of, VIII.
Rufford *or* Rufforth, township and chapelry of Croston: account of, XXII; hall, description of, XXII.
Ruffyn, saynt, brother of saynt Werburge: legendary account of, XV.
Rufus, ℜ, XX.
Rugeley, Luke, M.D., XIII.
Rugg (captain) and his great bottle nose, I.
Rughehaye, XX (*tit.* Eston).
Rugheued, XX (*tit.* Croenton).
Rugheyes, XX (*tit.* Halghton).
Rughschaghbrok, XX (*tit.* Acton).
Ruhlie. *See* Rowley hall.
Rulice, Mr., XIII.
Rullos, Richard de, VIII.
Rump parliament, notices of, IV, XXVII.
Rumword, villa de, XX.
Rumworth, township of Dean, XIX; school, account of, XIX.
Runcorn, XVII; built by Elflede daughter of kyng Alured, XV; general account of, VIII; priory, account of, VIII.
Runcorn, Samuel, VIII.
Runic inscription on font in Chipping church, XXII.
Running pump, Warrington, XVII.
Rupert, prince, I, IV, XIII, XIV, XVIII; his conduct of the war in Cheshire and Lancashire, II; barbarity at Liverpool, XII.
Rural deans, VIII.
Rushall hall in Golborn, Tattenhall: notice of, VIII.
Rush bearing, XIV.
Rushen (abbey of St. Mary of), isle of Man: notice of, XXII.

Rusholme *or* Rusham, township of Manchester, xix.
Rushout, James, xxviii.
Rushton in Tarporley, viii.
Rushton 𝔑, vi, xxii.
Rushworth, ix, xii, xviii.
Rusland, township of Cartmel: St. Paul's chapel in, xxii.
Russel, 𝔑, i, viii, ix, xii, xx, xxv, xxvii.
Russum, xx.
Rust, George: account of, xiii.
Rutland, Edward Manners earl of, and Elizabeth his daughter, xiv.
Rutter, Samuel, bishop of Man: notice of, ii.
Rutyngesik, xx (*tit.* Whelton).
Ruyl *or* Ruyll, 𝔑, xvii, xx.
Ruyssheton, 𝔑, xx.
Rycot, xiv.
Rycroft, 𝔑, viii, xxii, xxvii.
Rydeng, Johannes, ix.
Ryder, 𝔑, xvii, xxii.
Ryding, Richard, xxii.
Rydings, Fra., xxvii.
Rydyngfelde in Farington, xxx.
Ryfield farm, viii.
Rygmaden, John, xxii.
Ryland *or* Rylands, 𝔑, xviii, xxvii.
Ryle (Hen.) de Styall, viii; his chapel in Wilmslow church, viii.
Ryley, 𝔑, xxii.
Rymour (Ricardus le) de Wythington, xx.
Ryselegh, Petrus de, xxx.
Rysseley 𝔑, xvii.
Rysshefeld broke, Warrington, xvii.
Rysshemersch, xx (*tit.* Staneye).
Ryshton, 𝔑, xiv.
Ryton *See* Royton.

SABBATH observance at Rotterdam, i.
Sabbath tides at Holy Isle, i.
Sabryne, water of (*i.e.* the Severn), xv.
Sabunde *or* Sabonde, Raymond de, xiii; character of his *Theologia Naturalis*, xiii.
Sacheverell, 𝔑, ix, xxii.
Sacheverell mobs, v.
Sachsen (*Geschichte von*), by Bottiger, xviii.
Sack and claret at a Manchester entertainment, xiv.
Sacraments, administration of, at Amsterdam, Edinburgh and Leyden, i; at Downham, xiv.
Sacraments, Newcome's reflections on the, xviii.
Sadberrie, earl of, bishop of Durham, i.
Saddleworth *or* Sadelword, xviii, xx; account of, xix.
Sadler, 𝔑, viii, xiii, xvii.
Saerdam, Holland, i.
Saffron, medicinal virtues of, iv.
Sagar, Mr., xxvii.
Sager, Mr., xxii.
Sagiensis, Johannes abbas sancti Martini, xx.
Saighton, co. Chester, viii. *See* Saughton.
Sailsbury *or* Salesbury hall, Blackburn: notice of, xxii.
Saints, stories of, wrought in arras, xv.
Saints' Inheritance after the Day of Judgment, notice of, xiii.
St. Alban's, xiii; first duke of, ix.
St. Anne's guild, Chester, viii.
St. Augustine, quotations from, xxv.
St. Bees, viii; prior of, xxii.
St. Bloys, co. Cornwall, xiii.
St. Bridget's parish, Chester, viii.
St. Buriens, co. Cornwall, xiii.
St. Chad, chapelry of Malpas: account of, viii.
St. Clare, co. Cornwall, xiii.
St. Cross, advantages of the mastership of, xxiv.
St. Domingo, island of, taken by Drake, xxiii.

St. Ebrulft, abbey of, in Normandy: notice of, VIII.
St. Edith, chapel of, VIII.
St. Edmund's Bury, the great fire of, XXVII.
St. Evremond's attacks on Isaac Vossius, XIII.
St. George, Ascham on the legend of, VII.
St. George, sir Richard, Norroy, XXIV.
St. George's church, Liverpool, IX, XII.
St. George's guild, Chester, VIII.
St. Helena, island of, IX.
St. Helen's, co. Lanc.: school of, IV.
St. John, sir Walter: notice of, XIII.
St. John Baptist's hall, Chester, VIII.
St. John's church, Chester, XV.
St. John's college, Cambridge, XIII, XVIII.
St. John's college, Chester, VIII.
St. John's hospital, Chester, VIII.
St. Leger, Thomas, XXIX.
St. Malo, Normandy, IX, XIII.
St. Martin, rectory of, VIII.
St. Mary's land, Warrington, XVII.
St. Mary's nunnery, Chester, VIII.
St. Michael's mount, Cornwall, XIII.
St. Olave's church, Chester, VIII.
St. Oswald's, Chester, VIII.
St. Peter and St. Paul's, Chester, XV.
St. Peter's, Rome, XVIII.
St. Peter's chapel, tower of London, XVIII.
St. Peter's church, Liverpool, IX.
St. Pierre, 𝔑, VIII, XX.
St. Vincent's rocks, Bristol, XIII.
St. Werburgh's monastery, Chester, VIII, XVII. *See* Werburgh, St.
Salaries of Manchester clergy, XVIII.
Sale, XX; township of Ashton-upon-Mersey, VIII; hall, account of, VIII.
Sale, 𝔑, XVII, XIX, XX.
Salebury, in Ribblesdale, XIV, XX.
Salebury, 𝔑, XX, XXII.
Saleford, Galfridus de, XX.
Salford near Manchester, II, XIII, XVIII; account of, XIX.
Salford bridge, chapel on, XIX.
Salford hundred, eleven parishes in, XIX.
Salghton, VIII.
Salisbury, XIII; a pryncypall cytee of the West saxons, XV; insurrection at, XVIII; chapter house of, I; destruction of an ancient painted window in St. Edmond's at, XIV.
Salisbury, marquis of, XXII.
Salisbury, earls of, I, XXVIII.
Salisbury, 𝔑, I, II, XXV.
Salkeld, 𝔑, V, VIII.
Salley, fox- and otter-hunting at, XIV; abbey of, XIV; abbots of, XX.
Salmasius, Claudius: account of, XIII.
Salmon fishing in the Tweed, I; in the Mersey, IX.
Salmon's *State Trials*, XIV.
Salop, 𝔑, XX.
Salopiensis, Robertus: account of, VII.
Salopessire, Adam de, XXX.
Salt, Richard, XXVII.
Saltash, co. Cornwall, XIII.
Salter's (Dr.) edition of Whichcote's *Aphorisms*, XIII.
Salterswall, Whitegate, co. Chester, VIII.
Saltes (the), two islands near Waterford, I.
Salthill, XIV.
Saltingstall *or* Saltonstall, 𝔑, XVIII, XXVII.
Saltney marsh, near Chester: notice of, I.
Salt-works at Dort, Shields and Musselburgh: description of, I.
Salvin, Mr., architect, VIII.
Samlesbury, chapelry of Blackburn, VI, XIV, XX; account of, XXII; capella, XX; witches of, VI, XIV; higher, lower and Salesbury halls, description of, XXII.

Samlesbury, 𝔑, XX, XXII.
Sammes, Mr., XIII.
Sampson, Richard, bishop of Lichfield. *See* Savensby.
Sampson subduing his enemyes, embrodred in ryche tysshewe, XV.
Samson, Mr., XIII.
Samuels (mother) executed for witchcraft, VI.
Sanballat, XIV.
Sanchy, colonel, XXVII.
Sancroft, 𝔑, XIII, XXII.
Sancto Andrea, Robertus de, XX.
Sancta Maria, Joh. et Andr. de, XX.
Sancto Petro, Joh. et Urianus de, XX.
Sancta Werburga, Hugo de, XX.
Sandbach, XVIII; proceedings at during the Civil war, II; general account of, VIII; hall, notice of, VIII.
Sandbach, Richard de, VIII.
Sandeforde, Mr., wife of, I.
Sander and George (? Assheton), XIV.
Sanders, 𝔑, II, XXII.
Sanderson, 𝔑, IV, V, XIII, XIV, XIX.
Sandes, William, mayor of Lancaster, VI.
Sandford, co. Somerset, I, XIII.
Sandford, 𝔑, VIII, XII, XVIII, XXVII.
Sand-hills on coast of Holland, I.
Sandiford, 𝔑, IX, XII, XXVIII.
Sandiforth, 𝔑, XIX.
Sandiway in Whitegate, VIII.
Sandon church, monumental inscription in, XIII.
Sands, 𝔑, XXII.
Sandy's *Olearius*, XIII; *Travels*, XVIII.
Sandyford, Miles, XVIII.
Sandys, 𝔑, XXII.
Sanesbery, Robertus de, XX.
Sankey, chapelry of Prescot, XVII; account of, XXII; bridge, XVII; gate, XVII; mills, XVII.
Sankey magna, XVII, XXII; parva, XXII.
Sankey, 𝔑, XXII.
Sants *i.e.* saints, old bed-carvings so called by Lancashire cottagers, XIV.
Sapieha, prince Eustace, XXII.
Sapy, Robertus de, XX.
Saracenus, 𝔑, XX.
Saragossa, wager respecting, IX.
Saravia, XIII.
Sarayna, Torelli: notice of, VII.
Sargeaunt of mace, XIV.
Sarospatak, Hungary, XIII.
Sarson, Laurence, XIII.
Sarum, John Davenant bishop of, XIV.
Satan's malice, XVIII.
Saterthwaite, chapelry of Hawkshead: account of, XXII.
Saterthwaite, Thomas, XXII.
Saughall, township of Bidston, VIII.
Saughall, great- *and* little-, townships of Shotwick, VIII.
Saughton, VIII.
Saull, kynge, wrought in arras, XV.
Saumur, France, XIII.
Saunders, 𝔑, VI, VIII, XXVII.
Saunderson, 𝔑, VIII, XIX.
Saundiford, Will., XIII (?).
Sauthorp, Rob. de, XX.
Savage, 𝔑, VIII, IX, XVII, XIX, XXII.
Savensby, Alexander, bishop of Lichfield: notice of, VIII.
Savidge, Richard, XXII.
Savigné, Normandy: monastery of, XXII.
Savile, 𝔑, XIV, XIX.
Saville, 𝔑, IX, XIII, XVII.
Savory, John, XVIII.
Savoy, persecution of protestants by the duke of, XIII.
Savoy, Amadeus de, XIX.
Savoy (the), London, XIX.
Savoy conference, XVIII; account of, XIII.
Sawer, Geoffrey, XVII.
Sawrey, 𝔑, XXII.
Sawyer, mother, a witch, XII.

Saxons enfect all Englande with apostasie, XV; their seuen kyngdomes, XV.
Saxton's *Map of Lancashire*, XIX.
Sayer, sir John, and Everild his daughter, XIV.
Sayes *or* Sagio, France: abbey of St. Martin de, XXII. *See* Sagiensis.
Sayes, Henry abbot of, XXII.
Saynte Mariden, capella de, XX.
Scadewallebrok, XX (*titt.* Bretharue, Wolueton).
Scales, ℞, XXX. *See* Seales.
Scaliger, ℞, VII, XIII.
Scamel, a fishing net, XIV.
Scarborough, XIV.
Scarborough, earl of, XXVIII.
Scarborough, ℞, IX.
Scarbrick, Jam., VIII.
Scarisbrick, ℞, IX, XII, XX, XXII, XXVIII.
Scarisbrick hall, Ormskirk: account of, XXII.
Scarr, George, XIV.
Scarsdale, sir Nathanael Curzon baron, XXII.
Scasbricke, ℞, XII.
Schagh, ℞, XX.
Schardeley, Joh. de, XX.
Schayerhalghes, XX (*tit.* Spotlond).
Schepens *or* Sckepens, Dutch town-officials, I.
Schickardus's *Horologium Hebræum*, notice of, IV.
Schiedam, Holland, I.
Schireburn, ℞, XX.
Schireland, Robert de, XX.
Schlezer, John Frederick, XIII.
Schofield, John, XXVII.
Scholefield *or* Scholfield, ℞, VIII, XIX, XXII.
Scholefield hall, Milnrow: account of, XIX.
Scholmondeley *error for* Scholumdesley, Rog. de, XX.
Scholes, ℞, XVIII, XIX, XXVII.
Schonaich, baron of, XIII.
Schoolcroft, Mr., curate of Caton, XXII.
Schoolmaster punysshed and restored to helthe by myracle, XV.
School mills, Manchester: rental of, XVIII.
Schor, XX (*tit.* Heleye),
Schorebank, XX (*tit.* Whiteword).
Schoresworth, ℞, XX.
Schrevelius, Ewaldus: notice of, I.
Schröder, Christopher, a favoured visitor of G. J. Vossius, XIII.
Schute *or* Scute, a Dutch river-boat, I.
Schutilisworth, Henr. de, XX.
Sciences (the seuen) preserued by lernynge, XV.
Scioppius, Gaspar: account of, XIII.
Sclater, ℞, XIII, XXII, XXVII.
Scloterdyke, near Amsterdam, notable for a woman who had twenty-four husbands, I.
Scoales, Jeremy, of Norton, Derbyshire, IV.
Scobell, XVIII.
Scofeild, Mrs., XVIII.
Scoffield (captain) serves in defence of Bolton, II.
Scholefeld, Johannes de, XX.
Scolefullache, XX (*tit.* Chadewyk).
Scoler (Bruin) *or* Fowler (Brian), VIII.
Scoles, ℞, II, XIII.
Scoles, XX (*tit.* Ynes).
Scolfeld, ℞, XIX.
Scolfield, James, and wife, XVIII.
Scone abbey, last coronation at, I.
Scot, ℞, VI, VIII, XX.
Scotch, notices of the, I.
Scotch church, XII.
Scotch prisoners, XVIII; bad treatment of, XXVII.
Scote gift, XII.
Scotland, coins current in, I; peculiarities of speech, I; bill for union of England with, IX; trade regulations for, IX; sad condition of clergy in, XVIII.

Scots, south-country: their proceedings during the Jacobite rebellion, V.
Scott, sir Walter, bart., I, VI, IX, XIV, XVIII.
Scott, William, sheriff of York, XIV.
Scottish antiquaries, society of, IX.
Scoute or baylie, a high Dutch official, I.
Scoutes, guillemots, I.
Scout-stones, XIV.
Scowles, John, IX.
Scroop, colonel, II.
Scrop, 𝔑, XX, XXII.
Scrope, 𝔑, VIII, XIV.
Scudamore, sir Barnaby, IX.
Sea, the: its reverence unto the sands, VII.
Sea-terms, explanation of, I.
Sea-bank, Liverpool, XII.
Seabroke, James, of Liverpool, XXII.
Seacombe in Wallezey, VIII.
Seacome, 𝔑, II, IX, XII, XXIX.
Seacome's *Siege of Lathom House*, quotations from, XIV.
Seal *or* sea-calf, description of, I.
Seales *error for* Scales, Robert, XXII.
Seaman, Dr. Lazarus, XIII, XXVII.
Seathwaite, chapelry of Kirby-Irelith: account of, XXII.
Seaton, 𝔑, I, II, XIV.
Seaton house, near Edinburgh: notice of, I; occupied and fortified by highlanders, V.
Sebonde, Raymond de, XIII.
Secker, archbishop, XXII.
Sects at Rotterdam and Dort, I.
Secular prestes expulsed from monasteries with great discrecion, XV.
Sedall, Henry, XIX.
Sedbury, XIX.
Seddon, 𝔑, II, IV, XII, XVIII, XIX, XXII, XXVII.
Sedehe, XX (*tit.* Bilyngton).
Sedewalhelinabbe, XX (*tit.* Spotlond).
Sedgwick, 𝔑, XIII, XIX.
Sedley, 𝔑, XIII.
Seel, T. Molyneux Unsworth, XXII.
Sees translated from borowes to famous townes, XV.
Sefton *or* Sephton, near Liverpool, IX; notice of, IV; general account of, XXII; hall, description of, XXII.
Sefton, earls of, XIV, XXII.
Segary, Will., that noted disciplinarian, XIII.
Segeleyclogh, XX (*tit.* Westewod).
Segelocum, a Roman station, XIV.
Segraue, Stephanus de, XX.
Seilerus (Wenceslaus) and his powder of projection, XIII.
Sekerstone, Ralph, M.P. for Liverpool: notice of, XII.
Selby, co. York, XIV.
Selby (Mr.) taken prisoner, V.
Selden, VI, VII, XIII, XVIII; his *Mare Clausum*, XIII; *Marmora Arundeliana*, VII; *Table Talk*, VI, XII, XVIII.
Sele, yoke for cattle: etymology of, VI.
Self-denying ordinance, XII.
Self-examination, XVIII; plan of, XXVII.
Self-knowledge *and* self-condemnation, XVIII.
Selfullache, XX (*tit.* Spotlond).
Seller, 𝔑, VI, VII.
Sellet hall, Whittington: notice of, XXII.
Selside church, Kendal, XIX.
Semerwater lake, in Wensleydale, XIV.
Sempill, Hugh eleventh lord, and Sarah his wife, XIX.
Senior, Mr., XXVII.
Separatists, IV.
Sepulchral stones found at Warrington, XVII.
Sequens (service-book) of saynt Werburge, XV.
Sequestrations of the estates of rebels and consequent confusion, V.
Sequestrators for Lancashire during

the Civil war, list of, II; at Manchester, XXVII.
Sergeant, ℞, VIII, XXVII.
Seriaunt, Mr., XVIII.
Serjeant, John, XIII.
Sermon, Henry Newcome's first, XVIII.
Sermons (*Farewell*) by the London ministers, XVIII.
Serocold *error for* Serowld, Mr., IX.
Service Books, new and old, XVIII.
Service silver, a Cartmel rent, XXII.
Sessay, XIV.
Sessions house, Manchester: situation of, XXVIII.
Sethe, XX (*tit.* Castelton).
Seton *otherwise* Lekelay priory, Cumberland, XXII.
Settle, co. York, XIV.
Settles in Eccles church, XIX.
Seuenlawes, XX (*tit.* Barton).
Sevarites, XIII.
Seven-oaks, hamlet of higher Whitley, Budworth, VIII.
Severn river, I.
Sevigné's (madame de) divine tabouret, XVIII.
Seward's donations to St. Werburgh's abbey, VIII.
Sewell, F. H., vicar of Cockerham, XXII.
Sexburge, saynt, maryed to Ercombert kynge of Kent: legendary account of, XV.
Sexwulfus *or* Saxwulf, bysshop of Lychefelde, XV.
Seybold's *Autobiography*, XIII.
Seycom, Thomas, IX.
Seymour, ℞, IX, XII, XXVIII.
Shackerley, ℞, IX, XIII, XXIII.
Shacklocke, Mr., XVIII.
Shadwell's (vice-chancellor) decree respecting Manchester school, XIX.
Shadwell's *Lancashire Witches*, extracts from, VI.
Shaftoe, captain John: his trial and execution, V.
Shaftesbury, lord, IX, XIII.
Shakerley, ℞, I, VIII, XVII, XXII, XXVIII.
Shakspeare, William, XXIX; illustrative references to, XIV; epitaph ascribed to him, XXIX; enquiry into the authorship of the lines signed J. M. S., VII.
Shakspeare Society's Publications, XXIX.
Shalcross, Mr., of Stockport, VIII.
Shane (captain) gives 1000 acres to found a college, XIII.
Shanton, Thomas, XIII.
Shardlowe, VIII.
Sharp, ℞, XIII.
Sharpe, Dr., I.
Sharples, ℞, IX, XIV, XXII.
Sharrock, ℞, XIX, XXII.
Shavington-cum-Greasby, township of Wibunbury, VIII; hall, notice of, VIII.
Shaw, ℞, II, VIII, IX, XII, XIV, XVII, XVIII, XIX, XXII, XXVII.
Shaw, chapelry of Prestwich: account of, XIX.
Shaw *now* Worden hall, near Preston, XIV.
Shaw's (Henry) *Specimens of Ancient Furniture*, XIV.
Sheale, Richard: notices of, XXIX.
Sheare Thursday, why so named, VI.
Shearson, Thomas, XXII.
Sheep *and* sheep pastures, I.
Sheerness, I, IX.
Sheffield, co. York, IV.
Sheldon, Gilbert, archbishop of Canterbury, XIII, XXII.
Shelley, baronets, XIV, XXII.
Shelley, quotation from, XVII.
Shellow-end, Gawsworth, VIII.
Shelmadine, Mr., of Mottram, IV.

Shelmardine *or* Shelmerdine, 𝔑, XVIII, XXVII.
Shelton, Mr., XIII.
Shelvocke, Dorothy, XII.
Shene monastery, co. Surrey, VIII.
Shepay monastery, Kent, buylded by saynt Sexburge, XV.
Shepe hey, XX (*tit.* Whalleye).
Shepherd, 𝔑, VIII, IX, XVIII, XIX, XXVII.
Shepherdes (*the*), a miracle play, XXIX.
Shepley, 𝔑, XIX.
Shepley hall, Ashton-under-Line: notice of, XIX.
Sheppy isle, Kent, I.
Sherard, Mr., XXVII.
Sherborne, co. Dorset, XIII.
Sherborne *or* Sherbourne, 𝔑, XIV, XXVIII.
Sherburn hospital, near Durham, XIX.
Sherburne, 𝔑, XXII.
Sherdley, James, XXII.
Sherfield, Henry, recorder of Salisbury: narrative of his window-breaking exploit, XIV.
Sheridan, XIV.
Sheriff (high) for Lancashire, his charges and disbursements, V.
Sheriffmuir, indecisive battle of, V.
Sherington, 𝔑, II, XIV.
Sherley, 𝔑, I.
Sherlock, 𝔑, VIII, XIII, XIX, XXII.
Sherman, 𝔑, XIII, XXVII.
Sherson, Thomas, XXII.
Sherwin, 𝔑, XII.
Sherwood, Mrs., VIII.
Shevington *or* Sherington, Francis: notice of, IV.
Shiblach, VIII.
Shields, description of the salt-works at, I.
Shierson, Thomas, XXVIII.
Shiffnall grange, co. Salop, XIV.
Shipbrook, township of Davenham, VIII; castle, VIII; barony of, VIII.
Shipley, near Delft, Holland, I.
Ship-money, tax of, I.
Shippon, a cow-house, I.
Shireburn, sir Nicholas, of Stonyhurst, XXII.
Shireshead *or* Shireside, chapelry of Cockerham: account of, XXII.
Shirley, sir Thomas, VIII.
Shocklach, co. Chester: account of, VIII; hall and castle, notices of, VIII.
Shocklach oviat, township of Shocklach, VIII.
Shocklach, Thomas de, VIII.
Shone, 𝔑, VIII, XXVIII.
Shooting flying, when introduced, XIV.
Shore, 𝔑, XIX, XXVII, XXVIII.
Shorpthursday, meaning of, XV.
Shorrock (Ralph) taken prisoner at Preston, II.
Shorteakyr, le, Warrington, XVII.
Shortgreues, XX (*tit.* Whiteword).
Shortstainfeld in Farington, XXX.
Shotwick, account of, VIII; hall and lodge, notices of, VIII.
Shovelars, wild fowl, I.
Shovel-board *or* shuffle-board, a game, XIV, XVIII, XXVII.
Shover *or* Sholver, XIX.
Showley hall, Blackburn: notice of, XXII.
Shrewsbury, XV, XVIII; description of, I; Sacheverell mob at, V; Henry Newcome's controversy with, XXVII; abbey of, VIII, XXII.
Shrewsbury, Charles duke of, XXII, XXVIII.
Shrewsbury, earls of, VIII, XXIII.
Shrigley family, notice of, VIII.
Shrigley, William, XVIII.
Shrine of St. Werburge, instances of its miraculous virtue, XV.
Shrubshall (captain) overturns Mainamber stone, XIII.
Shurlach, township of Davenham, VIII.
Shute, 𝔑, VIII, XIII.

Shutlings loe, hill in Macclesfield forest: description of, XXIII.
Shuttelisworth, Joh. de, XX.
Shuttleworth, 𝔑, II, V, VI, IX, XII, XIV, XIX, XXII, XXVIII.
Shuttleworth hall, Padiham: notice of, XXII.
Shyreburn, Robertus de, XXX.
Sibs' *Workes*, XVIII.
Sibson, Edmund, vicar of St. Thomas's, Ashton-in-Makerfield: character of, XVII.
Sibyls, David Blondel's treatise of the, XIII.
Sickness sent in answer to Newcome's prayers, XVIII.
Siddall, 𝔑, V, VIII, XVIII, XIX.
Siddington, chapelry of Presbury: account of, VIII.
Sidebottom, 𝔑, VIII, XIX.
Sidegraves, Isabel, accused of witchcraft, VI.
Siden's *History of the Sevarites or Severambi* probably written by Isaac Vossius, XIII.
Sidesman, a corruption from synodsman, VIII.
Sidley, Mr., XIII.
Sidney, 𝔑, VIII, XII, XIII, XXV.
Sidney-Sussex college, Cambridge, XIII.
Sieges of Damietta, Haerlem and Leyden, I.
Sikemanesty, XX (*tit.* Croenton).
Sikes's (George) *Life and Death of sir Henry Vane*, XIII.
Silklinghale, Thomas de, XX.
Silche (the), a drain or syke in Warrington, XVII.
Silesia, cloister for religious education in, XIII.
Silkeston, Osbertus persona de, XX.
Sill, Mr., minister of Gressingham. *See* Still.
Sillesby, Mr., XIII.
Sillito, Randal, XVIII, XXVII; his account of a fatal thunder-storm, XXVII.
Silverdale, chapelry of Warton: account of, XXII.
Simister's wife, XVIII.
Simkin, Jo., VIII.
Simmonds, Robert, rector of Middleton, II. *See* Symonds, XIX.
Simmons, Nevill, London bookseller, XVIII.
Simmon wood, near Liverpool, XII.
Simnel, Lambert: invasion of, XXII.
Simon, father Richard: notice of, IV.
Simon, monke of Chestre, comforted by saynt Werburge in vision, XV.
Simpkin, Anne, IV.
Simpson, 𝔑, XIX, XXII, XXVIII.
Simson, 𝔑, XIII.
Sinclair's *Satan's Invisible World Displayed*, extract from, VI.
Singleton, 𝔑, VI, IX, XIV, XX, XXII, XXIV, XXX.
Singleton, great, chapelry of Kirkham: account of, XXII.
Singleton *or* Gingle hall, in Whittingham, Kirkham: notice of, XXII.
Singleton-thorpe (village of) washed away by the sea, XXII.
Sinner's Hope by Henry Newcome, publication of, XXVII.
Sion abbey in Middlesex, XXII.
Sir, a prefix to names of ecclesiastics, XIV.
Sire, John, an ancient servant, XII.
Sirleg, Sewallus de, XX.
Sirmond, XIII.
Sir Thomas's buildings *and* street, Liverpool, XII.
Sisson, Tho., XXIV.
Sithridhruydyng, XX (*tit.* Bilyngton).
Siwardescroft, XX (*tit.* Salebury).
Siwardus filius Antonij, XXX.
Sixlandes, XX (*tit.* Whalleye).
Sixsmith, 𝔑, IV, XXII.
Skelfshaw fells, XIV.

Skelmersdale, township of Ormskirk: notice of, XXII.
Skelmersdale, Edward Booth Wilbraham baron, XIV, XIX, XXII.
Skelton, engraver, XIV.
Skelton, poet laureate, XV; latin elegy by, XXIX.
Skinner *or* Skynner, Willmus, XX.
Skippul, XX (*tit.* Ynes).
Skipton, II, XIV; castle, XIV; inventory taken at, XIV.
Skipton, Ric. de, XX; James, XXII.
Skogan, Henry, an old poet, XIV.
Skydamore, lady, XXIV.
Skylyngton, Ad., XX.
Skytte, lord, a Swedish nobleman, XIII.
Slade, ℞, VIII, XVIII, XIX.
Slade *or* Milkwall-Slade hall, notice of, XIX.
Sladeburne in Bowland, XIV.
Slakk, ℞, XX.
Slane river, Ireland, I.
Slaney, John, XIII.
Slare, Dr., a London physician, XIII.
Slate's reprint of *Memoirs of Rev. Nathaniel Heywood*, XVIII.
Slater, ℞, XIII, XXII, XXVII.
Slaueden, Cecilia uxor Ade de, XX.
Slavery in Virginia, XVIII.
Slawright, Richard, prior of the hermit friars of St. Augustine, Warrington, XVII.
Sledde, kynge. *See* Fledde.
Sleperesgrene, XX (*tit.* Croenton).
Slingsby, ℞, XIII, XIV.
Sluices near Haerlem, I.
Slygcher-lane-end, Warrington, XVII.
Slytchers-lane, Warrington, XVII.
Smalebrok, XX. *See in same volume* Westewod.
Smaleschagh, XX (*tit.* Spotlond).
Smaleschagheued, XX (*tit.* Whiteword).
Smaleschaghsik, XX (*tit.* Whiteword).
Smalesik, XX (*tit.* Bilyngton).
Smaleys, XX (*tit.* Hulton).
Smalley, VIII.
Smallplace, widow, IX.
Smallpox in Manchester, XXVII.
Smalls (the), dangerous rocks off Pembrokeshire, I.
Smallwood, ℞, IV, VIII, XXII, XXVII.
Smallwood, township of Astbury, VIII.
Smalshaw, township of Ashton-under-Line, XIX.
Smalshaw, Chr., VIII.
Smeathes, probably smews, wild fowl, I.
Smeatonwood, township of Wrenbury, VIII.
Smekergill, Mrs., XIII.
Smereshalgh, Ad. de, XX.
Smersall, Laurence, XIX.
Smethedon, XX.
Smethills hall, Dean: account of, XIX.
Smethlage, Isabel daughter of Richard, VIII.
Smethurst, ℞, XXII, XXVII.
Smethurst hall, Middleton: notice of, XIX.
Smethwick, near Brereton, Cheshire, VIII.
Smethwick, ℞, I, XIII, XXVII.
Smith, ℞, I, II, III, IV, VII, VIII, IX, XII, XIII, XIV, XVIII, XIX, XXII, XXIV, XXV, XXVII, XXVIII.
Smith's *Compendium of Logic*, IV.
Smith's *Patriarchal Sabbath*, IV; schismatic effect of his writings, IV.
Smithcumberode, XX (*tit.* Castelton).
Smoke money, an ecclesiastical tax, VIII.
Smollett's *History of England*, IX.
Smyth, ℞, VIII, XIII.
Smythe, ℞, XVII.
Smythes howse, XX (*tit.* Whalleye).
Smythick, co. Cornwall, XIII.
Snell, George, D.D.: notice of, VIII.
Snelleshou, XX.
Snelleshou, ℞, XX.
Snelson, township of Rosthorne, VIII.

Snelston, township of Over-Peover, VIII.
Sneyd, ℞, VIII, XVIII.
Snidale hall, Westhoughton, XIX.
Snoddeword, Ricardus de, XX.
Snoddeword, XX (*tit.* Bilyngton).
Soame's *Mosheim*, XII.
Soap-making in Bristol, I.
Socage tenure, XIV.
Society for propagating the gospel in foreign parts, XVIII.
Society, royal; rise and progress of, XIII.
Sodehull, Thom. de, XX.
Sodon, Elizabeth, XII.
Solan geese, extreme fatness of, I.
Solarium *or* sollar, definition of, XVII.
Soldiers, a roman-catholic view of, XXV.
Solms, count of: notice of, I.
Solomon, kynge, purtrayed in arras, XV.
Someraikis, XX (*tit.* Whiteword).
Somerford of Somerford, pedigree, XX.
Somerford-Booths *and* Somerford-Radnor, townships of Astbury, VIII; hall and park, notice of, VIII.
Somers, ℞, IX, XXVIII.
Somers' *Tracts*, IX, XII, XVIII.
Somerset, William duke of, XII.
Somerset, Sarah duchess of: notice of, XIX; founds four exhibitions to Brazenose college from Manchester school, XIX.
Somerset, Charles earl of, XIV.
Somerton, Thomas, minister of Todmorden and blacksmith, XIX.
Somner, Mr., of Canterbury: notice of, XIII.
Sond *or* Sonde, Mr., minister of Caldecot, XVIII, XXVII.
Sondebache, Ricardus de, XX.
Sondediche, XX (*tit.* Bacford).
Sondeford, XX (*tit.* Bilyngton).
Sondeforth, Ralph, D.D., XIX.
Song, political, XII.
Sonkey *or* Sonky, ℞, XVII, XXII.
Soothill hall, near Dewsbury, XIV.
Sophia, electress, mother of George I., I.
Sophisters' schools, Cambridge, XIII.
Sorbière's (Samuel) remark on Brazenose college, XII; his interesting picture of Salmasius, XIII.
Sorocold, ℞, IX, XVIII, XIX, XXVII.
Sorocole, Mrs., XIV.
Sorsby, Mr., XIII.
Sory *or* Sawry, John, XVIII.
Sothden, aqua de, XX.
Sotheworthe *or* Sothewurthe, ℞, XVII.
Sothurn *or* Sothurne, ℞, XVII.
Sothword, Gilbertus de, XX.
Sotterley *or* Soterlegh, Edmund de, VIII.
Sotyndon, Willus de, XX.
Soueracre, township of Ashton-under-Line, XIX.
Soureby, ℞, XX.
Sourquedry, XIV.
Southampton, XIII.
Southampton, earls of, XII, XIV.
Southern, James, bailiff of Liverpool, XII.
Southernes, Elizabeth, *alias* Old Demdike: account of, VI.
Southey, Robert, XIII; his *MS.* Index to Scaliger's *Epistolæ*, XIII.
Southseller yarde, XX (*tit.* Whalleye).
Southsex, realme of Saxons, endured but short tyme, XV.
South-side, *error for* North-side, township of St. Oswald's, Chester, VIII.
Southwell, collegiate church of, XIX.
Southwell, Robert, XIII.
Southworth, ℞, VI, XIV, XVII, XXII, XXV.
Southworth hall, Winwick: account of, XXII.
Sowerbuts, Grace daughter of Thomas: her evidence at a witch trial, and recantation, VI.

Sowerby, C. B., incumbent of Ashton-upon-Mersey, VIII.
Sowle, a quaker publisher, XIII.
Spagnoli, J. Baptist: notice of, IV.
Spain, XII: affairs of, IX.
Spakeman, Richard and Katherine, XXII.
Spalato, archbishop of, and dean of Windsor, XIII.
Spanish armada, XII.
Spanish and French ambassadors, their sanguinary fight for precedency, XVIII.
Sparke, ꝑ, XXVII.
Sparks, Mr., VIII.
Sparrow, ꝑ, II, XIII.
Spatzenhaus at Constantinople, XVIII.
Speare, Baly, XII.
Spearing, Mr., senior proctor, Cambridge, XIII.
Speech in Scotland, peculiarities of, I.
Speech (poetical) made to kinge James at his comeinge to Hoghton tower, XIV.
Speeches (Latin) at Cambridge University, XIII.
Speeches of the Regicides, XVIII.
Speed, ꝑ, VIII, XIII, XXII.
Spek, Gilbertus de, XX.
Speke, township of Childwall, XII, XXII; various notices of, IX.
Speke hall, IX; account of, XXII.
Speke leet jury, presentment of, IX.
Speke, sir John: his chantry in Exeter cathedral, XIX.
Speke, William, XXVIII.
Spelman, sir Henry, VII; notice of, XIII.
Spence, XIII.
Spencer, ꝑ, VI, VIII, XIII, XIV, XVIII, XXII, XXIX.
Spense, Joseph, cook, XIII.
Spenser, ꝑ, VIII, XIII, XVIII, XXIX, XXX.
Sperthe, a piece of land, XVII.
Spicer, Ric. le, vic. Cestrie, XX.
Spina's (Alphonsus de) *Fortalitium Fidei*, XIII.
Spinning place, Liverpool, XII.
Spinosa, Benedict, XIII.
Spinx, Mr., XXVII.
Spiridion, bishop of Cyprus, XIV.
Spirits or ghosts, stories of, I; Dr. Henry More's view of the occupations of disembodied spirits, XIII.
Spital-Boughton, VIII.
Spittle, medicinal virtues of, I.
Spofforth, Richard, vicar of Dalton, XXII.
Sporis, William, XVII.
Sports, old English, XIV.
Sports (Book of), II, XIV.
Spotbrok, in Spotlond, XX.
Spotland, ꝑ, XIX, XX.
Spotlond and its divisions, XX.
Spottiswoode, John, archbishop of St. Andrew's: notice of, I.
Spottiswoode, sir Robert, I.
Sprat's (Dr.) *History of the Royal Society*, XIII.
Sprenger, VI.
Sproston, township of Middlewich, VIII.
Spryng, Johan, XX.
Spurstow, township of Bunbury, VIII; hall, notice of, VIII.
Spurstow, Dr. William, IV, XIII, XXVII; notice of, VIII.
Spurstow, ꝑ, VIII.
Spycer, John, XVII.
Squire, ꝑ, VIII, IX.
Squire-street, Liverpool, XII.
Stable, XX (*tit.* Whalleye).
Stable oak, XIV. *See* Staple oak.
Stables at the Hague and in Dublin, description of, I.
Stabliclogh, XX (*tit.* Sadelword).
Stackhouse, captain William, II.
Stadaghe *or* Stadaugh, Laurence, XXII.
Stafford, repared by Elflede duchesse

of Merciens, xv; priory of St. Thomas near, viii.
Stafford, lord, xxviii.
Stafford, ꝑ, viii, xix, xxviii.
Staffordshire, its connexion with Liverpool, ix, xii.
Stafforth, ꝑ, xx.
Stage-coaches to London, xii.
Staineton, John, curate of Rampside. xxii.
Staining, township of Poulton-in-the-Fylde, xxii; hall, notice of, xxii.
Stair brook divides Marbury and Norbury, viii.
Staley, township of Mottram, viii; hall, notice of, viii.
Staley *or* Staveley, Ralph, viii.
Stalmine, chapelry of Lancaster: account of, xxii.
Stalmine, ꝑ, xxii.
Stamford *or* Stanford, in Christleton, viii.
Stamford, earls of, iv, viii, ix, xiv, xix.
Stamford, Mr., xxviii.
Stamford- *or* Standford-bridge, in Barrow, viii.
Stamp *or* Stampe, ꝑ, xxvii.
Stananought, Edward, xxii.
Stanbury, John, bishop of Hereford, i.
Stand hall *otherwise* Pilkington tower, Prestwich: account of, xix.
Standard, battle of the: notice of, vii.
Standen, ꝑ, xx.
Standen felde, xx (*tit.* Whalleye).
Standen heye, xx (*tit.* Whalleye).
Standish, ꝑ, ii, v, ix, xiv, xviii, xx, xxii, xxvii, xxviii; pedigree, xxviii.
Standish-cum-Langtree, account of, xxii; grammar school, endowment of, xiv.
Standish hall, notice of, xxii; seditious meeting at, xxviii.
Staned, Ric. de, xx.
Stanedis, ꝑ, xxx.
Stanegge, xx (*tit.* Sadelword).
Staneye and its divisions, xx.
Staneye, ꝑ, xx.
Stanfeld, in Warrington, xvii.
Stanford, ꝑ, xx.
Stanhope, ꝑ, viii, xiv.
Stanhope's dragoons retreat before the rebels, v.
Stanlawe abbey, xix, xx; account of, viii; abbates, priores, sub-prior et alii, xx.
Stanlegh, Johannes de, xx.
Stanley, ꝑ, ii, iv, viii, ix, xii, xiii, xiv, xvii, xviii, xix, xxii, xxv, xxvii, xxviii, xxix.
Stanley-street, Liverpool, xii.
Stanney, viii. *See* Staneye.
Stanney parva, township of Stoke, co. Chester, viii; hall, notice of, viii.
Stannicliffe hall, Middleton, xiv; notice of, xix.
Stannynought, ꝑ, viii, xiii.
Stansfeld, ꝑ, xx, xxii.
Stanthorn, township of Davenham, viii.
Stanton, El., viii.
Stanwix, Thomas, governor of Carlisle: his account of the result of Preston fight, v.
Stanword and its divisions, xx.
Stanword, ꝑ, xx.
Stanwordle, xx (*tit.* Stanword).
Stanyclyf, xx (*tit.* Bilyngton).
Stanyhurst, Richard, xiii.
Stanymengate, xx (*tit.* Bilyngton).
Stanyord, xx (*tit.* Bacford).
Stanys, xx (*tit.* Bilyngton).
Stanystrete, xx (*tit.* Workedelegh).
Stapeley, township of Wibunbury, viii; hall, notice of, viii.
Stapeley family, viii.
Stapelford, ꝑ, xx.
Staple for English cloth at Delft, i.
Staple-oak, Bowland, xiv. *See* Stable oak.

Stapleford, co. Wilts, XIII.
Stapleton, 𝔓, I, XIII, XX.
Stapylton, 𝔓, XIII, XIX.
Star and dove sent as signes of consolacion to Chestre, XV.
Starbottom, XIV.
Star-chamber, court of, XII, XIV, XXIV.
Star-inn, York, XIV.
Starkey, 𝔓, II, VIII, XVIII, XX, XXII. XXVII.
Starkie, 𝔓, II, VI, XIV, XIX, XXII, XXVIII.
Starky, 𝔓, IX, XIX.
States-general of Holland, IX; constitution and military strength of, I.
Statham, John, XXVII.
Stations (holy) of the cytee of Rome, XV.
Staundon, William de, XXII.
Staunton, Dr., XXVII.
Staunton-Harold, co. Leicester, IX.
Staveley, chapelry of Cartmel: account of, XXII.
Staveley *or* Stauele, 𝔓, XX.
Stavenby, 𝔓, VIII, XX.
Staynol, Rogerus de, XX (?).
Stead, Samuel, of Rochdale, and Judith his wife, XIX.
Steam-engine, origin of the idea of the, XVIII.
Stearne's *Confirmation of Witchcraft*, extract from, VI.
Stedham near Runcorn, VIII.
Steel, 𝔓, VIII.
Steele, 𝔓, XVIII, XXVII.
Steelefoxe *or* Stealefoxe, Mr., XVIII.
Steers, Spencer, of Halewood, XII.
Steimson, Mr.: strong probabilities why he was a murderer, XXVII.
Stenrisiche, XX (*tit.* Spotlond).
Stephen, St.: why inferior to saynt Werburge, XV.
Stephens, 𝔓, VIII, XIII.
Stephenson, John, curate of Kirkby-Irelith, XXII.
Stepkins, Peter, XXVIII.
Sterne, 𝔓, XIII.
Sterry, Mr., XIII.
Steven, Mr., a chief Moscovy pilot, XXIV.
Stevenedge, co. Hertford, XIII.
Stevenson, 𝔓, IV, XIII, XXVII.
Stewart, 𝔓, I, VII, XIII.
Steyninges, XX.
Stidd *or* Stede, chapelry of Ribchester: account of, XXII.
Still, *error for* Sill, Mr., minister of Gressingham, XXII.
Stilton, Angel inn at, XIV.
Stirling castle, I.
Stirrop, XIV.
Stirrup, 𝔓, VIII, XXII.
Stock, 𝔓, XIX.
Stockdale, William, XVIII.
Stockham, near Runcorn, VIII.
Stockholm, a great statesman's letter from, XIII.
Stockport, IV, IX, XIV, XVIII; account of, VIII; storm and occupation of, II. *See* Stopford.
Stockport, 𝔓, VIII, XVIII, XXII, XXVII.
Stocks at Street-yate, reflections on the, XXVII.
Stockton, township of Malpas, VIII.
Stockton, 𝔓, VIII, XXVII.
Stockton's barn used as a chapel, XVIII.
Stodlee, Joh. de, XX.
Stodton, Robertus de, XX.
Stoke, co. Chester: account of, VIII.
Stoke, 𝔓, XIX, XX.
Stoke castle, co. Salop, VIII.
Stoke hall, near Nantwich, VIII.
Stokeport, 𝔓, XX.
Stokeworth, VIII.
Stokley, Nicholas, IX.
Stokton, 𝔓, XX.
Stokyngbrigie, XX (*tit.* Carleton parva).
Stone, co. Stafford: legendary notices of and origin of the name, XV.

Stone, Gilbert de: his manner of writing legends, VII.
Stone, Thomas, citizen of London, II.
Stonehenge, XIII.
Stone plate on Liverpool moss, XII.
Stones, 𝔑, I, XIX, XXII, XXVIII.
Stonlegh, XX (*tit.* Chadewyk).
Stonor *or* Stonore, 𝔑, XIX, XX.
Stonyhurst, XIV; account of, XXII; occupied by Cromwell, II.
Stony Stratford, XIV.
Stool of repentance, Grey-friars, Edinburgh, I.
Stopford (? Stockport), XVIII.
Stopford, 𝔑, XVIII, XXII, XXVII.
Stopport. *See* Stockport.
Storer, Arthur: tomb of, VIII.
Storeton, great *and* little, townships of Bebington, VIII.
Storey, Thomas, bailiff of Liverpool, XII.
Stories, strange, XIII.
Storks in Holland, I.
Storms, violent, I, XVIII.
Storrs hall, Arkholme, Melling: notice of, XXII.
Storts, sea-fowl, I.
Story, 𝔑, IX, XIII.
Stotfold, stall of Lichfield, VIII.
Stourbridge. *See* Sturbridge.
Stourton, XXIX.
Stourton, Charles lord, and his daughter Katherine, XIV.
Stout, William: extracts from his *MS. Journal*, VIII, XXII.
Stow *or* Stowe-nine-churches, near Bugbrook, Daventry, XV.
Stowe, historian, IX, XXIX.
Stowey, co. Somerset, I.
Strada, XIII.
Strafford, sir Thomas Wentworth earl of, IX, XII, XIII, XIV, XXIX; as lord-deputy in Ireland, I; extracts from his letters, XIV.
Strain or breed of horses, I.
Straingeways, Mr., IX.
Stralsund, discovery of a murdering inn near, I.
Strangawre channel in Irish sea: rush of the tides at, I.
Strange, lords, II, IV, VIII, IX, XII, XIV, XVIII, XXII, XXIII, XXV, XXVIII.
Strange, 𝔑, VIII, XXIV.
Strangeways, 𝔑, I, XVIII, XIX.
Strangeways hall, Manchester, XVIII; notice of, XIX.
Stranraer *or* Chapel, Galloway, I.
Straselius desires Dr. Dee's acquaintance, XXIV.
Stratford, 𝔑, VIII, XIX, XXII, XXVII.
Strathmore, earl of, and his highland regiment, V.
Straytburel, Robertus et Radulphus filii Henrici, XXX.
Street, Mr., XXVII.
Street, in Heath-Charnock, XIX.
Streete, 𝔑, XIV.
Streete-Hough, in Pilsworth near Prestwich, XIX.
Streeting, John, VII.
Streets in Liverpool, XII.
Strenyshalt, now called Whytby, XV.
Strete, Thomas, XIX.
Stretford, chapelry of Manchester: account of, XIX.
Stretton, XIV.
Stretton, chapelry of Budworth: account of, VIII.
Stretton, township of Tilston, VIII; hall, notice of, VIII.
Stretton, 𝔑, XX, XXVII.
Stretwell, William, XXVII.
Strickland, 𝔑, II, IX, XII, XIV, XXII, XXIX.
Stringer, 𝔑, VIII, XIII, XXVII.
Stroud, 𝔑, I, IX.
Stroyer *for* destroyer, XXIII.
Strutt's *Sports and Pastimes*, XVIII.
Stryall, Dr., XVIII.
Stuart, 𝔑, IX, XIII, XIV.

Stubbe, Henry: account of, xiii.
Stubbins, Dr., xiii.
Stubbs, 𝔑, i, viii.
Stublach, township of Middlewich, viii.
Stubley, 𝔑, xix.
Stubley hall, Littleborough, xiv; account of, xix.
Studley's (Peter) *Looking-glass of Schism*, i.
Stukely, sir Lewis, xiii.
Sturbridge and its fair, xiii.
Sturzaker, John, bailiff of Liverpool, xii.
Styall, township of Wilmslow, viii.
Styche, co. Salop, xix.
Styshall, near Coventry, viii.
Stythe, Mr., ix.
Suarez's (Francesco) *Disputationes Metaphysicæ*, iv.
Subjects of prayer, xviii.
Subsidy bill, debate on, ix.
Suckling, sir John, xiii.
Sudall, 𝔑, xiv.
Sudden *or* Southden, mill of, xx.
Sudell, 𝔑, xxii.
Sudlow, part of Tabley, Rosthorne, viii.
Sudmore, xx (*tit.* Ynes).
Suffield, lords, xiv, xix.
Suffolk *or* Southfolke under the sufferaynte of Uffa, xv.
Suffolk, dukes of, xiv, xxii.
Suffolk, earls of, i, xiv.
Sugar house, Liverpool, ix.
Sugar-house close, Liverpool, xii.
Sulingneia, Alur. de, xx.
Summer game, xiv.
Summer-greenes, xiv.
Sumner, J. B., bishop of Chester, xix.
Sumpter cloth, description of a, xiv.
Suna *or* Sunnah, its place in Mahometan theology, xiii.
Sunday, St., vii.
Sundays misspent, xviii.
Sunderland, lord, xxii.
Sunderland, countess of, viii.
Sunderland, grangia de, xx.
Sunderland hall, Ashton-under-Line, xix.
Suns (seven) seen together at Dantzig, xiii.
Superstitions, i; puritan, xviii.
Supervisor, legal origin and tenacious holding of the word, xxiv.
Surat, ix.
Surcease, to cease, iii.
Sureis, Rob. le, xxx.
Surius, Laurentius: account of, vii.
Surplice, disuse of the, xii, xiv. *See* Cirploise.
Surquedrie, Chaucer's definition of, iii. *See* Sourquedry.
Surrey, earl of, at Flodden, xxix.
Surreys, Thom. le, xx.
Surtees's *History of Durham*, xiv.
Survey (Domesday) of Bowland, xiv.
Susenbrotus, Johannes, iv.
Sussex, ix; seconde realme of Saxons, endured but short tyme in myght, xv.
Sussex, earl of, xxii.
Sutch, William, xxii.
Sutcliffe, Dr. Matthew, xiii; his benefactions to Chelsea college, xiii.
Suterdale, xx (*tit.* Merton).
Suthewyk, Guyd prior de, xx.
Sutton, 𝔑, viii, xii, xiii, xvii, xix, xx, xxii, xxviii.
Sutton, xviii.
Sutton, in Runcorn parish, viii.
Sutton, township of Middlewich, viii.
Sutton, township of Prestbury, viii.
Sutton-cum-Winkle, township of Macclesfield, viii.
Sutton-Coldfield, co. Warwick, xiv.
Sutton, gilden- *or* golden-, Cheshire: account of, viii.
Sutton magna *and* parva, townships of Eastham, viii; hall, notice of, viii.
Sutton grange, Whitegate, viii.
Swain *or* Swaine, 𝔑, viii, xxvii.

Swainemote, keeping the, XIV.
Swainson, John, of Halton hall, XXII.
Swallow, Will. de, XXII.
Swammerdam, Holland: rape mill at, I.
Swanley, captain, XII.
Swanlow, township of Over, VIII.
Swann *or* Swanne, ℞, VIII, XVII.
Swann inn, Talk-o'th'-hill, XIV.
Swansea, I.
Swarbrick, Mr., IX.
Swartmoor hall, Ulverston: account of, XXII.
Swaynesmore, XX (*tit.* Bilyngton).
Sweden, non-intervention policy of, XIII.
Sweetenham, Mr., XXVII.
Sweeting, ℞, IX, XII, XIII.
Sweeting-street, Liverpool, XII.
Swein, ℞, XXX.
Swein Child, ℞, XXX.
Swereford, Alex. de, XX.
Swettenham, co. Chester; account of, VIII; hall, XXVII, notice of, VIII.
Swettenham, ℞, IV, VIII.
Swift, dean, IX, XII.
Swillerst, Swingleherste *or* Swindlehurst, ℞, VIII.
Swillyngton, Rob. de, XX.
Swinden, co. York, XIV.
Swinerton *or* Swinnerton, ℞, VIII, IX.
Swinfield, Rich., bishop of Hereford, I.
Swinghurst, Tho., XXVIII.
Swinglehurst, ℞, XIV, XXII. *See* Swillerst.
Swinlegh *for* Swynlegh, John de, vicar of Warrington, XXII. *See* Swynlegh.
Swinnow, colonel, of Chatton, co. Northumberland: prosecution of his wife for witchcraft, VI.
Swinshead in Rosthorne, VIII.
Swinton, township of Eccles, XVII, XIX, XX.
Swinton *or* Swynton, ℞, XVIII, XIX, XX, XXVII.
Swordes, Ireland, I.
Swyer, ℞, VI.
Swyndeley, Hugh, IX.
Swyneflet, Richart de, XX.
Swyneford, XX (*tit.* Barue).
Swyneheued, XX (*tit.* Whiteword).
Swynesheued (? Swynerootings near Healey), XX.
Swyneshead abbey, co. Lincoln, XXII.
Swynlegh, John de, vicar of Warrington, XXII. *See* Swinlegh.
Sydales, XX (*tit.* Cliderhou).
Sydall, ℞, XIX.
Syddall, ℞, II, XVIII, XIX, XXVII.
Syde, XX (*tit.* Reued).
Sydenham, ℞, XIII, XXVII.
Sydney, ℞, XXIV.
Sygebert, kynge of eest Englande, subdued by Penda, XV.
Sykeston garthe, XX (*tit.* Whalleye).
Sylcock, Thomas, chaplain of Clitheroe, XXII.
Syleing, straining, VI.
Sylvester, Mrs., of Weeford, IV.
Sylvester's *Du Bartas*, XVIII.
Sylvius (Jacobus) desires Dr. Dee's acquaintance, XXIV.
Symcock, Mathew, XVIII.
Symmons *or* Symonds, sir James, XXVIII.
Symonds, ℞, XVIII, XIX. *See* Simmonds.
Symondeston, XX.
Symondeston, ℞, XX.
Sympson, ℞, I, XXVII, XXVIII.
Syngleton, ℞, XX, XXII.
Synod (*Infamous History of Sir Simon*), XVIII.
Synode, William, I.
Synods and Synodals, account of, XIX.

TABBEL, Rob. de, XX.
Tabeley, Willus de, XX.
Table Talk by Selden, XVIII.
Tables and tabling, XIV.
Tabley, township of Rosthorne, IV,

VIII, XVII; chapel, IV; hall, notice of, VIII.
Tabley, lords de, VIII, XXII.
Tabley, 𝔓, VIII.
Tabley, lower-, township of Budworth, VIII.
Tabley, over-, VIII.
Tachelache, XX (*tit.* Chaderton).
Taddeley in Acton, VIII.
Tadrid Eighes, XX (*tit.* Aluetham).
Taffe, John, IX; notice of, XXVIII; his evidence at the Jacobite trials, XXVIII.
Taillour, 𝔓, XXX.
Talæus, Andromarus: notice of, IV.
Talbot, 𝔓, II, V, VII, VIII, XIV, XIX, XXII, XXIII.
Talbot Papers, XXIX.
Talebote, Edmundus, XX.
Talboys, sir Gilbert, and Elizabeth his daughter, XIV.
Talents, Fra., XXVII.
Talk-o'th'-Hill, Taylor (the water-poet)'s anecdote respecting, XIV.
Tallebois, Ivo, XIX.
Tamysmouth, arrival of great hoosts of pagans at, XV.
Taneth, Miche de, XX.
Tanewrth, Rogerus de, XXX.
Tannfeld *error for* Townfeild, in Penwortham, XXX.
Tansy of gooseberries, receipt for, I.
Tapestry or arras depaynted with pyctures and hystoryes manyfolde, description of, XV.
Tapp-house at Delft, its strange privilege, I.
Tarbock, Tarbok *or* Tarbuck, 𝔓, II, XXII, XXVII.
Tarbock, township of Huyton, XXII; hall, notice of, XXII.
Tarbotte *or* Starbottom, co. York, XIV.
Tardy, John, XXX.
Tardy's tenement (? Tardy-gate in Farington), XXX.
Tarleton, 𝔓, IX, XII, XXII.
Tarleton, chapelry of Croston: account of, XXII.
Tarleton's fields, Liverpool, XII.
Tarleton-street, Liverpool, XII.
Tarnacara *or* Tarnaker, Willmus de, XX.
Tarporley, co. Chester, XIII; account of, VIII; marble medallion at, XIV.
Tarporley, Hugh de, VIII.
Taruin, Radulphus rector de, XX.
Tarvin, co. Chester: account of, VIII; notice of, XX; church, XIV; lecture, XXVII; wakes, how John Bruen tried to put them down, XIV.
Tasbrough, Mr., XXVIII.
Tasker, Jo., XXVII.
Tassis, Jean Baptiste: notice of, XXV.
Tateshale, Rob. de, XX.
Tatham, 𝔓, XX, XXII.
Tatham, co. Lanc.: account of, XXII; hall, description of, XXII.
Tatham-fell chapel, account of, XXII.
Tatlock, 𝔓, IX, XII, XXVIII.
Tatlowe, John, IX.
Tattenhall, account of, VIII; church, VIII; hall, notice of, VIII.
Tattenhall, 𝔓, VIII.
Tattersall, 𝔓, XXII.
Tatton, township of Rosthorne, IV, VIII; Conigree close in, IV; hall and park, account of, VIII.
Tatton, 𝔓, VIII.
Taunton, co. Somerset, XIII.
Taunton, 𝔓, VIII, XXII.
Tavy river, I.
Tawell, A. de, XX.
Tawnton *or* Tongton hall, Ashton-under-Line: notice of, XIX.
Taxall, co. Chester: account of, VIII.
Taylor, 𝔓, VIII, IX, XIII, XIV, XVIII, XIX, XXII, XXVII, XXVIII.
Taylour, Timothy, IV.
Teal, wild fowl, I.
Tedworth, the dæmon drummer at, XIII.

Tekely, Drabicius's guess with regard to, XIII.
Telesius, Bernardinus: account of, XIII.
Temperance of modern tables due to the French, XIV.
Tempest, ℞, II, XIV, XIX, XXII.
Templer, Mr., XXVII.
Templeton, first viscount, XIV.
Tenant-services, XVII.
Tenantsside, Beechton, Sandbach, VIII.
Tenby, I.
Tenison, archbishop, V, XXII.
Tennis court, Cambridge, XIII.
Tenths, account of, VIII.
Tenures of land, XV, XVII.
Terence, IV.
Terick, Mr., VIII.
Terms, nautical: account of, I.
Terrouane, battle of, XXIX.
Teruen, XX; Robertus de, XX.
Testa de Nevill', XIV, XIX.
Testamenta Vetusta, XXIX.
Testamentary burial, XIV.
Tetlow, township of Manchester, XIX.
Tetlow, ℞, XIX.
Tetton, township of Warmingham, VIII.
Teutonicus, ℞, XX.
Thacke, to thwack or beat hard, XXIII.
Thame river, XX.
Thamys (water of) bounds the south parte of Mercyens, XV.
Thane, John, D.D : account of, VIII.
Thanet, isle of, I.
Thaneth, Mich: de, XX.
Thar-cakes, oat-cakes, I.
Thatcher, Mr., I.
Thelwall, ℞, XVII, XX, XXVIII.
Thelwall chapel, Daresbury, Runcorn: account of, VIII.
Theobalds, XIV.
Theodorus, archebyssop and prymate, XV.
Theognis, a Greek poet, IV.
Therwin, Mr., XII.
Thetford priory, visits of players to, XXIX.
Thevet's *Cosmographye*, where he hath a speciall discourse of yᵉ vnicorne, VII.
Thief-leaders, under-bailiffs, I.
Thingwall, township of Woodchurch, VIII.
Thirlewind, John, IV.
Thirsclogh, XX (*tit.* Bilyngton).
Thistelrode, XX (*tit.* Castelton).
Thistelruyding, XX (*tit.* Bilyngton).
Thistelyruyding, XX (*tit.* Reued).
Thistleton, James, of Wrea, XXII (?).
Thom., clericus, fil. Gaufridi, XXX.
Thomas, ℞, VIII, XII, XVIII, XIX.
Thomas-a-Kempis, XVIII.
Thomasson, ℞, IV, IX.
Thomastown, XIV.
Thomecokfeld, XX (*tit.* Bilyngton).
Thomlinson, Mr., VII.
Thompson, ℞, IV, VI, VIII, XIII, XXII, XXVII.
Thomson, ℞, XII, XVIII.
Thomwort towne repared by the lady Elflede, XV.
Thoresby, John, cardinal and archbishop, XXII.
Thorn (Christmas-blossoming) at Glastonbury, description of, I.
Thorn, sad news from, XIII.
Thorn, Mr., XIII.
Thornborough, John, D.D., bishop of Worcester, XIV.
Thornburrow, Francis, of Selset hall, Kendal: his escape from Wigan, V.
Thorncliffe hall, Mottram: notice of, VIII.
Thorndike, Herbert: account of, XIII.
Thornelegh, sir Oliver, clerk, XIX.
Thorneton, ℞, XX.
Thornham, township of Middleton, XIX.
Thornhaugh, colonel: his death and eulogy by Cromwell, II.
Thornhill, near Wakefield, XIV.
Thornicroft, XX (*tit.* Meluer).

Thornicroft *or* Thornycroft, 𝔓, VIII, XXVII.
Thornscow, co. York, XIX.
Thornton, 𝔓, VIII, XIX.
Thornton, co. Chester: account of, VIII; hall, notice of, VIII; parsonage, XVIII; school, VIII.
Thornton in Neston, VIII.
Thornton in Coxwold, co. York, birth-place of John Webster, VI.
Thornton in Craven, XIV.
Thornton-Steward, co. York: leases of, VIII.
Thorold, sir John, bart., VIII.
Thorp, 𝔓, XIII, XVIII, XXIX, XXX.
Thounleye, Ricardus de, XXX.
Thraso, a character in Terence's *Eunuch*, XXIII.
Threap, rebuke or censure, VII.
Threlfall, 𝔓, XXII, XXVIII.
Threpfeld, XX (*tit.* Merland).
Threplondes, XX (*tit.* Bacford).
Thristcross, Mr., XIII.
Throgmorton, 𝔓, II, VI, XXVIII.
Throgmorton, Mr.: fiendlike children of, VI.
Thropp, Roger, XIX.
Thrush, John and Thomas, of London, woolpackers, VIII.
Thuanus, XIII.
Thunderbolt, virtues of a, I.
Thunderstorm at Lawton, Cheshire: its fatal effects, XXVII.
Thurgarton priory, co. Notts., XXII.
Thurland castle, Tunstall, XII; descriptions of, II, XXII; taken and retaken, II.
Thurledak, XX (*tit.* Riblecestria).
Thurles, Ireland, XIV.
Thurlow *or* Thurloe, 𝔓, IX, XII, XIII, XVIII, XXII.
Thurly, co. Bedford, XIII.
Thurneschagh, XX (*tit.* Spotlond).
Thurnham hall, Cockerham: account of, XXII.
Thursby, 𝔓, XXII, XXVII.
Thursday before Easter called Shorp-thursday, XV.
Thurstanton, Will. son of Matthew de, VIII.
Thurstaston *alias* Thurstanston, co. Chester: account of, VIII; church, VIII; hall, notice of, VIII.
Thurston, Mr., XXVII.
Thynne, 𝔓, XVIII.
Thysius, Antonius: notice of, I.
Tib, a low woman, XXIII.
Tibb, a familiar spirit, VI.
Tibbols, 𝔓, VIII.
Tichborne, Tichbourne *or* Tichburn, 𝔓, XII, XXII, XXVIII.
Tickle, Thomas, of Altcar, IX, XXII.
Tick-tacke *i.e.* tric-trac, a game of tables, XXIII.
Tides at Holy-isle, I.
Tidnock-end, in Gawsworth, VIII.
Tieys, Henr. de, XX.
Tildesley, township of Leigh, XIX. *See* Leigh, account of, XXII.
Tildesley, 𝔓, II, V, VIII, XIV, XVIII, XIX, XXII, XXVIII.
Tilebur *or* Tillesbur, Waltus de, XX.
Tiles (painted) for fire-places, at Amsterdam: description of, I.
Tillesley, Mr., a presbyterian divine, II.
Tilleson, Tho., XXIV.
Tillotson, archbishop, XIII, XXVII.
Tilsley, 𝔓, II, IV, XIII, XVIII, XXVII.
Tilson, 𝔓, XIV.
Tilston parish, co. Chester: account of, VIII.
Tilston, township of Bunbury, VIII; hall, notice of, VIII.
Tilston, Mr., VIII.
Timber trees, paucity of, in Scotland, I.
Time, poetical uses of, XXIII.
Timmis, Randle, XXIV.
Timperley, township of Bowden, VIII; hall, notice of, VIII.
Tine river, description of mouth of, I.

Tinemouth, I; castle, I. *See* Tynmouth.
Tintern *or* Kinneagh abbey, co. Wexford: notice of, I.
Tintwistle, co. Chester, VIII.
Tipping, 𝔑, VIII, XIX, XXVII.
Tirel *or* Tyrel, Hug., XX.
Tireman, Mr., of York, XIV.
Tisser, rev. John, XXII.
Tithebarn (the) in Dale-street, Liverpool, XII.
Tithebarn lane, Liverpool, XII.
Tithebarn-street, Liverpool: tenancies in, XII.
Titherington, township of Prestbury, VIII.
Tithes, difficulty about, XXVII.
Titley, township of Audlem, VIII.
Tiverton, township of Bunbury, VIII.
Toad, strange story of a, VI.
Tobaco smoking, XVIII; trade, IX.
Tockholes, chapelry of Blackburn, XIX; account of, XXII.
Tocstath, 𝔑, XX.
Todd hall, XIX.
Todd's *Life af Milton*, XXIV, XXIX.
Todegreue, XX (*tit.* Aluetham).
Todmarsden, 𝔑, XX.
Todmorden, chapelry of Rochdale, XX; account of, XIX; hall, XIV, description of, XIX.
Todson, Geffrey, XIX.
Toft, XIII.
Toft, township of nether Knutsford, VIII.
Toft, township of Rosthorne, VIII; hall, notice of, VIII.
Toft, 𝔑, VIII, XX.
Toland's *Life of Milton*, XXIV.
Tole, Ann daughter of John, XIV.
Toleration, want of, XVIII.
Toleration act, XVIII.
Tollemache, 𝔑, VIII.
Tolson, Dr., VII.
Tombert, duke, of the eest regyon of England, XV.
Tomkins, 𝔑, XVIII, XXIV.
Tomkinson, 𝔑, VIII.
Tomlinson, 𝔑, XXII, XXVIII.
Tompson, Joseph, minister of Sefton, XXII.
Tomson, James, mariner: information of, XXVIII.
Ton, 𝔑, XIX, XX.
Tonbrok in Hunresfeld, XX.
Tong *or* Tonge-end near Whitworth, XX.
Tonge in Prestwich, XIX; hall, account of, XIX.
Tonge, 𝔑, XIV, XIX, XX, XXVII.
Tongton hall. *See* Tawnton.
Tongue, Dr. Esrael: account of, XIII.
Tonson, Jacob, bookseller, XXIV.
Tonstal, Dr., XXVII.
Toone, 𝔑, XVIII.
Topclyffe, abbot of Whalley, XXII.
Tophail's (Ebn) Arabic fiction of *Hai Ebn Yokdhan:* notice of, XIII.
Topham, Mr., of Windsor, IX.
Topiary work, I.
Topliffe, co. York, I.
Toppeclif, 𝔑, XX.
Topping, 𝔑, VIII, XII, XVIII, XXVII.
Torald, Henricus, capellanus, XVII.
Torbay, IX.
Torbock, 𝔑, XIX, XXII.
Torbok, Hyton-, near Liverpool, IX.
Torbok, 𝔑, IX, XX.
Torboke, dame Cecill of, XVII.
Tordalesik, XX (*tit.* Eccles).
Torelli. *See* Sarayna.
Torfote, 𝔑, XVII.
Tories *and* Toryism, V, IX.
Torington, co. Devon., XIII.
Torre's *Catalogue of Incumbents*, XXII.
Torriano, Gio.: notice of, XIII.
Torthalen, XX (*tit.* Eccles).
Torver, chapelry of Ulverston, XIV; account of, XXII.
Tospot, Jem, a masque character, XIV.
Toster *for* Uttoxeter, XIV.
Totnes, co. Devon, XIII.

Tott, earl of, XIII.
Totteridge, XIV.
Tottington, township of Bury, XIX; hall, account of, XIX; royal manor of, XIX.
Touch, a term for granite or marble, I.
Touchet, ꝶ, VIII, XVIII.
Toulson, ꝶ, XXII.
Tounested, XX (*tit.* Aluetham).
Tournay, wager respecting, IX.
Tournourfall, XX (*tit.* Bilyngton).
Tower of London, alleged plot for seizing, XXVIII; confinement of Oldenburg in, XIII; records in, XII.
Tower hill, lord Strafford beheaded on, XIII.
Tower garden, Liverpool, XII.
Towers, ꝶ, XXII.
Towgood, John, of Wrightington, XXII.
Town hall, Liverpool, XII.
Town house near Littleborough: account of, XIX.
Towneley, ꝶ, VI, XIV, XVIII, XX, XXII, XXVIII.
Towneley hall, Burnley: description of, XXII.
Townleian marbles, XXII.
Townley, ꝶ, II, V, VIII, IX, XIII, XIX, XXII, XXIV, XXVIII.
Towns in Holland that elect the states-general, I.
Townsend, ꝶ, VIII, XXII.
Townshend, Mr., IX.
Toxliche, John and Anne, XXII.
Toxstath, Jacob, IX.
Toxteth park, IX, XII, XX; chapel, account of, XXII.
Toxton, XX (*tit.* Gerstan).
Tozier, captain, XXVIII.
Tradescant *or* Tredeskin, John, XVIII, XXVII; account of, VII.
Trafford, ꝶ, II, VIII, XIV, XVIII, XIX, XX, XXII, XXIII, XXVII, XXVIII; etymology of the name, XXIII.
Trafford, township of Manchester, XIX; hall and park, Eccles, account of, XIX.
Trafford, mickle, Plemstow, VIII.
Trafford (bridge-) hall, Plemstow: notice of, VIII.
Trafford (Wimbalds-) hall, Thornton: notice of, VIII.
Trafford chapel in Plemstow church, VIII.
Tranent, arrival of highlanders at, V.
Tranmere, township of Bebington, VIII, XII.
Tranmulle, Bernard lord of, VIII.
Translacion of the corps of saynt Werburge, description of, XV.
Transport debt, IX.
Transted ruined by the papists, XIII.
Transylvania, prince of, XIII.
Traquair, sir John Stewart earl of: notice of, I.
Trathorne, XX (*tit.* Etheleswyk).
Travelling in Bohemia, its dangers and expenses, XXIV.
Travers, ꝶ, IX, XII, XX, XXII.
Travis, ꝶ, VIII, XIX, XXII, XXVII.
Travis mill, XVIII.
Trawden forest, VI.
Traylebew family, VIII.
Trease, milk-pail, I.
Treasurers and collectors of subsidy, lord Derby's appointment of, II.
Treasury, petition to lords of the, XXVIII (?).
Treaty of Newport, XVIII.
Trebon castle, Bohemia, XXIV.
Treby, chief justice, IX.
Tredaugh. *See* Drogheda.
Tredeskin, John. *See* Tradescant.
Tremouille, duc de: notice of, I.
Trenchard, sir John: account of, XXVIII.
Trent, city of, XIII.
Trent river, XIV.
Trentam monastery, legendary notices of, XV.

Tresham, Mr., XXVII.
Trevor, 𝔑, IX, XII.
Trevoux, journalists of, XIII.
Trials (Jacobite) at Manchester, XXVIII.
Trim, Ireland, XII.
Trinity college *and* hall, Cambridge, XIII.
Trithemius (abbot) on the sex of angels, XIII.
Triumphs *or* pageants, value of, III.
Troghbrok, XX (*tit.* Whiteword).
Trollop *or* Trollope, 𝔑, II, VIII, XXVII.
Troms-Booth, lands in Bradshaw, Bolton, XIX.
Trot, 𝔑, XIII, XXVII.
Troutbeck, 𝔑, VIII, XVII.
Trowbridge, XII.
Trumbull, William, envoy at Brussels, IX.
Trumpington, 𝔑, VIII, XX.
Truro, co. Cornwall, XIII.
Trussel *or* Trussell, 𝔑, VIII, XX.
Tuball *and* Tubalcain, inventours of musyke, purtrayed in arras, XV.
Tuchet, 𝔑, XX.
Tucker, J., under-secretary of state: his letter to the mayor of Liverpool, IX.
Tuckney, Dr. Anthony, XXVII; account of, XIII; his *None but Christ*, XVIII.
Tudor, Gabriel, and Mary his wife, XIX.
Tufton, 𝔑, XIV.
Tulips in Holland, price of, I.
Tulket in Aundirnesse, XXII.
Tulketh, Marmaduke de, XXII.
Tulketh hall, Preston: notice of, XXII.
Tullianum (the) at Rome, XVIII.
Tully, Dr., XXVII.
Tumblers at court, XIV.
Tunfeld *i.e.* Townfield, in Whiteword, XX.
Tunneworth heye, XX (*tit.* Whalleye).
Tunneworth hyghe, XX (*tit.* Whalleye)
Tunneworth ryddynge, XX (*tit.* Whalleye).
Tunstall, 𝔑, V, XX, XXII.
Tunstall, account of, XXII; formation of the deanery of, XIX.
Tunstede, XX (*tit.* Etheleswyk).
Tunwalclif, XX. *See in same volume* Whiteword.
Tubervile, Dr., VIII.
Turenne, 𝔑, XVIII.
Turf moss, XVIII, XXVII.
Turin, siege of, IX.
Turkey (Christians in) reverence the English liturgy, IX.
Turks or pirates in the Bristol channel, dread of, I.
Tum-crook-hey, a meadow in Wallesey, VIII.
Turnebus, XXIV.
Turner, 𝔑, I, VIII, IX, XII, XVIII, XIX, XXII, XXVII.
Turnhagh, 𝔑, XX.
Turnogh, sir Robert, priest of Littleborough, XIX.
Turton, township and chapelry of Bolton: account of, XIX; tower, description of, XIX.
Turton, 𝔑, IX, XVII, XXII, XXVIII.
Tussingham, township of Malpas, VIII.
Tweed river, at Berwick, I.
Twelfth-day, celebration of, XIV.
Twells, Rob., XIII.
Twelves, Mr., XIII.
Twenge, 𝔑, XXII.
Twiggen nests and baskets, I.
Twine, Brian, vicar of Rye: notice of, VII.
Twis *or* Twisse, 𝔑, XX, XXVII.
Twisleton, 𝔑, II, XII.
Twiston *or* Twyston, XIV.
Twofoldhee, XX (*titt.* Castelton, Chadewyk, Merland, Spotlond).
Twyselton, Joh. de, XX.
Twysse, 𝔑, XVII.

Twystes (le) in Warrington, XVII.
Tydd rectory, near Wisbeach, VIII.
Tyeth barn, XX (*tit.* Whalleye).
Tyldesley, 𝔉, II, IX, XII, XIV.
Tyler, Wat: insurrection of, XXII.
Tylney, master of the revels, XXIX.
Tylston, vicar of Rochdale, XIX.
Tyne river. *See* Tine.
Tynhead, co. Wilts., XIII.
Tynmouth abbay distroied by Danes, XV.
Tynwald court, isle of Man, IX.
Tyrefford, Symon de, XX.
Tyrehare, John, XVII.
Tyrer, 𝔉, IX, XII.
Tyrer-street, Liverpool, XII.
Tyringham, sir Arthur: notice of, I.
Tyrwhitt, Grace daughter of Robert, XIV.
Tyson, 𝔉, XXII.
Tytylus, kynge of eest England, XV.

UGGECOTELAWE, XX (*tit.* Whiteword).
Uhtredus filius Sweyn, XXX.
Ulf, son of Turulf. *See* Machel and Ulf.
Ulkel, Nich., XX.
Ulminus, chanon of Chestre, having his leg and thie broken, is restaured to helth by saynt Werburge, XV.
Ulverston, account of, XXII; church dependent upon Urswick, XXII.
Umble pye, XIV.
Umfraville *or* Umphraville, 𝔉, XIV, XIX.
Uncanonical conduct, XIV.
Unccyon, holy: saynt Werburge requyres the spyrytuall sufferage of, XV.
Underley park, co. Westmorland, XIV.
Uniacke, Mr., of Carincham, I.
Unicorn, virtues of the horn of the, VII.
Uniformity, act of, IV, XII.
Union street, Liverpool, XII.
University of Cambridge: feud between the Fellows of St. John's college, XXVII. *See* Cambridge.
Unsworth, township of Prestwich, XIX.
Unsworth, Anne, XVIII, XXVII.
Unton, sir Henry, ambassador in France, XXIX.
Unton Inventories of furniture, XIV.
Unwyn, 𝔉, XVIII, XXVII.
Upcott, Mr., XIII.
Upham's (C. W.) *Life of Sir H. Vane*, XIII.
Uphaven, co. Wilts., XIII.
Up-Holland, chapelry of Wigan: account of, XXII. *See* Holland near Wigan.
Upshan, Mr., vicar of Acton, XXVII.
Upton, 𝔉, XIII, XXVIII.
Upton, co. Chester, XX.
Upton, township of St. Mary's, Chester, VIII; notice of, XV; park miraculously protected by saynt Werburge, XV.
Upton, township of Overchurch, VIII; church, VIII; hall, notice of, VIII; rectory, VIII.
Upton, township of Prestbury, VIII.
Upton in Woodchurch, VIII.
Urmston in Flixton, XIX; hall, account of, XIX.
Urmston, 𝔉, IV, VIII, XIX, XX, XXII.
Ursewyk, Eswardus de, XX.
Urswick, account of, XXII; church, XXII.
Urswick, 𝔉, XXII.
Urston, John, IV.
Ushant, IX.
Usher, archbishop, XIII; personal notices of, I; letters of Dr. Thomas James to, VII; *Sermons*, XVIII; *Works*, XIII.
Usk river, I.
Utica in Normandy, notices of the abbey of St. Ebrulft at, VIII.
Utkinton manor, Tarporley, IX, XIV, XVII; notice of, VIII.

Utley, hanged for witchcraft, VI.
Utrecht, cities and political power of, I.
Uttoxeter, colloquial abbreviation of, XIV.
Uty, Dr., XIII.
Uxbridge, co. Middlesex, XIII.
Uxbridge commission, XIV.

VACCARIES of Rossendale forest, XXII.
Vadcó, Alexius, XIV.
Vaile, to yield, III.
Val, Hugh de la, XXII.
Valentia, wager respecting, IX.
Valentia, Willus de, XX.
Valentia, lord, XIII.
Valentine, 𝔑, XIX, XXVII.
Valentinus, Michael Bernhard, XIII.
Vale-Royal, Whitegate, VIII, XIV; description of the hall, VIII.
Vale-Royal abbey, XXII; account of, VIII.
Valesius *or* De Valois, Henry: account of, XIII.
Valiers, captain, I.
Vallibus, Nich. de, constab. Cestrie, XX.
Valor of Pope Nicholas, XIX.
Vanasembla, Ingelo's country of, XIII.
Vandenberg, grave Henry of, I.
Van Druske, general, II.
Vane, 𝔑, XIII, XVIII, XXVII.
Van Helmont, John Baptist, VI; account of and extracts from his writings, XIII.
Van Helmont, Francis Mercury, XIII.
Vanity, poetical exhortation against, XV.
Vasnaer's (Nicolai) *Relationes Historicæ*, XIII.
Vatteville, Spanish ambassador: his sanguinary contest for precedency, XVIII.
Vaudrey *or* Vawdrey, 𝔑, VIII, XVIII.
Vaughan, 𝔑, XIII, XVIII, XXVII.
Vaulting a Sunday sport, XIV.
Vause, Thomas, of Garston, XXII.
Vaux, lord, XIV.
Vaux hall, near Blackpool, XIV.
Vavasour, 𝔑, XIV, XX.
Veal, John, XXVIII.
Veasie, Mrs., a most mighty fat woman, I.
Vecta, ilande, called the yle of Wyght, subdued by Wulfer kynge of Mercyens, XV.
Venables, 𝔑, II, IV, VIII, IX, XVII, XX, XXII, XXVII.
Venator, 𝔑, VIII, XX.
Vendeville, Dr., XXV.
Venetian ambassador, IX.
Venice, public agent at, XIII; Scotch prisoners sent to, XII, XVIII.
Venn, 𝔑, IX.
Venner, XVIII; mad prank of, IV.
Venour, Willus, XX.
Verdugo, 𝔑, XXV.
Vere, 𝔑, VIII, XIII, XVIII, XXIX.
Vergil, Polydore, XIV.
Verney, Mr., XIII.
Vernon, 𝔑, VIII, IX, XIII, XIV, XX.
Vernon's *Cheshire Collections*, XXIV.
Versailles, XVIII.
Vesey *or* Vescy, 𝔑, XIX, XX.
Veterinary practice, I.
Veterinus opposes Drabicius, XIII.
Veysey, John, LL.D., VIII.
Vicarages, one of Henry the Eighth's, an ironical phrase, XXII.
Vicar's-hill house, near Lymington, XIX.
Vicar's lane, VIII.
Vicomercatus courts Dr. Dee's acquaintance, XXIV.
Vicqueford, monsieur, XIII.
Vienna, siege of by the Turks, XIII.
Vigiliæ and Encœnia, patristic condemnation of, XIV.
Villemandy, editor of *Bochart*, XIII.
Villers, 𝔑, IX.

Villiers, ℞, XIV, XXII.
Vincent, saynt, depaynted on arras, XV.
Vincent, Mr., preacher at Dort, I.
Vincent's *MS. Collections* in college of arms, XIV.
Vincentius Lirinensis, notice of, XII.
Vindiciæ Academiarum, critical notice of, VI.
Viner, ℞, VIII.
Vines, Richard, XIII, XVIII.
Violett, Massted, incumbent of Milnrow, XIX.
Vipers, vulgar error concerning, XXIII.
Vipont, Rogerus de, XX.
Virgil, IV; *Inferno* of, XVIII.
Virginia, IX, XII; its slave trade, XVIII.
Virginia company sell the Bermudas, XIII.
Virgin Mary depaynted on arras, XV.
Virgin queen, dream respecting a, XXIII.
Virgins crowned with the lyly or with rooses, embrodred purtrayture of, XV.
Visitations of Lancashire, XIV. *See* vol. XXIV, art. 3.
Visitelli, Barbara, XXII.
Vitæ Patrum caused to be redde for a pastyme by saynt Werburge, XV.
Vitalis, Ordericus, XIV.
Viviani, geometer, XIII.
Vocabularies of sea and Scotch terms, I.
Vodka, Alexius, M.D.: notice of, XIV. *See* Vadco *and* Wadko.
Voetius, XIII, XVIII.
Voght's *Catalogus Librorum Rariorum*, XIII.
Voltaire's philanthropist, XII.
Von Hammer, XVIII.
Vornscapps, Dutch common-councilmen, I.
Vorstius, Adolphus, doctor of physic: his mode of lecturing, I.
Vortiger, kynge of Britons, invites over duke Hengyst, XV.
Vossius, Gerard John: account of, XIII.
Vossius, Isaac: account of, XIII.
Vyne, Rich., XIII.

WAAL river, Holland, I.
Wabewell, Willmus de, XX.
Waddington, XIV.
Waddington, ℞, II, XX, XXII.
Waddow hill, near Clitheroe, XIV.
Wade, ℞, VIII, XII, XIII.
Wadfurthlong, XX (*tit.* Etheleswyk).
Wadko, Dr., XIV.
Wadley, co. Berks., XIV.
Wadyngton, Thomas, XVII.
Waet, Tho., VIII.
Wagers, political, IX.
Wagner's (Adolphus) *Giordano Bruno*, XIII.
Wagstaffe, ℞, VI, VIII, XXVIII.
Wailes of Newcastle, stained glass by, XIX.
Wainesford, Mr., XIV.
Wainhouse, ℞, XXII.
Wainman, colonel: notice of, II.
Wainwright, ℞, II, VIII, XII, XIX, XXII.
Wait *or* Waite, ℞, VIII, XVIII.
Wakefeld, Alexander de, vicar of Ormskirk, XXII.
Wakefield, co. York, I, II, IV, XIV.
Wakering, John, bishop of Norwich, XXII.
Wakes and rushbearings, XIV, XXIII.
Walays, ℞, XXII.
Walbank, William, XIV.
Walchius's *or* Walch's *Biblia Theologica Selecta*, XIII.
Walden, XIII.
Waldenses, books of the, I; collection in England for, XIII.
Wale *or* wall, a wave, VII.
Walensis, ℞, XX.
Wales, IX; Brytons expulsed to, XV; dytche Offa dyvydes it from Englande, XV; English princes of, VIII.

Wales, north: its connexion with Liverpool, XII.
Wales, Mr., XVIII.
Waleton *and* Waletone, 𝔑, XX, XXII, XXX.
Waley, township of Taxall, VIII.
Waley, Thoma de, XVII.
Waleya, William son of Richard de, VIII.
Waleys, 𝔑, XX.
Walgrave, Mr., XXVIII.
Walkden, 𝔑, XIV.
Walker, 𝔑, I, V, VIII, IX, XII, XIII, XIV, XVIII, XIX, XXII, XXVII, XXVIII.
Walker's *History of Independency*, XII; *Sufferings of the Clergy*, XII, XIX.
Wall, to boil, I.
Wall, 𝔑, VIII, XIII, XIV, XXII, XXIV.
Wallæus, 𝔑, I.
Wallasey, VII; account of, VIII; church, VIII; leases of, VIII.
Wallasey-leasowe, IX.
Wallasey-race, IV; meaning of, VII.
Wallaston, township of Acton, VIII.
Wallbank, a messuage in Rochdale, XIX.
Walle, Will., prebendary of Chester, VIII.
Wallensis, Richard, lord of Litherland, XXII.
Waller, 𝔑, XII, XIII, XVIII.
Wallingford, William Knollys viscount: account of, XIV.
Wallis, 𝔑, I, IV, IX, XIII, XXII, XXIX.
Wallons, Mr., minister of Coulton, XXII.
Walloons, I.
Wallop, sir Henry, of Farley Wallop: notice of, I.
Walloper well, XIV.
Walls, ancient, viz., Picts', Graham's, Berwick, Chester, Newcastle, York, I.
Walm, a salt-measure, I.
Walmersley, township of Bury, XIX; school, notice of, XIX.
Walmsley, chapelry of Bolton: account of, XIX; becke *or* brook, XIX.
Walmsley *or* Walmesley, 𝔑, IX, XIV, XIX, XXII, XXVIII.
Walney island, chapelry of Dalton: account of, XXII.
Walnut-tree hey, Liverpool, XII.
Walnut-trees, Christmas-blossoming, I.
Walpole, 𝔑, IX, XIII, XXII.
Walpole's *Anecdotes of Painting*, XIV; *Letters to Mann*, IX.
Walschagh, Ad. de, XX.
Walsh, 𝔑, VIII, XIV, XVII, XXII.
Walshman, 𝔑, VI.
Walsingham, sir Francis, XXIV.
Walter, 𝔑, VIII, XIX, XXII, XXX.
Walthall, 𝔑, VIII.
Walthew, 𝔑, II, XXII.
Walthewyscroft, XX (*tit.* Swynton).
Walton, 𝔑, V, VIII, XIII, XIV, XVII, XVIII, XIX, XXII, XXVII, XXVIII, XXX.
Walton, XX; capella, XX.
Walton, near Liverpool, IX, XII; account of, XXII; hall, XXII.
Walton-le-Dale, XIV; account of, XXII; hall, notice of, XXII.
Walton, over- and nether-, Daresbury, Runcorn, VIII.
Walton bridge, military occupation and passages of, II.
Walton's *Polyglot Bible*, notice of, XIII.
Waltuna *or* Waleton, Ulf. de. *See* Wartuna.
Walworth, co. Hants., XIV.
Walworth, 𝔑, XIX, XXVII.
Wambewell, Willyam de, XX.
Wandsford, Christopher: notice of, XIV.
Wanklyn, J. B., VI.
Wantage, co. Berks., XIII.
Wango, Dolly, a masque character, XIV.
Wapentake, keeping a, XIV.
Wapping, IX.
Warburton, chapelry of Lymm, IV, XVII; account of, VIII; priory, VIII.

Warburton, 𝔓, VIII, XII, XIII, XIV, XVII, XIX, XX, XXIII, XXVII.
Warch, a pain, VI.
Warcoaste, Dr., physician of Leyden: his singular prescription, I.
Ward, 𝔓, II, VI, VII, VIII, IX, XII, XIII, XIV, XVIII, XXII, XXIII, XXVII.
Wardell, Math., XIII.
Wardens of Manchester, XVIII, XXVII.
Wardens (church-), swearing in, XVIII.
Wardhull parva, villa de, XX.
Wardle, township of Bunbury, VIII; hall, notice of, VIII.
Wardleworth, 𝔓, XIX.
Wardley hall, Eccles, XIV; account of, XIX.
Wardul, 𝔓, XX.
Ware, co. Herts., XIII, XIV; park, XIV.
Ware, sir John la, XIX.
Ware's (Dr. Hibbert-) *History of Collegiate Church of Manchester*, XIV, XIX.
Ware's (sir James) *History of Ireland*, XIV.
Wareham, William, XXVII.
Wareing *or* Waring, 𝔓, VIII, XIV, XXII.
Waretre, assessment of, IX.
Warford, township of Alderley, VIII.
Warinus, 𝔓, XXX.
Warkworth occupied by the Northumbrian rebels, V.
Warkworth castle, I.
Warmakysholt, XX (*tit.* Spotlond).
Warmingham, account of, VIII.
Warmingham, 𝔓, XII, XXVIII.
Warminster, XIII.
Warner, 𝔓, I, II, XIII.
Warnsfeld, battle of, XXV.
Warr (de la), 𝔓, XIX, XXII.
Warrant, sir John, knt., IX.
Warren, 𝔓, VIII, XIV, XVIII, XXII, XXVII.
Warriner, 𝔓, XIV, XXII.
Warrington, IV, VI, VIII, IX, XIII, XVIII, XIX; account of, XXII; description of, XVII; military struggles at, II, V, XII; inquisition at, XXVIII; bridge, early history of, XVII; heath, high church, museum, rectory, windmill, XVII; Grey-friars' monastery, VIII; Trinity chapel, XIX, account of, XXII. *See* Weryngton.
Warrington, earls of, IV, VIII, IX, XIX, XXII, XXVII.
Warthe (le) in Arpeley field, Warrington, XVII.
Warton in Kendal, account of, XXII; ruins at, XXII.
Warton, township and chapelry of Kirkham, XX; account of, XXII.
Warton, 𝔓, VIII, XXII, XXIV, XXIX.
Wartuna *error for* Waltuna, Ulf. de, *and* Waleton, Hulf. de, XXX.
Warwick repared by Elflede duchesse of Merciens, XV.
Warwick, earls of, II, VIII, XII, XV, XX.
Warwick, countess of, XXIV.
Waschett, William de, knt., lord of Copenhall, VIII.
Wash (the) near Latchford, XVII.
Washing (sluttish mode of) in Scotland and Ireland, I.
Waspetub, XX (*tit.* Croenton).
Waste, XXX (*tit.* Farington).
Watchet, co. Somerset, I.
Water, medicinal value of, I.
Waterfall, Rob. de, XX.
Waterford, IX; description of, I.
Waterford, S. episcopus, XX.
Waterfordleye, XX (*tit.* Wolueton).
Water-garth *or* -yarth, great and little, Liverpool, XII.
Watergate-strete, XX (*tit.* Cestria).
Waterhouse, 𝔓, XXII, XXVII.
Waterhouses, township of Ashton-under-Line, XIX.
Waterland's (Dr.) *Moyer Lectures*, XIX.
Water-street, Liverpool: tenancies in, XII.

Waterworks, curious, at Amsterdam, I.
Watfield, township of Astbury, VIII.
Watford, co. Herts., XIII.
Watkins, Mr., XIII.
Watkinson, N., XXVII.
Watling-street, I, VIII.
Watlondeswoderod, XX.
Watlondewod, XX (*tit.* Spotlond).
Watmough, N., XIV, XIX.
Wats, Rob., a godly minister, XIV.
Watson, N., I, IV, VIII, XIV, XVIII, XIX, XXIV, XXVII.
Watson's *History of Halifax*, XIV.
Watt, N., IX, XXII.
Watts, N.; VIII, IX, XIII, XXVII.
Watt's (Rev. Thomas) *Life of Dr. Assheton*, XIX.
Waverham, account of, VIII; church, VIII.
Waverley abbey, co. Sussex, XXII.
Waverton, account of, VIII.
Wavertree, Richard de, prior of St. Oswald of Nostell, XXII.
Wavertree lane, Liverpool, XII. *See* Waretre.
Wax-penny, an Easter due, XXII.
Wax-work at Amsterdam, I.
Way, Albert, XXIV; his *Catalogue of Antiquities, &c.*, XIV; *Promptorium Parvulorum*, VI.
Waynegate, XX (*tit.* Wlipshire).
Waynwright, William, IX.
Wearden, Rob., cook, XXII.
Weardley, a seat of the Tyldesleys, XIV.
Wearyall hill, near Glastonbury, XIII.
Weaver, captain, IV.
Web, Webb *or* Webbe, N., II, VIII, XIX, XXII, XXIV, XXIX.
Weber, Mr., XXIX.
Webster, N., VI, VIII, IX, XIII, XVII, XXII.
Webster's *History of Metallurgy*, XIV.
Wedacre *or* Woodacre hall, Garstang: notice of, XXII.
Wedon, co. Northampton: legendary account of saynt Werburge's residence there, XV.
Weest party of Mercyens (*i.e.* Cheshire) in all actes marcyall ever have the victorye, XV.
Weever, township of Middlewich, VIII.
Weever family, VIII.
Weever's *Monuments*, XXIX.
Weidler's *Hist. Astron.*, XIII.
Weimar, ghosts at, I.
Weimar, dukes of, I, XIII.
Welch, N., XXII.
Welchman, N., XIII, XXVII.
Weld, N., XXII.
Weldon, N., XIV, XXII.
Weldon's *Court of James I.*, XVIII.
Well in More street, Liverpool: account of, XII.
Wellar, Mr., XIII.
Wellegate, XX (*tit.* Cliderhou).
Wellesik, XX (*titt.* Cliderhou, Whelton, Whiteword).
Wells, XIII; description of, I; cathedral, VIII.
Wells, N., VIII, XXVII.
Welsby, J., VIII.
Welsh, N., XVIII, XIX.
Welsh evidences *or* title-deeds, XXIV.
Welsh Inventory, XVIII.
Weltby, Joseph, VIII.
Wemyss, earls of, XXII.
Wenborough, co. Devon., I.
Wendebrok, XX (*tit.* Bilyngton).
Wenedocie, bishopric of all South Wales, XV.
Wenefryde (saynt) depaynted on arras, XV.
Wenlecence (place of) founded by erle Leofric, XV.
Wensleydale, a little war in, XIV.
Wentworth, N., IX, XII, XIII, XIV, XIX, XXII.
Weobley, IX, XVIII.

Werbode, a fals knyght of kynge Wulfer: legendary account of, xv.
Werburge *or* Werburgh, St., I; *Holy Lyfe and History of*, VIII, XV; her eulogistic titles, XV.
Werburgh's (St.) abbey, Chester, I, VIII; foundation and endowment of, XV. *See* St. Werburgh.
Werburgh's (St.) church, Dublin, I.
Werden, 𝔓, XII, XXII.
Werdul, 𝔓, XX.
Werford, little-, township of Over-Peover, Rosthorne, VIII.
Werneth manor, VIII.
Werneth *for* Wornyth, Ric. de, XX.
Weryngton, XX.
Weryngton, 𝔓, XX.
Weseham, Rog. de, bishop of Lichfield, XIX.
West, 𝔓, IX, XIII, XVIII, XIX, XXII, XXVII.
Westby, 𝔓, II, XIV, XXII, XXVIII.
Westby hall, Kirkham: notice of, XXII.
Westchester (Speech of the Mayor of), a poetical satire, XIV.
West-Derby, IX, XII.
Westeighes, XX (*tit.* Aluetham).
Westeleye, 𝔓, XX.
Western, Mr., fellow of Manchester collegiate church, XVIII.
Westewod and its divisions, XX. *See in same volume* Eccles.
Westfaling, Herbert, bishop of Hereford: notice of, I.
Westhoughton *or* Westhalghton, township and chapelry of Dean, XX; account of, XIX.
West Indies, IX.
West-Kirby, VIII.
West-Lavington, co. Wilts., XIII.
West-Leigh, township of Leigh, XIX, XXII.
Westley, Mr., XXVIII.
Westmarches endure moche turment from the Danes, XV.
Westmariland *or* Westmoreland, origin of the name, XV.
West Mercia. *See* Weest.
Westminster, IX; abbey, XIV; school, Henry Stubbe's education at, XIII.
Westminster, Robert first marquis of, XIX, XXII.
Westmoreland, earls of, XIV, XIX.
Westmoreland militia run away from the rebels, V.
Weston, township of Runcorn, VIII.
Weston, township of Wibunbury, VIII, XII; hall, notice of, VIII.
Weston *and* Weston house, co. Derby, VIII.
Weston, 𝔓, VIII, XVIII, XX, XXVII.
West-Saxons, famous and myghty, thyrde realme of Saxons, XV.
Westslak, XX (*titt.* Eccles, Westewod).
Westwood, XX (*tit.* Whalleye).
Weteakyrs, Warrington, XVII.
Weteleye, XX (*tit.* Spotlond).
Weteleye (now Whiteleys in Spotland), Henricus de le, XX.
Wetenhalenes, ancient name of Vale Royal, VIII.
Wetenhall, chapelry of Over, VIII; hall, notice of, VIII.
Wetenhall, 𝔓, VIII, XIII, XX.
Wetherley, William, vicar of Blackburn and custos regalitatis of duchy of Lancaster, XXII.
Wethney- *probably* Whittern-abbey in Galloway, XXII.
Weverham, township of Whitegate, VIII.
Wexford, XII; description of, I.
Weyme, David, I.
Weymouth, XIII.
Weys- *or* orphan-houses, in Holland, I.
Weysmaisters, I.
Whaley, Dr., XIII.
Whalley, 𝔓, II, VIII, IX, XIV, XIX, XX, XXII, XXVIII.

Whalley, VI, XII, XIII, XIV; account of, XXII; battle at, II; divisions and bounds of the parish, XX; its original extent, XIV; impoverished state of the chapels, VII; church and church-yard, XIV; school, XIX, XXII; church-wardens' accounts, XIV; abbates, decani, portarius, procurator, rector *et* vicarii de, XX.
Whalley abbey, VI, XVII; description of, XXII; notice of, VIII; arms of, XIV.
Whalley Coucher Book, XVII, XIX.
Wharton, township of Davenham, VIII.
Wharton, lords, II, IX, XXVIII.
Wharton, ℞, I, XII, XVIII.
Wharton's *Troubles and Trial of Archbishop Laud*, XIII.
Whatcroft, township of Davenham, VIII.
Whatton, ℞, IX, XVIII.
Wheate, sir Thomas, XXII.
Wheatley, XX (*tit.* Whalleye).
Wheatley-lane in Pendle, VI.
Wheatley's *Moyer Lectures*, XIX.
Wheeler, Mr., XIII.
Wheel-horses, their mode of working, I.
Wheelock, township of Sandbach, VIII; hall, notice of, VIII.
Wheelock, Hugh, VIII.
Wheelton, near Rivington, XIX.
Whelcroft, XX (*titt.* Whelton, White-word).
Whelps, ships of war: notices of, I.
Whelton and its divisions, XX.
Whetstone, George, XIII.
Whichcote, ℞, XIII, XXVII.
Whigs, IX; their history and principles, V.
Whilton, Mat., VIII.
Whirley rents, in Halton, VIII.
Whispering place in Gloucester cathedral: description of, I.
Whiston hall, Prescot, IX; notice of, XXII.
Whiston's *Memoirs*, XIII.
Whitacre, XX (*tit.* Liuesay).
Whitacre orchard, XX (*tit.* Whalleye).
Whitacre, Thomas, of Holme, XIV.
Whitacres, ℞, XX.
Whitaker, ℞, I, VI, XII, XIV, XIX, XXII, XXVII.
Whitakers, Anne, VIII.
Whitborne, near Bromyard, XVIII.
Whitbrok, XX (*tit.* Sadelword).
Whitby, Edward, antiquary: notice of, VII.
Whitby in Stoke, VIII.
Whitby abbey, foundation and endowment of, XV; formerly called Strenyshalt, XV.
Whitchurch, co. Salop, I, VIII; taken by the parliament's forces, II.
Whitchurch, Mr., minister of St. Peter's, Nottingham, XXVII.
White, ℞, VII, VIII, XIII, XIV, XVIII, XXII, XXVII, XXX.
White's *Bampton Lectures*, XVIII.
Whiteby, XX.
White-chapel in Goosenargh *alias* Threlfall chapel, chapelry of Kirkham: account of, XXII.
Whitechapel, Liverpool, XII.
White cross, Liverpool, IX, XII.
White cross, Warrington, XVII.
Whitefeld, XX (*tit.* Wolueton).
Whitefield in Pilkington, Prestwich, XIX.
Whitefield, ℞, XXII, XXVIII.
Whitegate *alias* Newchurch, account of, VIII.
Whitehall, London: Sunday performances at, XIV.
Whitehall in Darwen, XXII.
Whitehall, Mr., of Pettles, XXVII.
Whitehaven, IX, XII, XIX.
Whitehead, ℞, XIV, XVIII, XIX, XXII, XXVII.
Whiteing, last abbot of Glastonbury, I.
Whitekar, XX (*tit.* Harwod).

Whitelegh, Agnes filia Henrici de, XX.
Whitelocke, Bulstrode, XII, XIII, XVIII.
Whitendale, XIV.
Whitendale, James, XIV.
White-parish, co. Wilts., XIII.
White-rent in Hale, XXII.
Whitesiche, XX (*tit.* Gerstan).
Whiteside, Richard: information of, XXVIII.
Whitestob, XX (*tit.* Wolueton).
Whitewell in Bowland, chapelry of Whalley, XIV; account of, XXII.
Whitewell chapel in Iscoyd, co. Flint, VIII.
Whitewellsike, XX (*tit.* Whiteword).
White Wolfe, a sermon by Stephen Denison, XIV.
Whiteword and its divisions, XX.
Whiteword, 𝕻, XX.
Whitewordbrok, XX (*tit.* Whiteword).
Whitfield, 𝕻, II, IV, VIII, XXVIII.
Whitfield hall in Crompton, Oldham, XIX.
Whitgift, archbishop, XIX.
Whitham, Dr., XXII.
Whithead, Jane, IX.
Whitley, over-, co. Chester, IV.
Whitley, higher-, township of Budworth, VIII.
Whitley, lower- *or* nether-, township and chapelry of Budworth: account of, VIII.
Whitley, 𝕻, II, VIII.
Whitlock, 𝕻, XIII, XXVII.
Whitloe, Thomas, of Bootle, XII.
Whitmore, 𝕻, VIII, XXII, XXV.
Whitney, highwayman: his pretended plot, XXVIII.
Whitson-ales, XIV.
Whittacre, 𝕻, XXII, XXVII.
Whittaker, 𝕻, XIV, XXII.
Whittakers *for* Whitacres, James, VIII.
Whittern abbey in Galloway, XXII.
Whittingham, 𝕻, XXII.
Whittington, co. Lanc.: account of, XXII; hall, notice of, XXII.
Whittington, Rev. T. J., of Winwick, XII.
Whittle, tithes of, XIX.
Whittle, 𝕻, VI, XII, XVIII, XIX, XXII, XXVII.
Whitworth, chapelry of Rochdale: account of, XIX.
Whitworth, 𝕻, XIV, XIX.
Whynn, Mr., XIII.
Whytehead, Robert, chantry priest of Downham, XXII.
Whythinfeld, XX (*tit.* Spotlond).
Whytingham, Warinus de, XX.
Wibunbury, co. Chester: account of, VIII.
Wichalgh *or* Wychough, township of Malpas, VIII.
Wich-Malbank, barony and chapel of, VIII. *See* Wych-Millbank *and* Wyco-Malbank.
Wickens *and* Wickyns, 𝕻, IV, XVIII, XXVII.
Wickham church, painted glass in, VII.
Wickliffe, John, XII; Richard James's justification of, VII.
Wickstead, 𝕻, VIII, XXIV.
Wickstead hall in Whitchurch, VIII.
Widdowes, John, IX.
Widdrington, lords, II, V.
Widdrington, 𝕻, V, XXVIII.
Wierus, lofty character of, VI.
Wife of twenty-four husbands, I.
Wigan, IV, XII, XIII, XIV; general account of, XXII; military proceedings at, II: rebel prisoners at, V; parliamentary election, IX; Benedictine priory, VIII; school, XIX, XXII; hall, notice of, XXII. *See* Wygan.
Wigan lane, battle of, XII, XIV.
Wigan, Mr., Independent minister, IV.
Wiggan, 𝕻, XVIII, XIX, XXVII.
Wiggin, major John, XIV.

Wigglesworth, John: his epitaph by Whitaker, XIV.
Wight, isle of, VII.
Wigland, township of Malpas, VIII; school, XIX.
Wigley, Mr., XXVII.
Wigmore, ℞, XXVII.
Wigstaston, township of Wibunbury, VIII.
Wigtoun, John Fleming earl of, I.
Wilaveston, the Norman name of Wirrall hundred, VIII.
Wilbraham, ℞, VIII, XIV, XVIII, XX, XXII, XXIV, XXVII.
Wilcocks, ℞, XIII.
Wilcox, ℞, VIII.
Wild, ℞, XVIII, XIX, XX.
Wildboar-clough, township of Prestbury, VIII; township of Macclesfield, VIII.
Wildbore, ℞, XXII.
Wilde, ℞, XII.
Wilderspool bridge, XVII.
Wilding, Isabel, XXII.
Wilfchristeland, XX (*tit.* Reued).
Wilkes, John, IX.
Wilkesley in Audlem, VIII.
Wilkin, Ricd., XIII.
Wilkins, John, bishop of Chester, VI, XVIII, XXII, XXVII; notices of, IV, VIII, XIII; his *Beauty of Providence*, XVIII.
Wilkins, Jos., IX.
Wilkinson, ℞, VI, VIII, XIV, XVII, XXII, XXVII.
Willaston, township of Neston, VIII.
Willbrake, Peter, XVIII.
Willesty, Joh., rector of St. Mary's, Chester, VIII.
William the Conqueror: causes why he came to this countre, XV.
William Rufus confirms and endows saynt Werburge's abbey, XV.
William III., IX, XII; plot to assassinate, XXVIII.
William of Nassau, prince of Orange: his murder and tomb, I.
William, St., archbishop of York, I.
William of Maluysburye (*i.e.* Malmsbury), XV.
William (son of Nigell) constable of Chester: his miraculous passage of the Dee, XV.
Williams, ℞, VIII, IX, XII, XIII, XIV, XXV, XXVIII.
Williamson, ℞, VIII, XII, XVIII, XIX, XXII, XXVII, XXVIII.
Williamson-street, Liverpool, XII.
Willis, ℞, VIII, IX, XIII, XIX, XXII.
Willisell, Thomas, XIII.
Willmot, rev. R. A., XIII.
Willmus, ℞, XXX.
Willoughby, lords, XIII, XVIII, XIX, XXII, XXVII, XXVIII.
Willoughby, ℞, II, XIII, XIX, XXVIII.
Wills, general: his military conduct and proceedings during the Jacobite rebellion, V.
Wilmesley, ℞, VIII.
Wilmslow, IV; account of, VIII.
Wilmslow, ℞, VIII, XIX.
Wilne in Weston, VIII.
Wilsey, James, VI.
Wilskley in Audlem, VIII.
Wilson, ℞, IV, VIII, XII, XIII, XIV, XVIII, XIX, XXII, XXVII, XXVIII.
Willson, ℞, XXIV.
Wilter, Mr., of Chester, IV.
Wilton, earl of Pembroke's house at, XIII.
Wilton, earls of, XIX, XXII.
Wilton, lord Grey de, XIX.
Wilton, Eustachius de, XX.
Wilvescomb *for* Wiveliscombe, co. Somerset, XIII.
Wimberley, aunt of H. Newcome, XXVII.
Wimbersley, township of Middlewich, VIII.
Wimbysh, ℞, XIV.

Wimmersley *or* Wimberley, XIV, XXII. *See* Winmerleigh.
Wincham, township of Budworth, VIII.
Winchester, I, XIII; a pryncypall cytee of West-saxons, XV; cathedral and school, VIII.
Winchester, marquess of, VIII.
Winckley, 𝔑, XXII.
Wincle in Macclesfield, account of, VIII.
Windebank, 𝔑, II, IV.
Windle in Prescot, XIX.
Windle, 𝔑, IX, XII.
Windmills in Holland, I; in Liverpool, XII.
Window in St. Edmond's church, Salisbury: fanatical destruction of, XIV.
Windsor, IX, XIII, XIX; castle, XVIII.
Winefride *or* Guinivere, the white hill-water, VII.
Wingate, 𝔑, IX, XXVIII.
Wingfield, sir Henry: his evidence at the Jacobite trials, XXVIII.
Winiffe, Thomas, bishop of Lincoln, XIII.
Winkleye, Mr., IX.
Winmerleigh hall, Garstang: notice of, XXII.
Winn, 𝔑, IX, XIV.
Winnington, 𝔑, VIII.
Winnington in Witton, Northwich, VIII.
Winnington bridge, battle of, IV.
Winstanley, township of Wigan, IV, XXII; hall, notice of, XXII.
Winstanley, 𝔑, II, IV, XII, XIX.
Winston, Dr. Thomas, XIII.
Winter, 𝔑, XVIII, XXII, XXIII, XXV, XXVII, XXVIII.
Win-the-fight's (Mrs.) case of casuistry, XIV.
Wintoun, earls of, I, V.
Winwick, VIII, IX, XII, XIV, XVII; general account of, XXII; fighting at, II; hall, notice of, XXII; school, notice of, IV.
Winwick church, description of, XXII; monuments to the Brothertons in, XII.
Winwick, 𝔑, XXII.
Wiresdale, chapelry of Lancaster: account of, XXII.
Wirrall, deanery of, VIII, XIX; rent paid by rural dean, VIII.
Wirrall, hundred of: its situation, I; Norman name, VIII; miraculously preserved by saynt Werburge, XV.
Wirrall, mayor of Chester, VIII.
Wisall, Margaret, of Wisall, XIV.
Wistanston, 𝔑, VIII.
Wistaston, co. Chester, XIV, XVII; account of, VIII; hall, VIII; Red hall, VIII.
Wisterson (? Willaston *or* Wistaston), co. Chester, XXIV.
Witches and witchcraft, I, VI, VII, XII, XXII, XXIV.
Witefeld, Robertus de, XVII.
Withalgh, Willmus de, XXX.
Withburge, saynt, daughter of kynge Anna of eest-England, XV.
Withenford, XX (*tit.* Wolueton).
Withens, willow trees, I.
Withenshaw chapel, Northenden, VIII; hall, notice of, VIII.
Withers, 𝔑, XXII.
Witherslack, in Beetham, co. Westmoreland, XIX.
Withington, VIII.
Withington, township of Didsbury, Manchester, XIX.
Withington, lower, township of Prestbury, VIII.
Withington, James, XXVII.
Withycomb, co. Devon, XIII.
Witnesses in *State Trials*, names of, XXVIII.
Witnesses in Jacobite trials, petition

that they might be examined apart refused, XXVIII.
Witney church, Oxfordshire: decorated window in, XIX.
Witter, Mr., VIII.
Witton, chapelry of Northwich: account of, VIII; school, VIII.
Witton, Robertus filius Roberti de, XX.
Witty, Dr., XXVII.
Wives in Scotland retain their maiden names, I.
Wladislas, fourth king of Poland, XIII.
Wlipshire, villa de, XX.
Wlipshire, 𝔑, XX.
Wodcokke, William, XXII.
Wode, John, XVII.
Wodechirche, 𝔑, XX.
Wodecok, Henry, XVII.
Wodemylne, XX (*titt.* Acton, Walton).
Woden, prynce, fifteenth from Noe: of whom our progenytours, Angles, Jutes and Saxons lynyally succeded, XV.
Wodenothe, Richard, bookseller, XIII.
Woderoue, 𝔑, XX.
Wofall, Thomas, IX.
Wogan, 𝔑, II, V.
Wolden hall, Eccles: notice of, XIX.
Wolf de Kyrkelanton, Willmus dictus le, XX.
Wolfall, 𝔑, IX, XX, XXII.
Wolfall hall, Huyton: notice of, XXII.
Wolfatt, George, rector of Ribchester, XXII.
Wolfenbuttell, duke of, IX.
Wolfenden, 𝔑, XVIII, XIX, XXVII.
Wolfgeatus, pater, XXX.
Wolfhouse hall, Chipping: notice of, XXII.
Wolfius's *Bibliotheca Hebraica*, XIII.
Wolgherton, township of Wibunbury, VIII.
Wollen, 𝔑, XVIII, XXVII.
Wolleston, sir John, alderman of London, II.
Wolley, 𝔑, XVIII, XXIV, XXVII.
Wolrych, Sarah daughter of Robert, VIII.
Wolseby (? Wolseley), sir Charles, bart., XVIII.
Wolsett *or* Woolsett, Dr., parson of Chipping, XXII.
Wolsey, cardinal, XXIX.
Wolslet *error for* Wolset, George, vicar of Ribchester, VIII.
Wolstanesholm, 𝔑, XX.
Wolstenholme, 𝔑, XIV, XIX.
Wolstenholme hall, Rochdale: account of, XIX.
Wolue, Robertus de, XX.
Wolueton (*i.e.* Woolton) and its divisions, XX.
Wolueton, Orm de, XX.
Woluetscoles, XX (*tit.* Cliderhou).
Wolveley, Alice de, and her son Thomas de Tonge, XIX.
Wolvesacre hall, Malpas, VIII.
Wolworth, Nich., XVIII.
Woman, whether a good angel can appear in the shape of, XIII.
Womball, 𝔑, XXVIII.
Wombwell, Mr., XXVII.
Wonderful News from the North, a witch pamphlet, VI.
Wood, value and use of, in Ireland, I; near Liverpool, origin and value of, XII.
Wood, 𝔑, II, VI, VII, VIII, XII, XIII, XIV, XVIII, XIX, XXII, XXVII, XXIX.
Woodacre *or* Wedacre hall, Garstang: notice of, XXII.
Woodbank in Shotwick, VIII.
Woodburn, John, XXII.
Woodchurch, account of, VIII.
Woodcock, 𝔑, XIII, XXII, XXVII.
Woodes, XX (*tit.* Whalleye).
Woodfen, Mr., XVIII.

Woodford in Prestbury, VIII.
Woodford hall, Over: notice of, VIII.
Woodhay chapel, Faddeley, Wrenbury, VIII; hall, notice of, VIII.
Woodhead in Mottram, notices of, I, VIII.
Woodhouse, ℜ, VII, VIII, XX.
Woodhouse-end, Gawsworth, VIII.
Woodhouses, township of Frodsham, VIII.
Woodka, Alexius, XIV. *See* Vodka.
Woodland, chapelry of Kirby Irelith: account of, XXII.
Woodmote, court of, XIV.
Woodnoth family, VIII.
Woodplumpton, chapelry of St. Michael's upon Wyre, XXII; hall, notice of, XXII.
Woodral *for* Woodnoth, VIII.
Woodroffe, Richard, of Burnley, XXII.
Woodroof, ℜ, XIV.
Woods, ℜ, IV, V, IX, XII, XXII.
Woodside, ℜ, XII.
Woodstock, Thomas of, earl of Lancaster, XXII.
Woodward, ℜ, VIII, XXVIII.
Woodyard *or* Ridyard, a little orchard in Chester belonging to the bishopric, VIII.
Wool of Cotswold the finest in the kingdom, I.
Wool-trade of Leyden, I.
Wooler, rebel forces at, V.
Woolfall, Richard, of Highton, XXVIII.
Woollavington, co. Somerset, I.
Woolmer, Samuel, XVIII, XXVII.
Woolrych *and* Woolrich, ℜ, VIII, XIII.
Woolset, George, parson of Cheapyn, VIII. *See* Wolslet, Wolsett, Wolfatt.
Woolton (much- *and* little-) in Childwall, VIII, IX. *See* W.olueton.
Woorall (lieut.) at Lathom siege, II.
Worcester, bishopric, XV; dean and chapter, patrons of Warton, co. Lanc., XXII; priory, XXII; poor of, VIII; battle of, IV, XII, XIV, XVIII, XXVII. *See* Wygornensis.
Worcester's (marquis of) invention of the steam-engine, XVIII.
Wordeleywall, XX (*tit.* Halghton).
Wordell, XX (*tit.* Whalleye).
Wordelword *i.e.* Wardleworth, XX.
Wordelword, ℜ, XX.
Worden, ℜ, XXII, XXVII.
Worden *or* Wearden hall, Leyland: account of, XXII.
Words, tenacity of, XXIV.
Wordsworth, ℜ, XXII.
Wordsworth's *Ecclesiastical Biography*, XIII.
Wordull *or* Wordehull, villa de, XX.
Wordull *or* Wordehull, ℜ, XX.
Workedelegh, XX.
Workedelegh, ℜ, XX.
Workesley, Jordan de, and his daughter Margaret, XXII.
Workington *or* Wirklington rectory, co. Cumberland: notice of, VIII.
World (the), curious paper in, XVIII.
Worldly interruptions of a divine, XVIII.
Wormall, Ciceley daughter of Mr., XIX.
Wormhill, XIX (?).
Wormhill family, VIII.
Wormius, Olaus, and his son William, XIII.
Worms-head, Glamorganshire, I.
Worneth, William de, XIX.
Worneth hall, Oldham: account of, XIX.
Worrall *or* Worrell, ℜ, XII, XXVII.
Worsewall in Wrenbury, VIII.
Worsley, township of Eccles, XIX; hall, account of, XIX.
Worsley, ℜ, VIII, XII, XIII, XVIII, XIX, XXII, XXVII.
Worsoe, XIV.

Worston, XIV, XX; hall, description of, XIV; house, manor, mill, wood, XIV.
Worston, Hugo fil. Radulphi de, XX.
Worswick *error for* Warwick, Mr., banker, XXII.
Worth in Prestbury, VIII.
Worth, count de, XIII.
Worth, ℞, VIII.
Worthington in Standish, XIII.
Worthington, ℞, VIII, IX, XIII, XVIII, XIX, XXII, XXV, XXVII, XXVIII.
Worthington's *Diary*, XVIII; *Miscellanies*, XIII.
Worthley, Grace: notice of and letter from, VIII.
Worton, Dr., XXVIII.
Worton hall in Wensleydale, notice of, XIV. *See* Morton.
Wotton, ℞, XIII, XIV.
Wotton's *Baronetage*, XIV.
Woulfe, Edward, XXVII.
Wra, Adam and Gerard de, XXII.
Wray, John, XIII.
Wray green, meeting-house, school, XXII.
Wren, ℞, I, XIII, XVIII, XXVII.
Wrenbury, account of, VIII.
Wrench, ℞, VIII.
Wrexham, co. Denbigh, VIII.
Wrigglewood, Mr., XIII.
Wright, ℞, IV, VIII, IX, XII, XIII, XVIII, XXII, XXIV, XXVII, XXVIII, XXIX.
Wright's *Chester Plays*, III.
Wrightington, ℞, XX, XXII, XXVIII.
Wrightington hall, Eccleston: notice of, XXII.
Wrigley, ℞, XVIII, XIX, XXVII.
Wrinehill, VIII.
Writhington, sir Edward, II.
Wro, ℞, XX.
Wroe (le) of Arpeley, Warrington, XVII.
Wroe, ℞, VIII, XIX, XXII, XXVII.
Wulfade, saynt and martyr, brother of saynt Werburge: legendary notices of, XV.
Wulfer, kynge of Mercyens: legendary account of, XV.
Wulstone, near Warrington, XVII.
Wulstone broke, XVII.
Wurzburg, bishop of: his chancellor and page burnt for witchcraft, I.
Wyatt, ℞, VIII, XVIII, XIX, XXII.
Wybba, kynge of Mercyens, XV.
Wybrant, William: information of, XXVIII.
Wyche, Thomas de, rector of Manchester, XIX.
Wych-Millbank, VIII.
Wycliff, Solom., VIII.
Wycoller *or* Wykeoller hall, Colne: notice of, XXII.
Wyco-Malbank *or* Nantwich, barony of, XX; pedigree, XX.
Wyddell near Bury, XIX.
Wydenhul, ℞, XX.
Wydnes, boscus de, XX.
Wye river, I.
Wyerwater, earl of Derby's disembarcation in, II.
Wygan, XXII.
Wygan, Willus de, XX.
Wygemora, Robertus de, XX.
Wyggelache, XX (*tit.* Croenton).
Wyght, yle of: historical notices of, XV.
Wygornensis, Maugerius episcopus, XXX.
Wylfryde, archbysshop of Yorke: notices of, XV.
Wylme *or* Wyllme, ℞, IX, XVII.
Wyn, sir Richard, M.P. for Liverpool, II.
Wynburn, Henr. de, XX.
Wyndeyates, XX (*tit.* Whelton).
Wyndham, sir Edward, of Orchard-

Wyndham, bart., and his daughter Jane, viii.
Wyndhul, 𝔑, xx.
Wyneton, Willmus de, xx.
Wynington, viii.
Wynkedelegh, 𝔑, xx.
Wynlaton, xx.
Wynlaton, Beatricia de, xx.
Wynn *or* Wynne, 𝔑, viii, ix, xii, xxviii.
Wynnewhike, 𝔑, xx.
Wynnington, Robertus de, xx.
Wynton, Joh. episcopus de, xx.
Wynwed, flood of, not ferre from Yorke: stronge myghty batell at, xv.
Wynynton, 𝔑, xvii.
Wyral, Rogerus decanus de, xx.
Wyresdale, xx.
Wyrvin, township and chapelry of St. Oswald's, Chester: account of, viii.
Wyrwal, 𝔑, xx.
Wyrwen, Willmus de, xx.
Wysewall, xx.
Wystanton *or* Wystoneston, Willmus de, xx.
Wyteleye, 𝔑, xx.
Wythenes, xx (*tit.* Cliderhou).
Wythenhull and its divisions, xx.
Wythenhull, 𝔑, xx.
Wythington, xx.
Wythington, 𝔑, xx.
Wythmor, Joh. de, viii.
Wytteworth, Ryc., xxii.
Wytton, boscus de, xx.

YACHTS, Dutch: description of, i.
Yale, Dr. David, viii.
Yannys, Mary, xxvii.
Yantunus, professor of Arabic at Leyden: his singular inventions, i.
Yarburgh, Mr., xiii.
Yarn-crofts at Dort, annual value of, i.
Yarnold, Thomas, mayor of Evesham, xxviii.
Yarwood, 𝔑, viii, xviii.
Yate, xx (*tit.* Spotlond).
Yate, Tristram, chantry priest of Padiham, xxii.
Yates, 𝔑, viii, xiii, xviii, xxii, xxvii, xxviii.
Yealand *or* Yelland, 𝔑, xxii.
Yealand-Conyers *and* Yealand-Redmayne, townships of Warton, xxii.
Yeardsley hall, Taxall: notice of, viii.
Yelverton, sir Henry, bart., viii.
Yenslow grange, viii.
Yeovil, co. Somerset: description of a strange disease in, xiii.
Yerwood, Randolph, xiii.
Yieldhouse, township of Manchester, xix.
Ynce, 𝔑, xxii.
Ynes and its divisions, xx.
Ynes, 𝔑, xx.
Ynis. *See* Ince.
Yoke, punishment of the, at Delft, i.
Yong, Mr., xiii.
Yong of Peters, xviii.
York, i, viii, ix, xiv; chyfe cytee of Northumberland and third archebisshops se under the Britons, xv; assizes at, vi; minster, i; ship money, i; siege of, iv.
York, archbishops of, xxii, xxvii.
York, James duke of: death of his only child, xiii.
York *or* Yorke, 𝔑, xiv, xxv.
York house, i.
Yorkshire, its connexion with Liverpool, ix, xii; noble spirit of the West-riding, iv.
Young *or* Younge, 𝔑, i, iv, viii, xii, xiii, xxvii, xxviii.
Ypres. *See* Ipres.
Yrefford, xx (*tit.* Spotlond).
Ythendalemore, xx (*tit.* Gerstan).

Yve, Roger, founder of Battlefield college, XXII.
Yrifford, XX (*tit.* Whiteword).

ZANCHIUS, Jerome: notice of, I. Zanchy, ꝑ, VIII, XVIII.
Zealand, chief towns of, and their political power, I.
Zeltner's (G. G.) *Historia Cryptosocinismi*, XIII.
Zepper's (William) *Ecclesiasticall Policye*, VII.
Zinzendorf, count, XIII.
Zouche, ꝑ, VIII, XIV.
Zuche, ꝑ, XX.
Zutphen, XXV.
Zutphen sconce, surrender of, XXV.
Zwicker, Daniel: account of, XIII.
Zwinger, the, XVIII.

INDEX TO VOLUME III.

Chester's Triumph.

Amery, or Amory, Robert, sheriff of Chester, notice of, viii–xiii, *Notes*, page 6.
—— family, viii, ix.
Amort, *Notes*, page 5.
Arneway, John, mayor of Chester, v.
Ancient (a flag, or standard), *Notes*, page 5.

Bandog, *Notes*, page 5.
Βασιλικον Δωρον, xv.
Bell, to bear the, *Notes*, pages 5–6.
Brereton, John, mayor of Chester, x.

Chester, pageants at, iii–vii; races at, ix, x; Water Tower at, x, xi; derivation of its name of Caerleon, *Notes*, page 1.
Chester's Triumph, rarity of the work, xvi, xvii.
Coghall, or Coughall, viii.
Collier's *Annals of the Stage*, vi.
Cross, High, Chester, when destroyed, xi.

Daniel, Samuel, xv.
Davies, Richard, of Chester, xi, xiii.
Dragon, artificial, *Notes*, page 3.

Ebranke, king, vii.

Green men, *Notes*, page 2.

Henry, eldest son of James I., xiv–xvi.

Imbarne, *Notes*, page 5.

Jacks, xii.

Lester, William, mayor of Chester, ix.
Lets, *Notes*, page 4.

Markland, Mr., v.
Marmoset, *Notes*, page 5.

Ormerod's *History of Cheshire*, viii, xvi.

Pageants, see Triumphs.

Religious dramas usually performed on St. George's Day, iv; stopped by the Reformation, vii.
Rogers, Rev. Robert, B.D., archdeacon of Chester, notice of, ix.
Rood-Eye, Chester, origin of the name, vi, *Notes*, page 4.

Smith, Sir Lawrence, mayor of Chester, vi.
Surcease, *Notes*, page 5.
Surquedrie, *Notes*, page 4.

Triumphs, or pageants, iv; their value, v.

Vaile, to yield, *Notes*, page 5.

Wright's *Chester Plays*, v.

INDEX TO VOLUME VI.

Potts's Discovery of Witches.

Ady, Thomas, his *Candle in the Dark*, xxiv, xxv.
Aghendole, xlviii, E 4, 23.
Agrippa, Cornelius, x, xviii.
Alker, William, his evidence, M 1.
Altham, Ja., baron of the Court of Exchequer, A 2, C 4, Y 2; notices of, 1, 50.
Amber Witch, lxxvii.
Anderton, James, of Clayton, B 4, I 4.
Anointing of witches, L 2, 32.
Assheton, Richard, of Downham, B 4; notice of, 15.
Astley, Elizabeth, C 4, X 1, 45.

Bacon, Lord, his *Sylva Silvarum*, v.
Baines's *Lancashire*, lix, lxxi, lxxiv; extracts from, 31.
Baldwin, Richard, miller, liv, B 3, C 1, D 3, 20.
Baldwyn, Mr., schoolmaster of Colne, D 4, 21.
Ball, a familiar spirit, F 4, G 1, G 2.
Bannister, Nicholas, C 3, E 4, F 4, G 3, *et passim*; notice of, 16.
Baptism of witches, 27.
Bartholinus, Thomas, the Dane, xl.
Baxter, Richard, xx.
Bernard's *Guide to Grand Jurymen*, 3.
Bierley, Ellen, lvi, C 4, K 3, Q 1, X 1; her trial, K 4–N 3.
——, Grace, L 2.
——, Henry, K 4.
——, Jennet, lvi, C 4, K 3, Q 1, X 1; her trial, K 4–N 3.
Bilson, boy of, xxix.
Birch, its value as a lamia-fuge, lxxi, lxxii.
Blackburn, L 2.
Bodin, John, xxviii; his *De Republica* and *Colloquium or Examination of Religions*, viii, *Demo-manie*, ix.
Boggard Hole, lxiii.
Booth, James, T 1.
——, Jennet, her evidence against Margaret Pearson, T 1.
Boothman, Jane, D 3, D 4,
Boyle, Robert, vi.
Brand's *Antiquities*, extract from, 9–11.
Bridgeman, Dr., bishop of Chester, lxxv.
Briercliffes, the, a fated race, lii.
Bromley, Sir Edward, baron of the Court of Exchequer, A 2, C 4, H 4, O 3, P 2, R 3, S 2, Z 2, *et passim*; his judgment on the witches, V 3; charge to the jury, Z 2; notice of, 1.
Browne, Sir Thomas, v, xl; fine exaggeration of, iii.
Bulcock, Christopher, G 4, I 3, Q 2.
——, Henry, S 2.
——, Jane, li, liv, C 4, Q 2–R 1, S 3, V 2, 39.
——, John, li, liii, C 3, G 4, I 3, Q 2–R 1, S 3, V 2, 39.
Bullock, Henry, C 2.
Bulloes (wild plums), lx.
Burnley, co. Lanc., Q 4.
Buys wife of Barrowford, lxix.

Casaubon, Meric, xviii; extract from, 12, 13; his reply to Wagstaffe, xxviii.
Chaddock, Peter, T 4, V 1; evidence against Isobel Robey, T 3.
Charles I., lxxv, lxxviii.
Charms, E 2, K 1, 22, 28, 29.
Chattox, Old, xlvi; *vide* Whittle, Ann.
Chester, lxxv.
Childers, —, S 4.

Chisnall, Edward, M 4, N 1, N 2.
Chrisom, 29.
Clegg, Miss, Hallfoot near Clitheroe, xlviii.
Clitheroe, xxx, xxxvi, V 4.
Cliviger, li.
Colne, R 3.
Communion, bread of the, H 3.
Confessions of witches, their visionary character, lxxvii.
Convention of witches at Malkin-Tower, l, lvi, C 3, F 3, G 2, G 3, G 4, I 3, O 3, P 1, P 4, Q 1, Q 4, Y 1, Y 3, Z 1, 40.
Corser, Rev. T., xli.
Cotta, John, his *Trial of Witchcraft* and other tracts, xx.
Covell, Mr., gaoler of Lancaster Castle, l, lviii, C 3, G 2, G 4, I 2, I 4, K 3, P 2, Q 2, S 3, V 1.
Cowell, Thomas, coroner, B 4, K 1.
Craven, R 1.
Crawford, Isobel, her execution, 40.
Crollius, xli.
Cronckshaw, Anne, G 3, R 2, 24.
Crooke, Margaret, 21; her examination against Ann Redfern, O 1.
Crosley, David, his *Triumph of Sovereign Grace*, li.
Cudworth, Dr. Ralph, vi.

Dandy, a familiar spirit, H 3, H 4, I 1, I 2, I 4.
Davies, Alizon; *vide* Device, Alizon.
——, Jennet; *vide* Device, Jennet.
——, William, lxviii.
Daylight gate, 4.
Deane, Jennet, Q 3, Q 4.
——, John, Q 4.
Dee, Dr., xxxiv.
De Lancre, x.
Delrio, x, xxviii.
Demdike, Old; *vide* Southernes, Elizabeth.
Derby, Ferdinando earl of, case of witchcraft, 51.
Dere, to hurt, 30.
Device, Alizon, xlvii, xlix, liii, liv, B 3, C 2, C 4, F 2, F 3, G 3, G 4, I 2, I 3, I 4, P 1, Q 2, Q 3, S 3, V 2, Y 3, 9, 20; her examinations, C 1, E 4; trial, R 2–S 3; confession, R 3.
——, Elizabeth, li, liii, B 3, C 4, I 1, I 3, O 4, R 1, R 2, V 2, 20; her examination, C 2; trial, F 2–H 1; verdict, K 2; evidence against others, I 4, O 4, P 4, Q 4, Z 1.
Device, James, li, liii, C 4, F 2, F 3, G 3, P 4, V 2, Z 1, 20, 27; examination, C 2; trial, H 1–K 2; evidence against others, E 3, G 2, G 4, O 2, O 4, P 1, P 4, Q 3, S 2, Y 3.
——, Jennet, li, lv, lvi, lxiii, lxvii, C 3, F 2, F 3, F 4, H 4, K 1, Z 2, 39; notice of, 24; evidence, F 4, G 1, G 3, H 4, I 3, P 1, Q 1, R 1, Z 1, 20; demeanour in court, I 1.
——, John, E 4, F 3, G 1, 20.
Devil is cloven footed, M 2.
Devil's marks, 4.
Dickonson, Frances, lxi, lxiii, lxvii, lxxv.
Digby, Sir Kenelm, extract from, 47.
Dodgson, —, S 4, Y 1.
Doewife, Old, K 4.
Drage, William, his *Treatise of Diseases from Witchcraft*, lxxi.
Duckworth, John, H 2, H 3, H 4.
Dyce, Rev. A., xli.

Elsen, an awl, 41.
Erastus, Thomas, viii, ix, x; his *De Lamiis*, x.
Erbury, William, his *Great Earthquake*, xxxii.

Fairfax, Edward, the poet, his witch prosecution and MS. *Discourse of Witchcraft*, 46.
Familiar spirits, their nature and arts, lxxiii, lxxv; afflicted with great scarcity of specie, 15; their names, 4; *vide* Ball, Dandy, Fancie, Mamilian, Tibb.
Fancie, a familiar spirit, B 4, D 3, E 3, M 2, 20.
Farrandly, meaning of, 29.
Fear, to frighten, lxiii.
Fence, the, in Pendle, B 2.
Ferriar *On Popular Illusions*, extract from, 26.
Filmer, Sir R., xii; his *Advertisement to the Jurymen of England touching Witches*, xxiii, xxiv; tract on Usury, xxiv.
Fludd, xxxiv.
Ford's *Witch of Edmonton*, extract from 6–9.
Foulds, Anne, of Colne, P 3, P 4, Q 1, 39.

Gaule, John, his *Select Cases of Conscience touching Witches and Witchcraft*, xx.
Gerard, Lord, R 3, S 2, 41.
——, Sir Thomas, T 3; notice of, 43.

Giffard, George, his *Dialogue concerning Witches and Witchcraft*, xix.
Gisborne in Craven, Y 1.
Glanville's *Sadducismus Triumphatus*, vii.
—— *Collection of Relations*, 2; extracts from, 42, 43.
Goldshaw (Gouldshey) in Pendle, B2, 3.
Good Friday a day for witch meetings, lxxiv, C 3, G 3, G 4, I 2, I 3, I 4, O 4, P 1, P 4, Q 1, Q 3.
Gray, Alice, C 4, G 4, I 3, P 4, R 1, X 1, 45.
——, Anne, P 4.
Greenhead in Pendle, liv, B 4.
Greyhounds and hare, a witch story, lxi.

Hale, Sir Matthew, v.
Hallam, the historian, ix.
Halseworths, —, T 4, 45.
Hanck, word used by witches, Q 4, Y 4, 39.
Hargreaves, Alice, widow, lxvii.
——, Blaze, I 1, I 2.
——, Christopher, of Thornyholme, G 3, G 4, I 4, P 1, R 1, 27.
——, Elizabeth, G 3, G 4, I 3, I 4, R 1.
——, Henry, E 3, Y 4; his evidence, Y 4.
——, Hugh, wife of, lxxv, G 3, G 4, I 3, I 4, P 1.
——, James, of Marsden, lxviii.
——, Jennet, R 1.
——, John, I 1.
Harne panne, cranium, 30.
Harsnet's (Archbp.) *Declaration of Popish Impostures*, extracts from, 3, 10.
Hartley, Edmund, hanged for witchcraft, 51.
——, Michael, P 4, 39.
Hasland Hall, Derbyshire, xxv.
Hawarden, John, T 3.
Hay, Grace, of Padiham, R 2.
——, Lawrence, C 4, X 1, 45.
Heber, Mr. Justice, Y 2; notice of, 47.
Hermetic school, philosophers of the, xxxiv.
Hewitt, Katherine, li, liii, C 4, G 4, I 3, Q 1, Q 4, R 1, V 2, Z 1; her trial, P 3–Q 1; notice of, 39.
Heywood and Broome's *Last Lancashire Witches*, a play, extracts from, lxv–lxx, 36–38.
Hearstones, a house in Pendle, lxii, lxxiii.
Hobbes, Thomas, of Malmesbury, v.
Holgate and his wife, lxix, 20.
Horace, extract from, 9.
Hopkins the witchfinder, xx, xxi, lxxix.
Houghton, Sir Richard, S 2.
Houlden, Robert, L 4; notice of, 33,
Howgate, Christopher, G 3, G 4, I 3, I 4, P 1, R 1, 20.
——, Elizabeth, G 3, G 4, I 3. P 1, R 2, 20.
Hutchinson, xxii, xxxix, lii.

Infants' corpses, magical use of, 32.

Jacks, Christopher, of Thornyholme; *vide* Hargreaves, Christopher.
——, Hen., lxviii.
——, John, lxviii.
James I., his *Dæmonologie*, lviii, T 2.
James, a glover, his remedy against witchcraft, T 3.
James' wife, lxviii.
Jesuits, good store of in Lancashire, K 3.
Johnson, Margaret, lix, lxxv, lxxvi; her confession, lxxii–lxxv.
Jonson, Ben., extracts from, 11, 12, 32.

Kildwick in Craven, xxix.
Knyvet, Thomas lord, notice of, 1.

Lancashire dialect, specimens of, lxv, 18.
—— witches, lxxviii.
Lancaster Castle, plot to blow up, C 3, G 2, G 4, I 2, I 4, P 1, Y 3.
Laund, the, D 3.
Law, Abraham, R 3; examination, S 1.
——, John, R 3, S 1, 42; evidence, R 4.
Leigh, William, parson of Standish, M 4, N 1, N 2, 45; notice of, 34.
Leonard's of the West Close, Little Robin wife of, lxx.
Lewis, parson, his execution for witchcraft, xxi–xxiii.
Libavius, xli.
Library, MS. catalogue of John Webster's, xli.
Lister, Leonard, Q 4, X 4, Y 1, Y 4, Z 1, 50.
——, Thomas, of Westby, C 3, G 3, I 3, I 4, Q 1, Q 2, Q 4, R 2, X 4, Y 1, Y 2, Y 3, Y 4, Z 1, Z 2, 40; notice of, 46.
Locke, John, xxiv.
Lomshawe, widow, of Burnley, B 4, D 3, D 4.
Loynd wife, lxiii, lxiv, lxv, lxix.
Lyon, Margaret, her evidence, T 4.
——, Thomas, T 3.

Malkin Tower, lvi, B 2; notices of, xlix, 16; *vide* Convention of witches.
Mamilian, a familiar spirit, lxxii.
Marsden in Pendle, lxxii.
Middleton's *Witch*, extract from, 9.
Miles, Dick, of the Rough Lea, his wife, lxviii, G 3, I 4, P 1.
Moore, Hugh, F 1.
——, John, E 4; his wife, E 2, E 3.
——, Sir Jonas, 23.
More, Dr. Henry, xli; character of, vi, vii; his *Collections of Relations*, vi, vii.
Morison's *Poems*, extract from, 16.
Morton, Dr., bishop of Durham, xxix.
Mouldheeles, wife of; *vide* Hewitt, Katherine.
Murderer, discovery of by touching the corpse, Y 3, Z 2, 47–50.
Mytton, Henry, of the Rough Lee, F 3, F 4, G 1, G 2, O 3, O 4.

North, Roger, as a biographer, v.
Nowell, Roger, of Read, xlix, lv, lvi, B 2, C 1, D 3, E 1, F 2, F 3, F 4, H 2, I 2, S 1; notice of, 3.
Nutter, Alice, li, liii, C 4, F 3, F 4, G 3, G 4, I 3, O 4, P 1, Q 1, R 1, V 2; notice of, 35, 36; special interest attaching to her fate, liv–lvi; her mansion still standing, liv; her trial, O 3–P 2; impenitence, P 2.
——, Anne, E 4, 20.
——, Anthony, E 3, E 4.
——, Christopher, E 1, N 4, O 1, 20, 21.
——, Elizabeth, D 3, 21.
——, John, of the Bulhole, C 1, F 1.
——, John, of Higham Booth, 21.
——, Mary, E 1, O 1, 21.
——, Miles, G 4, I 3, P 1.
——, Richard, F 4, G 3, O 4.
——, Robert, the elder, of Pendle, D 3, E 2, 21.
——, Robert, of Greenhead in Pendle, liv, B 4, D 2, D 3, D 4, E 1, E 2, N 4, O 1, 20, 21.
——, Mr., lx.
—— family, 20, 21.

Ollers, a field so called, lxiv.
Ormerod, George, the historian, li.
Osbaldeston, K 4.

Padiham, co. Lanc., lx, Q 4, V 4.
Paracelsus, xxxiv.
Parker, Henry, lx.
Parkinson, Rev. Richard, xxviii, xlv, 23.
Parre, Hugh, V 1.
——, Margaret, her evidence, V 1.
Paulinus, the Crosses of, xxxix.
Pearson, Edward, of Padiham, S 3.
——, Margaret, C 4, S 3, V 1, V 4, 42; account of her, S 3; trial, S 3 – T 1.
Peaseley Cross, T 3.
Pedigree of two witch families, 20.
Pendle Forest, xlviii, lviii; notice of, xliii, xliv; character of its inhabitants in the seventeenth century, xliv, xlv.
Pictures of clay (witch spells), B 3, E 1, E 3, E 4, F 4, G 2, H 3, N 4, O 2, 9–14.
Piggin, C 1, 16.
Pitcairne's *Criminal Trials*, 3, 5; extracts from, 13 – 15, 48 – 50.
Placita Coronæ, C 4.
Potts, Thomas, xlviii, xlix, li, liii, 50.
Prayer to get drink, K 1.
Preston, co. Lanc., L 1, L 4.
——, Jennet, C 3, G 4, I 3, P 1, P 4, Q 1, Q 2, Q 4, R 2; her trial, X 4 – Z 3.
Priestley, Henry, lxvii.
Priests and Jesuits, their character, N 2.

Raleigh, Sir Walter, his *History of the World*, v.
Ramsden, John, C 4, X 1, 45.
Reade, co. Lanc., C 1.
Redfern, Ann, xlix, liii, C 2, C 4, D 3, E 1, E 2, F 1, G 4, I 2, P 1, Q 1, Q 3, V 2, Y 3, 20; her trial, N 3 – O 2.
——, Mary, O 2, 20.
——, Thomas, D 4, E 1, E 2, N 4, O 2, 20.
Remigius, x.
Reynolds, Dr., xviii.
Ribble, water of, L 2, L 3.
Robey, Isobel, of Windle in Prescot, liv, C 4, S 3, V 2; notice of, 42; her trial, T 2 – V 1.
Robinson, Anne, Y 2.
——, Edmund, of Pendle, his examination, lxxi, lxxii.
——, Edmund, of Pendle Forest, mason, his examination, lix–lxxii; confesses his imposture, lxxvi; Webster's account of him, lix, lx.
——, James, 21; his examination, E 1, E 2.
——, alias Swyer, James, F 3, G 1.
——, alias Swyer, John, F 3, F 4, G 1, G 2, I 2, I 3; note on the name, lxi.
——, Mr., lx, lxiv.
Roby's *Antiquities of Lancaster*, lii.
Romilly's or Rumbles moor, G 4, I 3, P 1, P 4, Y 4, 27.

Rough Lee, description of, liv.
Rushton, Rev. John, D.D., xliv, xlvi, xlviii.

Samlesbury, L 4, 30, 31.
—— boat, L 1.
—— witches, lvi, C 4; their trial, K 3–N 3.
Samuels, Mother, iii, iv.
Sandes, William, mayor of Lancaster, B 4, I 4.
Saunders "sicut credit," and Lawrence his wife, lxix.
Scot, Reginald or Reynold, 2; notice of, xii, xiii; character and scope of his *Discoverie of Witchcraft*, xiii–xix.
Scott, Sir Walter, lii, lvii, lxii.
Selden's *Table Talk*, v.
Sele (yoke for cattle), lxiv.
Seller, —, F 4.
Shadwell's *Lancashire Witches*, extracts from, 17, 18.
Sheare Thursday, H 3, 28.
Shuttleworth, Sir Richard, E 2, O 2, 21.
——, Richard, of Gawthorp, notice of, lx.
Sidegraues, Isabel, C 4, X 1, 45.
Sinclair's *Satan's Invisible World Displayed*, extract from, 28, 29.
Singleton, John, N 1; his evidence, L 4.
Southernes, Elizabeth, xlvi–xlviii, xlix, liii, liv, B 1, C 4, D 2, E 3, F 2, F 3, F 4, G 2, G 4, H 3, I 1, I 2, I 4, O 4, P 2, Q 3, R 2, R 3, S 2, Y 3, 2, 17, 20; account of, xlvi–xlviii; description of, B 1; declaration respecting, B 1–B 2; evidence against her, B 2–C 2; her evidence against others, E 1, N 4.
Southworth, Christopher; *vide* Thompson *alias* Southworth.
——, Jane, lvi, C 4, K 3, Q 1, X 1; her trial, K 4–N 3.
——, Sir John, Knt., L 4, M 1; notice of, 33.
——, John, K 4.
Sowerbuts, Grace, lvi, K 3, K 4, L 4, N 1; her evidence, K 4–L 3; analysis of it by Potts, M 1–M 3; recantation, M 4.
——, Thomas, K 4, M 1, M 4.
Spencer, Mary, lxxv.
Sprenger, x.
Starkie, John, notice of, lx.
Stearne's *Confirmation of Witchcraft*, 4, 5; extract from, xxi, xxii.
Swinnow, Colonel, of Chatton, Northumberland, unsuccessful plot against his wife, lv.
Swyer; *vide* Robinson.
——, Christopher, of Barley, G 3.
Syleing, lxiii.

Thompson *alias* Southworth, Christopher, lvi, M 1, M 3, M 4, N 1, N 2, 31.
Thornton in Coxwold, co. York, the birthplace of John Webster, xxviii, xxix.
Throgmorton, Mr., of Warbois, fiendlike skill of his children, iii, iv.
Tibb, a familiar spirit, B 2, B 3, B 4, E 1, N 4.
Toad, story of a, 42.
Towneley, Henry, of the Carre, H 2, 28.
——, Anne, his wife, H 2, H 3, H 4, 28.
Trawden Forest, R 4.

Utley, hanged in 1630 for bewitching Richard Assheton of Middleton, 51.

Van Helmont, xxxiv, xli.
Vindiciæ Academiarum, xxxv.

Wagstaffe, John, xii; account of, xxv, xxvi; his *Question of Witchcraft Debated*, xxv; extract from, xxvi, xxvii; his *Historical Reflections on the Bishop of Rome*, xxv; Meric Casaubon's opinion of him, xxviii.
Walshman, Hugh, L 1, 32.
——, Thomas, L 1, L 2, L 3, M 1, M 3, M 4; evidence, L 4.
Wanklyn, J. B., xlv.
Warch, a pain, T 3, 45.
Ward, Bishop, xxxiv.
Warrington, co. Lanc., T 4.
Way's *Promptorium Parvulorum*, 4, 30, 41.
Webster, John, of Clitheroe, xii, xvii; his *Displaying of Supposed Witchcraft*, xxviii, xxxvi, xxxviii, xxxix; extracts from, lix, lx, lxxi, lxxvi; *Saints' Guide*, xxx; *Judgment Set and Books Opened*, xxx, xxxiv, xxxvii; extract from, xxxv, xxxvi; *Academiarum Examen*, xxxiii, xxxiv; *Metallographia*, xxxvi, xxxvii; MS. catalogue of his library, xli; anecdote of him, xxxix; his favourite walk, xl; not identical with the dramatist, xli; inscription on his monument, xlii.
——, the dramatist, extract from, xl.
Whalley, xxxix, V 4.
—— Abbey, xl.

Wheatley Lane in Pendle, lx.
Whitaker, Dr., xxxv, xxxvi, xxxix, xliii, li, lxxvi; his *History of Whalley*, lviii, lix; extract from, lxxv, lxxvi.
Whittle, Ann, xlvi–xlviii, xlix, liii, C 2, C 4, D 1, F 3, G 4, I 2, N 4, O 2, P 1, P 2, Q 3, V 2, Y 3, Y 4, 19, 20, 21; her examination and confession, B 4, D 3, E 2; trial, D 1–F 1; description of her, D 2; found guilty, K 2; evidence against Margaret Pearson, S 4.
——, Elizabeth, F 1.
Wierus, x, xi, xviii.
Wilkins, Bishop, xxxiv.
Wilkinson, Francis, T 4.
——, Jane, V 1; her evidence, T 4.
Wilsey, James, F 4.
Witches, lists of, lxxi, lxxiv, C 4.
——, pedigree of two families of, 20.
——, anointing of, L 2, 32.
Witches, examination of by Charles I., lxxv, lxxvi.
——, baptism of, 27.
—— of Pendle, their feuds, 22.
——, their Sabbath, 24–27.
Witchcraft, motives to its practise, O 3; the dark shadow it throws on human nature, iii, iv; the mighty intellects it has enslaved, v–x; its opponents and exposers, xii–xlii; its special habitat in England, xliii–xlv; commonness of confessions of, lxxvii; its history still a desideratum, lii; list of victims of, 44.
Wonderful News from the North, a pamphlet, lv.
Wood, Anthony à, xxv, xxix; extracts from, xii, xiii, xxxi, xxxii.

York assizes, C 3, G 4, I 3, Y 2, Y 4.

INDEX TO VOLUME XXIII.

A Golden Mirrour.

Alliteration, singular specimen of, 31.
Alton, co. Stafford, v.

Botfield, Beriah, xxi.
Brereton, George, of Ashley, 83; verses on, 43.

Chaule (?jowl), a jaw or jaw bone, 74.
Cheshire, character of the gentry of, xxvii–xxviii.
Cho ho, a falconer's call, 87.
Churchyard's *True Discourse Historicall of Government in the Netherlands*, xii.
Clawback, a backbiter, xxix, 66.
Cloutshoes, wooden clogs tipped with iron, 71.
Cogging, cheating, 58, 59.
Collier, J. Payne, xiv, xvi, xvii, xxi.

Davenports of Cheshire, proverb respecting, 80.
Derby, Henry 4th earl of, 3, 69.
Dimble (?dimple), a hollow, 5, 69.
Drake, Sir Francis, 70.
Dunstable road, proverb on, 89.

Egerton, Lady Mary, 80–81; verses on, 35.
Elizabeth, Queen, 2, 4, 7, 68, 69, 70; characteristic answer of, xi.

Fortune, lines on, 47.
Frobisher, Sir Martin, 71.

Glass of skill, probably the beryl, 87.
Gleides (gledes), red hot coals, 35, 82.
Golden Mirrour, account of, 66–67, 72, and Introduction *passim*.
Good counsel, poems of, 43, 44, 45, 46, 47–50.

Halton Castle, co. Chester, v.
Harre, higher, 48, 86.
Haslewood, Mr., xiii.
Hawkins, Edward, xix, xx.
Heber, Richard, xix.
Hespias, 22, 76.
Hexte, highest, 85.
Holcraft, Lady Julian, 76, 85; verses on, 20, 47.
Hunting match, dream of a, 11–14.

Johnson, Samuel, author of Hurlothrumbo, his singular burial place, 68.
Jumps, shifts, expedients, 59, 89.

Lamb, dream of a, 51–59, 86.
Lambe, Dr., astrologer, 87.
Legh, John, of Ridge, 72.
Leigh, Sir Peter, of Lyme, 27, 78.
——, Peter, verses on, 27.
——, Thomas, of Adlington, verses on, 31, 33.
Leighs of Cheshire, proverb respecting, 80.
Lennow, lean, feeble, 61, 89.

Madden, Sir Frederick, xiii.
Marfield forest, 1, 67.
Mars, dream of, 35–37.
Mary, queen of Scots, vi.
Merula (merle), the blackbird, 20, 76.
Mort, a musical hunting term, 14, 75.

Papists, 3, 5, 69, 70.
Perfit, a term of chase, 74.

Pick-thank, a parasite or flatterer, xxix, 49, 66, 86.
Poor Knight's Palace of Pleasures, xxi, 11, 73–74; probable author of, xv–xvii.
Pranck, to dress ostentatiously, 88.
Proctor, John, iv, viii, 66.
Proverbs: Davenports and Leighs, of Cheshire, 80; Dunstable road, 89.
Psalms, 33–34, 57–60, 61.

Quirry (quarry, *Fr.* carrée), a square enclosure for slaughtered game, 14, 74.

Rechat, a musical hunting term, 13, 74.
Retchless (reckless), 59, 89.
Ridge Hall, 72.
Ridley pool or mere, 37, 82.
Robinson, Richard, of Alton, account of, iv–ix, xv–xviii; his "name in verdict," iv. 59; *Golden Mirrour*, viii, ix, xvii, xix, xx, account of its discovery, xviii–xix; *Rewards of Wickednesse*, vi, xvii–xviii; *Ruefull Tragedie of Hemidos and Thelay*, vi, extract from, vii–viii.
——, Richard, of London, account of, ix–xiv, 70; his *Auncient Order*, &c. *of Prince Arthur*, xiii; *Eupolemia*, x; *Harmony of King David's Harp*, xi; *Ruby, an Historicall fiction*, xviii; *Life, Actes*, &c. *of Prince Arthur*, xiv.
——, Richard, actor, xiv.
Rodd, Mr., bookseller, xix.

St. Domingo, 71.
Shackerley, Hugh, 84; verses on, 45.
——, Jeffrey, of Holme, 83; verses on, 44.
——, Jeffrey, verses on, 46.
Shrewsbury, George Talbot 6th earl of, vi, 3, 69; motto of, 6, 70.
Shutlings loe, 1, 67–68.
Strange, Ferdinand lord, 75; verses on, 15.
Stroyer, destroyer, 18, 75.

Talbot, Lord Gilbert, dedication to, xxv; notice of, 65.
Thacke, (thwack), to beat hard, 31, 80.
Thraso, a character in Terence's *Eunuch*, xxix, 66.
Tib, a low woman, 87.
Tick tacke (tric trac), a game of tables, 88.
Time, dreams of, 24–26, 27–30, 31–33; quaint personification of, 24, 27, 31, 77, 79; poem on, 38–42.
Trafford, etymology of, 78.
—— family, antiquity of, 26, 78.
——, Sir Edmund, 77; verses on, 24.

Vipers, vulgar error concerning, 4, 69.
Virgin queen, dream of a, 1–10.

Wakes, 88.
Warburton, Peter, of Arley, 82; verses on, 38.
Ward, Roger, xviii, xx.
Winter, Sir William, 70.

INDEX TO VOLUME XXIV.

Chetham Miscellanies, Vol. I.

NOTE.—*The numerals in this Index refer to the order in which the five Tracts composing the volume are given, the paging of each being independent.*

Acton, Samuel, i, 32, 33; notice of, 25.
Addison, Galston, i, 20.
——, Joseph, i, 20.
Agar, Thomas, i, 18.
Allecock, John, i, 33.
Ancient monuments, plan for the recovery and preservation of, v, 48, 49.
Apslow, Dr., v, 12.
Arms, college of, iii, 5.
Asheley, John, v, 20.
Athenæum, i, 4.
Aubrey, MS. notes of, i, 3, 7, 11.
Awbrey, Dr., v, 15.

Babeau, Monsieur, v, 8.
Balthrop, Mr., v, 12.
Bayly, Dr., physician to Q. Elizabeth, v, 22.
Bendger, Sir Thomas, v, 20.
Bennet, Dr., v, 16, 17, 44.
Benoilt, Thomas, Clarencieux, iii, 7, 8.
Birch, Dr., i, 20; his *Life of Milton*, 12.
Bonner, bishop, v, 20.
Borowgh, William, v, 59.
Boswell's *Sale Catalogue*, extract from, i, 1, 2.
Bosworth, Hen., i, 18, 19.
——, Jacob, i, 18, 19.
Bourne, Sir John, v, 20.
Broke, lord, v, 20.
Bruarne, Dr., v, 10.
Brydges, Sir Egerton, i, 7.
Burrough, John, i, 20.

Cæsar, Dr. Julius, v, 11.
Calendar, reformation of the, v, 14, 22.
Canterbury, archbishop of, v, 13, 14, 16.
Capito, Joannes, v, 7.
Cecil, Mr. secretary, v, 10, 16, 18, 19.
Chancellor, Richard, v, 28, 59.
Charles, V. of Germany, v, 6, 19.
Cheke, Mr., v, 9.
Christoferson, John, v, 9.
Clarke, Abraham, release of portion of Milton's estate, 1, 19–23.
——, Caleb, and his family, i, 20.
——, Deborah, i, 1, 17; notice of, 19, 20.
Clavell, Mr., ii, 14.
College of Arms, iii, 5.
Comet of 1577, v, 21.
Commander, Hercules, ii, 5, 11.
Cook, Richard, i, 34.
Crewe, John, of Utkinton, ii. 11; notice of, 5.
——, Sir Randolph, ii, 12.

Dallaway's *Heraldic Enquiries*, iii, 6, 7.
Danesius, v, 8.
Darlington, John, i, 14, 26; assignment of lease to Elizabeth Milton, 29–32.
Dati, Carlo, i, 2.
DEE, Dr. John, his education, v, 4; love of study, 5; visit to the Low Countries, 5; preferment at Cambridge University, 5; wonderful "scarabœus," 5, 8; made M.A. 6; studies at Lovayne, 6; his wide fame, 6, 7, 8, 33, 34; studies

civil law, 7; visit to Paris, 7; success with the public and the learned, 7, 8; invitation from the Moscovite emperor, 9; testimonials, 9-11; made rector of Upton on Severn, 10-12; and of Long Lednam, 12, 13; enters Q. Elizabeth's service, 11; diappointed of certain preferments, 12; declines a bishopric, 13; loses his rectories, 14; works at the reformation of the calendar, 14, 22; visit to the Emperor Maximilian, in Bohemia, 14, 19, 23; his poverty, 13, 14, 15, 35 *et seq.*; some profitless advowsons assigned to him, 15; promised the mastership of St. Cross, 15, 16; his (? first) wife's death, 17, 19; his famous glass, 17; reception by Q. Elizabeth, 18; his mother's death, 18; imprisoned for treasonable enchantments, 20; counterworks some treasonable witchcraft, 21; winter journey for the queen's health, 22; account of his library, &c., 27-31; his losses, 31, 32; travelling expenses beyond sea, 32-34; liberality of his friends, 35, 36; housekeeping expenses, 36; slanders against him, 52 *et seq.*; rapidity of composition, 61; styles himself a Christian Aristotle, 63; his own notions of himself and his works, 52-67; addresses to Q. Elizabeth, 3, 45; plan for recovery of ancient monuments and old writers, 48, 49; works on navigation, 60; on famous and rich discoveries, 61; letter to Archbishop of Canterbury, 71-83; catalogue of his works, 24-27, 73-76.

Dee, Rowland, v, 4.

Dibbley, watchmaker, v, 29.

Disney, John, i, 21.

Dodsworth's *Collections*, ii, 9, 10.

Done, Abraham, i, 29, 32.

Dower, custom of London with respect to, i, 13.

Dugdale, William, Norroy, his letters to John Crewe, ii. 5-7, 11-13; *Monasticon*, 7; visitation of 1664-5, iii, 7, 11, 22-26; high notions, iv, 7, 8.

Dunne, Thomas, v, 6.

Dysart, Lyonnel, earl of, i, 14.

——, Grace, countess of, i, 30.

Edward VI., v, 10.

Elizabeth, queen, v, 10, 11, 17, 19, 22; her personal kindness, 12, 13, 14, 44; affability, 18; belief in astrology and witchcraft, 21; ill health, 22; ambition, 22.

Fairfax, lord, ii, 9, 10, 11.

Fernelius —, v, 8.

Ferrys, George, v, 20.

Flower, William, Norroy, iii, 7, 10.

Foster, Elizabeth. i, 12, 18; notice of, 20.

——, Thomas, i, 20, 21.

Frisius, Gemma, v, 5.

Fromonds, Jane, second wife of Dr. Dee, v, 44.

——, Nicholas, v, 31.

Godwin's *Lives*, i, 7, 34.

Gogava, Antonius, v, 5.

George, Sir Thomas, v, 4, 17, 44, 45.

Goupylus, Jacobus, v, 8.

Grene, Barthlet, v, 20.

Hackett, Thomas, i, 23.

Hacus, Mathias, v, 7.

Haley, Richard, i, 2.

Hamelius, Paschasius, v, 8.

Harrison, William, i, 25.

Hatton, Sir Christopher, v, 11, 13.

Hayley's *Life of Milton*, i, 11.

Henshaw, George, i, 24.

Heraldic Visitations, iii, iv; mode of proceeding in, iii, 6; their value, 7; lists of, where recorded, 7; caution respecting omitted names in, 12, 13; disregard of, iv, 7, 8.

Heraldic Visitation of 1533, note on, iii, 8; calendar of names of families in, 14, 15; ordinaries of arms in, 15-17.

—— of 1567, note on, iii, 10; calendar of pedigrees in, 17-19.

—— of 1613, note on, iii, 10; calendar of pedigrees in, 19-21.

—— of 1664-5, note on iii, 11; calendar of names of families in, 22-26; fragment illustrative of, iv.

Hollins, John, i, 29.

Holme, Randle (second), ii, 7; third, 13.

Howard, Lord Admiral, v, 44, 45.

Hudson, Mr., v, 19.

Hunter's *Sheaf of Gleanings*, extract from, i, 44, 45.

Irish territories, evidences (title deeds) of, v, 29.

Ivimey's *Life of Milton*, i, 20.

Jenkinson, Mr., ii, 11.

Johnson's *Lives of the Poets*, i, 11.

King, Daniel, ii, 9, 10; letter to Rev.

Henry Fairfax, 10, 11; his meanness, 14; *Vale Royal*, 6, 14.
Kuerden, Dr., letter to Randle Holme, ii, 7-10.

Laskey, lord, v, 13.
Leicester, Robert earl of, v, 11, 12, 13, 17, 21, 22.
Leycester, Mr., of Tabley, ii, 6.
——, Sir Peter, of Tabley, letter to third Randle Holme, ii, 13-15; copy of his Latin dedication to the *Antiquities*, 14.
Loftus, Edmond, i, 23.

Mackintosh, Sir James, i, 20.
Magnionus, Jo., v, 8.
Mallet, Dr., v, 11.
Man, Mr., v. 12.
Mantua, duke of, v, 6.
Mary, queen, v, 20.
Maximilian II. of Germany, v, 19.
Maynard, Henry, v, 16.
Meakin, William, i, 24.
Medina Cœli, duke of, v, 6.
Mercator, Gerardus, v, 5, 28, 56.
Merian, Mrs., i, 19.
Milton, John, commonness of the name near Nantwich, i, 5.
—— papers, notice of, i, 1-14.
—— testamentary papers, copy of, i, 36-44.
Milton, his domestic life misrepresented, i, 3, 4; portraits of him, 14; date of his death, 18; his seal, 21; undutifulness of his daughters, 12, 17; their defective education, 15.
——, Elizabeth, his widow, i, 16, 17, 21, 24; her connexion with Nantwich, 5, 6; humble origin, 9, 10; vindication of her character, 10-13; copy of her lease and release of Brindley farm, 26-32; death, 33; will, 33-35; pedigree, 45, 46.
——, Anne, eldest daughter, i, 1, 12, 15, 17, 18; notice of, 16; release from, 16-18; bond from, 25.
——, Mary, second daughter, i, 1, 12, 15, 17; notice of, 18, 19; release from, 18.
——, Deborah, youngest daughter, *vide* Clarke, Deborah.
——, Christopher, i, 2, 13, 16, 17, 18, 22.
——, Sir Christopher, 18.
——, Richard, i, 2, 18, 19.
——, Thomas, i, 18.
Minshulls of Stoke, i, 7, 8, 9.
—— of Wistaston, i, 44, 45.
Minshull, Edward, i, 24.
Minshull, Elizabeth, *vide* Milton, Elizabeth.
——, Mary, i, 24.
——. Richard, i, 7, 9, 14; bond from, 23, 24.
Mirica, Gaspar à, v, 5.
Mist's *Weekly Journal*, i, 20.
Mizaldus, v, 8.
Monluc, Monsieur de, v, 8.
Montaureus, Petrus, v, 8.
Moreton, John earl of, ii, 8.
Mortlake, v, 4, 17; account of Dee's library at, 27-31.

Nantwich, tradition respecting Milton at, i, 5.
Newbrenner, Conradus Justus, v, 34.
Newton, Bishop, i, 20; his *Life of Milton*, 18.
Nicolai, Nicholaus Grudius, v, 19.
Nicolas, Sir Harris, his List of Heraldic Visitations, iii, 7.
Nonsuch, court at, v, 16, 17.
Northampton, marchioness of, v, 12, 22.

Offhuysen, Joannes Franciscus van, v, 58.
Oldenburgh, earl of, v, 33.
Ormerod's *Cheshire*, i, 5, 6, 8, 9.
Orontius, —, v, 8.
Osborne, Peter, v, 9.
Oxford, earl of, v, 10.

Paget, Dr., i, 7.
Parry, Blanche à, v, 13, 16.
Peck's *Memoirs*, i, 7.
Pembroke, earl of, v, 12, 19.
Pena, Johannes à, v, 8.
Pennant's *Journey*, i, 7, 10.
Pezelius, Dr. Christopher, v, 33.
Philips' *Life of Milton*, i. 3, 7, 13.
Postellus, Gulielmus, v, 8.
Powell, Richard, i, 2, 16, 17, 22.
——, Mr., i, 17.
——, Mr., v, 30.
Price, John, i, 23.
Prideaux, v, 20.
Pykering, Sir William, v, 7.

Ramus, Petrus, v, 8.
Ranconetus, v, 8.
Richardson's *Life of Milton*, i, 10, 12.
Richmond, v, 18, 22.
Robinson, Thomas, jun., i, 18, 19.
Rohan, Monsieur de, v, 8.
Rowley, Uriah, i, 34.

St. Cross, advantages of the mastership of, v, 39–41.
St. George, Sir Richard, Norroy, iii, 7, 10.
Singletons of Lancashire, ii, 9, 10.
Sisson, Thomas, i, 23.
Skydamore, lady, v, 16, 21.
Smith, rouge dragon, ii, 6.
——, Dr., v, 10.
Star Chamber, v, 20.
Steven, Mr., v, 59.
Strange, Richard, v, 20.
Straselius, v, 8.
Supervisor, tenacity of the word, i, 27.
Sydney, Lord, v, 12.
——, Sir Henry, v, 11.
Sylvius, Jacobus, v, 8.

Tilleson, Thomas, ii, 9.
Timmis, Randle, i, 14, 25.
Todd's *Life of Milton*, i, 1, 2, 7, 10.
Toland's *Life of Milton*, i, 7.
Tomkins, Joseph, i, 34.
Tonson, Jacob, i, 20.
Townley, Christopher, ii, 8, 9.
Travelling expenses and dangers, v, 32–34.
Trebon Castle, Bohemia, v, 32.
Turnebus, v, 8.

Vernon's Cheshire Collections, ii, 6.
Vicomercatus, v, 8.

Wall, William, of Shingle Hall, ii, 9.
Walsingham, Sir Francis, v, 11, 22.
Warton, Mr., i, 3, 4, 11.
Warwick, countess of, v, 15, 16, 17, 45.
Watson, Dr., v, 16.
Way, Albert, i, 21.
Web, Mr., ii, 6.
Welsh evidences (title deeds), v, 29.
Wickstead, Ri., i, 25.
Wilbraham, Sir Thomas, bart., i, 24.
Willson, Dr., v, 11.
——, Mr. Secretary, v, 21.
Wisterson, co. Chester, note on, i, 23.
Witchcraft, case of, v, 21.
Woolley, Sir John, v, 4, 10, 13, 17, 45.
Words, tenacity of, i, 27.
Wright, Thomas, i, 24.

INDEX TO VOLUME XXV.

Allen on Surrender of Deventer.

Aldersey, Hugh, of Chester, ii.
Alençon, duke of, 15.
Allens of Buckenhall, lxi, lxii.
—— of Rossall, lxii, lxiii.
Allen, Elizabeth, lii, lxxi, lxxiv.
——, Gabriel, lxiii.
——, George, lxiv.
——, John, lxiii.
——, Mary, lxiv.
——, Richard, lxiii, lxxi.
——, Thomas, lxiv.
ALLEN, William (Cardinal), xx, xlv, 35; birth, lxiii; education, lxiv; made fellow of Oriel Coll. lxv; enters the priesthood, lxv; principal of St. Mary's Hall, and proctor, lxvi; retires to Louvain, and engages in theological controversy, lxvi; visit to Lancashire, lxvii; motives and occurrences of the visit, lxix, lxx; consequences of the visit, lxxii–lxxv; returns to the Netherlands, lxxii; institutes the seminary system at Douay, lxxv; made canon of Cambray, lxxv; D.D. lxxvi; in the pay of Philip of Spain, lxxvi; meets Persons, the jesuit, at Rome, lxxix; made rector of the English college, lxxx; publishes his *Apologie*, lxxx; health fails, lxxxv, xcv; made cardinal and archbishop of Mechlin, lxxxvi; revises the translation of the Bible, and the text of the Fathers, xcii; quarrels with the jesuits, xcii; his last occupations, xciv; death, xcvi; epitaph, lxvi, xcvi, xcvii; character, lxxx, xcvii, xcviii; beloved by the soldiery, 5; marvellous power of writing, lxxiii; political character of his writings, lxxxv; proofs of inconsistency, lxxxi–lxxxiv; biographies of him, lxiv; his *Admonition*, lxxxix, xc; *Apologie*, lxxi, lxxx, xciv; extracts from it, lxxvii, lxxviii, lxxix, 19, 21; *Defence of the Surrender of Deventer*, i, lxxxix; *Declaration of Sixtus Quintus his Bull*, lxxxix; extract from his book *On Purgatory*, lxxii.
Ashton, Roger, xxxvi, xliii; notice of, xxii, xxiii.
Assassination justified, l.

Babington conspiracy, xii.
Bamvile family, lix.
Bath a focus of papal intrigue, lxvii.
Bentivoglio (Cardinal), lxxxviii.
Blount, Christopher, ix, lxvi, lxix.
Burleigh, lord, 36.
Campion the jesuit, lxxiv, lxxx, lxxxiv.
Catholic soldiers more capable of reason than others, 18; practised on by heretics, 20; better soldiers, 27; God fights for them, 28–30.; a training college for, 32; *vide* Soldiers.
Cicero *De Republica* quoted, 14.
Cosby, Arnold, notice of, xxxv, xxxvi.
Crossley, James, lxxiii.
Cundy, Patrick, xliii.

Derby, earl of, xlii, lxviii, xciii.
Deventer, lxxxviii; its importance, xvii; capture by Stanley, xviii; account of its surrender, xxv–xxxiii; variety of opinions thereon, 6; justified by Allen and Parsons, 12.
Doesborg, capture of, xv.
Doleman's *Conference*, xcii.
Douay college, lxxv, lxxvi.

Drury, Sir William, notice of, v.
Dutch service unpopular, xxxii.
Dutch venality, xli.

Egerton, Sir John, iii, iv.
Elizabeth, queen, 35, 36; her parsimony, vii; well-being of England under, 16; inability as a heretic to make lawful war, 22; extract from her letter to Downham, bishop of Chester, lxxiii.
English atheism, 17.
—— catholics, loyalty of, lxxxiv.
—— college, disunion in, lxvii, lxxxvi.
—— refugees, their miserable condition, lii.
Essex, earl of, vii.
Excommunicated sovereigns, condition of, 22–26.

Fawkes, Guy, xlvii, lii, liii, liv.
Fitzherbert, Nicholas, lxiv, 35; extracts from his account of Allen, lxix, lxx, 36; character of his book, xcvii.
Fitzmaurice, John, iv.
Flud, John, xxxi, xxxii, xlvi; his depositions, xxxiv–xliii; execution, xliv.

Glasier, Thomas, iv.
Government of Ireland, extract from, xi.
Grey, lord, v.
Griffiths, Sir William, ii.
Groningen, 28.
Gunpowder Plot, liii, liv.

Hatton, Sir Christopher, xl, lxvi.
Haydock, Vivian, lxxi.
Heresy maketh infamous, 25.
Heretic armies always overthrown, 28, 29; miseries they endure, 31.
Hesketh, Thomas, lxiv.
Heskeths of Aughton, lxxiv.
Hocknell, Mr., xl.
Holt, William, li, lii.
Hovenden, Captain, xxxv.
Huntingdon, Lord, iii.

Irish soldiers, xiii; cost of recruiting, viii; description of, xii, xviii; their subordination, xxix; bravery and sufferings, xlvii.

Jackson, Francis, xxxix.
James, Thomas, xxxix.
Jaques, Francesco, xlvii; notice of, xxxvii, xxxviii.
Jesuits, power and influence of, xxii, xliv; injure the English Roman-Catholics, lxxxvii, lxxxviii; their bitterness against Cardinal Allen, xcv; treachery, xcvi.

Kerns, *vide* Irish soldiers.

Lancashire, state of religion in, lxviii, lxix, lxxii–lxxv.
Leicester, earl of, vii, xxvi, xxxiv, 27; his weakness, ix; ambitious schemes, xiii; vanity and incompetence, xx, xxi; improvidence, xxvii; praise of Sir William Stanley, xvi; strange confidence in him; xix, xxx, xxxi.
Lewis, Dr. Owen, bishop of Casano, lxxvii, lxxviii, lxxxvi.
Lilly's *Midas* quoted, 16.
Low Countries, injustice of the English wars in, 14.

Mansfeldt, Agnes de, xv.
Massey, Richard, notice of, xl.
Molyneux, Sir Richard, vi.
Morgan the sophister, lxiv, lxv, lxxv; his letter to the Queen of Scots, ix.
Munster, distribution of forfeited estates in, vi.

Nice, council of, 22.
Norfolk, duke of, lxxi, lxxii.
Norris, Sir John, vii, xv, xvi, xxi, xxv, xxvi, xxvii, xxxi, xxxiv.

O'Roghan, Dennis, his evidence against Sir John Perrot, ix, x.

Parma, duke of, vii, xvii, xxii, xlix, 5, 27, 31.
Parsons, Father, xxxix; *vide* Persons, Rev. F. R.
Paulet, Amyas, 35.
Pelham, Sir William (judge), notice of, xii.
Perrot, Sir John, vi, vii, viii, x; his alleged treason, x; training of soldiers, xii.
Persons, Rev. F. R. (jesuit), xxix, xxxi, xlii, xlvii, xlix, lxiii, lxv, lxxxiv, lxxxvi, lxxxviii, xci, xcii, xciii; his epitaph, xcvii.
Philipps, Peter, musician, liii.
Poole, John, of Capenhurst, iii, xxxviii; notice of, xxxv.

Raleigh, Sir Walter, v, xli.
Ratcliffe, Egremont, account of, 35–38.

Rich, Barnaby, v.
Russell, Sir William, vii.

St. Augustine quoted, 15, 21, 23, 31, 32, 33.
Salisbury, ——, xxxvi.
Sidney, Sir Philip, vii; his friendship with traitors, xx.
Smith, Sir Thomas, ii.
Soldiers honoured by the Church, 11; bound to a tender conscience, 20; must not serve heretics, 21; their rule of duty, 27; *vide* Catholic soldiers.
Southworth, Sir Thomas, notice of, lxvii.
Stanleys of Hooton, ii, iii.
Stanley, Edward, xvi.
———, Harry, of Crosshall, xl.
———, Robert, xxxix.
——— the jesuit, lx.
STANLEY, Sir William, lxxxvii, 5, 7; his birth, iii; marriage, iii; children, iv; longevity, iv; serves under the Duke of Alva, iv; is charged with desertion, iv; serves in Ireland, v, vi; discontent, vi; sent into Holland, vi, vii, xiii; first signs of disloyalty, vii; influence with the earl of Leicester, viii; dishonesty, viii; disloyalty, x, xi, xix; concerned in the Babington conspiracy, xiii; dislike to Leicester and Essex, xv; valour, xvi; takes Deventer, xviii; appointed its governor, xix; connected with the jesuits, xxii; plans the surrender of Deventer, xxv; Flud's depositions against him, xxxiv–xliii; his fortune confiscated, xxxvii; grief and discontent, xxxvii; remorse, xlvi; visits Philip of Spain, xlviii; plans to assail England, xlviii; returns to the Low Countries, xlix; goes to Madrid and Rome, xlix; concerned in a plot to murder Queen Elizabeth, l; and Maurice of Saxony, li; his poverty, li, lvi; neglect of art, liii; shuns the Gunpowder Plot, liv; aids the jesuits, lv; becomes a Carthusian monk, lvi; death, lvii; details of his funeral, lvii –lxi; his wife's epitaph, xxxvii.
Strange, Ferdinando lord, xli; notice of, xlii.

Tassis, Jean Baptiste, xxv, xxvii, xxviii, xxix, xxxiii, xxxvi, xlvi; notice of, xxiv.

Vendeville, Dr., lxxv.
Verdugo, xxxiii, xlvi.

Warnsfeld, battle of, xvi.
Whitmore, Mr., xl, lv.
Williams, Roger, l.
Winter, ——, liii, liv.
Worthington, Thomas, of Blainscow, notice of, xliv, xlv.

York, Sir Rowland, xxx, xxxiii, xxxvi, xliii, xlv, xlvi; notice of, xxiii, xxiv.

Zutphen, xv, xxv, xxvii; surrender of, xlv.

CPSIA information can be obtained
at www.ICGtesting.com
Printed in the USA
LVHW110934160522
718424LV00014B/289

9 783375 000790